Wide Awake in the Pelican State

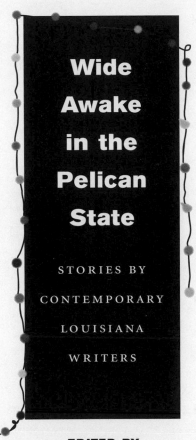

Wide
Awake
in the
Pelican
State

STORIES BY

CONTEMPORARY

LOUISIANA

WRITERS

EDITED BY

Ann Brewster Dobie

WITH A FOREWORD BY

Ernest J. Gaines

LOUISIANA STATE UNIVERSITY PRESS)|(BATON ROUGE

Published by Louisiana State University Press
Copyright © 2006 by Louisiana State University Press
All rights reserved
Manufactured in the United States of America
An LSU Press Paperback Original
FIRST PRINTING

DESIGNER: *Amanda McDonald Scallan*
TYPEFACE: *Minion*
TYPESETTER: *The Composing Room of Michigan, Inc.*
PRINTER AND BINDER: *Edwards Brothers, Inc.*

Library of Congress Cataloging-in-Publication Data

Wide awake in the Pelican State : stories by contemporary Louisiana writers / edited by Ann Brewster Dobie ; with a foreword by Ernest J. Gaines.
    p. cm.
  ISBN 0-8071-3034-6 (pbk.)
  1. Short stories, American—Louisiana. 2. Louisiana—Social life and customs—Fiction. I. Dobie, Ann B.
PS558.L8W54 2006
813'.01089763—dc22

2005020317

Pages 331–32 are an extension of the copyright page.

Contents

Foreword

Ann Dobie has in this volume compiled another superb group of stories by Louisiana writers, complementing her fine collection that came out in 1991, *Something in Common*. As in that collection, in this book you will find stories by writers whose names are not household words as well as stories by Pulitzer Prize winners. The authors have different backgrounds and the subjects are quite diverse, yet all the stories have come out of Louisiana, at least in some way.

Perhaps because of the direction the world is going, nowadays it sometimes seems difficult to distinguish a Louisiana writer from a writer from any other part of the country. When most outsiders think of Louisiana, they still think of New Orleans, the French Quarter, jazz, dancing, Cajuns, Creoles, spicy food. You will find some of this in a few of these stories, but not in most of them.

At their heart, nearly all these stories are not about externals; they are about intractable personal problems that may be universal. A theme I find in several of them is the struggle between father and son in an effort to form a binding relationship. Robert Olen Butler's "Crickets" and Richard Ford's "Calling" are two examples.

Of the three stories by the Pulitzer Prize winners—Butler, Ford, and Shirley Ann Grau—only Ford's story is immediately identifiable as Louisianian. It is a son's flashback to a family in a large house in New Orleans with its garden and gardener, and much fast living followed by a divorce. It is a contemporary story of New Orleans in all its splendor and decadence. Grau's absorbing story, "Letting Go," could have taken place almost anywhere. It is another story about the breakup of a family, with parents and in-laws involved. Butler's "Crickets" concerns a Vietnamese father and son. The father has brought with him from the old country the tradition of capturing crickets and now wishes to teach his son the art of capturing them and distinguishing one group from another. But the son has no interest in the past, and the father must realize that this is the United States of America, a different world from the one he left, and he must accept his son's world or lose him.

If you read a number of stories about Louisiana, you are bound to find some involving ghosts, voodoo, the supernatural. My own story in this book, "A Long

Day in November," is about a man who has more interest in his car than he does in his wife and son. He is a good man, a simple man who loves his family very much. But the car takes up almost all of his time—until his wife decides to leave him and take their son with her. This he cannot bear, and he tries everything to get her back. His last hope is a visit to the old voodoo woman who lives far back in the swamps. She tells him how to bring the family back together, but he refuses to take her advice—until he realizes there is no other way out of his predicament. The story is told by a six-year-old child who knows that lots of things are happening around him but he doesn't understand any of them.

Another story about the supernatural is John Dufresne's tightly woven little piece "The Freezer Jesus," in which an image of Christ appears on the refrigerator door of a poor family. People from all around—educated and illiterate, religious believers and nonbelievers—visit the house to see the image. The tone is comic, religious, yet also serious, skeptical—until the refrigerator is moved.

Ellen Gilchrist's "Rich," with its careful craftsmanship, reminds me of F. Scott Fitzgerald's "The Rich Boy" and his novel *The Great Gatsby,* in that not one word is wasted. Unnecessary narrative and dialogue have been shucked off to leave the bare kernel. The two main characters are Tom and Letty Wilson. They are rich in almost every way that one can be rich. They have money, they have friends in power, they have position. Letty is vice-president of the Junior League of New Orleans, and a picture of her at the symphony is in *Town and Country* magazine every year. Her husband, Tom, is vice-president of one of the largest banks in Louisiana. They know all the best people; they do all the right things. Yet there is a flaw—within the family—that will cause great changes.

"The Convict," by James Lee Burke, looks at racism in Louisiana head-on. When it comes to race relations, Will Broussard is in a small minority in his community—perhaps a minority of one, among whites at least. The story takes place just before the beginnings of school desegregation, and Will asks the old question: What is wrong with it? The blacks work for us, they cook our food, they look after our children, they nurse us when we're ill. We trust them in every way. So what is wrong with black children going to the same school as whites? Later, a black convict escapes from the state prison and ends up at Will Broussard's back door. Will's wife tells him to call the sheriff, but instead Will gives the convict food and money and directions to help him escape. The convict flees, but then returns, demanding more. The story is narrated by Will's young son, Avery. It is about a test of human values—whether one can stand alone or must surrender to the will of the community.

As I said before, though all these stories are by Louisiana writers, there is no single common theme or bunch of closely related themes running through them. They are richly varied. Alongside the Burke story is a fine one by John Biguenet that could hardly be more different—"The Work of Art." Like some of the other stories in the book, it could have been done by a writer from Atlanta or the Midwest or New England. Peter Lagarde, an attorney, sells everything he owns and borrows $125,000 from his grandmother to buy a statue by Degas. The grandmother lends him the money on the condition that he will have to pay back only $100,000 should he marry the girl with whom he is in love. If he doesn't marry her, then he must pay back the entire $125,000. Almost everything about this story makes me feel that O. Henry would have had fun writing it.

As writer-in-residence at the University of Louisiana at Lafayette, I have always told my students that the opening sentences are the most important element in a work of fiction. Because so many books are published each year, you must get the reader's attention immediately or you're going to lose him. All these stories have good beginnings, and perhaps the best is in Tim Gautreaux's "Welding with Children": "Tuesday was about typical. My four daughters, not a one of them married, you understand, brought over their kids, one each, and explained to my wife how much fun she was going to have looking after them again. But Tuesday was her day to go to the casino, so guess who got to tend the four babies? My oldest daughter also brought over a bed rail that the end broke off of. She wanted me to weld it." In just those few lines, Gautreaux makes the reader want to know the whole story— and conjures up an entire world in the process.

There is not space enough here to mention all the stories in this collection. I stress that those not mentioned are not less important than the others, but the ones I did touch on are, I feel, a good sample of the lot. So I will leave you to discover the pleasures of the others entirely on your own. And I hope you enjoy all these stories. I did.

ERNEST J. GAINES

Preface

It isn't news that Louisiana is a state richly endowed with natural resources. Oil, gas, timber, rivers, ports—it has just about everything except mountains laced with silver and gold. Equally valuable, but sometimes overlooked for inclusion in the usual lists of "greats," are the writers who have claimed Louisiana as home.

All states boast a few well-known writers, or a school of writing that flamed brightly for a short time, but Louisiana's poets and fiction makers have long been a part of its history. Even where literacy was scarce, stories flourished in the well-established tradition of storytelling. African Americans listened to the *griot,* who preserved the narratives that gave them an identity and history, and their white counterparts turned local events and characters into folktales and heroes. By the middle of the nineteenth century the works of George Washington Cable, who is sometimes called the first modern southern writer, began to appear in print, making them available to readers everywhere. He was a social reformer, a storyteller who dealt with the need for racial justice, the inequality of social classes, and the burdens of the past, but it was his descriptions of New Orleans's colorful inhabitants and Old World ambience that appealed to the reading public. The growing interest in narratives with local color attracted readers to Cable's world, a world that seemed foreign and romantic to people living in places like Kansas or South Dakota. Kate Chopin, following his lead, created characters based on the Catholic Creoles she met when she moved to New Orleans as a newlywed. With their quaint, old-fashioned, European manners and speech, they seemed to exist in a world apart, and the semitropical landscape she described only added to their exoticism. Although Chopin lived in Louisiana for little more than a decade, throughout her writing life she drew heavily on her experiences there to compose what were then thought to be scandalous tales of women seeking social and economic equality. In contrast to Chopin, Grace King, who called herself a "southern woman of letters," began her writing career in an attempt to offset Cable's portrayals of Creole society. Although both were natives of New Orleans, she was offended by what she judged to be Cable's pejorative depictions of the city and its people.

The twentieth century brought with it a flood of Louisiana writers, some of them popular successes, others recipients of the highest honors given in the literary world. Some even managed to fit into both categories. They included natives, but many, attracted by the unique culture they found in Louisiana, came from other places. In the 1920s Louisiana even laid claim to William Faulkner and Sherwood Anderson, who chose to spend considerable time during that decade living in New Orleans's French Quarter, a long cultural distance from their native Mississippi and Ohio.

The new century's writers explored every genre: fiction, poetry, drama, biography. For the stage, Tennessee Williams created Blanche DuBois, Maggie the Cat, and Amanda Wingfield, characters whose names are as well known as those of historical figures. Maggie even won Williams a Pulitzer Prize for *Cat on a Hot Tin Roof*. Lillian Hellman, too, made her name as a playwright, winning the New York Drama Critics Circle Award for *Watch on the Rhine*. Better known today for *The Little Foxes, The Children's Hour,* and her memoirs, she remains a colorful personality whose life is still the subject of films and plays by contemporary writers. (No doubt her lifelong relationship with mystery writer Dashiell Hammett, her witty but sharp-tongued verbal duels with Mary McCarthy, and her being blacklisted by the Un-American Activities Committee continue to generate some of the interest in her.)

In the field of fiction, Robert Penn Warren, who taught at Louisiana State University from 1935 to 1942, made news when he published *All the King's Men*, the novel in which the protagonist Willie Stark is a thinly veiled portrait of Huey Long. Warren, and Willie, managed to focus the attention of the entire nation on power and politics in Louisiana. The author also founded the *Southern Review*, one of the leading literary journals in the country, in addition to writing poems that earned him a Pulitzer, making him the only writer to receive that prize for both poetry and for a novel.

In the second half of the twentieth century, Louisiana's fiction writers assumed an increasingly high profile. Not only were they breaking into print at a rapid clip, they were also winning more prizes. In 1962 Walker Percy won the National Book Award for his first novel, *The Moviegoer,* following it with a steady stream of philosophical fiction and nonfiction that explores the human condition. André Dubus received a MacArthur "Genius" Award and the Rea Award for his fictional depictions of flawed human beings—wounded and weak and stubborn—and for the sheer beauty of his prose. Ernest Gaines too was named a MacArthur Fellow for his stories depicting the African American experience. Pulitzers became almost routine, with Shirley Ann Grau winning one in 1965 for her novel *The Keepers of the House,* followed by Katherine Anne Porter in 1966 for her *Collected Stories.* (Though not technically a Louisianian, Porter spent several years living and writing in New Orleans.) In 1981 the trend continued when John Kennedy Toole was posthumously awarded a Pulitzer for *A Confederacy of Dunces,* the novel that brought us yet another memorable New Orleanian, Ignatius Reilly.

The new millennium has seen no decline in the number of Louisiana writers receiving recognition from critics and the general reading public. Neither has it seen any decrease in the quality of the work they are producing. In fact, finding stories for *Something in Common,* a volume of fiction by Louisiana writers published a decade ago, involved searching for new and unknown writers to add to a few recognized ones. In contrast, so many stories by reputable writers were available for this collection that they alone could have filled more than a single volume would hold. The situation made the selection process at once simple and complex. It was simple because it involved little more than reading all the stories one could find by Louisiana writers and choosing those that stood out. That was a pleasure. On the other hand, there were so many well-crafted, deeply thoughtful pieces that deciding which among them were the front-runners became difficult. While one might lament not discovering fresh new talent, having so many successful practicing writers to draw from affirms the health of Louisiana's literary scene.

Although the stories in *Wide Awake in the Pelican State* could be said to emanate from a shared cultural tradition, they are, in fact, marked by their diversity. Their writers have lived all or some part of their lives in Louisiana, but they speak with many voices created by gender, race, education, religion, and travel—sometimes making it difficult to identify their intersections, always making the subsuming culture richer and more complex. The wide range of their focus is evident in the cultural environments found in the stories by Ernest Gaines, James Lee Burke, and Robert Olen Butler. In "A Long Day in November" Gaines finds humor in the rural world of African American culture. Burke, best known for his Dave Robicheaux detective novels, in "The Convict" shows us south Louisiana as a young boy sees it. And Butler introduces us to the Vietnamese who settled in Louisiana after the fall of Saigon in the story he calls "Crickets." Some of the stories do not take place in the state or anywhere in particular, but have unidentified settings. The King of Slack in Louis Gallo's story of the same name, for example, could live in any state. In "Mink" Joan Arbour Grant's Gloria could agonize over owning her fur coat anywhere it is cold enough to wear one. And Albert Davis's Mondebon exists in the imagination.

The commonality of these works lies in the fact that, like all good fiction, they are about human beings. They are about love, betrayal, family, about foolishness and wisdom, dreams and reality, giving up and hanging on. In the end they are important because they are probing, insightful descriptions of people who are living in complex worlds that they try to survive and understand. Now that's a natural resource.

ANN B. DOBIE

Wide Awake in the Pelican State

The Work of Art

JOHN BIGUENET

Denn das Schöne ist nichts
als des Schrecklichen Anfang, den wir noch grade ertragen. . . .
—RAINER MARIA RILKE

For Beauty is nothing
but the beginning of terror, which we just barely can still endure. . . .

The young man, lost in the warren of dingy dentist offices, import companies, and commercial insurance agencies on the eighth floor of the old Effinger Building, was attempting to deliver contracts to a ship chandler. He was sure that the directory beside the florid bronze elevator doors downstairs had listed the chandler in 817. But the last door on the dim hall was 815. He tried the knob. It was locked. He tapped on the milky glass pane with his law school ring just below an arc of golden letters that spelled J. GRUEN.

A thin voice answered his knock. Though the door opened only slightly, the overheated air of the office swarmed over him in the chilly hallway. "I'm looking for Hugo Fernandez, the ship supplier," he explained. "I'm Peter Lagarde. An attorney." He passed his business card to the old man peering at him from behind the door.

"Not on this floor. No Fernandez."

Lagarde looked past the old man into the office. Its walls were covered with paintings.

The thin voice strengthened. "You collect?"

"Collect art? A bit." Lagarde had learned in his four years as an associate at Daigle, Johnson to present a version of himself in matters of taste that might win the confidence of the clients and, especially, of the partners of the firm. He could be quite convincing; as an undergraduate, he had taken a minor in art history. But the small house he had bought and the stocks in which he had invested the proceeds of his trust fund left no capital for speculation in the art market. "Actually," Lagarde continued, "I've been thinking about expanding my collection."

"Perhaps I have something that might interest you." The door swung open.

Lagarde entered the small office, crowded with nineteenth-century portraits and religious works. It had been designed for a secretary; another door opened on a larger second room, where he glimpsed an ornately framed landscape. "Ah, the Impressionists." He was on safe ground; he remembered the movement because he had found its works so painfully absent of interest and so resistant to study for examinations.

"Actually, they're Postimpressionists." The old man pushed farther open the door into the other room. "Here, take a closer look."

Lagarde was surprised: the names of the artists were familiar. "I didn't know there were any galleries in this building," he said.

"Gallery? You call this a gallery? In Philadelphia for thirty years, there I had a gallery. But Hedda dies, God rest her, and my daughter makes me move here to New Orleans. I'm too old to live alone, she says. But I'm not going to retire, am I?"

The young man, half listening, surveyed a group of charcoals above a file cabinet.

"No, I sell what I can get a decent price for, the rest I take with me. Now I peddle masterpieces by phone to cowboys in Oklahoma. But it makes my Sarah happy to have me here, so what can I do?" Even as he talked, he urged his guest toward the drawings with a gentle push. "She makes me crazy, though, that girl. The door I have to keep locked, she says. What kind of business keeps its door locked? Bookies, they keep their door locked."

Lagarde recognized a Degas. He flipped the tag dangling at the bottom of the frame and gasped.

"Don't worry, that was just for the insurance during shipping. I can take ten percent off the top. No problem."

"No, I don't think so. And I've got to find Fernandez. He's expecting these papers."

"Wait. I have something for you." The old man was trying to lift a large, shallow box. Lagarde took the crate from him and put it down on a desk full of magazines. "You like Degas. I can tell. Here is something special. I got it cheap, just before I left Philadelphia."

Gruen had trouble flicking open the rusty latch that fastened the plywood top. "Wait a minute." He took a small hammer from a file cabinet and tapped open the hook. The top creaked back on dry hinges. "This is something a young man would like."

As Lagarde looked down, his breath caught in his throat. A small, exquisite woman gazed up at him from her bath.

"A Degas maquette. It's called *The Tub*. 1889, I think." They both regarded the sculpture. "She's charming, isn't she? I knew you'd like her."

Though the old man wore a cardigan with a high collar that was much too big for him, the musty heat made Lagarde almost dizzy. "How much?" he whispered.

"Let me see." As Gruen lifted the edge of the lead pan that Degas had used as the tub, his bony left hand crawled under like a spider. Slowly it withdrew with a yellow stub dangling a green string. "160,000. But minus the ten percent, it's yours for 144. A steal, let me tell you."

Lagarde was pale. His heart shook his chest.

"If it were a bronze, you couldn't touch it for under 750 these days. But it's wax and plaster. The way Degas is going, I ought to hold on to it. Give it five years, it'll double, triple, who knows? But forget the money. Just look at her."

Lagarde had not taken his eyes off her. She stared up at him over crossed legs, her left foot cupped in her right hand as she lolled in her bath.

"Too much? You could buy on time. By the month."

Her left hand held a sponge. Her hair was like a clump of wet, thick cloth. Lagarde was taking deep, quiet breaths, trying to calm himself. Degas had worked a reddish brown pigment into the wax to resemble bronze; why hadn't he cast the piece? Lagarde guessed without bothering to calculate that he couldn't afford it even if he sold everything: the house, the stocks, the car. "It's very nice, very fine. But I've really got to find Fernandez. It was a pleasure meeting you." Lagarde had already backed into the outer office and was feeling for the door. "Perhaps I'll stop back when I have more time." He closed the door before the old man could speak. His breath burst from him in little white clouds as he hurried down the cold hallway.

As the elevator descended, he leaned against a carved walnut panel. He left the papers for the ship chandler with the guard at the information desk.

Peter Lagarde busied himself for the next few weeks with a complex lawsuit arising from the grounding of a barge near White Castle in Iberville Parish. He had been accompanied on the site visit by a young Baton Rouge attorney representing some of the underwriters. She was a second-year associate named Lauren and, like him, a graduate of Tulane. The litigation kept them in frequent communication, and among the marine surveys, the depositions, and the motions for summary judgment, a friendship began to emerge. Lagarde found himself scheduling their appointments late in the afternoon so she might be more likely to stay for dinner. He surprised her with symphony tickets one night, but she couldn't stay—she had to prepare for a trial the next morning. He worried over whether he could give her a Christmas present without embarrassing her.

Just before the holidays, an envelope arrived for him at the firm. There was a Canal Street return address. Inside, a photocopied letter from the Gruen Gallery announced a Christmas sale. At the bottom of the letter was a handwritten note: "For tax purposes, I can let you have the Degas for $125,000 until the end of the year." He felt something like panic overtaking him. How had Gruen gotten his address? He remembered the business card he had offered the old man.

In fact, despite his work and despite his colleague from Baton Rouge, he had been unable to force the woman in the tub from his mind. At odd moments, he discovered himself imagining her. He had even spoken with a real estate agent and his broker. After expenses, he could expect $85,000 from the house and his investments. The car was only a year old; he would certainly clear $15,000. He had been relieved to realize that he really couldn't afford the piece. Where would he find $44,000? But now, thanks to Gruen's tax man, he was only $25,000 short, and Lagarde knew where he could find $25,000.

He picked up the phone and called his grandmother. He didn't mention the money. He wished Nana a merry Christmas and told her about his progress at Daigle, Johnson. He hinted at a romance with Lauren. He admitted that he couldn't get away to join his parents in New York for the holidays, but he knew they would understand. Nana insisted that he have Christmas dinner with her at the Wharton; he gracefully accepted.

He was ashamed even before he had hung up. But, he told himself, he wasn't going to ask his grandmother for the money because he wasn't going to buy the Degas. Even if it were the great investment Gruen suggested, it was insane for him to consider buying such a work of art. It would cost him everything he owned, plus a great deal more. And all he would have to show for it was an exquisite lump of wax.

That night, after a quick dinner at a new Mexican restaurant on Magazine, Lagarde stopped by the Tulane library. The reference librarian showed him the registers of prices paid at auction for artworks. Gruen had not exaggerated, but there was nothing like the maquette in the records. He could only guess that the enormous prices fetched by Degas bronzes could make his sculpture worth a quarter of a million in the right auction. Again, for the second time that day, he felt shame. But to his surprise, he realized that he was ashamed of thinking of his little bather in terms of money. He put his hands on the red cover of the closed volume before him and stared at his reflection in the window.

The next morning, Lagarde had coffee with Tommy Hinton, a friend in his firm's business section who specialized in estates. He explained his father wanted to surprise his mother with a fiftieth birthday present, a Degas sculpture. The colleague offered to check it out. "No sweat, we handle stuff like this all the time. You can't imagine the crap we have to do for the old farts we represent. Just get me the papers on it—and the price."

At lunch, he walked over to Gruen's. His heart was beating faster and faster as he rode the current of holiday shoppers. He noticed a legless beggar with a dog in the alcove of a bankrupt department store. The peeling sheets of brown paper revealed glimpses of mannequins in summer smocks; he recalled from his childhood the Christmas window displays of the store.

He pulled his coat closed against the cold, damp gusts. A ragged preacher with a plastic loudspeaker attached to his belt berated the crowds hurrying past. Lagarde tried to avoid the man's attention as he slipped into the Effinger Building.

As the old, ornate elevator creaked toward the eighth floor, he realized that he wouldn't have time for lunch. He was hungry, but this was more pressing.

The door to 815 was ajar. Lagarde peeked in. Gruen and another man were eating sandwiches on a crate. "Come in, come in," the old man insisted, rewrapping his food as he spoke. "This is my neighbor, Mr. Ruiz. He has the business next door." The lawyer nodded to the small dark man. "You're here for the Degas, am I right?"

"No, not today. I just wanted to ask you a few questions about it."

"Questions? Yes, ask me questions," the old man said, motioning to Ruiz to stay.

"First, could I have a copy of the papers?"

"The papers?"

"You know, to authenticate the piece." Lagarde saw the old man stiffen. "Not that there's any question."

The slightest smile creased Gruen's face. "Of course. I don't buy without papers." He turned to Ruiz and winked. "Well, maybe if it's really cheap, I make an exception."

"You have my address," the attorney reminded him.

"I'll put a copy in the mail this afternoon, no problem," the old man promised, still smiling.

"Also, I was wondering—and I'm not sure I want to go ahead with this—but I was wondering whether you needed all the money by the first of January?"

"December thirty-first. Not January."

Lagarde corrected himself. "Yes, all the money by the end of December?"

"If I wait until January, I may as well wait another year. Taxes. You're a lawyer; you know."

"Midnight on the thirty-first," Ruiz interjected.

"So you need everything?" Lagarde tried one last time.

Gruen shrugged. "Of course everything. If you want to buy on time, then we have to go back to the first price. But come see her again. Look here." The old man had shuffled into the back room and was struggling with the lid of the container.

"No, no, it's not necessary," Lagarde protested, weakening.

"Come, come see."

While Lagarde hesitated, Ruiz got up to view the piece.

"Oh, beautiful," he said with a vague Latin accent. "Look at her. And served up on a platter."

"It's a tub," Lagarde objected as he joined the two men peering into the low crate. The plaster podium of crumpled canvas on which Degas had set the piece swirled with the frozen folds of the cloth, like a woman's robe dropped carelessly on the bathroom floor. There was something terribly brazen—or innocent— about the girl.

"Oh, yes, a bath," Ruiz whispered. He reached into the box and stroked the bottom of her thigh with his finger. "Lovely, no?"

Lagarde was offended. It was ridiculous, he knew, but he felt a kind of jealousy overwhelm him. He repressed an urge to insult the little man.

Turning to Gruen, he asked, "Will you be here on the thirty-first?"

"Where else would I be?"

"I have to go. I'm late," Lagarde said, still flustered by his emotions.

"I'll see you then, yes?" The old man followed him with small steps out into the hall.

"We'll see," the attorney said as he hurried toward the elevators. "Maybe."

Lauren slept with Lagarde for the first time a week before Christmas. Two days of depositions from crewmen of the beached barge and its tug had been scheduled at Daigle, Johnson, and she had arranged to spend the intervening Thursday night in New Orleans. Finishing their work about eight, the two attorneys treated themselves to an expensive dinner in the French Quarter. They laughed easily with each other, and by the time one of them looked at a watch it was well past eleven. Lagarde offered to walk his colleague back to her hotel on Canal Street. She took his arm, and they huddled together against the cold wind that shook the shop signs of the Quarter. In the lobby of the hotel, Lauren kissed him on the cheek. He smiled as he waved good-bye from the revolving doors.

By the time they had concluded the last deposition late Friday afternoon, Lauren had already called her roommate in Baton Rouge to say she would not be home that night. In fact, she did not see her roommate again until Sunday evening, when, giddy and exhausted, she announced that she was in love.

For Lagarde, the weekend had disturbed and then simplified everything. The furtive glances across the conference table Friday morning, his clumsy invitation at lunch to stay through the weekend, the shy and tender smile with which she accepted, the interminable afternoon of lawyerly questions and answers, the confusion about what to do with her car at the hotel—everything, all the complexities and awkwardness and impatience of sudden love, fell with their clothes to the floor when at last, after dinner and a few fortifying drinks, the young couple shut the door of Lagarde's house behind them and put out the lights.

The next Thursday, Christmas Eve, the attorney slipped away early from the firm's holiday party to meet Lauren in Baton Rouge for dinner and to exchange gifts. Before he left, though, Tommy Hinton pulled him aside. "Listen, I got the report back from our appraiser this morning," his friend whispered conspiratorially over a half-empty glass of bourbon. "That statue, you know, for your daddy, it checked out. And it's worth at least 175, maybe 200,000. A hell of a deal." Clapping his friend on the back for the favor, Lagarde realized that he had almost forgotten about the sculpture during the last few days.

The following morning, snuggling beneath a comforter that had belonged to the girl's grandmother, the two lovers kissed and teased. Lauren wanted him to join her family for Christmas dinner that afternoon, but he had promised to celebrate the holiday with Nana at the hotel where she lived in New Orleans. "Well," said the young woman, struggling into her nightgown beneath the covers, "at least we can have a Christmas breakfast together."

By the time Lagarde had dressed, Lauren's roommate and her boyfriend had emerged from their room and were stumbling around the kitchen, begging for coffee. They had come in late, and so Lagarde had not yet met them. Stephanie, a friend from Lauren's undergraduate days at LSU, was a medical technician; her fiancé, Vic, was an intern at Our Lady of the Lake Hospital. The four shared a quiet breakfast. While Stephanie and Vic stared off into the flowering vines and blue lattice of the kitchen wallpaper, Lauren slipped her hand into Lagarde's beneath the table.

Nana was waiting in the lobby of the Wharton when her grandson arrived. "I would've come up and gotten you," Lagarde said, embracing the old woman gently.

"No, the reservations were for 12:30. I didn't want them to give our table away."

"Nana, it's just 12:30 now."

"Good, then we can go right in." She took her grandson's arm.

Seated near the small fountain at the rear of the dining room, Lagarde was pleased to be spending Christmas with his grandmother. With his parents' move to New York and the death of his aunt last year, he was the last of Nana's family still in the city. Sooner or later, his father would insist on bringing the old woman north to live with them. But for another year or two, she could manage on her own—with Lagarde's occasional help. Indulging finally in champagne and the restaurant's famously excessive desserts, grandmother and grandson enjoyed a merry afternoon, with the conversation somehow always returning to Lagarde's new friend in

Baton Rouge. The young man insisted on paying for the meal, and Nana invited him up to her rooms for coffee.

As an ancient bellhop brought them to the top floor of the hotel in the small elevator, Lagarde's grandmother whispered discreetly how pleased she was that he had found a young lady. "It's about time," she said.

Lagarde protested that they had just met and who could say what would come of it.

Nana gave him one of the smirks he remembered from childhood. "Who are you trying to fool? You're going to marry this girl."

They had reached her floor. As the old woman stepped out into the hall, Lagarde stayed in the elevator. *She's right,* he thought to himself with a start.

The bellman turned to his passenger. "Top floor," he wheezed. "Going down."

Lagarde followed his grandmother to her door. The furniture from the big house on Prytania looked odd squeezed into the apartment. Nana had moved here a few years after the death of Lagarde's grandfather. Four or five other elderly New Orleanians kept apartments at the Wharton; it was an old tradition that only a few hotels in town still honored. She picked up the phone and ordered coffee from room service.

Lagarde had managed to avoid the subject of the sculpture, but as they waited for the coffee to be delivered, he offhandedly mentioned the Degas he had been offered. Nana, enamored of the French, recalled her honeymoon in Paris.

"Your grandfather never had a taste for it, but he bought me my little Renoir pastel as a wedding present. It was our last day before coming home. The weather was terrible, but we were walking on the Rue Rivoli when I saw it through a window. I dragged him into the shop. Oh, it made me weak, I loved it so much. But he said no, absolutely not. I was furious with him—what a spoiled young thing I was. Then, that night, when we got back from dinner, there was the little drawing propped against the pillow of our bed. He was such a stinker, your grandfather."

Lagarde tried to change the subject. The last thing he wanted was to trade on his grandmother's happy memories. But Nana refused to talk about anything else. She demanded all the details. She even dragged from him the financial arrangements he might make.

"So you need a loan of $125,000 by next week," the old lady said, nodding her head, "but you'll pay back $100,000 as soon as you sell the house."

"And the car and the stocks," Lagarde added, with growing anxiety.

"Why not?" Nana smiled mischievously. "Why not?"

Lagarde felt his heart beating too quickly in his chest.

"And I'll tell you what," his grandmother continued, "if you marry Lauren, the other $25,000 will be my wedding present to you." Then wagging her finger at him, she said laughing, "But if you don't get married, you'll have to pay back every penny." She instructed him to call Deacon Gilbert, the family's attorney, on Monday afternoon. "Deek'll make the arrangements," she promised.

After they had had their coffee, Nana took Lagarde into her bedroom to show him the Renoir. He had not seen it since he was a child. It left him, as it had his grandfather, absolutely cold. The pretty young girl, smudged in pink and purple and blue, touched nothing within him, but his grandmother, standing next to him, brushed tears from her cheeks with a pale, wrinkled hand.

He had just gotten home from Nana's when there was a knock at the door. He peeked out through the living room window. "Surprise," Lauren shouted from the porch.

Once inside, she explained that she had gotten back to her apartment after lunch with her family and couldn't think of anything to do except to work on an admiralty case she was handling that involved a barge and a sandbar. So she had popped down to New Orleans to see if her cocounsel might want to spend the weekend collaborating with her on some legal research.

"Oh, I see. You want to get into my briefs, huh? Well, come on then," Lagarde agreed, pushing her into the bedroom, "we'd better get to work."

As the evening progressed to several courses of Chinese food, an old movie on cable, and finally a few hours of intermittent sleep in each other's arms on the sofa, their playfulness yielded to passion.

Lagarde woke to the rush of water. Wrapping himself in a blanket, he pushed open the bathroom door. Lauren, reclining in the huge, old tub with ball-and-talon legs, instinctively tried to cover her nakedness. Then she smiled at herself and shyly let her hands slip back into the water.

Dropping the blanket around his feet, Lagarde joined her in the tub. The water rushed up to her throat as he sat down across from her. She tried to lift her long hair out of the water; it lay along her shoulder like wet, dark silk.

"Give me your foot," he said.

She slid her foot along the porcelain until it slipped into the stirrup of his hand. Lifting it up on to his stomach, he cupped the top of it with his other hand and massaged it till she closed her eyes and sighed.

As his grandmother had promised, her attorney had the check waiting for him when he called Monday afternoon. Deek knew better than to ask what the money was for. "Can you pick it up tomorrow?" the old lawyer wondered. "I was just leaving for the club."

So after lunch on Tuesday, Lagarde returned to work with a check for $125,000 in his pocket. He was most afraid that someone in the office might see it; such a check would be difficult to explain, particularly if he tried to tell the truth about it.

He drove around for a long time before going home that night. In fact, he even took a ride out to Lake Pontchartrain. He knew he was approaching the moment when he would have to make a decision. He had only two days left.

A 5 P.M. filing deadline for a motion in a wrongful death suit brought by the widow of an oil rig worker occupied the attorney's attention for most of the next day. By the time a messenger had hurried off with the motion, Lagarde was almost relieved to discover that it was too late to make it over to Gruen's.

That night, he had trouble sleeping. He would make up his mind to buy or not to buy the sculpture; then, almost asleep, he would have second thoughts and roll onto his back to rethink the whole decision. As he grumpily ordered coffee and a blueberry muffin at the breakfast shop in his office building on New Year's Eve, Lagarde made up his mind for the last time.

He called Gruen at ten o'clock and arranged to pick up *The Tub* at the end of the day. Having committed himself to the purchase, he grew more and more excited as the morning matured into afternoon and the afternoon steeped into early evening. By four, most of the partners had already left for the long weekend. A few minutes after the hour, Lagarde pulled out of the parking lot and fought the early traffic to the Effinger Building. Finally finding a space, he dumped a handful of change in the meter and hurried into the building.

Gruen, already in his worn overcoat, was waiting. Somehow, he had dragged the unwieldy crate into the front room. His daughter, he explained, was picking him up downstairs in fifteen minutes. He handed over the authentication papers.

"Well," said Lagarde, taking a deep breath, "here's the check." Endorsing it with his Montblanc, he presented the old man with the slip of paper he had carried in his wallet for the last two days.

"But the tax," stammered Gruen. "Where's the tax?"

"I thought it was included."

"Included? Do you think I could sell you a Degas for $115,000? Even a maquette?" The old man leaned against the crate.

"It's all I've got." Lagarde realized in a kind of terror that he was in danger of losing her, but he bluffed anyway. "If it's not enough, I'll understand." He held out his hand to take back the check.

The old man folded the check and put it in his shirt pocket. "You're robbing me," he complained.

Lagarde had seen this before in negotiations for settlements. He sensed that even without the tax, the dealer was still making a comfortable profit. The lawyer wondered how cheaply the old man had gotten the piece in the first place.

Now that he had the money, Gruen was impatient to close up. Still grumbling, he locked the door behind him as Lagarde struggled down the hall with the crate. He held the elevator for the young man, who carefully placed the container onto the carpeted floor as they made their slow descent. Gruen said nothing, and when the elevator doors opened on the first floor, he hurried off without even a good-bye.

Lagarde muscled the crate into the trunk of his car but had to use a rope to tie it shut. Driving home, he avoided as many bumps as he could, afraid he would find the sculpture cracked in half when he pulled into his driveway.

It seemed to take forever to get home, but once he did struggle through the door with the heavy container, he felt a secret joy begin to seep through him. He gently lowered his burden onto the floor. Unlatching the top and stooping over the statue, he felt the weight of it along his spine as he began to lift. He stopped and bent his knees. As the bottom of the statue cleared the edge of the box, he quickly set the sculpture down on a kilim he had gotten at auction. Lagarde hadn't considered where he might put the piece. He had very little furniture, though what he had was of value, antiques carefully collected in the dusty warehouses of the city's oldest dealers.

Surveying the room, he chose as the statue's pedestal the nineteenth-century gaming table he had found the year before at an estate sale. He covered the polished mahogany with a table cloth and thick towels. Then he lifted the sculpture onto its center. He pulled the sturdy cockfighting chairs, upholstered in green leather, away from the table and adjusted the dimmer on the little chandelier. In the shimmering light of the crystal lamp, he admired *The Tub*.

Now that the work was his, he examined it more closely. He was shocked to discover the lips of a vulva pinched between her fleshy thighs and curls of thick hair scored across her pubes. But there were secrets, hidden by the bronze patina of the wax and the shadows of her raised legs.

For the first time, he touched the body of the bather. It looked so much like bronze, his fingers were surprised that the breast was not cool. The hardened wax of the figure felt like flesh grown suddenly taut under an unexpected hand.

Lagarde opened a small cabinet and withdrew a bottle of brandy. Pouring himself a snifter, he sat across the room admiring his sculpture. But in the midst of his pleasure, he began, inexplicably, to sadden.

Even after he had gone to his bedroom to dress for the evening, he could not shake the melancholy that had tainted his happiness. In fact, as he buttoned the leather thongs of his braces to the black, satin-striped pants and as he fumbled with the unfamiliar knot of a silk bow tie, his mood worsened, like the storm whipping out of the Gulf and across the marshes.

A cold rain lashed his windshield by the time he reached the interstate. Having promised Lauren that he would be in Baton Rouge by nine o'clock, he had to drive faster than he would have liked in such nasty weather. Her parents were hosting their annual New Year's Eve party, and she was eager for them to meet her new friend. Though he had hinted at his misgivings about being introduced to them at a party, Lauren was confident her mother and father would love him as much as she did. He almost hadn't noticed her use of "love." It was the first time either one of them had said the word. To his surprise, it left him not—as he would have expected—peevish, but rather calm, almost placid, as if it were the right word, after all, to describe the pleasure he felt in her company. It might have slipped by unnoticed in the distraction of his concern about meeting her parents if Lagarde hadn't caught Lauren's slight pause and sidelong glance as she said it.

He repeated her sentence as his car skimmed over the slick concrete of the highway.

"But why do you have to leave so early?" Lauren asked groggily. Then, sitting up in the bed and brushing the sleep from her eyes, she realized, "It's still dark outside."

As he gathered up his cummerbund and bow tie from the floor and stuffed them into a pocket of his dinner jacket, Lagarde explained that he had to go.

"I thought we were going to spend the weekend together," Lauren said, the hurt creeping into her voice. "Didn't you have a good time last night?"

Lagarde sat down beside her on the bed. "I had a wonderful time."

"Were my parents awful?"

"I love your parents," he said, then added after a pause, "and I love you."

Lauren strained in the darkness to see his eyes.

He bent and kissed her. "But I have to go," he whispered.

"At least let me make you breakfast."

He relented. "Just coffee."

They did not say much as they sipped from steaming mugs beneath the harsh kitchen light. Lagarde tried to find a way to explain why he had to return to New Orleans immediately, but with only a few hours sleep and still a bit dazed from the New Year's Eve festivities, he couldn't think how to make Lauren understand his anxiety about his statue.

In fact, he hadn't yet told her anything about the Degas. When he considered what he had done—spending $125,000 on a work of art—and even more when he considered what remained to be done—selling his house, his car, and his stocks to pay back his grandmother's loan—he began to see how foolhardy it would all appear to the woman whom, yes, he loved.

"I could come with you," she suddenly said, interrupting his thoughts. "We can call my mother from New Orleans and tell her we can't come to dinner. She won't mind; they're having a whole house of friends over to see LSU in the Cotton Bowl. It's just going to be a buffet."

"No, I wouldn't take you away from your family on a holiday," Lagarde protested. "Why don't you come tomorrow?"

"I can't. We have the firm's touch football game tomorrow. I have to play. Remember? You were going to be my cheerleader. Anyway, what's so important in New Orleans on New Year's morning?"

"I can't tell you. It's a surprise."

As they stood at the door, Lauren gave Lagarde a small, pouting kiss. He wanted to explain, but instead he hurried down the steps and out to his car.

Driving back to the city as dawn began to stain the horizon, he had a long conversation with himself, trying to ferret out the diverse sources of his worry. The most obvious was practical: he might not have insurance on the piece. It hadn't occurred to him that he might need a rider on his policy to cover such an expensive addition to his household furnishings, but at 4:30 A.M., tossing restlessly in Lauren's bed, the thought had suddenly pierced him. A second arrow of anxiety followed the first. The sculpture was still sitting on his dining room table, unprotected and exposed. His neighborhood, though relatively safe, had witnessed its share of crime since he had moved in. The piece might already have been stolen; surely burglars realized many people were away from their homes on New Year's Eve. Or it might even have been vandalized by teenagers hopped up on booze and drugs. Lying awake in the dark, Lagarde had taken a deep breath and made himself admit that his fears were exaggerated. Still, his insurance agent wouldn't be in the office until Monday; he decided he had to stay with the statue until then.

But money wasn't the only source of concern. He had felt guilty in Lauren's arms. In part, he was troubled by keeping a secret from her; however, he was too embarrassed and too uncertain of her response to reveal his purchase. There was another barb of guilt, though, that he was less ready to acknowledge. Smothering Lauren in his kisses, he had felt somehow unfaithful to the woman in *The Tub*. It was ridiculous, he knew, and as soon as he realized what had been rasping his conscience, it ceased to trouble him. But now, driving through the damp pine forests west of New Orleans, he recognized that he was as much owned by the work of art as owner of it. He could not imagine it as less than a petulant mistress, lolling indifferently in her bath. It was no mere lump of wax, of plaster, of canvas. It was a small, exquisite woman with a claim on him.

Lost in thought, he nearly hit an armadillo, dead on the highway.

When Lagarde left for work Monday morning, he hid the statue—replaced in its crate—among some empty boxes in the laundry room. Even once the insurance had been secured, Lagarde rarely removed the woman from her hiding place, particularly after his real estate agent began to show the house to prospective buyers.

It did not take long to sell the house, though the price was less than he had hoped. An antiques dealer made up the difference but left Lagarde with only a mattress, a chair or two, a small table. He waited until he had moved to his new apartment on the streetcar line before he sold his car. The stocks were worth a bit more than the last time he had checked, but with commissions and fees and all the unexpected costs of divesting oneself of material possessions, Lagarde found he still had to withdraw most of his $5,000 in savings to equal the $100,000 he owed his grandmother.

When he telephoned to let Nana know he'd sold his house, she dismissed his concerns about the money. "Just send the check to Deek after the closing," she said, making clear her indifference about the matter. But she was insistent on one point. "When am I going to get to see this beautiful woman of yours?"

"Well, I've got her in a crate right now," Lagarde said, trying to put his grandmother off.

"In a crate?" Nana repeated, horrified. "The poor girl. You should be ashamed."

Lagarde suddenly realized what his grandmother was talking about. "Oh, you mean Lauren."

"Of course I mean Lauren. You're not seeing someone else, are you?"

"No, no," Lagarde protested, "I thought you wanted to see the sculpture, the woman by Degas that I bought."

"Yes, her, too," the old lady said, still a bit disconcerted.

"I promise, as soon as I've got my new apartment all straight, you'll come for dinner. You can meet both women at the same time."

Nana laughed lightly. "So what did Lauren say when she found out you'd sold everything to buy a work of art?"

Lagarde coughed. "I haven't told her yet. I want it to be a surprise."

There was a silence on the other end of the line. Finally, the old woman said, "It's none of my business, of course, Peter. And I think it's utterly charming what you've done. And daring. But . . ."

"Yes," he said resignedly, "you're right."

He had joked to himself that he might have to marry Lauren just to avoid paying back the other $25,000 Nana had given him, but he began to wonder whether Lauren would have him after weeks of inexplicable behavior. She had sympathetically accepted one excuse after another. He was tired of worrying about a house; he preferred an apartment. His antique furniture was oppressive. He wanted a less cluttered, more minimalist look. The car was too much trouble, too ostentatious, and he insisted that the weekend trips to Baton Rouge he now made on the bus were preferable to driving—they gave him a chance to catch up on his reading. But when at last he allowed Lauren to see his bare new apartment, she betrayed her misgivings.

Standing in the doorway, she looked for something to admire in Lagarde's new place. Two wooden chairs faced each other across the gray carpet of an otherwise empty living room. There was nothing upon which to place the crystal vase she had brought as a housewarming present. She handed the wrapped package awkwardly behind her to Lagarde, who still stood in the hall.

"Let me show you the rest," he said without much confidence.

The gray carpet lapped at the white floor tiles of a tiny kitchen. A counter jutting out past the far wall of cabinets concealed a windowless dining alcove. There, a small black table plunged its stubby legs into another swatch of gray carpet.

Beyond lay the bath and bedroom, where a mattress sprawled on the floor. The phone rested on a book beside the simple bed.

Still holding the gift, he sighed. Lauren took his hand, and she made him sit with her on the edge of the mattress.

"I just want to tell you," she said, taking a deep breath, "that I've managed to save some money over the last two years. If you're having trouble right now, I want you to have it. It's not much—"

Lagarde interrupted her. "Thank you," he said.

"No matter how it happened—gambling, or whatever. It's yours, all of it."

Lagarde shook his head. "No, that's not it," he began. "I have to show you something." He stood up. "I want you to wait in here until I call you. OK?"

He closed the bedroom door behind him and unlocked the large hall closet, on which he had had a dead bolt installed before he moved in.

When Lauren emerged from the bedroom, Lagarde had extinguished all the lights except for three track lamps in the breakfast nook. In dimmed incandescence on the black table rested the sculpture. The shafts of muted light fell upon the wax face, a breast, and the legs of the nude woman. Slight shadows gave weight to her small body.

Lauren walked silently around the statue, once pausing to shyly touch the hand of the figure. Coming round to where she had started, she looked to Lagarde for an explanation.

"It's a Degas. It cost me everything." He couldn't bring himself to excuse it as an investment. "I just thought . . ." He stopped and sighed.

"She's exquisite," Lauren said. Her voice trembled as if she had been wounded in some way. "But you gave up everything for her."

Lagarde understood, all at once, that he was about to lose her. Without warning, he took Lauren in his arms, kissing her hard and unyieldingly as she tried to break free of him. He pressed her against the wall and slipped a hand inside her blouse. Then she was unbuckling his pants, pulling his shirt up. They fell to the floor and entwined beneath the indifferent gaze of the brazen nude woman.

Hours later, exhausted and bruised, the couple slept on the mattress in the back room. Just before dawn, Lagarde rolled awake from restless sleep and walked to the kitchen for water.

The dimmed lights still illuminated the statue. Naked, he stood before the work of art, his weariness swelling into fury over the sacrifices required of him by the woman in the tub, forever bathing, forever demanding his attention.

He began to see the folly of his devotion. For a moment, he could have done anything; he could have smashed the mocking face, the teasing body. But he was already too ridiculous, and he could not bring himself to hurt the beautiful creature.

He fled into the bedroom. The fringes of light from the other room cast themselves over Lauren, who had twisted free of the covers. The hair curling like cloth against the face, a breast cupped in her hand, the legs bent to expose the dark frills of her genitalia, a long arm dangling over the edge of the mattress onto the floor— Lagarde recognized, with a slight shudder, who lay asleep at his feet.

He wavered. "So this is love," he said, hopelessly, then knelt among the sheets frothing about her ankles and touched her.

The Convict

JAMES LEE BURKE

for Lyle Williams

My father was a popular man in New Iberia, even though his ideas were different from most people's and his attitudes were uncompromising. On Friday afternoon he and my mother and I would drive down the long, yellow, dirt road through the sugarcane fields until it became a blacktop and followed the Bayou Teche into town, where my father would drop my mother off at Musemeche's Produce Market and take me with him to the bar at the Frederic Hotel. The Frederic was a wonderful old place with slot machines and potted palms and marble columns in the lobby and a gleaming, mahogany-and-brass barroom that was cooled by long-bladed wooden fans. I always sat at a table with a Dr. Nut and a glass of ice and watched with fascination the drinking rituals of my father and his friends: the warm hand-shakes, the pats on the shoulder, the laughter that was genuine but never uncontrolled. In the summer, which seemed like the only season in south Louisiana, the men wore seersucker suits and straw hats, and the amber light in their glasses of whiskey and ice and their Havana cigars and Picayune cigarettes held between their ringed fingers made them seem everything gentlemen and my father's friends should be.

But sometimes I would suddenly realize that there was not only a fundamental difference between my father and other men but that his presence would eventually expose that difference, and a flaw, a deep one that existed in him or them, would surface like an aching wisdom tooth.

"Do you fellows really believe we should close the schools because of a few little Negro children?" my father said.

"My Lord, Will. We've lived one way here all our lives," one man said. He owned a restaurant in town and a farm with oil on it near St. Martinville.

My father took the cigar out of his teeth, smiled, sipped out of his whiskey, and looked with his bright, green eyes at the restaurant owner. My father was a real farmer, not an absentee landlord, and his skin was brown and his body straight and hard. He could pick up a washtub full of bricks and throw it over a fence.

"That's the point," he said. "We've lived among Negroes all our lives. They work in our homes, take care of our children, drive our wives on errands. Where are you going to send our own children if you close the school? Did you think of that?"

The bartender looked at the Negro porter who ran the shoeshine stand in the bar. He was bald and wore an apron and was quietly brushing a pair of shoes left him by a hotel guest.

"Alcide, go down to the corner and pick up the newspapers," the bartender said.

"Yes suh."

"It's not ever going to come to that," another man said. "Our darkies don't want it."

"It's coming, all right," my father said. His face was composed now, his eyes looking through the opened wood shutters at the oak tree in the courtyard outside. "Harry Truman is integrating the army, and those Negro soldiers aren't going to come home and walk around to the back door anymore."

"Charlie, give Mr. Broussard another Manhattan," the restaurant owner said. "In fact, give everybody one. This conversation puts me in mind of the town council."

Everyone laughed, including my father, who put his cigar in his teeth and smiled good-naturedly with his hands folded on the bar. But I knew that he wasn't laughing inside, that he would finish his drink quietly and then wink at me and we'd wave goodbye to everyone and leave their Friday-afternoon good humor intact.

On the way home he didn't talk and instead pretended that he was interested in mother's conversation about the New Iberia ladies' book club. The sun was red on the bayou, and the cypress and oaks along the bank were a dark green in the gathering dusk. Families of Negroes were cane fishing in the shallows for goggle-eye perch and bullheads.

"Why do you drink with them, Daddy? Y'all always have an argument," I said.

His eyes flicked sideways at my mother.

"That's not an argument, just a gentleman's disagreement," he said.

"I agree with him," my mother said. "Why provoke them?"

"They're good fellows. They just don't see things clearly sometimes."

My mother looked at me in the backseat, her eyes smiling so he could see them. She was beautiful when she looked like that.

"You should be aware that your father is the foremost authority in Louisiana on the subject of colored people."

"It isn't a joke, Margaret. We've kept them poor and uneducated and we're going to have to settle accounts for it one day."

"Well, you haven't underpaid them," she said. "I don't believe there's a darkie in town you haven't lent money to."

I wished I hadn't said anything. I knew he was feeling the same pain now that he had felt in the bar. Nobody understood him—not my mother, not me, none of the men he drank with.

The air suddenly became cool, the twilight turned a yellowish green, and it started to rain. Up the blacktop we saw a blockade and men in raincoats with flashlights in their hands. They wore flat campaign hats and water was dancing on the brims. My father stopped at the blockade and rolled down the window. A state policeman leaned his head down and moved his eyes around the inside of the car.

"We got a nigger and a white convict out on the ground. Don't pick up no hitchhikers," he said.

"Where were they last seen?" my father said.

"They got loose from a prison truck just east of the four-corners," he said.

We drove on in the rain. My father turned on the headlights, and I saw the anxiety in my mother's face in the glow from the dashboard.

"Will, that's only a mile from us," she said.

"They're probably gone by now or hid out under a bridge somewhere," he said.

"They must be dangerous or they wouldn't have so many police officers out," she said.

"If they were really dangerous, they'd be in Angola, not riding around in a truck. Besides, I bet when we get home and turn on the radio we'll find out they're back in jail."

"I don't like it. It's like when all those Germans were here."

During the war there was a POW camp outside New Iberia. We used to see them chopping in the sugarcane with a big white P on their backs. Mother kept the doors locked until they were sent back to Germany. My father always said they were harmless and they wouldn't escape from their camp if they were pushed out the front door at gunpoint.

The wind was blowing hard when we got home, and leaves from the pecan orchard were scattered across the lawn. My pirogue, which was tied to a small dock on the bayou behind the house, was knocking loudly against a piling. Mother waited for my father to open the front door, even though she had her own key, then she turned on all the lights in the house and closed the curtains. She began to peel crawfish in the sink for our supper, then turned on the radio in the window as though she were bored for something to listen to. Outside, the door on the tractor shed began to bang violently in the wind. My father went to the closet for his hat and raincoat.

"Let it go, Will. It's raining too hard," she said.

"Turn on the outside light. You'll be able to see me from the window," he said.

He ran through the rain, stopped at the barn for a hammer and a wood stob, then bent over in front of the tractor shed and drove the stob securely against the door.

He walked back into the kitchen, hitting his hat against his pants leg.

"I've got to get a new latch for that door. But at least the wind won't be banging it for a while," he said.

"There was a news story on the radio about the convicts," my mother said. "They had been taken from Angola to Franklin for a trial. One of them is a murderer."

"Angola?" For the first time my father's face looked concerned.

"The truck wrecked, and they got out the back and then made a man cut their handcuffs."

He picked up a shelled crawfish, bit it in half, and looked out the window at the rain slanting in the light. His face was empty now.

"Well, if I was in Angola I'd try to get out, too," he said. "Do we have some beer? I can't eat crawfish without beer."

"Call the sheriff's department and ask where they think they are."

"I can't do that, Margaret. Now, let's put a stop to all this." He walked out of the kitchen, and I saw my mother's jawbone flex under the skin.

It was about three in the morning when I heard the shed door begin slamming in the wind again. A moment later I saw my father walk past my bedroom door buttoning his denim coat over his undershirt. I followed him halfway down the stairs and watched him take a flashlight from the kitchen drawer and lift the twelve-gauge pump out of the rack on the dining room wall. He saw me, then paused for a moment as though he were caught between two thoughts.

Then he said, "Come on down a minute, son. I guess I didn't get that stob hammered in as well as I thought. But bolt the door behind me, will you?"

"Did you see something, Daddy?"

"No, no. I'm just taking this to satisfy your mother. Those men are probably all the way to New Orleans by now."

He turned on the outside light and went out the back door. Through the kitchen window I watched him cross the lawn. He had the flashlight pointed in front of him, and as he approached the tractor shed, he raised the shotgun and held it with one hand against his waist. He pushed the swinging door all the way back against the wall with his foot, shined the light over the tractor and the rolls of chicken wire, then stepped inside the darkness.

I could hear my own breathing as I watched the flashlight beam bounce through the cracks in the shed. Then I saw the light steady in the far corner where we hung the tools and tack. I waited for something awful to happen—the shotgun to streak fire through the boards, a pick in murderous hands to rake downward in a tangle of harness. Instead, my father appeared in the doorway a moment later, waved the flashlight at me, then replaced the stob and pressed it into the wet earth with his boot. I unbolted the back door and went up to bed, relieved that the convicts were far away and that my father was my father, a truly brave man who kept my mother's and my world a secure place.

But he didn't go back to bed. I heard him first in the upstairs hall cabinet, then in the icebox, and finally on the back porch. I went to my window and looked down into the moonlit yard and saw him walking with the shotgun under one arm and a lunch pail and folded towels in the other.

Just at false dawn, when the mist from the marsh hung thick on the lawn and the gray light began to define the black trees along the bayou, I heard my parents arguing in the next room. Then my father snapped: "Damn it, Margaret. The man's hurt."

Mother didn't come out of her room that morning. My father banged out the back door, was gone a half hour, then returned and cooked a breakfast of *couche-couche* and sausages for us.

"You want to go to a picture show today?" he said.

"I was going fishing with Tee Batiste." He was a little Negro boy whose father worked for us sometimes.

"It won't be any good after all that rain. Your mother doesn't want you tracking mud in from the bank, either."

"Is something going on, Daddy?"

"Oh, Mother and I have our little discussions sometimes. It's nothing." He smiled at me over his coffee cup.

I almost always obeyed my father, but that morning I found ways to put myself among the trees on the bank of the bayou. First, I went down on the dock to empty the rainwater out of my pirogue, then I threw dirt clods at the heads of water moccasins on the far side, then I made a game of jumping from cypress root to cypress root along the water's edge without actually touching the bank, and finally I was near what I knew my father wanted me away from that day: the old houseboat that had been washed up and left stranded among the oak trees in the great flood of 1927. Wild morning glories grew over the rotting deck, kids had riddled the cabin walls with .22 holes, and a slender oak had rooted in the collapsed floor and grown up through one window. Two sets of sharply etched footprints, side by side, led down from the levee, on the other side of which was the tractor shed, to a sawed-off cypress stump that someone had used to climb up on the deck.

The air among the trees was still and humid and dappled with broken shards of sunlight. I wished I had brought my .22 and then I wondered at my own foolishness in involving myself in something my father had been willing to lie about in order to protect me from. But I had to know what he was hiding, what or who it was that would make him choose the welfare of another over my mother's anxiety and fear.

I stepped up on the cypress stump and leaned forward until I could see into the doorless cabin. There were an empty dynamite box and a half-dozen beer bottles moted with dust in one corner, and I remembered the seismograph company that had used the houseboat as a storage shack for their explosives two years ago. I stepped up on the deck more bravely now, sure that I would find nothing else in the cabin other than possibly a possum's nest or a squirrel's cache of acorns. Then I saw the booted pants leg in the gloom just as I smelled his odor. It was like a slap in the face, a mixture of dried sweat and blood and the sour stench of swamp mud.

He was sleeping on his side, his knees drawn up before him, his green-and-white, pin-striped uniform streaked black, his bald, brown head tucked under one arm. On each wrist was a silver manacle and a short length of broken chain. Someone had slipped a narrow piece of cable through one manacle and had nailed both looped ends to an oak floor beam with a twelve-inch iron spike. In that heart-pounding moment the length of cable and the long spike leaped at my eye even more than the convict did, because both of them came from the back of my father's pickup truck.

I wanted to run but I was transfixed. There was a bloody tear across the front of his shirt, as though he had run through barbed wire, and even in sleep his round, hard body seemed to radiate a primitive energy and power. He breathed hoarsely through his open mouth, and I could see the stumps of his teeth and the snuff stains on his soft, pink gums. A deerfly hummed in the heat and settled on his forehead, and when his face twitched like a snapping rubber band, I jumped backward involuntarily. Then I felt my father's strong hands grab me like vice grips on each arm.

My father was seldom angry with me, but this time his eyes were hot and his mouth was a tight line as we walked back through the trees toward the house. Finally I heard him blow out his breath and slow his step next to me. I looked up at him and his face had gone soft again.

"You ought to listen to me, son. I had a reason not to want you back there," he said.

"What are you going to do with him?"

"I haven't decided. I need to talk with your mother a little bit."

"What did he do to go to prison?"

"He says he robbed a laundromat. For that they gave him fifty-six years."

A few minutes later he was talking to mother again in their room. This time the door was open and neither one of them cared what I heard.

"You should see his back. There are whip scars on it as thick as my finger," my father said.

"You don't have an obligation to every person in the world. He's an escaped convict. He could come in here and cut our throats for all you know."

"He's a human being who happens to be a convict. They do things up in that penitentiary that ought to make every civilized man in this state ashamed."

"I won't have this, Will."

"He's going tonight. I promise. And he's no danger to us."

"You're breaking the law. Don't you know that?"

"You have to make choices in this world, and right now I choose not to be responsible for any more suffering in this man's life."

They avoided speaking to each other the rest of the day. My mother fixed lunch for us, then pretended she wasn't hungry and washed the dishes while my father and I ate at the kitchen table. I saw him looking at her back, his eyelids blinking for a moment, and just when I thought he was going to speak, she dropped a pan loudly in the dish rack and walked out of the room. I hated to see them like that. But I particularly hated to see the loneliness that was in his eyes. He tried to hide it but I knew how miserable he was.

"They all respect you. Even though they argue with you, all those men look up to you," I said.

"What's that, son?" he said, and turned his gaze away from the window. He was smiling, but his mind was still out there on the bayou and the houseboat.

"I heard some men from Lafayette talking about you in the bank. One of them said, 'Will Broussard's word is better than any damned signature on a contract.'"

"Oh, well, that's good of you to say, son. You're a good boy."

"Daddy, it'll be over soon. He'll be gone and everything will be just the same as before."

"That's right. So how about you and I take our poles and see if we can't catch us a few goggle-eye?"

We fished until almost dinnertime, then cleaned and scraped our stringer of bluegill, goggle-eye perch, and sacalait in the sluice of water from the windmill. Mother had left plates of cold fried chicken and potato salad covered with wax paper for us on the kitchen table. She listened to the radio in the living room while we ate, then picked up our dishes and washed them without ever speaking to my father. The western sky was aflame with the sunset, fireflies spun circles of light in the darkening oaks on the lawn, and at eight o'clock, when I usually listened to "Gangbusters," I heard my father get up out of his straw chair on the porch and walk around the side of the house toward the bayou.

I watched him pick up a gunny sack weighted heavily at the bottom from inside the barn door and walk through the trees and up the levee. I felt guilty when

I followed him, but he hadn't taken the shotgun, and he would be alone and un-armed when he freed the convict, whose odor still reached up and struck at my face. I was probably only fifty feet behind him, my face prepared to smile instantly if he turned around, but the weighted gunny sack rattled dully against his leg and he never heard me. He stepped up on the cypress stump and stooped inside the door of the houseboat cabin, then I heard the convict's voice: "What game you playing, white man?"

"I'm going to give you a choice. I'll drive you to the sheriff's office in New Iberia or I'll cut you loose. It's up to you."

"What you doing this for?"

"Make up your mind."

"I done that when I went out the back of that truck. What you doing this for?"

I was standing behind a tree on a small rise, and I saw my father take a flash-light and a hand ax out of the gunny sack. He squatted on one knee, raised the ax over his head, and whipped it down into the floor of the cabin.

"You're on your own now. There's some canned goods and an opener in the sack, and you can have the flashlight. If you follow the levee you'll come out on a dirt road that'll lead you to a railway track. That's the Southern Pacific and it'll take you to Texas."

"Gimmie the ax."

"Nope. You already have everything you're going to get."

"You got a reason you don't want the law here, ain't you? Maybe a still in that barn."

"You're a lucky man today. Don't undo it."

"What you does is your business, white man."

The convict wrapped the gunny sack around his wrist and dropped off the deck onto the ground. He looked backward with his cannonball head, then walked away through the darkening oaks that grew beside the levee. I wondered if he would make that freight train or if he would be run to ground by dogs and state police and maybe blown apart with shotguns in a cane field before he ever got out of the parish. But mostly I wondered at the incredible behavior of my father, who had turned Mother against him and broken the law himself for a man who didn't even care enough to say thank you.

It was hot and still all day Sunday, then a thundershower blew in from the Gulf and cooled everything off just before suppertime. The sky was violet and pink, and the cranes flying over the cypress in the marsh were touched with fire from the red sun on the horizon. I could smell the sweetness of the fields in the cooling wind and the wild four-o'clocks that grew in a gold-and-crimson spray by the swamp. My father said it was a perfect evening to drive down to Cypremort Point for boiled crabs. Mother didn't answer, but a moment later she said she had promised her sister to go to a movie in Lafayette. My father lit a cigar and looked at her directly through the flame.

"It's all right, Margaret. I don't blame you," he said.

Her face colored, and she had trouble finding her hat and her car keys before she left.

The moon was bright over the marsh that night, and I decided to walk down the road to Tee Batiste's cabin and go frog gigging with him. I was on the back porch sharpening the point of my gig with a file when I saw the flashlight wink out of the trees behind the house. I ran into the living room, my heart racing, the file still in my hand, my face evidently so alarmed that my father's mouth opened when he saw me.

"He's back. He's flashing your light in the trees," I said.

"It's probably somebody running a trotline."

"It's him, Daddy."

He pressed his lips together, then folded his newspaper and set it on the table next to him.

"Lock up the house while I'm outside," he said. "If I don't come back in ten minutes, call the sheriff's office."

He walked through the dining room toward the kitchen, peeling the wrapper off a fresh cigar.

"I want to go, too. I don't want to stay here by myself," I said.

"It's better that you do."

"He won't do anything if two of us are there."

He smiled and winked at me. "Maybe you're right," he said, then took the shotgun out of the wall rack.

We saw the flashlight again as soon as we stepped off the back porch. We walked past the tractor shed and the barn and into the trees. The light flashed once more from the top of the levee. Then it went off, and I saw him outlined against the moon's reflection off the bayou. Then I heard his breathing—heated, constricted, like a cornered animal's.

"There's a roadblock just before that railway track. You didn't tell me about that," he said.

"I didn't know about it. You shouldn't have come back here," my father said.

"They run me four hours through a woods. I could hear them yelling to each other, like they was driving a deer."

His prison uniform was gone. He wore a brown, short-sleeved shirt and a pair of slacks that wouldn't button at the top. A butcher knife stuck through one of the belt loops.

"Where did you get that?" my father said.

"I taken it. What do you care? You got a bird gun there, ain't you?"

"Who did you take the clothes from?"

"I didn't bother no white people. Listen, I need to stay here two or three days. I'll work for you. There ain't no kind of work I can't do. I can make whiskey, too."

"Throw the knife in the bayou."

"What 'chu taking about?"

"I said to throw it away."

"The old man I taken it from put an inch of it in my side. I don't throw it in no bayou. I ain't no threat to you, nohow. I can't go nowheres else. Why I'm going to hurt you or the boy?"

"You're the murderer, aren't you? The other convict is the robber. That's right, isn't it?"

The convict's eyes narrowed. I could see his tongue on this teeth.

"In Angola that means I won't steal from you," he said.

I saw my father's jaw work. His right hand was tight on the stock of the shotgun.

"Did you kill somebody after you left here?" he said.

"I done told you, it was me they was trying to kill. All them people out there, they'd like me drug behind a car. But that don't make no nevermind, do it? You worried about some no-good nigger that put a dirk in my neck and cost me eight years."

"You get out of here," my father said.

"I ain't going nowhere. You done already broke the law. You got to help me."

"Go back to the house, son."

I was frightened by the sound in my father's voice.

"What you doing?" the convict said.

"Do what I say. I'll be along in a minute," my father said.

"Listen, I ain't did you no harm," the convict said.

"Avery!" my father said.

I backed away through the trees, my eyes fixed on the shotgun that my father now leveled at the convict's chest. In the moonlight I could see the sweat running down the Negro's face.

"I'm throwing away the knife," he said.

"Avery, you run to the house and stay there. You hear me?"

I turned and ran through the dark, the tree limbs slapping against my face, the morning-glory vines on the ground tangling around my ankles like snakes. Then I heard the twelve-gauge explode, and by the time I ran through the back screen into the house I was crying uncontrollably.

A moment later I heard my father's boot on the back step. Then he stopped, pumped the spent casing out of the breech, and walked inside with the shotgun over his shoulder and the red shells visible in the magazine. He was breathing hard and his face was darker than I had ever seen it. I knew then that neither he, my mother, nor I would ever know happiness again.

He took his bottle of Four Roses out of the cabinet and poured a jelly glass half full. He drank from it, then took a cigar stub out of his shirt pocket, put it between his teeth, and leaned on his arms against the drainboard. The muscles in his back stood out as though a nail were driven between his shoulder blades. Then he seemed to realize for the first time that I was in the room.

"Hey there, little fellow. What are you carrying on about?" he said.

"You killed a man, Daddy."

"Oh no, no. I just scared him and made him run back in the marsh. But I have to call the sheriff now, and I'm not happy about what I have to tell him."

I didn't think I had ever heard more joyous words. I felt as though my breast, my head, were filled with light, that a wind had blown through my soul. I could smell the bayou on the night air, the watermelons and strawberries growing beside the barn, the endlessly youthful scent of summer itself.

Two hours later my father and mother stood on the front lawn with the sheriff and watched four mud-streaked deputies lead the convict in manacles to a squad car. The convict's arms were pulled behind him, and he smoked a cigarette with his head tilted to one side. A deputy took it out of his mouth and flipped it away just before they locked him in the back of the car behind the wire screen.

"Now, tell me this again, Will. You say he was here yesterday and you gave him some canned goods?" the sheriff said. He was a thick-bodied man who wore blue suits, a pearl-gray Stetson, and a fat watch in his vest pocket.

"That's right. I cleaned up the cut on his chest and I gave him a flashlight, too," my father said. Mother put her arm in his.

"What was that fellow wearing when you did all this?"

"A green-and-white work uniform of some kind."

"Well, it must have been somebody else because I think this man stole that shirt and pants soon as he got out of the prison van. You probably run into one of them niggers that's been setting traps out of season."

"I appreciate what you're trying to do, but I helped the fellow in that car to get away."

"The same man who turned him in also helped him escape? Who's going to believe a story like that, Will?" The sheriff tipped his hat to my mother. "Good night, Mrs. Broussard. You drop by and say hello to my wife when you have a chance. Good night, Will. And you, too, Avery."

We walked back up on the porch as they drove down the dirt road through the sugarcane fields. Heat lightning flickered across the blue-black sky.

"I'm afraid you're fated to be disbelieved," Mother said, and kissed my father on the cheek.

"It's the battered innocence in us," he said.

I didn't understand what he meant, but I didn't care, either. Mother fixed strawberries and plums and hand-cranked ice cream, and I fell asleep under the big fan in the living room with the spoon still in my hand. I heard the heat thunder roll once more, like a hard apple rattling in the bottom of a barrel, and then die somewhere out over the Gulf. In my dream I prayed for my mother and father, the men in the bar at the Frederic Hotel, the sheriff and his deputies, and finally for myself and the Negro convict. Many years would pass before I would learn that it is our collective helplessness, the frailty and imperfection of our vision, that ennobles us and saves us from ourselves; but that night, when I awoke while my father was carrying me up to bed, I knew from the beat of his heart that he and I had taken pause in our contention with the world.

Crickets

ROBERT OLEN BUTLER

They call me Ted where I work and they've called me that for over a decade now and it still bothers me, though I'm not very happy about my real name being the same as the former President of the former Republic of Vietnam. Thiệu is not an uncommon name in my homeland and my mother had nothing more in mind than a long-dead uncle when she gave it to me. But in Lake Charles, Louisiana, I am Ted. I guess the other Mr. Thiệu has enough of my former country's former gold bullion tucked away so that in London, where he probably wears a bowler and carries a rolled umbrella, nobody's calling him anything but Mr. Thiệu.

I hear myself sometimes and I sound pretty bitter, I guess. But I don't let that out at the refinery, where I'm the best chemical engineer they've got and they even admit it once in a while. They're good-hearted people, really. I've done enough fighting in my life. I was eighteen when Saigon fell and I was only recently mustered into the Army, and when my unit dissolved and everybody ran, I stripped off my uniform and put on my civilian clothes again and I threw rocks at the North's tanks when they rolled through the streets. Very few of my people did likewise. I stayed in the mouths of alleys so I could run and then return and throw more rocks, but because what I did seemed so isolated and so pathetic a gesture, the gunners in the tanks didn't even take notice. But I didn't care about their scorn. At least my right arm had said no to them.

And then there were Thai Pirates in the South China Sea and idiots running the refugee centers and more idiots running the agencies in the U.S. to find a place for me and my new bride, who braved with me the midnight escape by boat and the terrible sea and all the rest. We ended up here in the flat bayou land of Louisiana, where there are rice paddies and where the water and the land are in the most delicate balance with each other, very much like the Mekong Delta, where I grew up. These people who work around me are good people and maybe they call me Ted because they want to think of me as one of them, though sometimes it bothers me that these men are so much bigger than me. I am the size of a woman in this country and these American men are all massive and they speak so slowly, even to one another, even though English is their native language. I've heard New Yorkers on television and I speak as fast as they do.

My son is beginning to speak like the others here in Louisiana. He is ten, the product of the first night my wife and I spent in Lake Charles, in a cheap motel with the sky outside red from the refineries. He is proud to have been born in America, and when he leaves us in the morning to walk to the Catholic school, he says, "Have a good day, y'all." Sometimes I say good-bye to him in Vietnamese and he wrinkles his nose at me and says, "Aw, Pop," like I'd just cracked a corny joke. He doesn't speak Vietnamese at all and my wife says not to worry about that. He's an American.

But I do worry about that, though I understand why I should be content. I even understood ten years ago, so much so that I agreed with my wife and gave my son an American name. Bill. Bill and his father Ted. But this past summer I found my son hanging around the house bored in the middle of vacation and I was suddenly his father Thiệu with a wonderful idea for him. It was an idea that had come to me in the first week of every February we'd been in Lake Charles, because that's when the crickets always begin to crow here. This place is rich in crickets, which always make me think of my own childhood in Vietnam. But I never said anything to my son until last summer.

I came to him after watching him slouch around the yard one Sunday pulling the Spanish moss off the lowest branches of our big oak tree and then throwing rocks against the stop sign on our corner. "Do you want to do something fun?" I said to him.

"Sure, Pop," he said, though there was a certain suspicion in his voice, like he didn't trust me on the subject of fun. He threw all the rocks at once that were left in his hand and the stop sign shivered at their impact.

I said, "If you keep that up, they will arrest me for the destruction of city property and then they will deport us all."

My son laughed at this. I, of course, knew that he would know I was bluffing. I didn't want to be too hard on him for the boyish impulses that I myself had found to be so satisfying when I was young, especially since I was about to share something of my own childhood with him.

"So what've you got, Pop?" my son asked me.

"Fighting crickets," I said.

"What?"

Now, my son was like any of his fellow ten-year-olds, devoted to superheroes and the mighty clash of good and evil in all of its high-tech forms in the Saturday-morning cartoons. Just to make sure he was in the right frame of mind, I explained it to him with one word, "Cricketmen," and I thought this was a pretty good ploy. He cocked his head in interest at this and I took him to the side porch and sat him down and I explained.

I told him how, when I was a boy, my friends and I would prowl the undergrowth and capture crickets and keep them in matchboxes. We would feed them leaves and bits of watermelon and bean sprouts, and we'd train them to fight by keeping them in a constant state of agitation by blowing on them and gently flicking the ends of their antennas with a sliver of wood. So each of us would have a stable of fighting crickets, and there were two kinds.

At this point my son was squirming a little bit and his eyes were shifting away into the yard and I knew that my Cricketman trick had run its course. I fought back the urge to challenge his set of interests. Why should the stiff and foolish fights of his cartoon characters absorb him and the real clash—real life and death—that went on in the natural world bore him? But I realized that I hadn't cut to the chase yet, as they say on the TV. "They fight to the death," I said with as much gravity as I could put into my voice, like I was James Earl Jones.

The announcement won me a glance and a brief lift of his eyebrows. This gave me a little scrabble of panic, because I still hadn't told him about the two types of crickets and I suddenly knew that was a real important part for me. I tried not to despair at this understanding and I put my hands on his shoulders and turned him around to face me. "Listen," I said. "You need to understand this if you are to have fighting crickets. There are two types, and all of us had some of each. One type we called the charcoal crickets. These were very large and strong, but they were slow and they could become confused. The other type was small and brown and we called them fire crickets. They weren't as strong, but they were very smart and quick."

"So who would win?" my son said.

"Sometimes one and sometimes the other. The fights were very long and full of hard struggle. We'd have a little tunnel made of paper and we'd slip a sliver of wood under the cowling of our cricket's head to make him mad and we'd twirl him by his antenna, and then we'd each put our cricket into the tunnel at opposite ends. Inside, they'd approach each other and begin to fight and then we'd lift the paper tunnel and watch."

"Sounds neat," my son said, though his enthusiasm was at best moderate, and I knew I had to act quickly.

So we got a shoe box and we started looking for crickets. It's better at night, but I knew for sure his interest wouldn't last that long. Our house is up on blocks because of the high water table in town and we crawled along the edge, pulling back the bigger tufts of grass and turning over rocks. It was one of the rocks that gave us our first crickets, and my son saw them and cried in my ear, "There, there," but he waited for me to grab them. I cupped first one and then the other and dropped them into the shoe box and I felt a vague disappointment, not so much because it was clear that my boy did not want to touch the insects, but that they were both the big black ones, the charcoal crickets. We crawled on and we found another one in the grass and another sitting in the muddy shadow of the house behind the hose faucet and then we caught two more under an azalea bush.

"Isn't that enough?" my son demanded. "How many do we need?"

I sat with my back against the house and put the shoe box in my lap and my boy sat beside me, his head stretching this way so he could look into the box. There was no more vagueness to my feeling. I was actually weak with disappointment because all six of these were charcoal crickets, big and inert and just looking around like they didn't even know anything was wrong.

"Oh, no," my son said with real force, and for a second I thought he had read my mind and shared my feeling, but I looked at him and he was pointing at the toes of his white sneakers. "My Reeboks are ruined!" he cried, and on the toe of each sneaker was a smudge of grass.

I glanced back into the box and the crickets had not moved and I looked at my son and he was still staring at his sneakers. "Listen," I said, "this was a big mistake. You can go on and do something else."

He jumped up at once. "Do you think Mom can clean these?" he said.

"Sure," I said. "Sure."

He was gone at once and the side door slammed and I put the box on the grass. But I didn't go in. I got back on my hands and knees and I circled the entire house and then I turned over every stone in the yard and dug around all the trees. I found probably two dozen more crickets, but they were all the same. In Louisiana there are rice paddies and some of the bayous look like the Delta, but many of the birds are different, and why shouldn't the insects be different, too? This is another country, after all. It was just funny about the fire crickets. All of us kids rooted for them, even if we were fighting with one of our own charcoal crickets. A fire cricket was a very precious and admirable thing.

The next morning my son stood before me as I finished my breakfast and once he had my attention, he looked down at his feet, drawing my eyes down as well. "See?" he said. "Mom got them clean."

Then he was out the door and I called after him, "See you later, Bill."

Where She Was

KELLY CHERRY

My mother was a child in Lockport, Louisiana, where there were six "good" houses distinguishable from the small row houses, each with a two-seated outhouse in the back yard, in which the unskilled workers, most of whom were Cajun, lived. To the east of the mill were houses for the sawyer and two mill officials; to the west, houses for the mill's bookkeeper, the commissary manager, and the filer, her father. Papa, she called him.

A wide veranda extended across the front of the house. Here my mother spent long hours in the lazy bench swing, saved from the fierce afternoon sun by a Confederate jessamine vine starred with small white fragrant flowers that relentlessly seduced big hairy black-and-yellow bumblebees and long-billed humming-birds whose rapidly vibrating wings seemed an excessive labor on such days. Beneath the house, which was set high on pillars, was a cool, dark place hidden from view behind a skirt of green lattices, where her papa built shelves to store her mother's Mason jars of mayhaw jelly and mustard pickle and brown paper bags of sugar beets.

Inside the house, in the living room, were the phonograph and the piano, the morris chair that was "Papa's chair," and several tall glass-enclosed bookcases containing, my mother remembered, illustrated editions of *Paradise Lost* and *Paradise Regained, A Child's Garden of Verse,* the family Bible, *Evangeline, Girl of the Limberlost,* complete sets of Scott, Hugo, and Dickens, and *The Princess and Curdie,* on the front of which was a picture of the princess in a gown of pale green silk that seemed to glow when she looked at it, like a will o' the wisp.

She was a shy child, my mother, easily embarrassed, a perfectionist at five, but she was also inventive, able to entertain herself happily, and able to abandon herself to her imagination. On rainy days she read the Sears, Roebuck and Montgomery Ward catalogues or the French book her sister, studying library science at Carnegie Tech, sent her, with the nouns depicted in garments that suited their genders ("*la fenêtre*" wore a ruffled frock). She played her autoharp or copied music onto homemade manuscript paper, though she could not yet read the notes. She played with Isaac, the little black boy who helped her mother with her gardening, or Charlie Mattiza, whom she summoned to his window by calling "Charlie Mattiza, Pigtail Squeezer!" from his yard.

The early evenings, the blue-to-lavender time between supper and bedtime, she spent on her papa's lap in the morris chair, listening to phonograph records. His phonograph was his prize possession. It was the first one in Lockport. He had records of *Scheherazade, Night on Bald Mountain,* Weber's *Invitation to the Dance* and overture to *Oberon.* (Later, he was to get Stravinsky's *Rites of Spring,* which he listened to over and over, until he felt he understood it.) She was her father's favorite, the two of them drawn powerfully to a world that did not even exist for the people around them, in Lockport, Louisiana, in the century's teens.

By the time my mother was in her seventies, living in England, she had come to believe that human beings were like cancer cells, destroying everything worthwhile—though she had her quarrels with nature too (eating, for example, was an essentially ugly act, whether performed by people or animals) and there were a few human achievements that conceivably validated our presence on earth (Bach's music). I think she felt that the life-processes had been devised purposely to humiliate her. She considered that sex was an invasion of privacy, sleeping was a waste of time, and having children was like signing a death-sentence for your dreams, whatever they might be. She told me these things while we were sitting in front of the television—the telly—flipping through the cable "videopaper" by remote control, to check out the temperature in Wisconsin, the exchange rate for dollars, the headlines. Emphysema and strokes had whittled her life down to the size of the screen. Despite my best intentions, I sometimes became irritated by her. I was at a point in my own life where what I wanted more than anything was to feel connected to other people, and I found it difficult not to feel bitter about a point of view that, I now say, had to a great extent ghostwritten, as it were, my autobiography. For I was my mother's daughter, as she was her father's, and I had tried to be the reflection of her dreams that she wanted me to be—as she had tried to be her father's.

Sometimes her papa brought scraps of wood home from the sawmill for his youngest daughter to play with. As the saw-filer, it was his important job to keep razor-sharp the teeth of the whirling, circular saw that the sawyer, riding his carriage back and forth, thrust the logs into. Out came boards, and the curls and scraps and shavings he took home to my mother. She laid them out on the front lawn like the floor plan for a schoolhouse, assigning a subject to each "room," and wrote a textbook for each subject, using Calumet Baking Powder memo books, which were distributed free at the commissary, and elderberry ink. Requiring a pupil, she invited Elise Cheney to her schoolhouse—having decided that Elise, of all her acquaintances, was most in need of an education. After a few sessions of trying to teach Elise how to spell "chrysanthemum," she renounced her teaching career in disgust—my mother was impatient with dullards—and turned her attention to the seven Henderson children, whose names, for some reason, she felt compelled to remember in chronological order. Pumping her tree swing to the top of the great oak in the front yard, she sang loudly and mnemonically, for hours on end,

> Oh the buzzards they fly high down in Mobile
> (Lalla, Lillie, Georgia, Billy, Flossie, Edna, Beth).
> Oh the buzzards they fly high down in Mobile
> (Lalla, Lillie, Georgia, Billy, Flossie, Edna, Beth).
> Oh the buzzards they fly high
> And they puke right out the sky
> (Lalla, Lillie, Georgia, Billy, Flossie, Edna, Beth).

One summer they rented a house on Lake Prien, where her father fished for tarpon by day and was in demand as a dancing partner by night, when the grown-ups paired off to the strains of Strauss waltzes, starlit breezes blowing in through the open windows, billowing the muslin curtains. He was a handsome man, serious and loyal, permanently dazzled by his lively wife, a petite redhead he'd courted for a year in Mobile, wooing her with a bag of grapes in his bicycle basket.

My mother was going to be a beautiful woman, a finer version of the young Katharine Hepburn, but she didn't know it yet. She was the baby—a tall, skinny baby, she thought, while her mother and two sisters were visions of stylishness. This was the summer her middle sister, about to join the flapper generation, launched a campaign to persuade her parents to let her have her hair cut short. When tears and tantrums failed, she began to pin it up in large puffs that stuck out over her ears. These puffs were popular with her classmates and were called "cootie garages." Each day, the cootie garages grew a little larger—and finally, when her head began to look as though it had been screwed on with a giant wing nut, her parents said to her, "Please, go get your hair cut!"

My mother was still in her Edenic chrysalis, fishing in doodlebug holes with balls of sand and spit stuck to the ends of broomstraws. She went fishing with her papa on his boat, *The Flick,* helping him to disentangle the propeller when it got caught in water hyacinths. The dreamy, wavy roots were like cilia or arms, holding up traffic. They passed the pirogues in which Cajun trappers push-poled their way through the bayous. Drying on the banks was the Spanish moss from which the Cajuns made their mattresses. Crawfish crept along the sandy bottom of the bayou, and water bugs skated on the surface. Cottonmouth moccasins slithered away in disdain. Hickory and hackberry, willow and cypress shut out the sun. Her papa pointed out birds that were like lost moments in the landscape, helping her to see what was almost hidden: white egrets, majestic as Doric columns, red-winged blackbirds, pelicans, and pink flamingos. This was my mother's world.

She had boyfriends. When she entered the consolidated school for Calcasieu Parish, at Westlake, which, like her pretend-school, had a different room and even a different teacher for each subject, she boarded the school bus at the commissary, always sitting next to Siebert Gandy, the sawyer's son, who never failed to save one of the choice end seats for her. From the two end seats, one could dangle one's legs out the rear of the van. On rainy days, the potholes filled up wonderfully with a red soupy mud that tickled one's toes.

Siebert was two years older than she was. He frequently handed her a five-cent bag of jawbreakers when she got on the bus. To cement their unspoken bond, my mother "published" a weekly newspaper, printed on wrapping paper from the butcher at the commissary. There was only one copy of each edition, which appeared at irregular intervals, and she delivered it surreptitiously to Siebert's front yard. After her family moved to Gulfport—the timber had been used up and oil had been discovered in the swamp and the mill closed down, scattering its employees—she received a letter from Siebert, whose family had moved to California, which began, "My dear little girl." She never got beyond the salutation. She burst into tears and handed the letter to her mother, who carried it off with her and never mentioned it again. So Siebert had loved her—but why had he waited until he was two thousand miles away to tell her? When she was in her seventies, living in England, she told me that she thought she really had loved Siebert. She never forgot him. He had been a part of the world that closed off after she left Lockport.

At first she loved Gulfport. They lived two blocks from the beach. She was growing up, and the freighters in the harbor, the sun flashing on the wide water that rolled across to Mexico, the white sand and palm trees and merchant seamen, all seemed like landmarks in her expanding horizon. But this new world was busy with other minds that had their own ideas about how things were to be done. She could no longer escape into private dreams, a secret music. A clamor began, and so did an unacknowledged rage at it—this infringement, this stupidity, this noise.

She did not let herself know how distressed she was. There was a glassed-in sleeping porch that became her bedroom; her middle sister was away at college, and her library-science sister had gotten a job in Tampa. It was a tiny, cramped porch, overlooking the back garden, and on the side, the alley that separated the lawn from the Everetts'. On the wall above her bed she pasted a picture she'd torn out of a magazine—white daisies, with yellow-button centers like butter in biscuits, on a field of green, a dark gray sky overhead like a monastery.

She was facing a whole new set of problems, worries she had not realized came with growing up: how to make her stockings stay up (garters were not yet available; stockings were rolled at the top, and then the rolls were twisted and turned under; the other girls' stayed up, but hers slid down her thin legs and finished up around her ankles, so that she had to keep ducking behind oleander bushes on her way home to pull them back up); what to do if she met a boy on the way, God forbid; and most of all, how to avoid being laughed at.

Despite the book of French nouns, she had gotten off to a bad start in French class in Gulfport. When she joined the class, skipping two grades, the students had already learned to answer the roll call by saying "Ici." She thought they were saying "Easy," and so when her name was called, she said "Easy." Everyone laughed. When she prepared her first assignment for English class, she thought her paper would look nice if she lined up the margins on the right side as well as on the left, which necessitated large gaps in the middle. The teacher held her paper up to the class as an example of how not to do homework.

That same English teacher terrified my mother by requiring every student, during senior year, to make a speech at morning assembly. My mother began to worry about her "Senior Speech" when she was still a sophomore. When senior Dwight Matthews walked out on the stage with his fiddle and said, "I shall let my violin speak for me," and then played "Souvenir," she fell in love with a forerunner of my father, and so my future began to be a possibility, an etiological ruck in the shimmery fabric of the universe.

My mother had inadvertently learned to read music back in Lockport when she'd entertained herself by copying the notes from her sister's piano étude books. The first time she attempted the violin, her fingers found their way by instinct to the right spots. Soon she was studying with Miss Morris at the Beulah Miles Conservatory of Music on East Beach. Miss Morris often carried her violin out to the end of the municipal pier in the evening to let the Gulf breezes play tunes on it. (She also recited poetry to the rising sun.)

My mother's violin was an old box that had belonged to her papa's father. Eventually, by winning the *New Orleans Times-Picayune*'s weekly essay contest, she saved up fifty dollars (though this took some time, as the prize for her essay on the Pascagoula Indians, for example, was fifty pounds of ice) and sent off to Montgomery Ward for a new violin, complete with case, bow, and a cake of genuine rosin (progress over her former sap-scraped-from-pine-bark).

Even with the new violin, there was time for boys. She and her best girlfriend, Olive Shaw, used to go cruising, though this activity was not much more sexual than crabbing, which they also did a lot of. Olive had an old Dodge that Mr. Shaw had named Pheidippides, after the Greek athlete who'd run himself to death. Olive was only thirteen, but no one needed a license to drive in Mississippi. They liked to drive out to the Gulf Coast Military Academy to watch the cadets' parade and hear the band play "Oh, the Monkey Wrapped Its Tail Around the Flagpole." She cannot have been as backward as she thought she was—when the marching was over, the boys gathered around the car, flirting like crazy.

But she knew nothing of sex, the mystery she and Olive were dying to solve. All the Zane Grey books ended with the hero kissing the heroine on the blue veins of her lily-white neck. My mother's neck was as brown as her cake of rosin, from her hours swimming in salt water and lying on the pier. She was not in danger of having her blue veins kissed—she examined her neck in the bathroom mirror, and not one blue vein showed under the light. Finally one of the cadets kissed her, after a movie date— on the mouth, not her neck. She worried that she might be going to have a baby, but her stomach stayed flat, and after a while she forgot to think about it.

Much social life revolved around church, which my mother nevertheless avoided as much as possible. When she did go—Sunday services were obligatory—

she tried to act as if she were not related to her family. Her mother's mother's hymn-singing sounded rather like Miss Morris's violin-playing (off-key), and her own mama, perky in a new bonnet, seemed to become a stranger to her, as if she belonged to other people instead of to her own daughter—busying herself with the flowers at the altar, saying "Good morning!" and "Isn't it just a lovely day!" to all and sundry. My teenaged mother cringed when her grandmother called across the street to her mama: "Hat-*tee,* when you come to lunch, bring the bowl of mayonnaise and the Book of Exodus!"

She survived these humiliations, and even her "Senior Speech" since she'd been lucky enough to be assigned a role in the school play. She had one line to speak: "I'm your little immortality," and after weeks of practice, she learned to say it loud enough to be heard by the audience. It came out "I'm your little immorality," but it satisfied the English teacher's requirement.

Her mama took her shopping in New Orleans for her graduation clothes: a green silk dress for Class Day, a white chiffon for graduation, and a pink organdy for the Senior Prom. But when the morning of the prom arrived, she still did not have a date. Her mama disappeared into the hallway to whisper into the telephone, and soon Alfred Purple, whose mother was, like my mother's mother, a member of the United Daughters of the Confederacy, called to ask my mother to go to the prom with him.

Alas, that night when Alfred called for my mother he had one foot done up in a wad of bandage, as if he had the gout. At the dance, they sat briefly on the sidelines; then my mother asked him to take her home. She hung the pink organdy prom dress on a satin-covered hanger. In two years, she would be one of the popular girls at LSU, dancing to all the latest tunes—but she had no way of knowing that that night. She was convinced Alfred had returned to the prom afterward, with both feet in working order. Anyway, she was done with high school. She was fifteen. This is a portrait of the girl who became my father's wife.

After my parents were married, and my mother was pregnant with my brother, they made a trip back from Baton Rouge to Gulfport. One day my mother and grandmother went for an afternoon outing in the Model-T Ford, my grandmother at the wheel. They drove past rice paddies and sugar cane fields, and cotton fields, the cotton bursting out in little white pincushions. As they scooted along the highway, relishing the breeze the car created for them, they chatted about love and marriage and impending babies. They stopped beside a deserted beach to eat the fried chicken wings and hard-boiled eggs that my grandmother had packed. From the car, the sparse dune grass seemed almost transparent in the haze of heat, like strands of blown glass. The gentle waves broke the water into smooth facets that flashed like the diamond on my grandmother's finger (my mother, a Depression bride, had only an inexpensive gold band). The salt in the air was so strong they said to each other that they could salt their hard-boiled eggs just by holding them out the window. My mother laughed. She felt so close to her mother, so free, now that she was grown up, about to have a baby, that she decided to ask her a question about sex. "Mama," she said, "isn't it supposed to be something people enjoy? Is something wrong with me?"

The gulls were diving off shore. My mother was aware of her heart beating like a metronome—she wished she could stop it, that determined, tactless beat. As soon as the question was out, she realized she had gone where you should never go— into your parents' bedroom. She blushed, thinking about the time she'd surprised her papa in the bathroom.

Her mother looked straight ahead, through the windshield, and drummed her fingers on the steering wheel. "Your father and I have always had a wonderful sexual relationship," she said firmly. "I'm sorry if it's not the same for you."

That was all. It was like a nail being driven in, boarding up a dark, hidden place. On Class Day, my mother's "gag" gift had been a hammer—because, as Bill Whittaker, the master of ceremonies, had explained, everyone knew my mother wanted something for her papa. She remembered how happy the little joke had made him as he sat in the school auditorium.

They fed the leftovers to the crying gulls. The sun was dropping in the west like an apple from a tree. On the way home, they talked about other things—her sisters, the apartment in Baton Rouge.

She had dropped out of graduate school to marry my father, at twenty. The apartment was in a building rented to faculty. My father taught violin and theory. In fact, my mother had been responsible for his coming to LSU: As the star violin pupil, she'd been asked to offer her opinion on the vitae the department had received. In those days, job applications were routinely accompanied by photographs. My mother instantly chose my father.

She was so pregnant—eight-and-a-half months, and it seemed to her that no one had ever been as pregnant as she. She felt like Alice after she'd bitten into the "Eat me" cake, grown too huge for the room. She thought she would never be pretty again—in less than a year, she'd become an old lady, almost a matron. Her dancing days were over. These were dull days. She had no friends, because any friendship one married woman had with another had to be shallow (you couldn't talk about your husband or your sex life or how much you hated having to cook three meals a day, or how you felt about anything). There was no money for movies or dresses—it was 1933, and only by the grace of Huey Long, who, demagogue though he might be, saw to it that not a single LSU faculty member was laid off, the only university in the country that was true of, did they have any money at all (but often it was scrip). She couldn't have gotten into a new dress anyway, not any dress she'd want to get into.

She couldn't even practice—her stomach didn't give her arms enough mobility. When she did the laundry in the bathtub, scrubbing shorts and socks on a grooved aluminum washboard, she felt so solidly planted on the tile floor that she envisioned getting up again as an uprooting.

In bed, she lay with her back to my father, facing the wall. Such long sticky nights, and then the barest increase in comfort with the coming of winter—but the emotional temperature in the room remained high. My mother did not understand what had happened to her, how just by loving music and my father she'd become enmeshed in misery, in a spartan orange-crate apartment, in a life that was devoid of the beautiful epiphanies of her childhood.

But she was too well trained to inflict her depression on my father. There were no tears—she was not one for self-pity. Even on Christmas morning, which felt as foreign to her as Europe, as exotic as Catholicism or snow, because this was the first Christmas she had not spent with her family, she made the bed and fixed my father's breakfast, no lying in or moping around. The tree reached almost to the ceiling, and the lights, which she had tediously tested one by one, were all shining. On top of the tree stood a gold star that lasted through the years until I got married and my parents began to dispense, a little bit at a time, with the ceremonies and symbols Christmas had acquired for them.

She and my father were awkward with each other that morning, addressing each other with a formal politeness better suited to guests. It seemed to them that every small choice they made was setting a precedent for Christmases to come—

and also represented a rupture from their pasts. They ate pain-du, day-old bread fried in egg yoke and sugar, a Cajun variant of French toast. My mother drank cocoa and my father drank coffee—choices that later became habits and eventually defining characteristics. In the early morning light, which temporarily softened the drab apartment, lending an impressionistic reticence to the sharp edges of the furniture, the scratchy upholstery, they sat self-consciously on the floor by the tree. My father kissed my mother and placed in her hands the present he had bought for her with a kind of desperate good will, searching all over New Orleans for something that would make her happy again, glad to be married to him. When he had bought it, leaning over the glass counter in Maison Blanche on a fall day that was hot even for Louisiana, conferring with the sales clerk while sweat ran down the inside of his shirt sleeves under his suit jacket, he had seen my mother gesturing gracefully with the little evening bag in her left hand like a corsage of sequins, her beautiful smiling face a sonata on a blessedly cool evening.

It was red. It seemed to slide under your fingers, the hundreds of tiny, shiny sequins as tremulous as water. It was as flirtatious as a handkerchief, as reserved as a private home. When my mother took it out of its box, the tears she'd been hiding from my father were released—they fell from her eyes like more sequins, silvery ones. She knew how she was hurting him, but there was nothing she could do about it. She tried to explain how ugly the evening bag made her feel, but the more she tried to explain herself, the more she seemed to be accusing him.

She ran to the bathroom, sobbing, where she could be alone. The red evening bag lay half in its box, half out, like a heart at the center of the burst of white tissue paper. My father's present waited under the tree. He went into the kitchen and sat at the formica table, drinking another cup of coffee. There were tears in his eyes too, behind his glasses. He blew his nose. He was drinking his coffee from a pale green cup with a V-shape, a brand of kitchenware that was omnipresent at the time. He felt wounded and frustrated and angry, and sad, and confused, and disgusted.

When I was seventeen, I took a train by myself from Virginia to New Mexico, having transferred for my sophomore year to the New Mexico Institute of Mining and Technology. On the way out there I stopped over in Gulfport to visit my mother's mother, Grandma Little. She was at the station to hug me hello. She was wearing white open-eyelet shoes and a lavender print and a pale pink straw bonnet and when she smiled her face turned a pretty shade of rose as if she were a bouquet all by herself. "You may call me Hattie now," she offered, meaning that if I was grown up enough to make a trip like this alone, I was grown up enough to be treated like an equal. She was eighty-two.

She was standing in front of the chest of drawers in the hallway, watching herself in the mirror as she took off her bonnet. Partly because her name was Hattie, she always wore hats—and also because they kept the sun off her face. She showed me where I could put my suitcase.

She still lived in the old house just a couple of blocks from the beach. The house had thick stone walls to keep the heat in in winter and the coolness in in summer. She had made up a bed for me on the sleeping porch and when I woke up the next morning the first thing I saw was a blue jay in the pecan tree. The second thing was Grandma Little brushing her long white hair. It fell almost to her waist, even pulled over her head from the back as she brushed the underside, and made me think of a bridal veil. She had been a widow for eight years. After she put her hair up, we ate breakfast in the kitchen. I had never been alone with her before. The day in front of us seemed as long as a railroad track.

She drew a map for me and I walked down to the beach. The sun on the water was as bright and sharp as knife blades. By the time I got back to the house, in the midafternoon, clouds had rolled in—they arrived on time, I learned, like a train, every day at this time of year, and it rained for an hour, and then the sun came out again, as nonchalant as if it had never been supplanted.

Grandma Little had her feet propped on a footstool Grandpa had made for her for Christmas one year. She was sitting in a deep, wide armchair. I sat on the couch and she told me about my mother. The light in the room grew heavier and slowly sank out of sight. I turned on the floor lamp.

"When we moved to Lockport," she said, "your mother was five. Up until then, we had been living in Lake Charles. Your mother had to leave her rabbits behind and she was very upset about that. She loved those rabbits. She always preferred animals to people. When she was *very* little, and we had company to dinner, she used to hide under the table, where no one could see her eat. She insisted that I hand her a bowl of oatmeal—that was all she would eat—under the tablecloth. Well, when we first moved to Lockport, she decided she was going to learn how to be sociable, and on her first day of school, she came home with all her classmates. She had told them it was her birthday. My goodness, I don't know how many children there were! I didn't want to embarrass her by telling them that it wasn't her birthday, but of course there was no ice cream or cake in the house. Why would there be? And we made our own ice cream in those days, don'tcha know. So I gave each of them a banana and a glass of lemonade and they all sang 'Happy Birthday' to your mother, and I think she felt very pleased with herself about what a grand occasion it was."

I blinked back tears. I was seventeen and homesick.

"Oh yes," she said, "your mother was a handful, strong-willed and skittish."

Grandma Little had gotten quite stocky and she had to work to get out of the enveloping armchair, but she refused to let me help her, saying it was better for her to make the effort. Finally she was standing in front of me, her hands on her hips, head cocked to one side. "Dinner is ready," she announced.

We ate chicken spaghetti off the Spode plates in the dining room. As we ate, it seemed to me that the room filled up with the ghosts of children. The air shimmered with their small shapes. Elise Cheney and Charlie Mattiza stood at the back of the room, and all seven Hendersons (Lalla, Lillie, Georgia, Billy, Flossie, Edna, Beth). Isaac was there with his trowel that was almost as big as he was. Siebert Gandy came with a bag of jawbreakers, his birthday present for my mother. Then things got mixed up and others crowded in—Olive Shaw, Dwight Matthews, the cadets. They were all so young that even I felt old. They were almost as young as the century had been. They seemed to be playing, or dancing in slow motion, and laughing—I could almost hear their laughter, as if it were an overtone, the music behind the music. Their faces were as translucent as wind.

I washed the dishes while Grandma Little went on ahead to bed. She got up at four every morning, to do the cleaning and most of the cooking while it was still cool. The hot, soapy water on my hands felt like a reprieve from a disembodied existence I was both tempted by and frightened of. I dried the dishes and returned them to their shelf on the china closet in the dining room. I remembered my mother's saying how she had found a secluded glen on the high ground on the far side of the narrow footbridge that crossed the swamp at the west end of Lockport, near, it seemed to her, where the sun went down. It was a circular clearing completely enclosed by leafy shade trees. Here she could lie on the grass, surrounded by wild violets and forget-me-nots and dandelions, and watch the clouds of yellow butterflies that drifted across the sky above her. As she lay there, she heard a symphony she had never heard before. It was not on any of her papa's records. It seemed to come from inside her head, and yet she didn't know how it could, since she couldn't write music. When she was in her seventies, living in England, she was to say, "I wished I could have written it down, because I wanted so much to remember it. It was the most beautiful symphony I have ever heard. After that first time, I spent many afternoons in the glen. No one ever disturbed me there. Nobody ever knew where I was."

Fever

MOIRA CRONE

I started out that morning as myself. As steady David Wheelock.

I'd been in my work, and I guess it took me a minute to answer the bell. She had already started to leave, she was walking away by the time I got to the door. I called out to her, "Yes?"

"Dr. Wheelock," she said, turning rapidly. "It's me!"

I nodded, neutrally. Then I said, "Yes," again, too loudly. She was a young woman, maybe twenty-five, lots of makeup, in a long-sleeved beige fitted tunic that flipped out over her black leggings.

"The other day I gave you something that wasn't yours."

I knew the voice. I knew this was a person who sort of did things I asked her to do. There were fewer and fewer such girls around, I even remarked to myself. But I had no idea in the world who she was.

"Uptown Insta Print? Ahnh?" she said. She took a lock of her hair and twisted it with her finger.

"Yes," I said, nodding. "You are the—"

"Over on Maple?"

Our fax machine had broken in the fall. So I had been using the copy shop's. I was writing an as-told-to for a Texas politician, Kleinert. This was the girl I sent the pages through, the one who collected my electronic mail, which was composed almost entirely of insults from Kleinert. The book was a soap job, but the guy wanted whipped cream. It was low work, but I had to do something.

"The other day, I mean right before Christmas, when you came in and I gave you that big stack from Austin? All those? I think I gave you papers of mine, Xeroxes—"

My daughter Charlotte started to wail from her high chair in the kitchen. This went through my mind: *Never leave infant unattended while seated in this device.* I sidestepped rapidly down the hall.

"By mistake," the girl called out, coming in.

I returned with my baby. The girl was standing there, in my foyerless little bungalow. Right inside. I hadn't asked her in.

"A bunch of lyrics. I was with Larry that day, and he's got the group together finally, Desire and the Wannabes. They need a woman vocalist." She took an index finger and stabbed the bony white indentation at the "v" of her dress. My wife Gwen used to call that place between her breasts "my swimming pool," in the long-ago days when she was deprecating about her body. "Me," the girl said, closing her eyes a little longer than needed. "I got my hair done like this."

The only thing I could think to do was to ask her to spell it.

"I look that different hanh?" she said. "Camille, c-a-m-i-l-l-e, A-bare, h-e-b-e-r-t."

I became conscious the baby clothes I'd washed were spilling out of a big basket on the fireplace seat. Charlotte started to squirm in my arms. Camille Hebert followed me down the hall to the kitchen saying, "I was named for the hurricane," and put one of her pastel lacquered fingernails in Charlotte's pink overalls. "The one nobody ever thought would hit Biloxi. Did I tell you that before?" She offered to change the baby, but I said I would do it.

"You are really something, Dr. Wheelock," she said, watching me handle the moist towelettes. I was a good father. I think she saw that, she liked it.

"I'll get the folder," I said, when I had finished taping the new Huggie. I had talked to her, I had. About my work, once, maybe more than once, about being an author. That was the word she used. Author. Then Camille opened her arms and took Charlotte. I didn't even think about it. I handed the baby to her. She didn't think about it either.

I went to my study, a little room beyond the kitchen. This was deep in the house. The wood floors were buckling and there was a leak in the back that was ruining the wallpaper Gwen had put up. She'd done as much of the work as I had, even when she was pregnant. I had always figured there was something agitating my wife at bottom, that she over compensated. For a long time I thought it was that we couldn't seem to have a child, but we finally did, and that just sped her up, gave her a whole new purpose. Lately she got better at everything she did. For example, she'd recently decided to lose twenty pounds to lower her chances of breast cancer. She just did it, no problem, even though we had moved to New Orleans, where overeating was really worth it. Lately she was leaner when I touched her.

We'd left upstate New York last spring when Gwen got the offer from her law firm here. I had lost my position. That was how we said it, my "position."

Thunderstorms in winter were still strange. In the park that afternoon, I'd been bitten by mosquitos. A voice in me said, there should be snow now. It is actually January. The weather didn't follow any rules. I wasn't accustomed to the South, let me put it that way. I was off my stride. I'm a New Yorker, Brooklyn, actually.

Then it was almost six in the evening and Camille had been sitting in my kitchen for over an hour, poring through several pages of lyrics she'd mixed in with a chapter Kleinert sent back. I was being civil. There had been some lightning, now rain was spraying across the windows.

"Is it cold in here to you?" she asked, finally.

I said no, and asked her if she needed a lift.

"No, I'm fine, maybe I could have a cup of tea? You got a microwave?"

"Camille, I'll have to let you go," I said. I was trying. It didn't work.

"You know what?" she said. "I had this flu last week, was really out of it, it seems like it will kill you."

"I see."

"And I was just fine Saturday, but I'm getting a relapse," she announced, then said nothing for a second. "You notice how people catch everything here? Now they got cholera in the oysters, or they say they do, plus I find out they have a leprosarium on the river." She made a weird bucktooth face, a goofy Charlie Chan.

"Aren't you from here?" I asked her.

"I'm from the prairie," she said. "Not New Orleans."

"The prairie?"

"I'm freezing," she shuddered. "My brother told me it could come back and knock you for one. Right out of nowhere. I guess I better call Larry, huh?"

"I'll take you wherever you want to go," I said. "Who is Larry?" Charlotte was approaching the threshold of the kitchen in her wheeled walker. *Never employ this device near stairs or on uneven surfaces.* Head injury or death may result. "The student infirmary?" I asked, blocking Charlotte's progress. Camille had told me she was taking a few courses at UNO.

"Nothing's open, no dorms, nothing—it's break," she shook her head. Her face darkened then, it was something visible. I assumed she was beginning to understand me. "My sister's ex-husband drove me here when I got the word about the gig. He's halfway to Gulfport by now, the jerk. He came on to me, can you believe it? I mean, I had to get out and hitch." She leaned in the alcove near the phone and dialed. She folded her arm across her waist, so I could have looked at the start of the crease in her bosom, but I chose not to. I thought of her standing on Highway 10, a storm blowing. That road wasn't even built on land, it stood in the midst of the swamp on pillars. There is a twenty-foot drop off the sides, beyond the railing. A person can fall into a swamp.

It crossed my mind, how did I ever forget her name?

"Larry's not there," she said, plopping back into the ash wood chair. Beads of perspiration sprouted out of every pore in her forehead at once. This was breathtaking. You know what that looks like? Like dew.

"You must have a fever," I said to her.

"No lie," she said, rolling her large dark eyes about.

"Can you go to your family?" I asked, directing Charlotte's walker carefully with my foot towards the center of the kitchen.

"Mamou?" she said, wagging her small head with its odd hair. No, no not beautiful, I corrected myself, made the effort: she looked like a cartoon, a shocked medieval page. She needed shoes that curled up at the toe.

"You came in from Mamou?" Her town was hours away, through the bayous, and past them. I'd read about it. A place where the ethnographers went. She was a real Cajun. So rare. I watched her color fade until she was white as the sink. Charlotte was below, reaching for the black lace cuffs on her legs. Somehow it was a nice moment. I couldn't help that.

"Larry's number has changed. And I have to sing in twenty-four hours," she exclaimed. "I guess I got to be more specific, huh? You have any powders and some oranges?" She said "ah-rahnges."

"Do your parents speak French at home?" I asked. I hadn't met one before, a Cajun. I was trying to figure out how to make her understand. The South was strange to me. I was curious. The boundaries were hard for me to find, but everybody else knew where they were. To me things were, well, fluid. As in, they ran together, as in, you didn't know how you were being read, or even what you were supposed to be reading.

"You are really a kick, you know that, Dr. Wheelock?" she said as she sat down on one of Gwen's new leather couches. Her tiny pointed hands tore open the fruit I gave her in a single motion.

When I took it I learned her temperature was 103 degrees. I put her under Gwen's afghan. "That's nothing," she said. "People in my family will cook."

She fell fast asleep without any warning, the way my baby did now and then.

"Everybody okay?" Gwen asked when she called.

She was in Fargo taking depositions for a product liability case. She hated to be away. That was what she said.

"Charlotte's doing fine all day," I came back, "but she can't sleep at night, when you are away, you know that."

"I'm really sorry they are keeping me here, that part is agony," she said.

She'd said she'd be away one night. This was her third. She'd done this before. I was imagining her standing there in her thick terry bathrobe, with a little gold chain around her neck. Did that robe have a monogram? Yes it did. The case she was working on was about beauty parlor chairs that snapped a few clients' necks.

"How's the book?" she asked.

"It's in the processor," I said. "Len sent me the new outline. I'll say what they want me to say. Kleinert is a weasel."

"Is it that bad? It's not," Gwen said.

"Never a discouraging word," I said to her.

"Oh, David," she said, disapproving. "How's our girl?"

"She crawled on the rug. She got a mosquito bite, bites, in the park. She gummed some biscuits. She tore around in her walker. She went through a lot of diapers."

"David," she said.

"What?" I said, really wanting her to say what.

Gwen talked mostly, and the more she went on, the more I felt like telling her things weren't going all that well. I was trying to decide how to make this subject apropos. It was okay that she talked, I thought. She was doing something. "Miss you much," I said.

Camille, her color back, her hair flattened, came back into the kitchen holding a Velvet Underground album I had forgotten I ever owned. She pointed to it in query, mouthing, "Can I play this?"

I said, "Sure, sure, go ahead," aloud.

"Who are you talking to?" Gwen said. "Me?"

"A girl. Camille Hebert."

"We are in the same time, aren't we?" Gwen asked.

"Central."

"What is a girl doing there at seven forty-five at night?"

"She works at the fax place. She gave me some pages that weren't mine. When she came to get them she passed out."

"From what?" Gwen said, a kind of laugh in her voice. "What is this, sweets?"

"She's ill. She has a bug." Camille went back into the other room so I continued. "I can't get her to leave. She's a child. She has nowhere to go. It's awkward."

It was awkward. It was damned awkward.

"Take her to the hospital," Gwen said.

"That's a good idea," I said. "I can't really talk right now. I hear Charlotte." This was a tiny lie. It was either Charlotte or Camille trying to sing.

"Call me tomorrow, huh. Touro Infirmary. Like the blues. It's the closest emergency room to us. The number is by the phone. I put it there in case—I'll be home Tuesday at eleven or something. I'm not sure what flight they put me on. I'll call. This is awful, isn't it?"

"Yes," I said.

Never look at her narrow nostrils, her mild French girl mustache while she is sleeping on your couch all night.

I was feeding Charlotte her instant cereal at seven when Camille came in, saying, "Thank you so much for that sleep. Could I take a shower? I saw where the towels are." She coughed. She sounded horrible. She went on, "Is your wife here? Dos she live here?"

I told her.

"And left you with the little baby?"

"It's the nineties," I said. "We do this."

"I have a boyfriend who was always leaving. Was working the oil fields until everybody had to leave. I mean Saudi. He was on every other month, and when he came back, he'd have this money, a ton of plans, wear me out going places. Gave me nice high-life albums, though."

"High life?"

"African music," she bit her middle fingernail, a long one. "Since July he's been living in St. Martinville, building a log house from a thirty-thousand-dollar kit. For us, he says. But this is all on his menu. You know what I'm saying?"

"I think so," I said. She looked older to me just then. She looked tired.

"You happy, Dr. Wheelock?" Camille asked me. "Over at Uptown we didn't put you in with the happy people."

"Why?" I said.

"When I'd ask you questions about yourself, you'd turn on like a light, for one thing."

"And?"

"Certain people, I pick up on."

"I am, really, I am," I said. "I am." I pointed to my baby, who just then spat up white rice cereal.

I changed Charlotte's clothes. Several days a week I took her to Mrs. Funes, her Nicaraguan sitter, so I could write. I told Camille, who seemed better, coming in after her bath, in a long white T-shirt, pink lace stockings, a white scarf tied around her head so she resembled Civil War wounded, that she could let herself out. I explained to her how to make sure the door was locked.

"I guess I can get a streetcar," she said. She was amusing but somebody ought to tell her, that's what I thought. I had plans. I had work to do. I usually wrote continuously for the first four hours of the day.

"Where are you exactly going?" I asked her.

"I have to sing tonight," she said. "That's why I am in New Orleans," as if this was news to everybody.

"Where?"

"I don't know."

"Well why don't you try Larry then?" I said, grabbing a fork out of Charlotte's tiny fist. *Keep sharp objects out of children's reach.* I lowered my daughter onto the floor, and she started to crawl across the white linoleum towards this houseguest. Uninvited, I guess I'll add. Uninvited houseguest.

She pointed at me the way people mime shooting an arrow. "You got it. I'm going to call his friend Adrian," Camille said.

Maybe she wasn't dumb, but just aesthetic. Or aggressive. This was some Cajun form of aggression. A gris gris. No, I needed the gris gris, to get rid of her, that's what I was thinking. Or a mojo. She would give me the mojo, the spell.

She hung up the phone. Obviously she had made some progress. "I need people who will give me advice. You have any more?"

She wasn't being sarcastic. I found that sweet. She didn't seem to know sarcasm existed.

"Don't take any more powders," I said. "It's aspirin. Your stomach will bleed."

"Yeah?" she said. "I never heard that before. Bleed?"

"Don't take a step," I said, pointing, "the baby, she's by your foot."

"I'm not going to kick her. I'm watching everything. I see what's going on." She took off her scarf, rubbed her temple, reached for the headache powders.

Tell me, then, I almost said. Tell me what's going on. Please be very clear.

Soapy. Fresh coriander, I decided: that was the scent in Mrs. Funes's house. I like it today, usually I couldn't stand it, I thought as I was driving Camille to the club where she was to practice with the band for a few hours. I was taking a break from Kleinert.

She took up much less room than Gwen, who is five seven and has no ankles. In the early eighties Gwen wore pants, to cover up what she referred to as her piano legs, which were once a secret, something tender between us. When she wore those clothes, I taught at the college near Utica that went broke.

Those were certain days. Those were days in a place that had seasons, like winter summer fall. A place that had rules. I was raised in Brooklyn. In those days in Brooklyn, you didn't go into anyone's house without being invited in a very formal, careful way. You talked on the porch. Everything took place on the porch, in people's driveways, on the sidewalk. Social life, kids playing, I'm talking about.

When I taught at that college, Gwen used to make so much food for faculty dinner parties nobody could eat half of it. Coquilles Saint-Jacques, followed by prime rib. When the place started folding, she would have done anything to keep it going. She was still calling alumni after the trustees had leased the campus buildings to a school for the deaf.

Since we'd moved to New Orleans, she let her legs show. She wore black stockings and short skirts and colors glaring enough to sober up world-famous drunks. A consultant she paid real money to told her to wear these hues.

I liked Magazine but it got a little redundant. There were patches of bad housing, followed by three distinct stretches of galleries and cafes, then a Shoetown, maybe. I couldn't get it. Where I came from you could tell right away if a neighborhood was good or bad, rich or poor, Irish, Italian, or Jewish, etcetera. In New Orleans this is all mixed up. I drove up and down the street several times before I found the place. While I was driving, I remember I felt inordinately sad. I noticed that a clinging, elaborate sadness had been a factor in my life since Charlotte was born, and we'd moved, since Gwen started working so much. Probably for a long time, I'd been attaching large emotions to little things, and feeling neutral about the big things—well, I say this now.

"Hey babes, it's the next-to-last Dixie Beer sign," she said. When she got out I wished her luck.

I felt a little odd then, even stricken, at ten o'clock in the morning on Magazine, to be alone in the car, to be without Camille Hebert. Again I saw her out on that road. I thought perhaps I'd abandoned her—this even though she'd invited herself to my place, this even though she'd barged in on my life, so to speak.

As if I didn't have enough to worry about.

Gwen had been wearing orange, red, popping blue, eye-peeling teal, and taxi yellow, without respite, of late.

This was the first outward sign, as I see it now: when I was supposed to, I didn't call her. I called her two hours later. She answered with a sweet, inquisitory "yes."

"I love you," I said. "I wish you were here."

"Me, too," Gwen answered. Then she was silent.

"What is it?" I said.

"What was going on last night?"

"Nothing, really, she's a singer. She came by to get some pages she'd given me by mistake. Lyrics—"

"Oh, don't tell me anything, just reassure me, okay? No, don't even do that. That would legitimize my asking."

"You can ask," I said.

"How is Charlotte?"

She wouldn't even ask. That struck me. Her discipline. She had more rules than ever, since we'd come to this lapsed sort of town, this southern city.

"She grows every day," I said. "Mrs. Funes swears she's less nervous."

"What do you mean 'less nervous.' Why do you say it that way?"

"What way?"

"David, let's not be like this. It isn't like us," she said softly, quietly. "Is something wrong? Tell me."

In our marriage were many givens, basic definitions. In our marriage, we had always been true. But this time I said, "Like what?"

"You know you can say anything."

"I'm keeping up my end," I said. I don't even know where that came from. Well, I'm not completely sure.

"This is hard too," she said, and then I listened to her recite what she had done the last twenty-four hours. She had a flair for detail. Whiplash at Margie's Hair Skin and Nails. "This never had to happen," she said.

"You believe that?" I asked.

"I believe that," she said. "I even know it. I am certain."

Ladies who leaned back for a blue rinse, in neck braces now for their trouble. I started to laugh. I did. I started to laugh.

"Do you think I am having fun?" Gwen said.

"I don't think you are having ordinary kind of fun," I said. There was a time when I adored her for throwing herself into things because it was obvious she had to. I always marveled. I thought about the old uncompromising New York winters, about the gallons of hot soup she made when she was a gung-ho wife. How she always used to ask, how is it? Do you like it?

"That's not where we are," she said. "I know it isn't. I just know it. You are just down."

"So?" I said, hearing in my own voice a certain invading zest.

That day, Charlotte didn't nap for Mrs. Funes, and then, when she got home, she was too wound up to fall asleep. I had to strap her in the Snugli and pace for hours. She wailed when I touched her, wailed when I let her alone. I didn't sleep at all, really, I just catnapped in the leather recliner while she fussed on my breast. The next day Kleinert woke me at eight, to tell me my prose was "shot full of holes. Is there something wrong with you? Don't you tape it when I tell you my story?"

Let me explain Kleinert's life: greed, boosterism, and impenetrable megalomania bred in sandy Waco. He goes on: "Can't you fill in with a little snazz? Have you ever been introduced to finesse? Why is the thing such a downer? You have a problem? Can't you stretch out the high spots?"

Charlotte was fast asleep when I gave her to Mrs. Funes, which meant she had gotten her days and nights "mixed up." This was a tendency I had gone to great lengths to set right months before.

Most of the day I napped, then I tried to work, but my eyes hurt me awfully. I couldn't even look at the screen. Charlotte was wide awake when I picked her up, not a good sign. I had a few beers while she was practicing her creeping. Early that evening she picked up a white scarf off the floor and handed it to her daddy, I mean, to me.

Never start car without securing your infant in the restraint system—that's what I was thinking.

But it was midnight and I thought the top of my head might float right off. I was driving down Magazine wearing Charlotte in a Snugli pouch underneath my gray windbreaker. In the infant seat beside us was the scarf and a brown paper bag from an all-night Walgreens. When I zipped the windbreaker up in front, I had a big belly, a real gut.

The place was only a quarter full, and Camille was sitting alone in the corner with a piano singing "Fever." She did this rather bravely, considering she wasn't in good voice. I wondered if it was just the flu.

The bartender was a heavy man with a T-shirt that read, "Boogie 'Til You Die." I was compelled to point to the downy head under my chin—but the man only shrugged.

Everything I saw, I heard a little voice saying, yes, yes, that too, yes, that, and why not. I was fighting this voice.

"Dr. Wheelock," she said, as if she had been expecting me, "How you-all are? Larry was dreaming. One guy showed up. So I asked for the piano, this old thing in the back. It was in tune. You know how unusual that is? This city is underwater. You generally have to tune a piano every two weeks."

"You mean below sea level?" I said, waiting to get the order to leave. Of course I was going to go. I didn't even have to reenforce this idea. *From myself* I would get the order to go. It was coming. I was waiting.

"My little sweetie in there?" She touched Charlotte's head with her small good-looking hand.

"This is for you," I said, "and you left this at my house."

She made the Charlie Chan face again and I remembered what it had looked like to me the first time she did it. This time it was charming, proof I was drunk, I thought, or worse.

She took the scarf and the paper bag. The Valentine's display had just gone up in the drugstore. I'd bought a five-pound heart of Pangburn's Chocolates. In the bag as well were two bottles of blue cold medicine. The labels read "No aspirin." These were small acts, at the time, spontaneous, unpremeditated. That's how I saw them.

"I have been thinking you should look out for yourself, huh? You could be getting it. Larry's supposed to come here. He's taking me to Opelousas in the morning. Wants to make up for the fiasco. It's not what you think, though," she said.

I realized I had no idea what she thought I thought.

"Larry's gay," she said.

Then I knew.

I hopped off the stool. I had to grab the edge of the bar with both hands. I was losing my balance, mostly because of the weight of my baby in the front, but this seemed desirable. I paused, not yet poised. I really didn't know what next. I had absolutely no plan, no projection, no outlook.

Yet, I felt great. There is something here, in this story, about intention and prevention, and rules and being alive, being fluid, but I haven't worked it all out completely yet. I've had too much else to deal with. Camille steadied me. I leaned forward and kissed her for this.

"Now, I've got feelings for you, Dr. Wheelock," she whispered, thickly sighing, as we started, "but I got to tell you it still hurts to breathe."

I thought this was very funny, this remark. Wasn't this funny, that she said it hurt to breathe. So did she. So did Camille.

I reached around her the way I might reach around Gwen, but there was so much less of her than there had ever been of my wife. My hands could find out so much in so little time. She had a tiny Braque collage of a body, a little cubist guitar, full of angles. Nothing, nothing at all, was where it was supposed to be.

Making out, leaning sideways on the bar, was a struggle. We had to devise a one-armed operation, like the sidestroke, alternating left and right, the kind lifesavers use in deep water. Charlotte squirmed between us, vital and fat. Camille's kisses were exactly what I had always wanted kisses to be: uncanny, how this was so.

At home, under my down comforter, the delight took over entirely, the deliciousness, the ease. I had forgotten what it was like to be desired in that way, to be convinced you are someone's elixir.

When she finally slept, her breath caught, faintly, in her chest. I loved this sound—muffled waters.

In the morning, on the way back from Mrs. Funes's house, I unrolled my Toyota windows. I kept telling myself to think about the night, what a horrendous thing had happened, but even though I wanted to, my mind kept following off down other paths. Nature was one. Half the trees on the streets were blooming and the other half were laden with dying, purplish leaves. The camellia bushes in the neighborhood were still going. Below them were puddles of pink blooms turning brown. In Louisiana everything was simultaneous. Nothing was chopped into seasons. Now I saw. A certain convergence of opposites. There was a mist so fine it was possible to inhale it, or maybe you just let it flow into your pores. Underwater. There was a way in which feeling bad, even hating myself a little, felt perfectly marvelous—was this something you could even say to another person? It doesn't make sense, does it, when I say it here. I was terribly aware of the beauty of the broken-down storefronts and houses, of the imperfect places, of the wounded, the flawed, the ugly, the never-very-good.

I think I even asked myself at this point, *what are you turning into?* But I had the feeling that answer would be delayed.

"Gwen called," Camille said. "That's your wife, isn't it?" She was sitting in the kitchen in a tiny yellow dress that looked to me like a nightgown, but it was obvious she thought she was dressed.

"You answered?" I said, alarmed. "What?"

"She said she'd be in at eleven-twelve. Delta. At the airport."

I just looked at her. "Go," I said.

"I said I was the maid," she said, nodding.

What maid? She was going, of course. I told her to go. I heard her getting her things together. In seconds I picked up in the kitchen, the bedroom, the other bedroom, the hall. I stripped the sheets off. But my head pounded. I was sick. I found all the small, dangerous toys. *Never leave small objects within infant's reach. Choking or strangulation may result.* I fixed myself some quick tea. *Never use metal utensils in the microwave. Never take four aspirin on an empty stomach.*

"Go!" I told her, when I saw her in the hall, in the bathroom. She was everywhere, suddenly, I couldn't get away from her.

Next thing, Mrs. Funes called, to say Charlotte was vomiting. She had a fever. I called the pediatrician, but I couldn't get through. Four times. The fifth time I picked up, there was no dial tone. It was Gwen, calling back, on the line.

"It didn't ring," she said.

"I'm psychic," I said.

"I'll just get a cab," she said. "I'm early. The plane landed early. You hired a maid?"

"What? No. Not a maid. Darling. Darling."

"Soon," Gwen said.

I piled Camille's things on the porch, handed her a stray Guess T-shirt. I had already said good-bye twice. But she was still sitting in the Adirondack porch chair under the stucco arch when I came outside on my way to retrieve Charlotte.

"Go," I said. "I'm sorry. I'm so sorry."

"I am too," she said with her interesting mouth. "I know. I get it."

"I mean it," I said. "When I say 'go' do you hear another word?" I meant this. I had serious doubts. This business about how I was being read. This was exactly what I was thinking. I wasn't angry, really. I didn't want her to ever go, actually.

"Sure," Camille said. "I'm going, okay? I'm going."

"I have to get the baby. She's coming down with something. I'll drop you off anywhere."

"No, no," she said, "there's a streetcar," with a certain kindness, "I GET IT," picking up herself and her things, and swinging her arms as she walked away down the street, like a young Audrey Hepburn rather, I thought. Good-bye, good-bye, I said under my breath. Better of course, if she were to leave. Better, of course. For her. Better. I was perfectly willing to say forever good-bye at that exact point, I think.

A little later I wondered if I had the same body as I had yesterday, the way this one hurt at every joint. Charlotte was hot when I got her. She fell fast asleep in the car.

When I drove up back at the house, Gwen was standing on the sidewalk with her suitcase that had wheels. Camille Hebert was in front of her, holding the box of chocolates, opened. Gwen had raised one hand the way Indians in old movies say how.

"What is this? Some kind of joke? David? Who are you? Are you David?" she said, pivoting around when I walked up. "Please tell me."

"This is a big mistake. This is Camille. She just came by—"

"Yes," Gwen said, waiting, expectant.

"I thought you had gone," I told Camille. "There was a streetcar, no?"

"I was going," Camille said, "but then I saw her—"

"Why does she call me 'her' like that?" Gwen asked, her eyes going to me. "Tell me right now."

Camille turned to Gwen, "Your baby is sick. She has the flu. It is going around. David too. Everybody here is coming down with something."

"How do you know?" Gwen said.

"I know, I know plenty," Camille said, popping a milk-chocolate-covered caramel in her mouth.

"The baby's sick? How sick? How could this happen?" Gwen stood there for a second, no words coming, in her impeccable red jacket, her chevron design pocket square. "This can't happen."

"It does," I think I sort of enjoyed saying. "It did. It does. It did."

Turning to get the baby out of the car, I found myself touching Camille's soft cheek. I didn't intend to do this in the way I intended customary things. It felt un-preventable. But of course, it was the awful breach. All things were set in stone, everything became perfectly clear, there was a straight line between all the events of the last three days, perfect cause and effect, the second I touched Camille's cheek. Behind me, waiting, was Gwen. All this time, I was breaking down, a perfect wreck, somehow I knew this, but I went forward, as if I were single-minded, as if I knew what the hell I was doing. That is what is asked of people, isn't it. That they know what the hell they are doing. It is a great deal to ask, I think now. I was running a fever at the time.

In this awful moment I somehow turned to philosophy. I had lots I wanted to say to Gwen, actually, but all that came out was, "It does, it did." This was incredibly stupid. I know that now. I meant to say much wiser things.

One of the aspects of this whole mess that strikes me lately—how I am outside it, watching so often, how I've started now to see everything coming, from both women, no surprises, when before I was totally unprepared. Very often it's as if I'm watching a character with whom I identify mildly, and when another awful thing is about to happen to him I groan in anticipation, I double over at the outrageous complications, at the melodrama, how terribly he's screwed up, but it doesn't always faze me that it's me: I don't feel it yet that way. I don't have that defining grief. I wonder sometimes when that recognition will come, that waking up. I even long for it. This distance, this sense of philosophy, began the second I touched Camille's cheek.

I wanted to tell Gwen then, "Don't you know we are lived as much as we live, we are driven as much as we drive? You can't prevent everything, darling, darling. There are things nobody can see coming."

She would have probably repeated herself, she was livid, not thoughtful, exactly. I don't blame her. This is what she keeps saying to me now: who are you? in her New York accent, are you David? How am I supposed to talk to you when I don't know who you are?

The Significance of Importance

ALBERT BELISLE DAVIS

We are flying due south, all of us, low above the white shells of Mondebon Road in a seaplane usually chartered by oilfield supervisors checking inland leases. Even on this gray day you can see, to your right, the *paw*-green, *paw*-blue decks of the Great Fleet behind the shrimpers' camps along Bayou Mondebon. Don't go telling me that's not something to talk about, those boats. The stern trawlers with masts, out-riggers, and booms to handle nets. The side trawlers with cranes for working nets over either side. All of them with high bows and square sterns, all wide-beamed with their wheelhouses well forward.

The road ends just up ahead at the jetty wall on the *Tee Co-to,* an arpent, ar-pent-and-a-half of hard naked earth that had once been an Indian-mound built on a natural levee. Oak trees used to grow on that levee all the way to the northern shore of Mondebon Bay. *Tee Co-to* separated from the rest of the levee when the bayou made a motion, and without waiting for a second, bolted toward the sexy new-dug trappers' ditch that soon became the Trappers' Canal you've been seeing running straight along the deserted strip of maidencane left of the road.

There, on the mound near the jetty wall. What looks like a penny almost touch-ing that rust-colored rectangle. Those are the tops of Vay's cistern and camp. Those two nubs protruding from each of the long sides of the rectangle are the ends of pontoons just like the pontoons below us on our plane. And that person there, wav-ing up at us, trying to run as fast as we are flying, circling as we circle, that's . . . Leroi. Now that's really something to talk about. On a day with more sun, you'd be able to see the deck tarp and blessing flags on his sunk oyster boat in the deep wa-ter on the other side of the jetty wall.

If we had time, I'd wait for clear sky and a spring tide, and I'd get us all up higher in the air, to the level of jets carrying tourists just like you from New Orleans 60 miles northeast to mostly Spanish-speaking lands far-far to the south. From up there, take my word, the road looks like a white thread floating on one great body of water, the body of Bay-Gulf. But we need to get to this place—my place—right now, right as Leroi is beginning his walk to Tah-loo's camp.

Why not jump?

Come on. Being a tourist takes great courage.

I know, I know. Falling's got to be stretching anybody's definition of travel or courage. But feel lucky for once in your lives, lucky as the Governor at his vacation ranch when he fell off his horse onto that mattress of sand between two rocks.

Close your eyes. Jump.

You see? Lucky as the Governor, you've landed in the softest marsh just east of the shallowest point of Trappers' Canal about half-way back up the road from the jetty wall. It's cold, *moo-dee* cold, a day with on and off rain in January, 1973. You heard that sound? *Moo-dee?* Memorize that sound. You'll need it down here. Now, wade across Trappers' Canal. We don't want to miss Leroi when he walks by. More than weather's about to change, for all of us.

You're in South Louisiana—say *L'sood d'lah loo-eez-yahn*—in the Great State of Louisiana. More specifically, you're in Mondebon, the southernmost settlement in the parish of Mondebon, the ball of the foot of that green wading boot most all schoolchildren can point to on maps. But you're also in a Louisiana that cannot be seen on maps, a Louisiana bordered by other Great States like the Great State of Joy, the Great State of Sadness, and the *moo-dee* Great State of Hope. A Louisiana divided into realms called protectorates.

No, don't laugh those of you from outside the Great State of Louisiana. Protectorates are those zones, traceable and non-traceable, that we from the settlement of Mondebon hold in common with every other region, state, or nation, whether geopolitical or natural, real or not-real in this good good world of people.

And after the hike you've just taken, you now know—it's possible to walk *through* parts of this place. You have landed in a place where you will always laugh at the word "ground."

Speaking of words—and we will, we will—what words of greeting should I choose for you? Down all the bayous all over the parish of Mondebon you will hear your hello probably coming at you as a question, something like "*Sah-vaw?*" How's it going? Here in the settlement of Mondebon, your greeting most often will be "*Kwo-sah-dee?*" What you say?

The Protector of Mondebon is a good and honest man with the nickname Tahloo and a family name that ends in *x* written down. Most of us in Mondebon would vote that *x* is the letter most of you expect to see at the end of our names written down. I bet when you see Tah-loo's family name written down, you would say it *Pe-ri-lo*. And that's good because that means, from the start, we have a lot in common. Most all of you, like most all of us from Mondebon, are some kind of smart.

Besides being good and honest, Tah-loo is related, mostly by marriage, to the Mondebon parish sheriff, who has the family name Gautier. Let me help you. *Go-chay.*

Aw-oh. You caught me. And it didn't take you that long at all. All of my words are being written down. Even the French called Our French. Which isn't Proper French, *an?* See that line I just went back and put through that *n* in the English word *an?* That means you never quite get to the *n* because the vowel went got itself trapped way-way up your nose. I can do it with the English word *on*, too. *On.* And if I go back and draw a line through two *o*'s, that's like the *o*'s in the word *look* are jumping up and down in socks on the roof of your mouth.

Try this:

Loo Bon Dee-oo. That's how we say the name of Our God in Mondebon. I've got my reasons for taking the time to do all this going back. And it's not to give a quick French lesson to tourists. We don't want your trip to sound too much like school. You'll know my reasons soon enough. What you need to know for now is that written-down's not so bad when you think about it. You can't see me, but you can still hear me.

Now let's go back to Tah-loo.

Tah-loo has eight surviving children. Those of you from outside Mondebon have no doubt heard that word "survive" used in front of the word "children." Those two words together can mean different things. Often, you use them to describe the children of a parent who has lived a long life and has reached that sad time where he or she's outlived some of his or her sweet *bay-bays.* Around here, up until about the end of the 1940s, you could rarely describe someone's children without using that before-word, no matter how old the parents were. Tah-loo, even as a young daddy five years after returning to Mondebon after the end of his war in 1918, the hair of the point of his widow's peak still a black arrow on his wide forehead, could say, "I have one surviving children, me."

But it's 1973 now. We even have a Cajun governor. In many medical-related ways, we're catching up to you outside of Mondebon. Even Tah-loo—the point of his widow's peak still sharp, or so we think. (Tah-loo's still strong enough to push you away before you get close enough to check out the white point in the middle of his thick gray crop.) Even Tah-loo's gotten old enough to where the odds are he's going to survive some sweet *bay-bays* breathing today just because his breathing's going on and on past theirs. A happy time for Mondebon when we can say our children—by the way, most all of them can read and write—are living to be old themselves. But what a dark time, too, just like the world outside of Mondebon, where one of Nature's cruelest jokes—watching your children die at any time, which is second only to knowing you have only so much time left to live—has become one of Nature's incomprehensible ironies—watching your children die just because you're out and out outliving them.

Tah-loo lives a little up the road from here—no, don't look yet. I'll tell you when—in a tin-roof palace on pilings, a palace of (front to rear) white-painted cypress walls, green-painted CDX plywood walls, and white-painted, special-treated particle board walls. The palace has doubled in size (front to rear) every decade through remodeling projects. For a decade—decade and a half, two decades?—the construction took place just to transform a sight already big and pretty into a sight that is big-big and pretty-pretty. Tah-loo has had the means to do this.

You all know what I mean by "means." Tah-loo's wife, Madame Tah-loo, she knows what I mean. Her whole Gautier family all at once knows what I mean.

Good Tah-loo had the means and the means were a certain kind of smart and a boat bigger than anyone else's, which means that good Tah-loo ended up with the goods, which means more shrimp than anybody else. Good Tah-loo would sometimes trade shrimp for nails. Or he could trade shrimp for cash, then cash for nails. Remember that time when cash and shrimp and nails all meant the same thing?

Then, somewhere along the line, Tah-loo's cash became Tah-loo's money. Somewhere after that, Tah-loo started thinking about all of his means and all of his goods in terms of his money. He could see his money in places other than his pocket—on paper. And whenever Tah-loo saw his money on paper, he saw numbers. And the more Tah-loo thought about those numbers, the more the numbers seemed to increase. Many of us like to think that Tah-loo learned all he knows about numbers from the Gautier family, but Tah-loo, like most people who end up with more than one boat, Tah-loo got to understand and recognize numbers on his own, which is not really at all like writing-down when you think about it. Memorize o to 9 and you just about got the possibilities covered.

For sure, Tah-loo knew about his numbers before he married into the Gautier family. Tah-loo is certain he knew about his numbers before he married into the Gautier family because he remembers talking about his numbers with the first Gautier he met, the Gautier who would one day be his brother-in-law, but who was not Tah-loo's brother-in-law when Tah-loo first met him. That was the same day that Tah-loo had his first erection since somewhere back before when his second wife died.

Tah-loo remembers meeting the Gautier who would one day be his brother-in-law in the early 40s. It had to be in the early 40s because the war had already started, the war with a "II" in its name. Almost all of that war took place in the early 40s.

This war is not the war Tah-loo calls *his* war—Tah-loo's war was the one before that, The Great War, which had a Roman numeral "I" attached to it as soon as the next one got the "II." Tah-loo, like most any of us, does not remember when the "II" got attached that made the "I" get attached. But the start, Pearl Harbor, and the end, VE Day—the end for one day, one day when we all together forgot that we still had a VJ Day to cross—were lines so deeply drawn in the shells that you know you're stepping over. All Tah-loo knows for sure about the start of his war is that it must have happened before that trip he took on that boat big enough to be called a ship. (No matter how big Tah-loo's boats get, they must never cross over that line where boats become ships. You can get vomited on right in your face sleeping on your back in a hammock in the hold of a ship.)

I mention all this war math not to criticize anybody's memory, but to show you how many of us in Mondebon try to keep track of when we did things. We, like everybody else in the good good world of people, cross over lines where the world is different all of a sudden. These lines are sometimes as invisible as white lines in white shells, and sometimes they are so deeply drawn that they scratch through the shells to the black-black clay below. That war, the second one, is a deep line that is easy for most of us still in Mondebon in 1973 to see when we look back, even those of us, like Tah-loo, who fought in the earlier war and whose surviving children were all daughters when the draft for the later one came around.

Like all male Gautiers, Tah-loo's brother-in-law—who wasn't, remember, Tah-loo's brother-in-law when Tah-loo met him—had not only completed all eleven years of high school but had attended at least a year in another school, most always in New Orleans. In New Orleans, Tah-loo's brother-in-law met a man who'd met a man named Higgins who'd been building some shallow-draft boats for trappers in South Louisiana.

Now let me tell you something about what we all have in common with Gautiers. Most all of us are always running into other people. All of the people in the Gautier family seem to meet up with somebody who met somebody like a Higgins from New Orleans who builds boats. You, too, could run into somebody who has run into these people, especially in South Louisiana. Everybody could.

But how many of us would know a Higgins from a Bo-lo Cunningham when we hear about them? After all, Bo-lo built boats for trappers, too. His whole family did. Good boats. Good and pretty boats. But Bo-lo's boats just got you from one wet here to one wet there. And Higgins would go and build a boat that would win a war. How to know? you ask. Indeed, how, how to know. And that's what makes most of us all so not-Gautier. Say that, "*paw*-Gautier."

Know another little thing that makes most of us *paw*-Gautier? When we invest—even those of us lucky enough to buy-in to boats that are about to turn into landing crafts—we invest in boats. A Gautier invests in people, people from all over South Louisiana. People like Tah-loo. Like the Governor, back when the Governor was just André Andrews with an office the size of a post office box.

And another little thing, no matter what you hear—and you'll hear a lot down here—investing in people, not education, is the Great On-going Gautier Experiment.

According to Tah-loo's brother-in-law, "importance" or "the perception of importance," was the "Law Number One" of "successful enterprise." And that's just how Tah-loo's brother-in-law said it to Tah-loo that day Tah-loo met him. From the start, the Gautiers didn't talk down to Tah-loo. And from that start, Tah-loo's brother-in-law kept adding on words until somehow "importance or the perception of importance" became attached to Tah-loo where he was standing in the room, to Tah-loo "someone who was blessed with both luck and a drive to work hard—"

That's right. Work hard. I hope you didn't come here thinking we eat and dance all the *moo-dee* time.

But back to Tah-loo, in the room that smelled like *fee-lay* was being sprinkled on gumbo in a kitchen somewhere. And figs? Someone cooking preserves? Back to

Tah-loo with a Gautier who had a forehead broad as Tah-loo's but without the widow's peak, a Gautier who was standing close enough to Tah-loo for Tah-loo to have taken a full step forward and to have pushed the Gautier back except that the Gautier's voice seemed to be coming from more one step and one arm length away. To Tah-loo:

"Besides luck and hard work, add in a boat bigger than anyone else's, and you've got someone on the road to wealth—not total wealth, which is having all, which no one except the Good God Above Us All . . ." God. That's how Tah-loo's brother-in-law said the name of God, by the way. In English. Gautiers did not and do not speak French, any kind of French, at business meetings.

"But just think, Boo," Tah-loo's brother-in-law said—how long ago? twenty, thirty years, yesterday?—"just think what a kick-ass businessman God, him, he could be if he could let go his goodness for just a day, just a day, to really go show everybody how it's all done. Not let go of his goodness enough to go to Hell, which is hard for him to do since he thought-up and built Hell from the ground up . . . But let his goodness go just enough, just enough to get ahead of everybody else, and then stop. Just look at Heaven, Boo, that kick-ass business he got going without even trying. Ah, you got to respect him. And you respect him and he respect you back. Especially if you've got the enterprise he gave to people and expects people to use it back."

Of all the words Tah-loo heard coming his way, Tah-loo did not choose to repeat the word "kick-ass." I might have chosen that one, but I know a lot more about significance than most. I'm not saying that a Gautier invented that word "kick-ass." But you can see for yourself that they were using it as far back as the early 1940s.

"Enterprise" is the word Tah-loo chose to repeat to his brother-in-law. "Enterprize," Tah-loo said. "Like go in and get a award. I see the merit part in it, but what exack it mean?"

"It doesn't matter what it means, Boo. What matters is that Law Number One is if you want to make it high-high in business you've got to be important and sound important."

"Who got the time to be 'portant?"

"You ask good questions, Boo. I heard you had a hatsize only a cast-net can measure. Like you say, who? Who really got the time?"

"My boats, they business? You mean something like that?"

"I mean more, me. I'm afraid, Boo, that you, Tah-loo yourself, are the business."

"You loss me there."

"Let's get back to sounding important, Boo."

"I understand that, me. What Coonass wouldn't want that, we had the time?"

"Don't ever say that word out loud anymore, Boo."

"Time?"

"That other word, Boo."

"Coonass?"

"That's the word."

"That ain't French. I was being careful, me, like you just say to be careful and not go use the French. Less try not to use the French at the business meeting, you say. So I say Coonass. I didn't go say it *chood-shah-wee*."

"Take my word, Boo. Some words are lower in English than in French. But since you went brought it up and not me, let me say that even a Coonass can do it."

"Do what again?"

"Say something that sounds important that means something else everybody can understand."

"I don't understand what you trying to say. That I can say."

At that first meeting, Tah-loo's brother-in-law did not go into the difference between importance and significance, which all Gautiers understand. In fact, that understanding is something I myself have in common with Gautiers. And think about it. A significant man is just not as important-sounding as an important man. Instead, Tah-loo's brother-in-law, still without speaking down, still close enough to have seen the white hair beginning to grow in the still-gray point of Tah-loo's widow's peak, but somehow still far enough away to be out of reach—by one step and one arm-length—for pushing away, which Tah-loo was known to have done if you made what looked like a twitch of a move toward him . . . Tah-loo's brother-in-law tried to help Tah-loo this way:

"So, Boo. You've got more than one boat? That's what you said?"

"*Sah-say*. I mean, correck. And not one ship, proud to say."

"How many boats does everybody else have, Boo?"

"Count the skiff?"

"Just boats, Boo. How many, everybody else?"

"'Bout one. Each a piece. And, like you say, I don't count the skiff."

"You a business, Boo."

"I'll be gotdam. You mean, all along, without me not even trying?"

"That's right, Boo. And I'm here to tell you more. You've moved past that. Into what we in my family call another phase."

"Another face?"

"Something like that. But not at all like that."

Tah-loo apologized, in his French, which is Our French. Then he apologized for forgetting himself and for using French.

After cautioning Tah-loo about apologizing at business meetings, in any language, Tah-loo's brother-in-law went on to something he called Tah-loo's "standing."

"I'm here to tell you, Boo. You've got what's called a standing, you, in Mondebon. And I hate to tell you. When you've got you a standing you're almost required to stand up with it."

"Hole on, hole on. This a business meeting you say?"

"That's right, Boo. That's why we sent you word to drive all the way to town to talk to us. My family's interested in you and your standing."

"Hole on again. This getting haywire. Less get this on back on down to the word *word*. That where we begun at, correck?"

"Yes, Boo, the important-sounding word."

"You say even I, Coonass that I am or not. Even I, you say, can sound 'portant? And go do that?"

"I was about to say more. I was about to say, you *should* do it. You've got to. Go do it. Because of—"

"How I stan'?"

"Correct, Boo. That's what we Gautiers call standing up to your standing."

"Could I just say. And don't go stop me if I get going good . . . Could you just tell me one, two, maybe three 'portant word right now? Then, when I catch on to all this, all this you saying, later. Then maybe I can go try use them like I want? If I got the time? Or can I just go hire me somebody? I catch on good while back to how 'portant hiring is, keeping all my boat going. Going good, too. Up till I can't get the gas. Can't get too much the gas with just a A-stamp. So for sure you can't go hire the gas . . . with a . . . I mean—"

"I think I know what you mean, Boo. But in all honesty, I had a little trouble following you there for a while, just a little. As for ration stamps and gasoline, there's something I'll tell you about later, something comes from standing."

"Save me some time. Tell me now."

"Important people have to have gas to run the boats or many people are hurt."

"You got you a word for that, I 'magine."

"Sure do, Boo. Privilege. Influence."

"Which mean I can get all the gas I need."

"See, Boo? You didn't have to hire anybody to understand those words."

"Can this in-flu . . . Can it git a name of somebody you know I can go hire that understand . . . What you call it? The face?"

"Sure. I have names. There's even ways you can hire somebody for free."

"You said free?"

"You heard me, Boo. There's even somebody close right now."

"You? I had a feeling you was too close."

"Let's just say for the right number, like you said, you can hire anybody you want. But not exact this Gautier you're talking direct to right now. You can't afford me, not even you, yet. And not because I have more boats or a hatsize to match—"

"You got the boat?"

"On paper, Boo. I'll explain. We'll explain. We Gautiers. And you'll understand. But we're betting you will. You even wore a white shirt to meet with—"

"I always wear me a white shirt."

"We know, Boo. We know. There's more to Tah-loo than nets. Again, that's why we called you to come see us here today. We're betting you will."

"The Gautiers bet, them?"

"A special kind of bet, Boo. A bet on paper. A kind of bet you call an investment."

"Sound 'portant."

"We Gautiers like to say we put the *im* in important."

"Sound like a waste of the time to me, making up long-ways when short-ways done the trick."

"Let's get this back to God, Boo. It always gets back to him. Never take him out. Look at all the angels God, him, he went and hired. All those angels flying pretty-pretty in all that bright sky at their backs. But look at all of them as the kind of workers he could get cause he knew how to look and sound important. He could hire the best. God doesn't run no poor-boy outfit. And we Gautiers don't invest in poor-boy outfits. You catching on now?"

"If I don't, I'm sure, me, I'll catch on all of it later."

So. So it was from his brother-in-law—who indeed did have, like Tah-loo, a special-order hatsize that made hats not worth Tah-loo's time—that Tah-loo heard about important-sounding words like "phases." It was Tah-loo's brother-in-law who told Tah-loo, also, that English words ending in *ity* are probably the most important-sounding English words of all. Unfortunately these same words of all English words are the ones that Tah-loo has always had the most trouble pronouncing.

But another word, the word "Boo," addressed to male-people who are listening to you at any particular time, was an important-sounding word Tah-loo admired immediately and adopted as his own almost immediately. "Immediate admiration" for Tah-loo usually meant within an hour, an hour-and-a-half, two hours. "Immediate adoption" is harder to put a specific time on when we speak of Tah-loo, but in this case we can be certain Tah-loo had crossed that line, had control of the word "Boo" in his own vocabulary, as early as 1944. And we have none other than the United States Coast Guard as witnesses. It was in 1944 that Tah-loo saw the German submarine periscope off Cheniere Cypremort and signaled the Coast Guard boat with his own shirt and told them "Quick-quick-quick, Boo," when they floated alongside.

(As everyone in Mondebon knows, by way of the same witnesses, the periscope turned out to be a galvanized pipe.)

From his brother-in-law, also, Tah-loo heard that even a little standing mixed with lots of money—importance or the perception of importance—will inevitably lead to something called politics.

"I know this word, me," Tah-loo said. "Who don't? The politic. But I'm too simple and humbling of a man, me, for sure to stand up *into* that."

"It's more than just standing—"

"Hope it ain't like taking a trip. I don't go on no trip, me. Not even on paper. I'm from Mondebon, like you know. All us got us a bag pack under the bed case of a 'mergency, but I ain't never had to go use mines. Even when I went oversea, on that . . . that ship, first name of George, in my unal-form. Talk about hell. Ever try sleepin' on your belly in a hamnit?"

"A hammock?"

"Like I say, even sick like the dog in a hamnit going all the way oversea, I didn't go say I was on no trip."

"I follow you there, Boo. War isn't like a trip. A trip is something you go on because you want to."

"And who want that? That be like somebody go tell you you got two, two-and-a-half, three week lef' to live. *Moo-dee* trip. And *moo-dee* more a vacation. I mean, gotdam trip, gotdam vacation."

"Exact, Boo. No need to correct yourself, by the way. A word, once out, is out. But politics isn't like a trip. For sure, not like a vacation. I swear. It's something like what you from down Bayou Mondebon call a white line in white shells. That kind of a passing."

"How you know about the white line?"

"Let's just say we check things out, Boo, and invest in those—"

"Never wrote not one check in my life, me. Proud to say. Not saying, now, 'cause I don't know how to write. Ain't so proud of that. I never been to the school from out of where the knowing how to write, it got to come. Not saying I'm proud of that, me, not doing a lick a—"

"But we Gautiers have done a lick. We kind of specialize in education. And you can hire us."

"I heard about your mama and her special school, me. Who ain't. She took children from every village for her school, correck?"

"Correct, Boo."

"Now back to the politic. You say people just natural pass over into it? Like I natural pass from boats to being a business without knowing I pass over till after? That?"

"Well, Boo. Politics . . . It's more like it gets down to you. From the top. You'll feel it falling down to you from the top."

"Like when I look up, I'm going to see it?"

"That's a good way to put it."

"Like a face? And what face I'm going to see, me, you think, when I look up and see the politic?"

"Probably a Gautier face, Boo. I'm just being honest when I say that."

"And what you Gautiers see when you look up? God?"

This was the first time Tah-loo's brother-in-law laughed, a real laugh that opened and closed the button placket of his starched white shirt, the cloth just above and a little to the right of about where his brother-in-law's *boo-deek* was probably located. (On his ride back to Mondebon after this meeting, Tah-loo would remember considering the probable location of his brother-in-law's *boo-deek*. Tah-loo would also remember remembering, that his mama had once told him, in French, "A navel's a navel, no matter exack where on or exack who on." Believe it or not, as far as Tah-loo could remember, that's all he'd ever heard his mother saying to him on the subject of importance.)

Then, still laughing, Tah-loo's brother-in-law reached over and touched Tah-loo on the back, a light smoothing-a-wrinkle kind of touch Tah-loo could feel from the base of his neck all the way to and a little over and down his left shoulder. (Tah-loo's white shirt was ironed, but not starched. *Paw*-Gautier or not, there was no way Tah-loo was going to let his youngest, unmarried, surviving daughter put starch in his shirt, importance or not.) As soon as Tah-loo felt the feel of the hand, a feel that meant someone was too close by at least one step and one arm-length, he raised both of his hands to push. But Tah-loo did *not* push. A *not* that means to me that Gautiers are indeed, as I've heard, *always away enough*.

"What so funny?" Tah-loo asked. "Just being honest back."

"Let's say you're just living up to your reputation, Boo. Good, honest, humble Tah-loo Perilleux."

"That mean?"

"Means you deserve an honest answer, Boo. As high-high-high as we Gautiers stand, there are still faces between us and God. I say that with all my humility."

"Your humil-i-ti-ty? I don't understand. For true, this time I don't."

"You will, Boo. And when politics fall and you understand—and you will. When it happens, just erase through the word 'importance,' long-ways or short-ways, everywhere I said it to you today and put in the word 'power' over the place where the word 'importance' used to be when I said it to you, and know what you got? You got Law Number One of Politics."

"Power? Like in my arm I just went'n raise jus' now. My arm into my hand kind of power? Or the kind of power my mama got when she read the card? Like your mama got a reputation for her school, my mama, her, she got a reputation for read-ing the card. She made a good living for my daddy by reading the card. Like I say, there so many kind—"

"Oh, we know, Boo. And we figure you know that, too. In your way."

"This kind of getting all real-real all-haywire. Could you talk that back at me in French just a little?"

"French? Aw, Boo, the world is bigger than Mondebon. Big-big bigger than Mondebon."

"I understand, me, the world got to be more big. I been oversea, like I say. Who the hell care the world more big?"

"The world, Boo, is like numbers."

"The number? *Ah-ret.* You know what that mean?"

"Means this meeting's over?"

"Correck. I know how to *moo-dee* count. Don't never go tell me about the num-ber."

"So what do you think, then, Boo? About all—"

"I'm not sure I even want to catch on to some of what you just said, but . . ."

"But what, Boo?"

"But I'm sure I will."

Indeed, within one, one-and-a-half, two-hours after that time Tah-loo spoke to the Gautier who would someday be his business partner and his brother-in-law, Tah-loo was certain he had not caught on to most of what his brother-in-law said about importance. In all honesty, beyond *boo-deeks,* the subject had never been worth his time.

So certainly he had not caught on to what his brother-in-law said about poli-tics. But within one, one-and-a-half, two-hours after that time Tah-loo spoke to the Gautier who would be his brother-in-law, Tah-loo was still certain that, if and when the time came, he eventually would catch-on. For a long time, Tah-loo had caught on to something significant about himself:

Catching on was certainly just a matter of time.

It is no slight on Tah-loo when I say that he caught on to ideas less quickly than he caught on to a joke and that he rarely caught on to a joke on the day it was spoken. As far as any of us know, Tah-loo only told one joke in his life, at his 60th birthday party, and it took him till his 65th birthday party to catch on that he had actually told a joke about five years before. If you get a chance while you're here to meet up with Tah-loo, he's bound to tell you his joke. So prepare yourself. Here's the joke:

I got me one of them photograph type of memory. I just can't remember the name of the people in the picture.

Tah-loo has almost always understood this slow-catching-on side of himself, as far back as the complicated rear-to-lateral trenches of his war. But perhaps his reputation for slowness in these areas is what has enabled him to take possession of the cash of other people around him who believe that he is still in the process of catching on when in fact he has already caught on.

I know that the words "slow-smart" seem to be at odds when I put them together for you. But such a thing exists in this world, and Tah-loo and his eventual acquisition of the cash of those around him are proof of slow-smart's being around.

The best example I can give you of Tah-loo's slow-smart is his marriage to the sister of the man who would one day be his brother-in-law. Now . . . How can I say this? I turn red as Vay's rusty cistern roof so easy. But I'm from Mondebon, so I've got to give a say a try.

It is no slight on Madame Tah-loo when I say that, besides the fact that she was her brother's sister, only her youthfulness—she was eleven-and-a-half, three-quarter, months younger than Tah-loo's youngest surviving daughter by his second wife . . . Only her youthfulness and her femaleness made her attractive to Tah-loo at that time in his advanced-along, half-century-old life when he met her. In fact, anyone who has seen Madame Tah-loo at any of the phases of her life would agree that there is little else besides the fact she is a Gautier and she is a female who was once youthful that could have made her attractive in any way to any man at any time in any light.

You follow, or do I have to say it insultingly plain?

And it is still no slight on Tah-loo when I say that when he finally realized that there was someone else sitting in the room with him and his future brother-in-law . . .

(His brother-in-law had given Tah-loo hints—angels flying in front of bright sky, people hiring other people for free—but Tah-loo had not caught on.)

It is no slight on Tah-loo when I say that when he finally looked at the future

Madame Tah-loo sitting in front of the window, she became more and more attractive to Tah-loo beyond her femaleness and her youth the more he listened to
her brother.

No. I am not saying that Tah-loo married Madame Tah-loo just because of the
ideas of her brother, especially his brother-in-law's idea about how marriage is a
way you can hire somebody for free to take care of some important things you
never had time for before. Let me try again:

Tah-loo, him, is slow-smart. And he is a male, which is a man. Which means he
is slow-smart and he has a penis—

I know that word is easy for most of you to say. After all, it is even all over your
televisions now. But that's the future, and we're still in 1973. And, even though I
might turn easily all red, you all by now must have figured out I'm not one to keep
a right word back. Let me now try to wrap this penis I just used—not *my* penis.
You don't know if I have a penis—wrap the word "penis," in a more civil cloak, a
cloak, as you know, that takes a hell of a few more stitches to weave than the *tee-
teet* piece of cloth called honesty . . .

The one thing that all kinds of male-smart have in common with Tah-loo's
slow-smart is in the relationship of desire for femaleness, any femaleness in most
any kind of light, to such ideas as Inner-Beauty and Respect. What I mean is, rarely
do such ideas like Inner-Beauty and Respect catch on before a man's desire for femaleness, most any femaleness in most any kind of light, has taken hold. There,
that sounded civil, and what is more, that sounded important. So let's go on.

Tah-loo married Madame Tah-loo a short time—three, three-and-a-half, four
months—after the incidence of his first erection, which, it is safe to say—because
it is a physical action that requires some kind of before-hand conscious or unconscious working of the mind—occurred somewhere after his mind caught on, in
some kind of conscious or unconscious way, that Madame Tah-loo was physically
a female. But he married her a long, long time before she had been fully realized
into the creature of Inner-Beauty that she would become for him in 1950, on the
eighth birthday of his first, last, and only surviving son Renard, when Tah-loo
looked from his son's face to his wife's face and saw that, above the soft, brown fleece
above her top lip, she had the same dark-sharpness on and in her eyes you could
see on and in the eyes of his son. Surely, Tah-loo thought on his son's birthday, that
dark-sharpness had been there on and in her before it had been on and in the eyes

of his son, who came out of her. Who among us would not bet that there would soon follow some kind of Respect? Some among us even call Respect itself a kind of Love. And, again. If you've seen Madame Tah-loo, you know:

If someone, even a Great Protector, links her to any kind of Beauty, even Inner-Beauty, there's got to be some kind of potential for some kind of Love going on.

What I'm trying to do here is give Tah-loo the credit he deserves beyond his penis and his craving for youthful femaleness. Even from the first day he saw her sitting, a picture of youth but little else, in the parlor as she silently read her Sunday Missal—from the left side where the Latin mass-words were, while she covered with her big right hand the right side where the English mass-words were—even as Tah-loo felt a heaviness for her in his pants that did not exactly coincide with the vision the lens of his two eyes projected on back to the front his brain, even while her brother talked in the same room about money and business and standing, Tah-loo had already caught on to how his mind worked, slow but certain, and thus Tah-loo trusted, in that same parlor at that same time, that after her youth was gone, some kind of significant idea or other would somehow get attached to this unattractive woman in some way somewhere down the line.

See, I told you Tah-loo is smart, maybe the smartest kind of smart, the smart that trusts, with a trust close to faith, that it will catch-on later.

I can imagine that maybe some of you see, too, by now, that with my ability to string more words than are necessary in my attempt not to insult, that I myself, whoever I am, must be some kind of smart, a wordy smart, but a smart just the same. And obviously, I can write it all down, too. Another significance.

One more significance that might have slipperied past you. And let me tell you now that we're on the subject of me—I cannot, red-faced or not, bare to have a significance slippery past anybody. But you've probably figured that out already, too, on your own. One more significance:

Give Madame Tah-loo and her brother credit for knowing when marrying a middle-aged man with an erection and a bunch of boats is also a wise financial arrangement. Give the entire Gautier family credit for being the first family in the parish, down to a man and a woman and a *bay-bay,* who understood all together at the same time that there is a difference between the word "job" and the word "business." Give them all credit, too, for not falling for the popular modern association of the words "romantic love" with the words "long-lasting marriage."

Am I saying that Madame Tah-loo and her brother and the entire family down to a man and a woman and a *bay-bay* planned to have Madame Tah-loo sitting in that room at that particular time reading her missal with the light at her back?

I *am* saying that. Yes.

Or as those of us from Mondebon say in English, "Yas." Or in Our French, "*Way*." Which just about almost rhymes with *Gautier,* which leads me to the two other things in Mondebon I've heard said on this particular subject of this particular family:

"A cent is a *soo* for some, but it's something else to a *Go-chay.*"

Another way to say it, again mixing Our French with English:

"Wars and depressions and ration stamps are the end of things for some, but are *ways* for Go-chays."

The Last Man on Earth to Play the Bones

CHARLES DEGRAVELLES

The first time you passed it, you missed it completely. Even cruising as you were at fifteen or twenty miles an hour, out for a Sunday, you and your new friend, exploring the country roads south of town. You'd instructed her that an essential part of learning any new place is getting lost in it, and you promised to arrange it. The way you'd done it on your first trip to London, you told her, in Seattle too, and on Crete: the trick, you said, is to let one road lead into another till you've no earthly idea where you are; then see if you can find your way back!

The very thought made you both kind of giddy, two women adrift in this strange flat land. Lean and black, the road staggered and looped away into the damp heat, following a levee which itself apparently followed the unseen and meandering river. Long stretches of field were interrupted only by an occasional farm house and the sudden looming of these bigger-than-any-tree-ought-to-be trees, like shadows fleshed and come to life. Both of you from elsewhere, in the South for the first time and less than a year, both of you teaching at the university. You agreed that anything seemed possible here, as if a mythological creature (and not a pair of crows) might suddenly rise up from behind one of those dilapidated barns or swoop down from an overhanging sycamore or water oak, the moss in its branches like someone's discarded underthings. From the front seat of your friend's convertible, through squinted eyes, the landscape swirled in tepid gusts (even at fifteen or twenty miles an hour) and you seemed to be sinking into rather than passing through it. The first time you passed it, you missed it entirely.

But that was before your friend's car threw itself suddenly into a series of spasms, lurched, boiling and hissing, into the roadside weeds. The engine would turn over, all right, but even you could tell its soul had fled—somewhere into these empty fields, maybe, or beyond that distant border of trees into who knows where. You fought with your friend over whether one or both of you should go for help and if one, which one.

So that, walking past it, a mile or more back up the road, you noticed it for the first time, a house trailer, set back off the blacktop in a muddy yard under a half dozen or so pecan trees with its little hatch-like door thrown open to catch what cool there might be in the patches of breeze floating down the long late summer afternoon.

You stood back and appraised: could have been pink once, but you wouldn't have bet money on it. Made when trailers were still *called* trailers. Tiny and leaning slightly, it seemed; you had the notion to reach out and set it straight as you would a picture on a wall. You heard yourself whisper, "must be like living in an abandoned refrigerator."

You approached cautiously, half-expecting a big black dog to bound out from under the trailer, snarling, to run you back up the road. But all you ignited was a storm of cackles and wild dodgings beneath your feet, the insanely confused running around for which chickens are famous. The roosters were almost too bright to look at, pacing nervously in scattered coops, crowing, their tails spouting geyser-like in dizzying colors. Their mean little heads twisted and turned to throw first one then the other beady eye cynically on you as if they could see under your clothes. You'd grown up in a city and could neither explain nor dispel your discomfort. It stung your nostrils. It was unpleasant. It was eerie.

You threaded through the wire coops which seemed to have sprouted haphazardly, like mushrooms after a rain. The flat tin roofs shed the day's heat, each in a separate vertical river of waves. Through the door you heard the low murmur of a TV and the sizzle of hamburgers frying in a pan. And, every now and again, a laugh (you guessed it was a laugh, but it was more like a shout, really, the kind of yahoo yell a cowboy makes when he's riding a bronco and staying on): "Hyahhh! Hyahhh!" It floated out into the muddy yard where you stood stiff-backed amidst the obscene crowing, the tin huts popping like knuckles as they cooled and contracted. "Hyyyahhh! Get him, coonass. Get him!"

Maybe you should try the next place down the road, you thought, however far that might be, but you only stood there. The chickens scratched and cackled and scurried. The TV gurgled like an underground stream, just beyond your understanding. The hamburgers sizzled. The tin roofs popped in the breeze. "Hyyyahhh! Hyyyahhh!"

Reed Langlois finally helped you too, though he was suspicious at first, leaning in the slender door frame, looking down at you hard from behind the torn screen. The shadow from the beak of his baseball cap cut his face in two—the half you could see was expressionless—and you thought for the moment after you'd explained your situation that he didn't speak English, that he would simply walk back into the trailer, leaving you there as if he hadn't understood a word you'd said.

But he nodded finally, a short decisive dip of the chin, pushed past without a word, and began what looked to you like a random rummaging around the open yard. Like one of his chickens, you thought, as he bent down and picked through scattered clumps of junk for this or that tool, laughing and mumbling to himself about whatever it was he'd been watching. You began to wonder if he remembered what it was he was doing.

His wife appeared in the doorway, pushed the screen door open to have a look at you, a spatula in her hand. Unlike her husband, she seemed serene, as if she were listening to something pleasant just beyond your hearing. Barefoot, in T-shirt and jeans, her bleached blonde hair pulled back away from a very nearly pretty face, she reminded you of someone from your childhood, the daughter of a couple who'd spent a summer working for your parents. You granted her the right to be suspicious, even hostile, about a lone woman showing up at her door, but she seemed to take your sudden appearance from out of nowhere as naturally as she would an afternoon thunderstorm. Still, she wouldn't look directly at you, seemed to watch you through her husband, the spatula in her hand like a wand.

He was talking to you now, up in your face and talking fast. He threw the tools recklessly, one by one, past you into the bed of a new Isuzu pickup: screwdrivers, wrenches, pliers sailing through the air. He was talking to you as if you were supposed to know what it was he was talking about. You wished that she'd come with you because you sensed that something in her, well, kind of held him in place, like a counterweight, kept him from floating up through the pecan limbs into the ragged clouds, mumbling and tossing tools around like popcorn. But you could see she wasn't coming, that she was the type who stayed behind.

He'd completely warmed to you now, was yakking on and on about what he'd been watching on television and what in the hell was so funny about it.

Because his right eye was made of glass, Reed Langlois had to lean forward and crane his neck to talk to you as he drove, as if his blindness were a fat person sitting between the two of you. Even then he wasn't really looking at you but right over your shoulder—which put another ghost, perhaps a skinny one, behind you. He was youngish, about your age, more or less, though it was hard to tell with country people. He shouted everything he said, snatched off his baseball cap from time to time and gave the dashboard a good beating with it. He reminded you of the spoiled kid who's got his mother where he wants her and keeps her there with a periodic tantrum whether she needs it or not.

". . . So the TV news guy is asking the old Cajun how it was he came to be playing the bones." He'd leaned over and put an imaginary mike in front of your face. For a moment neither of his hands was on the steering wheel; the truck dipped off the shoulder and sprayed gravel after which he guided it, one-handed, back onto the blacktop without ever taking his good eye off (near) you. Everything he said assumed you knew all about him, that you were somehow acquainted with every detail of his background and personal life—not like you were friends, not like that at all, but that you just somehow knew. It kept you dizzy, off-balance.

"And I know right away by the look of this old coonass (you know how Daddy makes that look when he's about to lay it on you thick) that this old man's gonna start playing more than the bones. But the reporter don't know it. He's taking the old coonass one hundred percent serious, like it's the King of Poland or somebody he's talking to. So the coonass gets this real serious expression on his face like, 'Ho-ho, cher, let me tell you all dere is to know about da bones,' and the reporter keeps on nodding and looking real, real interested, see, like playing the bones is gonna be the next stage of the space program or something, and I'm thinking to myself, 'Go get him, coonass, lay it on him!' Jesus Christ, you really did walk a piece, didn't you? Where you from? You're lucky I was home today and not fishing. I'm on my seven-off. Go back offshore Sunday. So the coonass starts in, kind of lightly at first, about how if you're gonna get the right sound not just any bones will do; you need cat bones! Oh, man, that reporter's just eating it like ice cream. He's thinking to himself how he's gonna win some awards for this one, you know, like the Best Report from the Backwoods Award or something like that. And so the reporter asks him, 'Well, sir, where *do* you get your cat bones?' And the old man kind of nods his head gravely and says how he wouldn't *kill* a cat of course but how everybody in his community saves up their dead cats for him and leaves 'em in his backyard, and how once you got your dead cat how only these special bones from the back legs—I forget what he called them—will do and how they got to be dried in the sun just so and you can't oven-cook 'em or microwave 'em 'cause that's not how his daddy did it or his granddaddy before that, and the reporter's just nodding like he's got a spring in his head, eating it up like ice cream, and, man, I'm killing myself laughing and screaming, 'Get him, get him!'"

When your friend's car finally came into sight, a blinking blue spot at the edge of the black strip of road, something strange happened. A dog appeared at the top of the levee and began down, making for the highway at a leisurely trot. Not that this was strange in itself; it's just that Reed nearly lost control of the truck in skidding to a stop. "What luck!" he whispered.

It happened very quickly. He seemed to have forgotten you were even there. He began inching the truck forward into position, his face, under the low beak of the baseball cap, pinched into a tight little knot of concentration. When the dog had just set its paw on the glistening blacktop and was starting to cross, Reed slammed the accelerator to the floor and the truck leapt forward, tires screaming like a witness.

It was hard to tell if he'd hit the dog or not because the last you saw, it was running back over the levee. You could tell Reed was wondering, too. He was breathing hard, teeth set, face flushed. He craned his neck slowly to peer around the invisible fat person who sat peacefully as ever between the two of you, focused on the lean ghost behind your right shoulder. His right hand reached up and stroked a twenty-two rifle in its rack behind the seat. "What do ya think?" he asked. He let the question hang there awhile for you to savor. "Naw," he said finally and turned back to the wheel (you'll swear now he winked his one good eye at you). "They'll do that sometimes. I think we got him."

Reed Langlois went on talking without a pause while he did whatever it was he was doing under the hood of your friend's convertible—hitting on it with a wrench or whatever as far as you knew. You and your friend were grateful enough, but you found yourself watching the sky go dark, and wishing like hell you were home.

"And so the reporter asks the old coonass how long he's been playing the bones and the old man, seeing now there's no way he can push the thing too far, says, 'Well, cher, it's like dis: it runs in da family. My daddy, he played *les os*—dat's what da ol' folks call 'em, *les os*—and his daddy before dat, and back and back like dat.' And the reporter's about to pee on himself he's so happy he's found the real thing, and he's already thinking he can get Charles Kuralt out of the midwest to come down here and do this thing, and I'm just screaming, I mean it, I'm screaming, 'get him, get him, coonass!' And so the old man tops it by telling the reporter how he's the last person on the planet earth to play the bones, and after him, the bones as a musical instrument is gonna be dead and buried forever. Like ice cream, I'm telling you. It was just too good."

"Maybe he is," your friend suggested.

Reed looked up from under the hood, up from under his cap, cocked his head like a rooster and stared in the general direction of your friend. "Maybe he's what?"

"The last man to play the bones."

Reed thought about this a moment. "Hell, I don't know, maybe he is. Okay, crank her up. Let's see if she'll fly."

He wouldn't take your money, and that's how you ended up back at the trailer having a beer with Reed and Julie. He wouldn't take money and he insisted, and your friend had said (you would thank her properly for this later), "Come on, what the hell." And he had, of course, after all, fixed the car.

Inside, the trailer was pretty much what you expected, hand-me-downs, mostly, jammed in so close together you could hardly move. A couple of chairs, a small sofa, a rickety kitchen table. The water bed looked new. A small stove and refrigerator pushed up near a sink made that side seem the kitchen, but pots and utensils were everywhere. The greasy smell of hamburger hung thick.

A small black-and-white television next to the bed was playing the "Andy Griffith Show"—an episode you remembered. Barney was demonstrating some kung fu moves he claimed to have mastered. "They're lethal," Barney was saying as he waved his hands back and forth in front of Andy's indulgent smile. "They're lethal weapons!" You expected Reed or Julie to turn it off, but they didn't seem to notice it was on.

On one wall was tacked the only piece of art work in the place, a poster of an enormous cartoon eagle, wings spread, talons open and extended as it dropped, about to snatch and devour a scrawny mouse. The mouse faced its awesome foe with chest out, an irreverent sneer on its mousy face, throwing with its paw the single-fingered salute you called in school "the bird." At the bottom of the poster, in bold red letters, the moral was spelled out: "Defiance!"

Reed, then Julie, each took a hit of pot and passed it your way. The marijuana joint was inserted behind the cocked hammer of a blown glass pipe shaped like an old-fashioned pistol. You took it as they had, inhaled through the barrel until the thick white smoke filled the transparent pipe, then released it into your lungs in a single blast. "Suicide sucking," Reed wheezed through the top of a held breath. You and your friend each sipped politely from a can of beer, did your best with small talk, explained that you had a long drive to get back to town.

Reed wanted you to know he *had* to kill the dogs because they killed his chickens. And it wasn't simply revenge, he said; he was protecting an economic asset. These were not your ordinary barnyard variety, your basic fat-assed egg layers or fryers; they were game cock, proud fighting chickens, some worth four or five hundred dollars each or more. They were his livelihood, he said, (that, and the marijuana). He'd tried pelting the dogs with rock salt from his shotgun, built a fence, even strung a strand of electric wire. Nothing had worked. They kept getting in. Nothing but killing them.

You looked at Julie to see how she was taking all this. She'd hardly opened her mouth since you'd walked in, but you could tell she wasn't stupid and knew exactly what you were thinking. "His nickname is 'Lack,'" she said. "Ever since his high school history teacher said he lacked all sense." Everyone laughed at this, especially Reed.

Reed said his father had fought chickens and his grandfather too. He pulled from his pocket a small black-handled pocket knife and opened it up. It was his grandpa's, he said, a Case knife with a real steel blade. "None of this stainless shit. It'll rust if you let it, but it holds an edge." When your friend betrayed doubt that he could split a hair with it, Reed was indignant. He reached over and pulled a hair from her arm (too surprised to scream, tears came to her eyes) and everyone laughed hysterically when he actually did it. You could see your friend framing the story to re-tell it just so when you got back to town.

When you finally got up to go, Reed stood in the doorway with a grin and wagged his finger. Not before you'd seen his pride and joy, he said. He assured you this would be the highlight of the evening, something you'd never forget, and he pushed through the hatch-like door out into the night.

"Most people put down chicken fighting without knowing the first thing about it," he said, squeezing back through the tiny door with a fierce, red-eyed bird under each arm. The trailer was small with two people in it. With four there was almost no room to move. Two chickens added and you had the feeling you were trapped inside Reed Langlois's skull.

This close, the chickens seemed more the size of hawks, almost as beautiful. They reminded you of missiles, torpedoes, fighter jets, with something overly alert, fanatical in their expressions, like bug-eyes soldiers run out of a foxhole. You'd always thought of farm animals as having something soft about them—sheep, calves, dogs—something warm. Or else stupid like a goose or the chickens you'd seen. But these eyes were both smart and malicious, not a glimmer of innocence. With his good eye, Reed stroked the length of each bird, from the small, nervous, bullet-shaped head with its razor beak down the tense wiry spine into the luxurious bloom of blue and green tail feathers gleaming with a metallic sheen.

At first they seemed only interested in each other, craning and twisting and wickedly jabbing. Reed held them just far enough apart to keep them from connecting. But when he shoved awkwardly past you, one of the birds lunged, a vicious stab of the beak that tore into your shoulder. "Good God!" you screamed, grabbing your arm, almost falling backwards in your chair. Reed nodded knowingly, approved of your judgment. His glass eye was milky, unreadable, but his good eye blazed. "They're mean, all right. Fine goddamned animals."

With some difficulty, Reed managed to back into his chair at the kitchen table, still holding the birds apart. They were nearly berserk now with crowing. Each darting head seemed to have a life of its own as it tried to outmaneuver the other. Julie took four small leather balls, each with a strap, from a box, placed them on the table. "Like boxing gloves," she explained, "so they won't kill each other." Then she reached under and lifted one of the chickens, expertly as her husband. The blood had risen in her face, you noticed, a peculiar luster in her eyes, and for the first time you thought, "Ah, yes, of course, husband and wife." She whispered to her rooster and it responded, calming, while she sheathed the spur of each foot into a glove. The man and the woman, each with an animal, faced across the table. "Now we're gonna have some fun," Reed said.

All at once you saw yourself with a curious amazement: the college professor, guzzling beer in some house trailer in who knows where, south Louisiana, holding your bleeding arm and muttering "good God" while two fighting chickens were passed, over and over, within pecking distance, then pulled away. Had he said fun?

You looked to your friend, expecting to share with her the irony, but she was lost in the spectacle. Her mouth hung open, and every time the birds got close enough to jab and scream, she winced, and shuddered. I'm free to leave, you told yourself with determination, and you sat up straight. I can walk out of here any time, right now if I want to. I ought to want to. I do. I am. (You didn't.)

At each pass, the birds became more frantic. Finally, when it seemed their handlers could hardly hold them, Reed yelled, "Let go!" The trailer exploded as the chickens threw themselves at each other in furious bursts, colliding mid-air, wings thrashing, legs extended and flailing with their gloved spurs at the head and chest of the other. There was no crowing now, only the thick, muscular thudding of crashing bodies, the rasping of beating wings. In the short intervals between collisions, they strutted and postured, parading with a breathless bravado around and around the table. Each blazing eye, set like a gem in the ever-shifting head, never left its opponent; each grim lean body swaggered this way and that, sizing up with the considered deliberation of a master craftsman the preciseness of the angle of advantage for the next sudden onslaught.

But if the birds were silent, their handlers were not. Reed seemed in the fight himself, bent at the waist, neck poking through his T-shirt, good eye lowered to the level of the circling, jabbing chickens. Every movement sent a tremor through him and when, in a furious flash, one attacked, he'd leap and holler, "Hyaaah! Get him, get him, get him, you bastard." He threw his fists, hopping and dancing, thrusting and jiggling in a wild pantomime of what he watched. Julie, too, red-faced now, teeth glistening, was totally immersed: "Now, gray, hit him! Look out, look out, blue. Hit him back. Hit him!" The trailer rocked in spasms. Feathers flew.

Then it was over. Julie and Reed were each holding a bird, and in the sudden eerie quiet, everybody in the room was panting and sweating. Julie seemed slightly overwrought, as if she'd only mislaid her composure. "Don't want them to hurt each other," she said, stroking her bird. She bent to baby talk to it, then dodged as it made a furious stab at her face. Reed positively shimmered with pride and exhilaration. He held up one of the leather gloves by its strap. "One of them would be dead by now if it weren't for these."

Neither seemed to notice (or care) that your friend had fallen over backward in her chair and sat, staring wide-eyed through pulled up knees, her back against the wall, or that your arm was still bleeding. The lamp had been knocked to the floor as well and threw onto the ceiling the bizarre looming shadows of the couple and their animals. "They drew blood as it was with just their beaks," Reed went on, and he thrust the chicken at you for inspection.

Without answering, you stumbled toward the door, your friend close behind you as she struggled to her feet, pushing to get out, both of you, as if it were a place on fire. Unfailingly polite, your friend turned to Reed and Julie as you neared the door and said, "Fascinating, really."

"War machines," Reed answered. "The ancient Romans got their inspiration from fighting cocks. That's how come they ruled the world."

"It's true," Julie said, "Reed read it in a book."

You threw the door open and ran into a tree. Had a tree grown in the doorway? A soft tree? The tree shoved you back into the trailer so that both you and your friend fell onto the floor. Then the tree stepped inside, squinting in the sudden light, holding one hand over its eyes till they became adjusted. It held in its other hand a large, gleaming, silver-plated pistol. The tree said, "I come to see about my dog."

The sudden silence was dizzying, as if everything everywhere had suddenly held its breath. Everything, that is, except the crickets. The crickets kept whining like a gear that keeps turning in the absolute silence after a watch has been smashed under an angry boot.

Two angry boots into which were crudely stuffed a dirty pair of khakis out of which overflowed a disheveled and misbuttoned short sleeve shirt out of which arose a human head, a big head whose hair stuck out crazily in patches as if it were blowing in a perpetual and sinister wind.

"I know you killed her," the old man said, waving the pistol. He was crying. "So don't bother trying to say nothing to me, boy. I been calling and calling and she ain't come back. Look here," he said, and in a strange theatrical gesture, stuck his head out the door, holding the gun on Reed the whole time. "Lucy! Lucy! God-damnit, Lucy!" He stuck his head back in. "You see," he said, "so don't think I don't know what you been up to, you little sonofabitch. You gone and killed her with the rest. I been out here my whole damned life, boy, born and raised right out here," he waved his free hand wildly to show you all where he'd been born and raised, "and you come in here and plop this fucking trailer down and commence to shooting dogs and poisoning dogs and running over dogs, and I warned you, didn't I, but now you gone and killed her with the rest, you killed her even though I warned you, you know I did, I warned you if you touched a hair on that dog's head, I was going to put you where a cat puts shit!"

Your first impulse was to explain everything—surely the old man, insane as he was, would understand a reasonable explanation for your presence here; it was all so simple, really, an afternoon drive, a broken-down car, a simple request for a little assistance . . . you were no dog killer! You wanted to show him. What? Your driver's license? Your diplomas? Your good will? Show him, by God, that this was none of your business! That you didn't belong here. To demonstrate the series of improbables that led to this improbable scene. To prove that your being here was a terrible, terrible mistake.

But then the old man, though you cowered on the floor at his big dirty boots, didn't seem to have noticed you yet. He'd lowered his hand from his eyes, was still talking (he'd never quit talking) and stretched out his other arm full length so that the end of the gun barrel wasn't three feet from the center of Reed's face.

Scared as you were, there was something left over to marvel at the way Reed was acting with a loaded revolver on him. Not nonchalance, exactly; more than that, more than matter-of-factness, more than cool. He was excited, almost eager, seeming to have fully anticipated this moment and been waiting for it, almost as if this stand-off was his idea, as if he'd invited the old man over for a fight and weren't they going to have some fun now. His hands rested lightly on his hips. The balance of his body was shifted to one straight leg while the other leg, slightly bent, might have been induced to tap its foot. Come on, it might have said, what's next? His head was oddly cocked to give his good eye full play. His lips were moist from licking and re-licking and seemed so much to be keeping a smile off, you thought for one strange moment it might all be a put-on, like those staged show-downs in tourist towns out west, a wild practical joke to poke at the city slickers.

That's when you saw Reed's right hand slide casually into his pocket and then you knew exactly what it was: he was crazy. While the old man kept raving about his dog and what he was going to do to Reed, aiming a loaded pistol at him the whole time, Reed, if you could believe your eyes, was, with one hand in the dark cramped pocket of his jeans, trying to open the blade of his pocket knife, inheritance of his grandfather; he was preparing to do battle.

And then another revelation shook you (though you'd been aware of it since you first laid eyes on him): he was crazy like his chickens were crazy. You're not sure if it was then or later that you made a mental note about "cock-sure," about how it was that this expression had somehow lost the connotation of irrationality, insanity, even, that it surely must have had for the people who first used it, people who must have known about fighting roosters.

But where *were* the chickens? Somehow they'd escaped the crowded trailer and you listened for them through the open door; yes, there they were, naked spurs now, you figured, the pointless flutter and thud of a battle to the death. You suddenly thought of Julie and found her crouched and cringing behind Reed. She knew what was about to happen. You could see that. Her eyes were closed, her head thrown back. One fist was pressed into her stomach as if she were about to be sick, one was pressed into her mouth. She knew. She knew.

You told and re-told the story for how many weeks? How many moths? for your friends, your colleagues, your family back home. Told and re-told till they were sick of hearing about it. Until they finally made you stop. How you simply crawled out on all fours, actually brushing the old man's legs, through the door, down the cinder block steps and into the night. How the old man kept raving, paying you no more attention than he had the chickens. How your friend had followed you, the two of you crawling across the floor like a couple of dogs, across the muddy yard, on your hands and knees like a couple of old dogs. How you got into your car and turned the key—it was running fine now—and simply drove away, drove in silence for miles, the lights of the city fanning the sky, the darkness behind you, behind you.

And then, months later, long after you'd forgotten it yourself, the telephone call. You answered. "Hello?"

"You're not going to believe this," someone said, "but he wasn't the last."

"What?"

"Like your friend said. He wasn't the last."

"Who is this?"

"Lack."

"Who?"

"Lack Langlois."

"Who?"

"Last night on TV, on the Grand Ole Opry, no less, there's this young kid, no kidding, couldn't have been a day over twelve, and there he is playing the bones like all get out."

"How did you get this number? I thought you were. . . ." You couldn't bring yourself to say it.

"That's what I wanted to tell your friend," Reed went on. "You tell her. I knew that old coonass was taking that reporter up river, but hell, what I didn't know was that I was right there in the boat with 'em." He laughed. "Can you imagine being the last of anything? Just when I was all set—had my cat and everything—here comes this young kid, on the Grand Ole Opry, no less, playing the bones like all get out. You tell your friend. Just when I was all set to be the last man on earth to play the bones."

The Freezer Jesus

JOHN DUFRESNE

Two days after we learned we had Jesus on our freezer, my sister Elvie had this dream where all the mystery was explained to her. Freezer's this ordinary, yellow Amana. Sets out there on the porch on account of we got no room for it inside the house. What Jesus explained to Elvie in the dream was that He supernaturally connected the porch light to the freezer and turned the freezer into a TV and on that TV was Jesus Himself. Elvie, He says to her, I've chosen you and your brother Arlis this time because you all been so alone and so good these fifty, sixty years and because your bean crop's going to fail again this spring. And tell Arlis, He said, to call the Monroe newspaper and tell them Jesus has come again and everyone should know what that means.

Now, I've never been a strictly religious person like most of my neighbors. Naturally, I believe in the Lord and salvation and Satan and all of that. I just never reckoned what all that had to do with planting beans or chopping cotton, you see. And then comes that Friday and I'm walking Elvie up the path from the bean field at dusk and I notice the porch light on and I tell Elvie we must have had a visitor stop by. As we get closer, I notice a blemish on the freezer door that wasn't there before. Then suddenly the blemish erupts like a volcano and commences to changing shape, and what were clouds at first become a beard and hair, and I recognize immediately and for certain that the image is the very face of Jesus right down to the mole near his left eye.

What is it, Arlis? Elvie says to me. Why you shaking? Of course Elvie can't see what I see because she's blind as a snout beetle. So I tell her about this Jesus, and somehow she knows it's true and falls to her knees and sobs. Praise God, Arlis, she says.

We're not accustomed to much excitement in Holly Ridge, Louisiana. Only time we made the news was seven years ago when a twelve-point buck jumped through Leamon Dozier's bathroom window while he was shaving and thrashed itself to unconsciousness. Still, the Dream Jesus had told Elvie we were to let the world know, so I called the paper. The boy they sent along didn't mind telling me he was mighty skeptical before he witnessed the freezer with his own eyes. Said, though, it looked more like Willie Nelson than Jesus unless you squinted your eyes, and then it looked like the Ayatollah of Iran. Of course, any way you look at it, he said, it's a miracle. He took out his little notebook and asked Elvie what she thought this means. She said, well, this here's Jesus, and evidently He has chosen Richland Parish for His Second Coming. My advice, she told the boy, is that people should get ready.

First off, just a few people came at twilight to watch the freezer erupt with Jesus. Then they brought friends. Then the gospel radio station in Rayville hired a bus and drove folks out here. Pretty soon, the Faulkner Road was crowded all the way to 138 with dusty pilgrims. I spent my afternoons and evenings trying to regulate the toilet line through the house. Either that or I'd be fetching water from the well for the thirsty or faint or trying to keep the cars off my melon patch. Anyway, I got little work done in the fields and soon the Johnson grass had choked the life from my beans. Elvie reminded me how the Lord had prophesied the crop failure, and she reassured me that He would provide.

Every night at nine-thirty, the Amana TV would begin to fade slowly and within minutes the divine image would be gone. Then I'd spend an hour or so picking up soda cans and candy wrappers all over the yard. Once in a while I'd find a pilgrim still lingering by the coop, up to something, I don't know what, and I'd have to ask him to leave. One time this Italian lady from Vicksburg says to me could she have a morsel of food that I kept in the freezer. She was sure if she could just eat something out of that holy freezer, she would be cured of her stomach cancer. I gave her a channel cat I'd caught in Bayou Macon and said I hoped it worked.

Then this TV evangelist drove up from Baton Rouge in a long, white limousine, walked up on the porch, looked the freezer up and down without a word, followed the arc of the extension cord plugged into the porch light, gazed out at the gape-mouthed crowd, turned to me, smiled sort of, said Praise Jesus in a whispery voice, combed his fingers through his long hair, nodded to his chauffeur, got back into the limousine, and drove away.

The TV minister wasn't the only preacher who came calling. The Reverend Danny Wink from the True Vine Powerhouse Pentecostal Church came every day and took to sitting beside Elvie in a seat of honor, I suppose he thought, up on the porch by the screen door. It was the Reverend Wink's idea to transfer the freezer to his church, where it could be worshiped properly before a splendid congregation and all, which was sure okay with me so long as the Reverend furnished us with another freezer. I had a shelf full of crawfish tails to think about. Elvie, though, told him she was waiting on a sign from Jesus. One evening, the Reverend Wink presented Elvie with a brass plaque that read: "This Freezer Donated by Elvie and Arlis Elrod," and pointed to where he'd screw it onto the freezer.

About a month after Jesus first appeared to us, I'm sleeping when I hear this racket out on the porch and I get up quietly, figuring it's one of the idolaters come back in the middle of the night to fool with the freezer. What I see, though, is Elvie kneeling in a pool of light from the open freezer door, holding handfuls of ice cubes over her eyelids, weeping, asking Jesus to scrub the cataracts from her milky old eyes. I watched Elvie for three nights running. On that last night, Elvie started jabbering in tongues the way the Reverend Wink does, and she's so like a lunatic there in her nightgown screaming at this big, old machine that I can't watch no more.

In the morning, I found Elvie slumped on the kitchen floor. She said, Arlis, I'm as blind as dirt and always will be. She called the Reverend Wink and had him haul off the freezer that morning. And then what happened was this:

Jesus never did reappear on that freezer, which made the believers at the True Vine Powerhouse Church angry and vengeful. Right from his pulpit, the Reverend Wink called me and Elvie schemers, charlatans, and tools of the Devil. Elvie, herself, grew bitter and remote, asked me did I do something clever with that Amana maybe. I said no I didn't and she said it surely wasn't kind of the Lord to give her hope and then snatch it away like He done. Our bean crop's ruined, cotton's all leggy and feeble, and I don't know what we'll do.

Can't even say the Lord will provide, but I do know that He's still here with us. I see Him everywhere I look, only this time I'm keeping the news to myself. I saw Him in that cloud that dropped a lightning bolt this afternoon. I see His face in the knot on the trunk of that live oak out back. What I notice this time is those peculiar wine-dark eyes, drunk with the sadness of rutted fields and empty rooms. I can squint my eyes and see Jesus smiling back at me from the dots on the linoleum floor, and I think He must be comforted by my attention. I hear His voice in the wind calling to me, and I feel calm. I hear Him whisper, Arlis, get ready. In her room, Elvie sits at the edge of the bed, coughs once in a while, and fingers the hem of her housedress.

Calling

RICHARD FORD

A year after my father departed, moved to St. Louis, and left my mother and me behind in New Orleans, to look after ourselves in whatever manner we could, he
called on the telephone one afternoon and asked to speak to me. This was before
Christmas, 1961. I was home from military school in Florida. My mother had begun her new singing career, which meant taking voice lessons at a local academy,
and also letting a tall black man who was her accompanist move into our house
and into her bedroom, while passing himself off to the neighborhood as the yardman. William Dubinion was his name, and together he and my mother drank far
too much and filled up the ashtrays and played jazz recordings too loud and made
unwelcome noises until late, which had not been how things were done when my
father was there. However, it was done because he was not there, and because he
had gone off to St. Louis with another man, an ophthalmologist named Francis
Carter, never to come back. I think it seemed to my mother that in view of these
facts it didn't matter what she did or how she lived, and that doing the worst was
finally not much different from doing the best.

They are all dead now. My father. My mother. Dr. Carter. The black accompanist, Dubinion. Though occasionally I will still see a man on St. Charles Avenue, in
the business district, a man entering one of the new office buildings they've built—
a tall, handsome, long-strided, flaxen-haired, youthful, slightly ironic-looking man
in a seersucker suit, bow tie, and white shoes, who will remind me of my father, or
how he looked, at least, when these events occurred. He must've looked that way
all of his years, into his sixties. New Orleans produces men like my father, or once
did: clubmen, racquets players, deft, balmy-day sailors, soft-handed Episcopalians
with progressive attitudes, good educations, effortless manners, but with secrets.
These men, when you meet them on the sidewalk, or at some uptown dinner party,
seem like the very best damn old guys you could ever know. You want to call them
up the next day and set some plans going. It seems that you always knew about
them, that they were present in the city, but you just hadn't seen a lot of them—a

glimpse here and there. They seem exotic, and your heart expands with the thought of a long friendship's commencement and your mundane life taking a new and better turn. So you do call, and you do see them. You go spec fishing off Pointe a la Hache. You stage a dinner and meet their pretty wives. You take a long lunch together at Antoine's or Commander's, and decide to do this every week from now on to never. And yet someplace along late in the lunch you hit a flat spot. A silent moment occurs, and your eyes meet in a way that could signal a deep human understanding you'd never ever have to speak about. But what you see is, suddenly—and it is sudden and fleeting—you see this man is far, far away from you, so far, in fact, as not even to realize it. A smile could be playing on his face. He may just have said something charming or incisive or flatteringly personal to you. But then the far, faraway awareness dawns, and you know you're nothing to him and will probably never even see him again, never take the trouble. Or, if you do chance to see him, you'll cross streets mid-block, cast around for exits in crowded dining rooms, sit longer than you need to in the front seat of your car to let such a man go around a corner or disappear into the very building I mentioned. You avoid him. And it is not that there is anything so wrong with him, nothing unsavory or misaligned. Nothing sexual. You just know he is not for you. And that is an end to it. It's simple, really. Though of course it's more complicated when this involves your father.

When I came to the telephone for my father's call—my mother had answered and they had spoken some terse words—my father began right away to talk: "Well, let's see, is it Van Cliburn, or Mickey Mantle?" These were two heroes of the time whom I had gone on about and alternately wanted to be when he was still in our lives. I had already forgotten them.

"Neither one," I said. I was in the big front hall where the telephone alcove was. I could see outside through the glass front door. William Dubinion was there on our gated lawn, on his knees in the monkey grass that bordered my mother's camellias. It was a fine situation, I thought—staring at my mother's colored boyfriend while talking to my father in his far-off new city, living as he did. "Oh of course," my father said. "Those were our last year's fascinations."

"It was longer ago," I said. My mother made a noise in the next room. I breathed her cigarette smoke, heard the newspaper crackle. She was listening to everything, and I didn't want to seem friendly to my father, which I did not feel in any case. I thought he was a bastard.

"Well now, see here, ole Buck Rogers," my father continued. "I'm calling up about an important matter to the future of mankind. I'd like to know if you'd care to go duck hunting in the fabled Grand Lake marsh. With me. I have to come to town in two days to settle some business. My ancient father had a trusted family retainer named Renard Theriot, a disreputable old yat. But Renard could unquestionably blow a duck call. So I've arranged for his son, Mr. Renard, Jr., to put us both in a blind and call in several thousand ducks for our pleasure." My father cleared his throat in the stagy way he always did when he talked like this—highfalutin. "I mean if you're not overbooked, of course," he said and cleared his throat again.

"I might be," I said, and suddenly felt strange even to be talking to him. He occasionally called me at military school, where I had to converse with him in the orderly room. He naturally paid all my school bills, sent an allowance, and saw to my mother's expenses. He probably paid for William Dubinion's services, too, and wouldn't have cared what their true nature was. He had also conceded us the big white Greek Revival raised cottage on McKendall Street in uptown. (McKendall is our family name—my name. It is such a family as that.) But, still, it was very odd to think that your father was living with another man, and was calling up to ask you to go duck hunting. And then to have my mother listening, sitting and smoking and reading the *States Item,* in the very next room and thinking whatever she must've been thinking. It was nearly too much for me.

And yet I wanted to go duck hunting, to go by boat out into the marshes that make up the vast, brackish tidal land south and east of our city. I had always imagined I'd go with my father when I was old enough. And I was old enough now, and had already been taught to fire a rifle—though not a shotgun—in my school. Also, when I spoke to him that day, he did not sound to me like some man who was living with another man in St. Louis. He sounded the way he always had in our normal life, when I had gone to Jesuit, and he had practiced law in the Hibernia Bank building, and we were a family. Something I think about my father, whose name was Boatwright McKendall, and who was only forty-one years old at the time: something about him must've wanted things to be as they had been before he met his great love, Dr. Carter. Though you could also say that my father just wanted not to have it be that he couldn't do whatever he wanted. He wouldn't credit that anything he did might be deemed wrong, or the cause of hard feeling or divorce or terrible scandal such as what sees you expelled from the law firm your family started a hundred years ago and that bears your name; or that you conceivably caused the early death of your own mother from sheer disappointment. And in fact if anything he did had caused someone difficulty, or ruined a life or prospects, or set someone on a downward course—well, then he just largely ignored it, or agreed to pay money for it, and afterward tried his level best to go on as if the world were a smashingly great place for everyone and we could all be wonderful friends. It was the absence I mentioned before, the skill he had not to be where he exactly was, and yet to *seem* present to any but the most practiced observer. A son, for instance.

"Well, now look-it here, Mr. Buck Rogers," my father said to me over the telephone from—I guessed—St. Louis. Buck is what I was called and still am, to distinguish me from him (our name is the same). And I remember becoming suddenly nervous, as if by agreeing to go with him, and to see him for the first time since he had left a New Year's party at the Boston Club and gone away with Dr. Carter—by doing these altogether natural things (going hunting) I was crossing a line, putting myself at risk. And not the risk you might think based on low instinct, but some kind you don't know exists until you feel it in your belly, the way you would if you were running down a steep hill and at the bottom there's a deep river or a canyon, and you can't stop. Disappointment was what I risked, I know now. But I wanted what I wanted and would not let such a feeling stop me. "I want you to know," my father continued, "that I've cleared all this with your mother. She thinks it's a wonderful idea." I pictured his yellow hair, his handsome, youthful, unlined face talking animatedly into the receiver in some elegant, sunny, high-ceilinged room, beside an expensive French table, with some fancy art objects beside him, which he would be picking up and inspecting as he talked. In my picture he was wearing a purple smoking jacket and he seemed happy to be doing what he was doing.

"Is somebody else going?" I said.

"Oh, God no," my father said, and laughed. "Like who? Francis is too refined to go duck hunting. He'd be afraid of getting his beautiful blue eyes put out. Wouldn't you, Francis?" It shocked me to think Dr. Carter was right there in the room with him, listening. My mother, of course, was also listening to me. "It'll just be you and me and Renard, Jr.," my father said, his voice going away from the receiver. I heard a second voice, a soft one, say something then where my father was, possibly some ironic comment about our plans. "Oh Christ," my father said in an irritated tone, a tone of his I didn't know any better than I knew Dr. Carter's. "Just don't say that. This is not that kind of conversation. This is Buck here." The voice said something else, and in my mind I suddenly saw Dr. Carter in a very unkind way, a way I will not even describe. "Now you raise your bones at 4 A.M. on Thursday, Commander Rogers," my father said in his highfalutin style. "Ducks are early risers. I'll collect you in front of your house. Wear your boots and your Dr. Dentons and nothing bright-colored. I'll supply the artillery for us."

It seemed odd that my father thought of the great house where we had all lived, and that his own father and grandfather had lived in since after the Civil War, as *my* house. It was not my house, I felt. The most it was was my mother's house, because she had married him in it and then taken it in their hasty divorce.

"How's school, by the way," my father said distractedly.

"How's what?" I was so surprised to be asked that. My father sounded confused, as if he'd been reading something and lost his place on a page.

"School. You know? Grades? Did you get all A's? You should. You're smart. At least, you have a smart mouth."

"I hate school," I said. I had liked Jesuit, where I'd had friends. But my mother had made me go away to Sandhearst because of all the upset with my father's leaving. There I wore a khaki uniform with a blue stripe down the side of my pants leg, and a stiff blue doorman's hat. I felt a fool at all times.

"Oh, well, who cares," my father said. "You'll get into Harvard the same way I did."

"What way," I asked, because even at fifteen I wanted to go to Harvard.

"On looks," my father said. "That's how Southerners get along. That's the great intelligence. Once you know that, the rest is pretty simple. The world wants to operate on looks. It only uses brains if looks aren't available. Ask your mother. It's why she married me when she shouldn't have. She'll admit it now."

"I think she's sorry about it now." I thought about my mother listening to half our conversation.

"Oh, yes. I'm sure she is, Buck. We're all a little sorry now. I'll testify to that."

The other voice in the room where he was spoke something then, again in an ironic tone. "Oh shut up," my father said. "Just shut up that talk and stay out of this. I'll see you Thursday morning, son," my father said, and he hung up before I could answer.

This conversation with my father occurred on Monday, the eighteenth of December, three days before we were supposed to go duck hunting in the marsh. And, for the days in between then and Thursday, my mother more or less avoided me, staying in her room upstairs with the door closed, and often with William Dubinion, or going away in the car to her singing lessons with William acting as her chauffeur—though she rode in the front seat. It was still the turbulent race times then, and colored people were being lynched and trampled upon and burnt out all over the Southern states. And yet it was just as likely to cause no uproar if a proper white woman appeared in public with a Negro man in our city. There was no rule or logic to any of it. It was New Orleans, and if you could carry it off you did. Plus Mr. Dubinion didn't mind working in the camellia beds in front of our house, just for the record. In truth, I do not think he minded about very much. He had grown up in the cotton patch in Pointe Coupee Parish, between the rivers, had somehow made it to music school at Wilberforce, in Ohio, been to Korea, and played in the Army band. Later, he barged around playing the clubs and juke joints in the city for a decade before he somehow met my mother at a society party where he was the paid entertainment and she was putting herself into the public eye to make the case that, when your husband abandons you for a rich queer, life will go on.

Mr. Dubinion never addressed much to me. He had arrived in my mother's life after I had gone away to military school, and was simply a fait accompli when I came home for Thanksgiving. He was a tall, skinny, solemnly long-yellow-faced Negro with sallow, moist eyes, a soft lisp, and enormous bony, pink-nailed hands he could stretch up and down a piano keyboard. I don't think my mother could have thought he was handsome, but possibly that didn't matter. He often parked himself in our long living room, drinking Scotch whiskey, smoking cigarettes, and playing tunes he made up right on my grandfather's Steinway concert grand. He would hum under his breath and grunt and sway up and back like the jazzman Erroll Garner. He usually looked at me only out of the corner of his yellow Oriental-looking eye, as if neither of us really belonged in such a dignified place as my family's house. He knew, I suppose, he would not be there forever and was happy for a reprieve from his usual life, and to have my mother as his temporary girlfriend. He seemed to believe I would not be there much longer, and that we had that in common.

The one thing I remember him saying to me was during the two days before I went with my father to the marsh that Christmas—Dubinion's only Christmas with us, as it turned out. I came into the great shadowy living room where the piano sat beside the front window and where my mother had established a large Christmas tree with blinking red lights and a gold star on top. I had a copy of "The Inferno," which I had decided I would read over the holidays because the next year I hoped to leave Sandhearst and be admitted to Lawrenceville, where my father had gone before Harvard. William Dubinion was again in his place at the piano, smoking and drinking. My mother had been singing "You've Changed" in her pretty, thin soprano, and had left to take a rest because singing made her fatigued. When he saw the red jacket on my book he frowned at me and turned sideways on the bench and crossed a long thin leg over his other one so his pale hairless skin showed above his black patent-leather shoes. He was wearing black trousers with a white shirt, but no socks, which was his normal way to be around the house.

"That's a pretty good book, isn't it," he said, in his lisping voice, and stared at me in a way that felt accusatory.

"It's written in Italian," I said. "It's a poem about going to hell."

"So is that where you expect to go?"

"No," I said. "I don't."

"'*Per me si va nella città dolente. Per me si va nell' eterno dolore.*' That's all I remember," he said, and played a chord in the bass clef, a spooky, rumbling chord like the scary part in a movie.

I assumed he was making these words up, though of course he wasn't. "What's that supposed to mean," I said.

"Same ole," he said, his cigarette dangling in his mouth. "Watch your step when you take a guided tour of hell. Nothing new."

"When did you read this book?" I said insolently, stopped between the two partly closed pocket doors. This man was my mother's boyfriend, her Svengali, her impresario, her seducer and corrupter (as it turned out). And he was a strange, powerful man who had seen life I would never see. I'm sure I was both afraid of him and afraid he would detect it, which probably made me seem superior and therefore made him dislike me.

Dubinion looked up over the keyboard at an arrangement of red pyracanthas my mother had placed there. "Well, I could say something nasty. But I won't." He took a breath and let it out heavily. "You just go ahead on with your readin'. I'll go on with my playin'." He nodded but did not look at me again. We did not have too many more conversations after that. My mother sent him away later in the winter. Once or twice he returned but then finally disappeared. Though by then her life had changed in the bad way it was probably bound to change.

The only time I remember my mother speaking directly to me during these two days, other than to inform me that dinner was ready or that she was leaving at night to go out to some booking Dubinion had arranged, which I'm sure she paid him to arrange (and paid for the chance to sing as well), was on Wednesday afternoon, when I was sitting on the back porch, poring over the entrance-requirement information I'd had sent from Lawrenceville. I had never seen Lawrenceville, or been to New Jersey, never been farther away from New Orleans than Yankeetown, Florida, where my military school was, occupying the buildings of a former Catholic hospital for sick and crazy priests. But I thought that Lawrenceville—just the word itself—could save me from the impossible situation I deemed myself to be in. To go to Lawrenceville, to travel the many train miles to New Jersey and to enter whatever complex place New Jersey was—all that coupled with the fact that my father had gone there and my name and background meant something—seemed to offer me an escape and a relief and a future better than the one I had at home in New Orleans.

My mother had come out onto the back porch, which was glassed in and gave a prospect down onto the backyard grass. On the manicured lawn was an arrangement of four Adirondack chairs and a wooden picnic table, all painted pink. The back yard was completely walled in, and no one but our next-door neighbors could see—if they chose—that William Dubinion was lying on top of the pink picnic table with his shirt off, smoking a cigarette and staring sternly up at the warm blue sky.

My mother stood for a while watching him. She was wearing a pair of men's white silk pajamas, and her voice was husky. I'm sure she was already taking the drugs that would soon disrupt her reasoning. She was holding a glass of milk, which was probably not just milk but milk with gin or Scotch or something in it to ease whatever she felt terrible about.

"What a splendid idea to go hunting with your father," my mother said sarcastically, as if we were continuing a conversation we'd been having earlier, though we had said nothing about it, despite my wanting to talk about it, and despite thinking I ought not go and hoping she wouldn't permit it. "Do you even own a gun?" she said, though she knew I didn't. She knew what I did and didn't own. I was fifteen.

"He's going to give me one."

She glanced at me where I was sitting, but her look didn't change. "I just wonder what it's like to take up with another man of your own social standing," my mother said, and ran her hand through her hair, which was newly colored ash blond and done in a very neat bob that had been Dubinion's idea. My mother's father had been a pharmacist on Prytania Street and had done well catering to the needs of rich families like the McKendalls. She had gone to Newcomb, married up, and come to be at ease with the society my father introduced her into. (Though I have never thought she really cared about New Orleans' society one way or the other—unlike my father, who cared about it enough to spit in its face.) "I always assume," she said, "that these escapades usually involve someone on a lower rung. A stevedore, or a towel attendant at your club." She was watching Dubinion. He must've qualified in her mind as a lower-rung personage. She and my father had been married for twenty years, and at age thirty-nine she had taken Dubinion into her life to wipe out any trace of a previous way of conducting her affairs. I realize now, as I tell this, that she and Dubinion had just been in bed together, and he was enjoying the dreamy aftermath by lying half-naked outside on our picnic table, while she roamed the house in her pajamas alone, and had to end up talking to me. It's sad to think that in a little more than a year, when I was just getting properly adjusted at Lawrenceville, she would be gone. Thinking of her now is like hearing the dead speak. "But I don't hold it against your father. The man part, anyway," my mother said. "Other things, of course, I do." She turned then, stepped over and took a seat on the striped-cushion wicker chair beside mine. She set her milk down and took my hand in her cool hands, and held it in her lap against her leg. "What if I became a very good singer and had to go on the road and play in Chicago and New York and possibly Paris? Would that be all right? You could come and see me perform. You could wear your school uniform." She pursed her lips and looked back at the yard, where William Dubinion was laid out on the picnic table like a pharaoh.

"I wouldn't enjoy that," I said. I didn't lie to her. She was going out at night and humiliating herself and making me embarrassed and afraid. I was not going to say I thought this was all fine. It was a disaster and soon would be proved so.

"No?" she said. "You wouldn't come see me perform in the Quartier Latin?"

"No," I said. "I never would."

"Well," she said and let go of my hand, crossed her legs, and propped her chin on her fist. "I'll have to live with that. Maybe you're right." She looked around at her glass of milk as if she'd forgotten where she'd left it.

"What other things do you hold against him?" I asked, referring to my father. The man part seemed enough to me.

"Oh," my mother said. "Are we back to him? Well, let's just say I hold his entire self against him. And not for my sake, certainly, but for yours. He could've kept things together here. Other men do. It's perfectly all right to have a lover of whatever category. So he's no worse than a lot of other men. But that's what I hold against him. I hadn't really thought about it before. He fails to be any better than most men would be. That's a capital offense in marriage. You'll have to grow up some more before you understand that. But you will." She picked up her glass of milk, rose, pulled her loose white pajamas up around her scant waist, and walked back inside the house. In a moment I heard a door slam, then her voice and Dubinion's voice, and I went back to preparing myself for Lawrenceville and saving my life. Though I think I knew what she meant. She meant my father did only what pleased him, and believed (completely wrongly) that doing so permitted others the equal freedom to do what they wanted. Only that is not how the world works, as my mother's life and mine were abundant proof. Other people affect you. It is really no more complicated than that.

My father sat slumped in the bow of the empty skiff at the end of the plank dock. It was the hour before light. He was facing the silent, barely moving surface of Bayou Baptiste, beyond which (though I couldn't see it) was the vacant, quaverous marshland that stretched as far as the Mississippi River itself, west of us, and miles away. My father was bareheaded and seemed to be wearing a tan raincoat. I had not seen him in a year.

The place we were was called Reggio dock, and it was only a rough little boat camp from which fishermen took their charters out in the summer months, and duck hunters like us departed into the marsh by way of the bayou, and where a few shrimpers stored their big boats and nets when their season was off. I had never been to it, but I knew about it from boys at Jesuit who had come here with their fathers, who leased parts of the marsh and had built wooden blinds and stayed in flimsy shacks and stilt houses along the single-lane road down from Violet, Louisiana. It was a famous place to me in the way that hunting camps can be famously mysterious, and seem to have a danger all about them, and represent the good and the unknown, which so rarely combine in life.

My father had not come to get me as he'd said he would. Instead, a yellow taxi with a light on top had stopped in front of our house and a driver came to the door and rang and told me that Mr. McKendall had sent him to drive me to Reggio— which was in St. Bernard Parish, and for all its wildness not very far from the Garden District.

"And is that really you?" my father said from the boat, turning around, after I had stood on the end of the wooden dock for a minute waiting for him to notice me. A small, stunted-looking man with a large square head and wavy black hair and wearing coveralls was lugging canvas bags full of duck decoys down to the boat. Around the camp there was activity. Cars were arriving in the darkness, their taillights brightening. Men's voices could be heard laughing. Someone had brought a dog that occasionally barked. And it was not cold, in spite of being the week before Christmas. The morning air felt heavy and velvety, and a light fog had risen off the bayou, which smelled as if oil or gasoline had been let into it. The mist clung to my hands and face, and made my hair under my cap feel soiled. "I'm sorry about the taxi ride," my father said from the bow of the aluminum skiff. He was smiling in an exaggerated way. His teeth were very white. He looked thin. His pale, fine hair was cut shorter and seemed yellower than I remembered it, and had a wider part on the side. It was odd, but I remember thinking—standing looking down at my father— that if he had had an older brother this was what that brother would look like. Not good. Not happy or wholesome. And of course I realized he was drinking, even at that hour. The man in the coveralls brought down three shotgun cases and laid them in the boat. "This little yat rascal is Mr. Rey-nard Theriot, Jr.," my father said, motioning to the small, wavy-haired man. "There are *some* people of course who know him as Fabrice. Or Fabree-chay. Take your pick."

I didn't know what this meant. But Renard, Jr., paused after setting the guns in the boat and looked at my father in an unfriendly way. He had a heavy, rucked brow, and even in that poor light a dark complexion, which made his eyes seem small and penetrating. Under his coveralls, he was wearing a red shirt that had tiny gold stars on it. "Fabree-chay is a duck caller of surprising subtlety," my father said too loudly. "Among, we say, his other talents. Isn't that right, Mr. Fabrice? Did you say hello to my son, Buck, who's a very fine boy?" My father flashed his big smile around at me, and I could tell he was taunting Renard, Jr., who did not speak to me but continued his job to load the boat. I wondered how much he knew about my father, and what he thought if he knew everything.

"I couldn't locate my proper hunting attire," my father said, and looked down at the open front of his topcoat. He pulled it apart, and I saw he was wearing a tuxedo with a pink shirt, a bright-red bow tie, and a pink carnation. He was also wearing white-and-black spectator shoes, which were wrong for the Christmas season and in any case would be ruined once we were in the marsh. "I had them stored in the garage at Mother's," he said, as if talking to himself. "This morning quite early I found I'd lost the key." He looked at me, still smiling. "You have on very good brown things, though." I had just worn my khaki pants and shirt from school—minus the insignias—and black tennis shoes and an old canvas jacket I'd found in a closet. This was not exactly duck hunting in the fashion I had heard about from my school friends. My father had not even been to bed, had been up drinking and having a good time. Probably he would've preferred staying wherever he'd been, with people who were his friends now.

"What important books have you been reading," my father said for some reason, from down in the boat. He looked around as a boat full of hunters with a big black dog motored slowly past down Bayou Baptiste. Their guide had a sealed-beam light he was shining out on the water's misted surface. They were going to shoot ducks, though beyond the opposite bank of the bayou was only the flat treeless expanse that ended in darkness.

"I'm reading 'The Inferno,'" I said and felt self-conscious for saying "Inferno" out here.

"Oh that," my father said. "I believe that's Mr. Fabrice's favorite book. Canto Five: those who've lost the power of restraint. I think you should read Yeats's autobiography, though. I've been reading it in St. Louis. Yeats says in a letter to his friend the great John Synge that we should unite stoicism, asceticism, and ecstasy. I think that would be good, don't you?" My father seemed to be assured and challenging, as if he expected me to know what he meant by these things, and who Yeats was, and Synge. But I didn't know. And I didn't care to pretend I did to a drunk wearing a tuxedo and a pink carnation in a duck boat.

"I don't know them. I don't know what those things are," I said and felt terrible to have to admit it.

"They're the perfect balance for life. All I've been able to arrange are two, however. Maybe one and a half. And how's your mother?" My father began buttoning his overcoat.

"She's fine," I lied.

"I understand she's taken on new household help." He did not look up, just kept fiddling with his buttons.

"She's learning to sing," I said, leaving Dubinion out of it.

"Oh well," my father said, getting the last button done and brushing off the front of his coat. "She always had a nice little voice. A sweet church voice." He smiled, as if he knew I didn't like what he was saying and didn't care.

"She's gotten much better now." I thought about going home right then.

"I'm sure she has. Now get us going here, Fabree-chay," my father said suddenly.

Renard was behind me on the dock. The other boats of hunters had already departed. I could see their lights twitching back and forth over the water, heading away from where we were still tied up, the soft *putt-putts* of their outboards muffled by the mist. I stepped down into the boat, and Renard came in behind me, and the boat tilted radically to one side as my father took a long drink out of a pint bottle he had stationed between his feet, out of sight.

"Don't go fall in, baby," Renard said to my father from the rear of the boat as he was giving the motor cord a strong pull, his voice tinged with sarcasm. "I don't know anybody who'd be willing to pull you out."

My father, I think, did not hear him. But I heard him. And I thought he was certainly right.

I cannot tell you precisely where we went in Renard, Jr.,'s boat that morning, only that it was out into the dark marshy terrain that is the Grand Lake and is in Plaquemines Parish. Later, when the sun rose and the mist was extinguished, what I saw was a great surface of gray-brown water broken by low, yellow-grass islands where it smelled like tar and vegetation rankly decomposing, and the mud was blue-black and adhesive. And on the horizon, illuminated by the morning light, were the visible buildings of the city—including the Hibernia Bank building, where my father's office had been—nudged just above the earth's curve. It was strange to feel so outside civilization, and yet to see it.

Of course, at the beginning it was dark. Renard, Jr., being small, could stand up in the rear of the sliding boat and shine his light over me, in the middle, and my father hunched in the bow. My father's blond hair lit up brightly and stayed back off his face in the breeze. We went for a ways down the bayou, then turned and motored slowly under a wooden bridge and then out along a wide canal bordered by swamp hummocks where white herons were roosting and the first ducks of those we hoped to shoot went swimming away from the boat and out of the light, springing suddenly up into the shadows and disappearing. My father pointed at these startled ducks, made a gun out of his fingers, and jerked one-two-three silent shots as the skiff hurtled along through the marsh.

Naturally, I was thrilled to be there—even in my hated military-school clothes with my drunk father dressed in his tuxedo and the little monkey that Renard was operating the boat. I believed, though, that this had to be some version of what the real thing felt like—hunting ducks with your father and a guide—and that anytime you went, even under the most perfect circumstances, there would always be something imperfect that would leave you feeling not exactly good. The trick was to get used to that feeling, or risk missing what little happiness there really was.

At a certain point when we were buzzing along the smooth surface of the lake, Renard, Jr., abruptly backed off the motor, cut his beam light, turned the boat's nose hard left, and let the wake carry us straight into an island of marsh grass I hadn't made out. I then saw this was not simply an island but also a grass-front blind, built of wood palings driven into the mud, and where peach crates were lined up inside for hunters to sit and not be seen by flying ducks. As the skiff nosed into the grass bank, Renard, now in a pair of hip waders, was out heeling us farther up onto the solider mud. "It's duck heaven here," my father said, then suddenly coughed densely, his young man's smooth face becoming stymied by a gasp, so that he had to shake his head and turn away.

"He means it's the place where ducks go to heaven," Renard said. It was the first thing he'd said to me, and I was surprised by how much his voice did not sound like the yat voices I'd heard and that supposedly sound like citizens of New York or Boston—cities of the North. Renard's voice was cultivated and mellow and inflected, I thought, like some uptown funeral director's, or a florist's. It seemed to be a voice better suited to a different body from the tough, muscular, gnarly little man up to his thighs in filmy, strong-smelling water, and with a long wavy white-trash hair style.

"When do the ducks come here," I said, only to have something to say back. My father was recovering himself, spitting in the water and taking another drink off his bottle.

Renard laughed a private little laugh he must have thought my father would hear. "When they ready to come. Just like you and me," he said, and began hauling out the big canvas decoy sacks, and seemed to quit noticing me entirely.

Renard had a wooden pirogue hidden back in the thick grasses, and, when he had covered our skiff with a blanket made of straw mats, he used the pirogue to set out decoys as the sky lightened, though where we were was still dark. My father and I sat side by side on the peach boxes and watched Renard tossing out the weighted duck bodies so as to make two groups in front of our blind, with a space of open water in between. I could see now that what I'd imagined the marsh to look like was different from how it was. For one thing, the expanse of water around us was smaller. A line of green trees had appeared in the distance across the marsh, closer than I had expected, and I could hear some music that must've come from a car at the Reggio boat dock. And eventually there was the sun, a white disk burning behind the mist, and from a part of the marsh entirely opposite from where I first expected it. In truth, though, all of these things—these confusing and disorienting and reversing features of where I was—seemed good, since they made me feel placed, so that in time I forgot the unsatisfactory ways I had been feeling about the day and about life and about my future, which did not seem so good.

Inside the blind, which was only ten feet long and four feet wide and had spent shells and candy wrappers and cigarette butts on the planks, my father displayed his pint bottle of whiskey, which was three-quarters empty. He sat for a time when we were arranged on our crates, and said nothing to me, or to Renard, who had finished distributing the decoys and climbed into the blind to await the ducks. Something seemed to have come over my father, a great fatigue or ill-feeling or a suddenly pre-occupying thought that removed him from the moment and from what we were doing there. Renard unsheathed the guns from their cases. Mine was the old A. H. Fox twenty-gauge double gun, heavy as lead, which I had seen in my grandmother's house many times and had handled enough to know the particulars of without ever shooting it. My grandmother had called it her "ladies' gun," and she had shot it when she was young and had gone hunting with my father's father. Renard gave me six cartridges, and I loaded the chambers and kept the gun muzzle pointed up from between my knees as we watched the sky and waited for the ducks to try our decoys.

My father did not load his gun but just sat propped against the wooden laths of the blind, with his shotgun leaned on the grassy mat. After a while of watching and seeing only a pair of ducks operating far out of range, we heard other hunters begin to take their shots, sometimes several at a terrible burst. I realized then that there were two other blinds across the pond we were set down on—three hundred yards from us, but visible when my eyes adjusted to the light and the distinguishing irregularities of the horizon. A single duck I'd watched fly across the sky flared at the other hunters' shooting but then abruptly collapsed and fell straight down, and I heard a dog bark and a man's voice, high-pitched and laughing through the soft air. "Hoo, hoo, hoo, ooh lawd," the voice said. "That mutha-scootch was all the way to Terrebonne Parish when I hit him." Another man laughed. It all seemed very close to us, even though we had not shot and were merely scanning the milky skies.

"Coon-ass bastards," my father suddenly said. "Jumpin' the shooting time. They have to do that. It's genetic." He was addressing no one, just sitting leaned against the blind's sides, waiting.

"Already been shootin' time," Renard, Jr., said. He was wearing two wooden duck calls looped to his neck on leather thongs. He had yet to blow one, but I wanted him to, wanted to see a V of ducks turn and veer and come into our decoy set, the way they were supposed to.

"Now, is that so, Mr. Grease-Fabrice, Mr. Fabree-chay," my father said. He wiped the back of his hand across his nose and up into his hair, then closed his eyes and opened them wide, as if he were trying to fasten his attention to what we were doing but did not find it easy. The blind smelled of his whiskey, and of whatever ointment Renard, Jr., used on his thick hair. My father had already got his black-and-white shoes muddy and scratched, and there was mud on his tuxedo pants and his pink shirt and even on his forehead. He was an unusual-looking figure to be where he was. He seemed to have been dropped out of an airplane on the way to a party.

Renard, Jr., did not answer back to my father's calling him Grease-Fabrice. It was clear he wouldn't like a name like that, and I wondered why he would even be here to be talked to that way. And of course there was a reason. Very few things in the world are actually mysterious. Most things have disappointing explanations somewhere behind them, no matter how strange they seem at first.

After a while, Renard produced a package of cigarettes, put one in his mouth, but did not light it—just held it between his damp lips, which were big and sensuous. He was already an odd-looking man, with his star shirt, his head too big for his body—a man who was probably in his forties and had just missed being a dwarf.

"Now, there's the true sign of the yat," my father said sarcastically. He was leaning on his shotgun now, concentrating on Renard, Jr. "Notice the unlit cigarette, pooched out of the front of the too expressive mouth. If you drive the streets of Chalmette, Louisiana, sonny, you'll see men and women and children who are all actually blood-related to Mr. Fabrice, standing in their little postage-stamp yards wearing hip boots with unlighted Picayunes in their mouths just like you see now. Ecce homo."

Renard, Jr., unexpectedly opened his mouth with his cigarette somehow stuck to the top of his big ugly purple tongue. He cast an eye at my father, leaning forward against his shotgun, smirking, and quickly flicked the cigarette backward into his mouth and swallowed it without changing his expression. Then he looked at me, sitting between him and my father, and smiled. His teeth were big and brown-stained. It was a lewd act. I didn't know how it was lewd, but I was sure it was.

"Pay no attention to him," my father said. "These are people we have to deal with. French acts, carny types, brutes. Now I want you to tell me about yourself, Buck. Are there any impossible situations you find yourself in these days? I've become expert in impossible situations lately." My father shifted his feet on the muddy board floor, and his shotgun, which was a beautiful Beretta over-under with silver inlays, suddenly slipped and fell right across my feet with a loud clatter—the barrels ending up pointed straight at Renard, Jr.'s, knees. My father did not even try to grab the gun as it fell.

"Pick that up right now," he said to me in an angry voice, as if I had dropped his gun. But I did. I picked the gun up and handed it back to him, and he penned it to the side of the blind with his knee. Something in the sudden, almost violent way he put his gun where he wanted it reminded me of himself before a year ago. He had always been a man for abrupt moves and changes of attitude and unexpected laughter and strong emotion. I had not always liked it, but I'd decided that was what men did, and accepted it.

"Do you ever hope to travel?" my father said, ignoring his other question, looking up at the low sky as if he'd just realized he was in a duck blind and, for a second at least, was involved in the things we were doing. His topcoat had sagged open, and his tuxedo front was visible, smudged with mud. "You should," he said before I could answer.

Renard, Jr., began to blow on his duck call then, and crouched forward in front of his peach crate. And, because he did, I crouched in front of mine, and my father—noticing us—squatted on his knees, too, and averted his face, as if he were praying. After a few moments of Renard, Jr.,'s calling, I peered over the straw wall of the blind and could see two black-colored ducks flying right in front of our blind and low over our decoys. Renard, Jr., changed his calling sound to a broken cackle, and when he did the ducks suddenly swerved to the side and began winging hard away from us, almost as if they could fly backward.

"You let'em seen you," Renard said in a hoarse whisper. "They seen that white face." I could smell his breath, crouched beside him. It was a smell of cigarettes and sour meat and must've tasted terrible in his mouth.

"Call, God damn it, Fabrice," my father said then, shouted really. I twisted around to see him, and he was right up on his two feet, his gun to his shoulder, his topcoat lying on the floor so that he was just in his tuxedo. I looked out at our decoys and saw four small ducks cupping their wings and gliding toward the water where Renard had left it open. Their wings made a pinging sound.

Renard, Jr., immediately started his cackle call again, still crouched, his face down. "Shoot'em, Buck, shoot'em," my father shouted at me, and I stood up and got my heavy gun to my shoulder, and without meaning to fired both barrels, pulled both triggers at once, just as my father (who at some moment had loaded his gun) also fired one then the other barrel at the ducks, which had briefly touched the water but were already heading off, climbing up and up as the others had, flying backward away from us, their necks outstretched, their eyes—or so it seemed to me, who had never shot at a duck—wide and frightened.

My two barrels, fired, had hit one of Renard's decoys and shattered it to pieces. My father's two shots had hit, it seemed, nothing at all, though one of the gray paper wads drifted back toward the water while the four ducks grew small in the distance until they were shot at by the other hunters across the pond and two of them dropped.

"That was completely terrible," my father said, standing at the end of the blind in his tuxedo and red tie, his hair slicked close down on his head in a way that made him resemble a child. He quickly broke his gun open and replaced the spent shells with new ones from his tuxedo-coat pocket. He seemed no longer drunk but completely engaged and sharp-minded, except for having missed everything.

"Y'all shot like a couple of ole grandmas," Renard said, disgusted, shaking his head.

"Fuck you," my father said calmly, and snapped shut his beautiful Italian gun in a menacing way. His blue eyes widened, then narrowed, and I believed he might point his gun at Renard, Jr. White spit had collected in the corners of his mouth, and his face had gone from looking engaged to looking pale and damp and outraged. "If I need your services for other than calling, I'll speak to your owner," he said.

"Speak to your own owner, snooky," Renard, Jr., said, and when he said this he looked at me, raised his eyebrows, smiled, and pushed his heavy lips forward in a cruel, simian way.

"That's enough," my father said loudly. "That is absolutely enough." I thought he might reach past me then and strike Renard in the mouth he was smiling through. But he didn't. He surprisingly just sat back on his peach crate, faced forward, and held his newly reloaded shotgun between his knees. His little pink carnation was flattened in the greasy mud.

I could hear my father's hard breathing. Something had happened that wasn't good, but I didn't know what. Something had risen up in him, some force of sudden rebellion, but it had been defeated before it could come out and act. Or so it seemed to me. Silent events always occur between our urges and our actions. These events are parts of our important hidden lives. But I did not know what event had just occurred, only that one had, and I could feel it. My father seemed tired now, and to be considering something. Renard, Jr., was no longer calling ducks, and was just sitting at his end, staring at the misty sky, which was turning dense and luminous red at the horizon, as if a fire were burning at the far edge of the marsh. Shooting in the other blinds had stopped. A small plane traced across the sky. I saw a fish roll in the water in front of the blind. I thought I saw an alligator. Mosquitoes appeared, which is never unusual in Louisiana.

"What do you do in St. Louis?" I said to my father. It was the thing I wanted to know.

"Well," my father said thoughtfully. He sniffed. "Golf. I play quite a bit of golf. Francis has a big house across from a wonderful park. I've taken it up." He felt his forehead where a mosquito had landed on a black muddy stain that was there. He rubbed it and looked at his fingertips.

"Will you practice law up there?" I asked.

"Oh lord no," he said and shook his head and sniffed again. "They requested me to leave the firm here. You know that."

"Yes," I said. His breathing was easier. His face seemed calm. He looked handsome and youthful. Whatever silent event that had occurred had passed off, and he seemed settled about it. I thought I might talk about going to Lawrenceville. Duck blinds were where people had such conversations. Though I thought it would've been better if we'd been alone, and didn't have Renard, Jr., to overhear us. "I'd like to ask you . . . ," I began.

"Tell me about your girlfriend situation," my father interrupted me. "Tell me the whole story there."

I knew what he meant by that, but there wasn't a story. I was in military school, and there were only other boys present, which was not a story to me. If I went to Lawrenceville, however, I thought there could be a story. Girls would be nearby. "There isn't any story," I started, and he interrupted me again.

"Let me give you some advice." He was rubbing his index finger around the blue muzzle of his Italian shotgun. "Always try to imagine how you're going to feel after you fuck somebody before you fuck somebody. *Comprendes?* There's the key to everything. History. Morality. Philosophy. You save yourself a lot of misery." He nodded as if this wisdom had become clear to him all over again. "Maybe you already know that," he said. He looked up above the front of the blind, where the sky had turned to fire, then looked at me in a way to seem honest and to say (so I thought) that he liked me. And then he said, "Do you ever find yourself saying things in conversations that you absolutely don't believe?" He reached with his two fingers and plucked a mosquito off my cheek. "Do you," he said and seemed amused. "Do ya, do ya, do ya?"

I thought of conversations I'd had with Dubinion, and some I'd had with my mother. They were that kind of conversation—memorable if only for the things I didn't say. But what I said to my father was "No."

"Convenience must not matter much to you then," he said in a friendly way.

"I don't know if it does or not," I said because I didn't know what convenience meant. It was a word I'd never had a cause to use.

"Well, convenience matters to me very much. Too much, I think," my father said. I thought then of my mother's assessment of my father—that he was not better than most men. I assumed that caring too much for convenience led you there, and that my fault in later life could turn out to be the same one because he was my father. But I decided to see to it that my fault in life would not be his, if I possibly could. "There's one ducky duck," my father said. He was watching the sky and seemed bemused. "Fabrice, would you let me apologize for acting ugly to you, and ask you to call. How generous that would be of you. How nice." My father smiled strangely at Renard, Jr., who had seemed to be brooding.

And Renard, Jr., did call. I did not see a duck. But when my father squatted down on the dirty planking where his topcoat was smeared and our empty shell casings were littered, I did, too, and turned my face toward the floor. I could hear my father's breathing, could feel the whiskey thick on his breath, could see his wet knuckles supporting him unsteadily on the boards, could even smell his hair, which was warm and musty. It was as close as I could come to him. And I decided that it would have to do, might even be the best there could be.

"Wait now, wait on 'im," my father said, hunkered against the rough planks but actually looking up from the tops of his eyes. He put his fingers on my hand to make me be still. I had not seen anything. Renard, Jr., was calling his long, high-pitched rasping incessant call, followed by many short bursts that made him grunt in his throat in a way I hadn't noticed before, and then the long high call again. "Not quite yet," my father whispered. "Not yet. Wait on him." I turned my face sideways to see up, my eyes cut to the corners to find something. "No," my father said, close to my ear. "Don't look up." I inhaled deeply and breathed in all the smells again that came off my father. And then Renard, Jr., said loudly, "Go on, Jesus! Go on! Shoot 'im. Shoot now. Whatchyouwaitin'on?"

And I stood up then without knowing what I would see, and brought my shotgun to my shoulder before I really looked. And what I saw, coming low over the decoys, its own head turning to the side and peering down at the brown water, was one lone duck. I could distinguish its green head and dark bullet eyes in the haze-burnt morning light and could hear its wings pinging. I did not think it saw me or heard my father and Renard, Jr., shouting, "Shoot, shoot, oh Jesus, shoot, Buck!" Because when my face and gun barrel appeared above the front of the blind, it did not change its course or begin the backward-upward maneuvering I'd seen, which was its way to save itself. It just kept looking down and flying slowly and making its noise in the reddened air above the water and all of us.

And, as I found the duck above my barrel tops, my eyes opened wide in the way I knew you shot such a gun, and I thought: It's only one duck. there may not be any others. What's the good of one duck shot down? In my dreams there'd been hundreds of ducks, and my father and I shot them so that they fell like rain, and how many there were would not have mattered because we were doing it together. But I was doing this alone, and one duck seemed wrong, and to matter in a way a hundred ducks wouldn't have, at least if I was going to be the one to shoot. So that what I did was not shoot, and lowered my gun.

"What's wrong?" my father said from the floor below me, still on all fours in his wrecked tuxedo, his face turned down, awaiting a gun's report. The lone duck was past us now, quickly out of range.

I looked at Renard, Jr., who was seated on his peach crate, small enough not to need to hunker. He looked at me, and made a strange face, a face I'd never seen but will never forget. He smiled, and he began to bat his eyelids in fast succession, and he raised his two hands, palms up, to the level of his eyes, as if he expected something to fall down into them, or as if he were praying. I don't know what that gesture meant, though I have thought of it often—sometimes in the middle of a night when my sleep is disturbed. Derision, I think; or possibly it meant he merely didn't know why I had not shot the duck and was waiting my answer. Or possibly it was something else, some sign whose significance I would never know. Fabrice was a strange man. No one would've doubted it.

My father was up on his muddy feet suddenly, although with difficulty. He had his shotgun to his shoulder, and he shot once at the duck. And of course it did not fall. Then he stared for a time with his gun to his shoulder until the speck of duck wings disappeared.

"What the hell happened," he said, his face red from kneeling and bending. "Why didn't you shoot that duck?" His mouth was opened into a frown. I could see his white teeth, and his two hands were gripping the sides of the blind. He seemed to be in jeopardy of falling down. He was, after all, still drunk. His blond hair shone in the misty light.

"I wasn't close enough," I said.

My father looked around again at the decoys as if they could prove something. "Wasn't close enough?" he said. "I heard the damn duck's wings. How close do you need it? You've got a gun there."

"You couldn't hear it," I said.

"Couldn't hear it?" he said. His eyes rose off my face and found Renard, Jr., behind me. His mouth took on an odd expression. The scowl left his features, and he looked amused, the damp corners of his mouth revealing a small, flickering smile I was sure was also derision and that represented his view that I had balked at a crucial moment, made a mistake, and didn't therefore have to be treated so seriously. This from a man who had left my mother and me to fend for ourselves while he disported without dignity or shame out of sight of those who knew him.

"You don't know anything," I suddenly said. "You're only . . ." And I don't know what I was about to say. Something terrible and hurtful. Something to strike out at him and that I would've regretted forever. So that I didn't say any more, didn't finish it. Though I did that for myself, I think now, and not for him, so that I would not have to regret more than I already regretted. I didn't really care what happened to him, to be truthful. Didn't and don't.

And then my father said, the insinuating smile on his handsome lips, "Come on, sonny boy. You've still got some growing up to do, I can see." He reached for me and put his hand behind my neck, which was rigid in anger and loathing. And, without seeming to notice, he pulled me to him and kissed me on my forehead, and put his arms around me and held me until whatever he was thinking had passed and it was time for us to go back to the dock.

My father lived thirty years after that morning in December, on the Grand Lake, in 1961. By any accounting he lived a whole life after that. And I am not interested in the whys and why nots of what he did and didn't do, or in causing that day to seem life-changing for me, because it surely wasn't. Life had already changed. That morning represented just the first working out of particulars I would evermore observe. Like my father, I am a lawyer. And the law teaches you that most of life is about adjustments, the seatings and reseatings we perform to accommodate events occurring outside our control and over which we might not have sought control in the first place. So that when I am tempted, as I was for an instant in the blind, or as I was through all those thirty years, to let myself become preoccupied and angry with my father, or when I see a man who reminds me of him, stepping into some building in a seersucker suit and bright bow tie, it is best just to offer myself release and to realize I am feeling anger all alone, and that there is no redress. We want it. Life can be seen to be about almost nothing else sometimes than our wish for redress. As a lawyer who is the son of a lawyer and grandson of another, I know this. And I also know not to expect it.

For the record—because I never saw him again—my father went back to St. Louis and back under the influence of Dr. Carter, who I believe was as strong a character as my father was weak. They lived on there for a time until (I was told) Dr. Carter quit the practice of medicine entirely. Then they left St. Louis and travelled to Paris and after that to a bright white stucco house near Antibes, which I in fact once saw, completely by accident, on a side tour during a business trip, and somehow knew to be his abode the instant I came to it, as though I had dreamed it— but then couldn't get away from it fast enough, though they were both dead and buried by then.

Once, in our newspaper, early in the nineteen-seventies, I saw my father pictured in the society section amid a group of smiling, handsome crewcut men, again wearing tuxedos, and red sashes of some foolish kind, and holding champagne glasses. They were men in their fifties, all of whom seemed, by their smiles, to want very badly to be younger.

Seeing this picture reminded me that in the days after my father had taken me to the marsh, and events had ended not altogether happily, I had prayed for one of the first times, but also for the last time, in my life. I prayed quite fervently for a while, and in spite of all, that he would come back to us and our life would begin to be as it had been. And then I prayed that he would die, and die in a way I would never know about, and his memory would cease to be a memory, and all would be erased. My mother died a rather sudden and pointless death not long afterward, and many people including myself attributed her death to him. In time, my father came and went in and out of New Orleans, just as if neither of us had ever known each other.

And so the memory was not erased. Yet, because I can tell all of this now, I believe that I have gone on beyond it, to a life better than one might have imagined for me. Of course, I think of that life—mine—as being part of their aftermath, part of the residue of all they risked and squandered. Such things can happen. Possibly they happen in some places more than in others. But they are survivable. I am proof, since, in truth, I have never imagined my life any other way than as it is.

A Long Day in November

ERNEST J. GAINES

1

Somebody is shaking me but I don't want to get up now, because I'm tired and I'm sleepy and I don't want get up now. It's warm under the cover here, but it's cold up there and I don't want get up now.

"Sonny?" I hear.

But I don't want get up, because it's cold up there. The cover is over my head and I'm under the sheet and the blanket and the quilt. It's warm under here and it's dark, because my eyes's shut. I keep my eyes shut because I don't want get up.

"Sonny?" I hear.

I don't know who's calling me, but it must be Mama because I'm home. I don't know who it is because I'm still asleep, but it must be Mama. She's shaking me by the foot. She's holding my ankle through the cover.

"Wake up, honey," she says.

But I don't want get up because it's cold up there and I don't want get cold. I try to go back to sleep, but she shakes my foot again.

"Hummm?" I say.

"Wake up, honey," I hear.

"Hummm?" I say.

"I want you get up and wee-wee," she says.

"I don't want wee-wee, Mama," I say.

"Come on," she says, shaking me. "Come on. Get up for Mama."

"It's cold up there," I say.

"Come on," she says. "Mama won't let her baby get cold."

I pull the sheet and blanket from under my head and push them back over my shoulder. I feel the cold and I try to cover up again, but Mama grabs the cover before I get it over me. Mama is standing 'side the bed and she's looking down at me, smiling. The room is dark. The lamp's on and the mantel-piece, but it's kind of low. I see Mama's shadow on the wall over by Gran'mon's picture.

"I'm cold, Mama," I say.

"Mama go'n wrap his little coat round her baby," she says.

She goes over and get it off the chair where all my clothes's at, and I sit up in the bed. Mama brings the coat and put it on me, and she fastens some of the buttons.

"Now," she says. "See? You warm."

I gap' and look at Mama. She hugs me real hard and rubs her face against my face. My mama's face is warm and soft, and it feels good.

"I want my socks on," I say. "My feet go'n get cold on the floor."

Mama leans over and get my shoes from under the bed. She takes out my socks and slip them on my feet. I gap' and look at Mama pulling my socks up.

"Now," she says.

I get up but I can still feel that cold floor. I get on my knees and look under the bed for my pot.

"See it?" Mama says.

"Hanh?"

"See it under there?"

"Hanh?"

"I bet you didn't bring it in," she says. "Any time you sound like that you done forgot it."

"I left it on the chicken coop," I say.

"Well, go to the back door," Mama says. "Hurry up before you get cold."

I get off my knees and go back there, but it's too dark and I can't see. I come back where Mama's sitting on my bed.

"It's dark back there, Mama," I say. "I might trip over something."

Mama takes a deep breath and gets the lamp off the mantelpiece, and me and her go back in the kitchen. She unlatches the door, and I crack it open and the cold air comes in.

"Hurry," Mama says.

"All right."

I can see the fence back of the house and I can see the little pecan tree over by the toilet. I can see the big pecan tree over by the other fence by Miss Viola Brown's house. Miss Viola Brown must be sleeping because it's late at night. I bet you nobody else in the quarter's up now. I bet you I'm the only little boy up. They got plenty stars in the air, but I can't see the moon. There must be ain't no moon tonight. That grass is shining—and it must be done rained. That pecan tree's shadow's all over the back yard.

I get my tee-tee and I wee-wee. I wee-wee hard, because I don't want get cold. Mama latches the door when I get through wee-wee-ing.

"I want some water, Mama," I say.

"Let it out and put it right back in, huh?" Mama says.

She dips up some water and pours it in my cup, and I drink. I don't drink too much at once, because the water makes my teeth cold. I let my teeth warm up, and I drink some more.

"I got enough," I say.

Mama drinks the rest and then me and her go back in the front room.

"Sonny?" she says.

"Hanh?"

"Tomorrow morning when you get up me and you leaving here, hear?"

"Where we going?" I ask.

"We going to Gran'mon," Mama says.

"We leaving us house?" I ask.

"Yes," she says.

"Daddy leaving too?"

"No," she says. "Just me and you."

"Daddy don't want leave?"

"I don't know what your daddy wants," Mama says. "But for sure he don't want me. We leaving, hear?"

"Uh-huh," I say.

"I'm tired of it," Mama says.

"Hanh?"

"You won't understand, honey," Mama says. "You too young still."

"I'm getting cold, Mama," I say.

"All right," she says. She goes and put the lamp up, and comes back and sit on the bed 'side me. "Let me take your socks off," she says.

"I can take them off," I say.

Mama takes my coat off and I take my socks off. I get back in bed and Mama pulls the cover up over me. She leans over and kiss me on the jaw, and then she goes back to her bed. Mama's bed is over by the window. My bed is by the fireplace. I hear Mama get in the bed. I hear the spring, then I don't hear nothing because Mama's quiet. Then I hear Mama crying.

"Mama?" I call.

She don't answer me.

"Mama?" I call her.

"Go to sleep, baby," she says.

"You crying?" I ask.

"Go to sleep," Mama says.

"I don't want you to cry," I say.

"Mama's not crying," she says.

Then I don't hear nothing and I lay quiet, but I don't turn over because my spring'll make noise and I don't want make no noise because I want hear if my mama go'n cry again. I don't hear Mama no more and I feel warm in the bed and I pull the cover over my head and I feel good. I don't hear nothing no more and I feel myself going back to sleep.

Billy Joe Martin's got the tire and he's rolling it in the road, and I run to the gate to look at him. I want go out in the road, but Mama don't want me to play out there like Billy Joe Martin and the other children. . . . Lucy's playing 'side the house. She's jumping rope with—I don't know who that is. I go 'side the house and play with Lucy. Lucy beats me jumping rope. The rope keeps on hitting me on the leg. But it don't hit Lucy on the leg. Lucy jumps too high for it. . . . Me and Billy Joe Martin shoots marbles and I beat him shooting. . . . Mama's sweeping the gallery and knocking the dust out of the broom on the side of the house. Mama keeps on knocking the broom against the wall. Must be got plenty dust in the broom.

Somebody's beating on the door. Mama, somebody's beating on the door. Somebody's beating on the door, Mama.

"Amy, please let me in," I hear.

Somebody's beating on the door, Mama. Mama, somebody's beating on the door.

"Amy, honey; honey, please let me in."

I push the cover back and I listen. I hear Daddy beating on the door.

"Mama?" I say. "Mama, Daddy's knocking on the door. He want come in."

"Go back to sleep, Sonny," Mama says.

"Daddy's out there," I say. "He want come in."

"Go back to sleep, I told you," Mama says.

I lay back on my pillow and listen.

"Amy," Daddy says, "I know you woke. Open the door."

Mama don't answer him.

"Amy, honey," Daddy says. "My sweet dumpling, let me in. It's freezing out here."

Mama still won't answer Daddy.

"Mama, Daddy want come in," I say.

"Let him crawl through the key hole," Mama says.

It gets quiet after this, and it stays quiet a little while, and then Daddy says:

"Sonny?"

"Hanh?"

"Come open the door for your daddy."

"Mama go'n whip me if I get up," I say.

"I won't let her whip you," Daddy says. "Come and open the door like a good boy."

I push the cover back and I sit up in the bed and look over at Mama's bed. Mama's under the cover and she's quiet like she's asleep. I get on the floor and get my socks out of my shoes. I get back in the bed and slip them on, and then I go and unlatch the door for Daddy. Daddy comes in and rubs my head with his hand. His hand is hard and cold.

"Look what I brought you and your mama," he says.

"What?" I ask.

Daddy takes a paper bag out of his jumper pocket.

"Candy?" I say.

"Uh-huh."

Daddy opens the bag and I stick my hand in there and take a whole handful. Daddy wraps the bag up again and sticks it in his pocket.

"Get back in that bed, Sonny," Mama says.

"I'm eating candy," I say.

"Get back in that bed like I told you," Mama says.

"Daddy's up with me," I say.

"You heard me, boy?"

"You can take your candy with you," Daddy says. "Get back in the bed."

He follows me to the bed and tucks the cover under me. I lay in the bed and eat my candy. The candy is hard, and I sound just like Paul eating corn. I bet you little old Paul is some cold out there in that back yard. I hope he ain't laying in that water like he always do. I bet you he'll freeze in that water in all this cold. I'm sure glad I ain't a pig. They ain't got no mama and no daddy and no house.

I hear the spring when Daddy gets in the bed.

"Honey?" Daddy says.

Mama don't answer him.

"Honey?" he says.

Mama must be gone back to sleep, because she don't answer him.

"Honey?" Daddy says.

"Get your hands off me," Mama says.

"Honey, you know I can't keep my hands off you," Daddy says.

"Well, just do," Mama says.

"Honey, you don't mean that," Daddy says. "You know 'fore God you don't mean that. Come on, say you don't mean it. I can't shut these eyes till you say you don't mean it."

"Don't touch me," Mama says.

"Honey," Daddy says. Then he starts crying. "Honey, please."

Daddy cries a good little while, and then he stops. I don't chew on my candy while Daddy's crying, but when he stops I chew on another piece.

"Go to sleep, Sonny," he says.

"I want eat my candy," I say.

"Hurry then. You got to go to school tomorrow."

I put another piece in my mouth and chew on it.

"Honey?" I hear Daddy saying. "Honey, you go'n wake me up to go to work?"

"I do hope you stop bothering me," Mama says.

"Wake me up round four thirty, hear, honey?" Daddy says. "I can cut 'bout six tons tomorrow. Maybe seven."

Mama don't say nothing to Daddy, and I feel sleepy again. I finish chewing my last piece of candy and I turn on my side. I feel good because the bed is warm. But I still got my socks on.

"Daddy?" I call.

"Go to sleep," Daddy says.

"My socks still on," I say.

"Let them stay on tonight," Daddy says. "Go to sleep."

"My feet don't feel good in socks," I say.

"Please go to sleep, Sonny," Daddy says. "I got to get up at four thirty, and it's hitting close to two now."

I don't say nothing, but I don't like to sleep with my socks on. But I stay quiet. Daddy and Mama don't say nothing, either, and little bit later I hear Daddy snoring. I feel drowsy myself.

I run around the house in the mud because it done rained and I feel the mud between my toes. The mud is soft and I like to play in it. I try to get out the mud, but I can't get out. I'm not stuck in the mud, but I can't get out. Lucy can't come over and play in the mud because her mama don't want her to catch cold. . . . Billy Joe Martin shows me his dime and puts it back in his pocket. Mama bought me a pretty little red coat and I show it to Lucy. But I don't let Billy Joe Martin put his hand on it. Lucy can touch it all she wants, but I don't let Billy Joe Martin put his hand on it. . . . Me and Lucy get on the horse and ride up and down the road. The horse runs fast, and me and Lucy bounce on the horse and laugh. . . . Mama and Daddy and Uncle Al and Gran'mon's sitting by the fire talking. I'm outside shooting marbles, but I hear them. I don't know what they talking about, but I hear them. I hear them. I hear them. I hear them.

I don't want wake up, but I'm waking up. Mama and Daddy's talking. I want go back to sleep, but they talking too loud. I feel my foot in the sock. I don't like socks on when I'm in the bed. I want go back to sleep, but I can't. Mama and Daddy talking too much.

"Honey, you let me oversleep," Daddy says. "Look here, it's going on seven o'clock."

"You ought to been thought about that last night," Mama says.

"Honey, please," Daddy says. "Don't start a fuss right off this morning."

"Then don't open your mouth," Mama says.

"Honey, the car broke down," Daddy says. "What I was suppose to do, it broke down on me. I just couldn't walk away and not try to fix it."

Mama's quiet.

"Honey," Daddy says, "don't be mad with me. Come on, now."

"Don't touch me," Mama says.

"Honey, I got to go to work. Come on."

"I mean it," she says.

"Honey, how can I work without touching you? You know I can't do a day's work without touching you some."

"I told you not to put your hands on me," Mama says. I hear her slap Daddy on the hand. "I mean it," she says.

"Honey," Daddy says, "this is Eddie, your husband."

"Go back to your car," Mama says. "Go rub against it. You ought to be able to find a hole in it somewhere."

"Honey, you oughtn't talk like that in the house," Daddy says. "What if Sonny hear you?"

I stay quiet and I don't move because I don't want them to know I'm woke.

"Honey, listen to me," Daddy says. "From the bottom of my heart I'm sorry. Now, come on."

"I told you once," Mama says, "you not getting on me. Go get on your car."

"Honey, respect the child," Daddy says.

"How come you don't respect him?" Mama says. "How come you don't come home sometime and respect him? How come you don't leave that car alone and come home and respect him? How come you don't respect him? You the one need to respect him."

"I told you it broke down," Daddy says. "I was coming home when it broke down on me. I even had to leave it out on the road. I made it here quick as I could."

"You can go back quick as you can, for all I care," Mama says.

"Honey, you don't mean that," Daddy says. "I know you don't mean that. You just saying that because you mad."

"Just don't touch me," Mama says.

"Honey, I got to get out and make some bread for us," Daddy says.

"Get out if you want," Mama says. "They got a jailhouse for them who don't support their family."

"Honey, please don't talk about a jail," Daddy says. "It's too cold. You don't know how cold it is in a jailhouse this time of the year."

Mama's quiet.

"Honey?" Daddy says.

"I hope you let me go back to sleep," Mama says. "Please."

"Honey, don't go back to sleep on me," Daddy says. "Honey—"

"I'm getting up," Mama says. "Damn all this."

I hear the springs mash down on the bed boards. My head's under the cover, but I can just see Mama pushing the cover down the bed. Then I hear her walking across the floor and going back in the kitchen.

"Oh, Lord," Daddy says. "Oh, Lord. The suffering a man got to go through in this world. Sonny?" he says.

"Don't wake that baby up," Mama says, from the door.

"I got to have somebody to talk to," Daddy says. "Sonny?"

"I told you not to wake him up," Mama says.

"You don't want talk to me," Daddy says. "I need somebody to talk to. Sonny?" he says.

"Hanh?"

"See what you did?" Mama says. "You woke him up, and he ain't going back to sleep."

Daddy comes across the floor and sits down on the side of the bed. He looks down at me and passes his hand over my face.

"You love your daddy, Sonny?" he says.

"Uh-huh."

"Please love me," Daddy says.

I look up at Daddy and he looks at me, and then he just falls down on me and starts crying.

"A man needs somebody to love him," he says.

"Get love from what you give love," Mama says, back in the kitchen. "You love your car. Go let it love you back."

Daddy shakes his face in the cover.

"The suffering a man got to go through in this world," he says. "Sonny, I hope you never have to go through all this."

Daddy lays there 'side me a long time. I can hear Mama back in the kitchen. I hear her putting some wood in the stove, and then I hear her lighting the fire. I hear her pouring water in the tea kettle, and I hear when she sets the kettle on the stove.

Daddy raises up and wipes his eyes. He looks at me and shakes his head, then he goes and puts his overalls on.

"It's a hard life," he says. "Hard, hard. One day, Sonny—you too young right now—but one day you'll know what I mean."

"Can I get up, Daddy?"

"Better ask your mama," Daddy says.

"Can I get up, Mama?" I call.

Mama don't answer me.

"Mama?" I call.

"Your paw standing in there," Mama says. "He the one woke you up."

"Can I get up, Daddy?"

"Sonny, I got enough troubles right now," Daddy say.

"I want get up and wee-wee," I say.

"Get up," Mama says. "You go'n worry me till I let you get up anyhow."

I crawl from under the cover and look at my feet. I got just one sock on and I look for the other one under the cover. I find it and slip it on and then I get on the floor. But that floor is still cold. I hurry up and put on my clothes, and I get my shoes and go and sit on the bed to put them on.

Daddy waits till I finish tying up my shoes, and me and him go back in the kitchen. I get in the corner 'side the stove and Daddy comes over and stands 'side me. The fire is warm and it feels good.

Mama is frying salt meat in the skillet. The skillet's over one hole and the tea kettle's over the other one. The water's boiling and the tea kettle is whistling. I look at the steam shooting up to the loft.

Mama goes outside and gets my pot. She holds my pot for me and I wee-wee in it. Then Mama carries my pot in the front room and puts it under my bed.

Daddy pours some water in the wash basin and washes his face, and then he washes my face. He dumps the water out the back door, and me and him sit at the table. Mama brings the food to the table. She stands over me till I get through saying my blessing, and then she goes back to the stove. Me and Daddy eat.

"You love your daddy?" he says.

"Uh-huh," I say.

"That's a good boy," he says. "Always love your daddy."

"I love Mama too. I love her more than I love you."

"You got a good mama," Daddy says. "I love her, too. She the only thing keep me going—'cluding you, too."

I look at Mama standing 'side the stove, warming.

"Why don't you come to the table and eat with us," Daddy says.

"I'm not hungry," Mama says.

"I'm sorry, baby," Daddy says. "I mean it."

Mama just looks down at the stove and don't answer Daddy.

"You got a right to be mad," Daddy says. "I ain't nothing but a' old rotten dog."

Daddy eats his food and looks at me across the table. I pick up a piece of meat and chew on it. I like the skin because the skin is hard. I keep the skin a long time.

"Well, I better get going," Daddy says. "Maybe if I work hard I'll get me a couple tons."

Daddy gets up from the table and goes in the front room. He comes back with his jumper and his hat on. Daddy's hat is gray and it got a hole on the side.

"I'm leaving, honey," he tells Mama.

Mama don't answer Daddy.

"Honey, tell me ''Bye, old dog,' or something," Daddy says. "Just don't stand there."

Mama still don't answer him, and Daddy jerks his cane knife out the wall and goes on out. I chew on my meat skin. I like it because it's hard.

"Hurry up, honey," Mama says. "We going to Mama."

Mama goes in the front room and I stay at the table and eat. I finish eating and I go in the front room where Mama is. Mama's pulling a big bundle of clothes from under the bed.

"What's that, Mama?" I ask.

"Us clothes," she says.

"We go'n take us clothes down to Gran'mon?"

"I'm go'n try," Mama says. "Find your cap and put it on."

I see my cap hanging on the chair and I put it on and fasten the strap under my chin. Mama fixes my shirt in my pants, and then she goes and puts on her overcoat. Her overcoat is black and her hat is black. She puts on her hat and looks in the looking glass. I can see her face in the glass. Look like she want cry. She comes from the dresser and looks at the big bundle of clothes on the floor.

"Where's your pot?" she says. "Find it."

I get my pot from under the bed.

"Still got some wee-wee in it," I say.

"Go to the back door and dump it out," Mama says.

I go back in the kitchen and open the door. It's cold out there, and I can see the frost all over the grass. The grass is white with frost. I dump the wee-wee out and come back in the front.

"Come on," Mama says.

She drags the big bundle of clothes out on the gallery and I shut the door. Mama squats down and puts the bundle on her head, and then she stands up and me and her go down the steps. Soon's I get out in the road I can feel the wind. It's strong and it's blowing in my face. My face is cold and one of my hands is cold.

It's red over there back of the trees. Mr. Guerin's house is over there. I see Mr. Guerin's big old dog. He must be don't see me and Mama because he ain't barking at us.

"Don't linger back too far," Mama says.

I run and catch up with Mama. Me and Mama's the only two people walking in the road now.

I look up and I see the tree in Gran'mon's yard. We go little farther and I see the house. I run up ahead of Mama and hold the gate open for her. After she goes in I let the gate slam.

Spot starts barking soon's he sees me. He runs down the steps at me and I let him smell my pot. Spot follows me and Mama back to the house.

"Gran'mon?" I call.

"Who that our there?" Gran'mon asks.

"Me," I say.

"What you doing out there in all that cold for, boy?" Gran'mon says. I hear Gran'mon coming to the door fussing. She opens the door and looks at me and Mama.

"What you doing here with all that?" she asks.

"I'm leaving him, Mama," Mama says.

"Eddie?" Gran'mon says. "What he done you now?"

"I'm just tired of it," Mama says.

"Come in here out that cold," Gran'mon says. "Walking out there in all that weather . . ."

We go inside and Mama drops the big bundle of clothes on the floor. I go to the fire and warm my hands. Mama and Gran'mon come to the fire and Mama stands at the other end of the fireplace and warms her hands.

"Now what that no good nigger done done?" Gran'mon asks.

"Mama, I'm just tired of Eddie running up and down the road in that car," Mama says.

"He beat you?" Gran'mon asks.

"No, he didn't beat me," Mama says. "Mama, Eddie didn't get home till after two this morning. Messing around with that old car somewhere out on the road all night."

"I told you," Gran'mon says. "I told you when that nigger got that car that was go'n happen. I told you. No—you wouldn't listen. I told you. Put a fool in a car and he becomes a bigger fool. Where that yellow thing at now?"

"God telling," Mama says. "He left with his cane knife."

"I warned you 'bout that nigger," Gran'mon says. "Even 'fore you married him. I sung at you and sung at you. I said, 'Amy, that nigger ain't no good. A yellow nigger with a gap like that 'tween his front teeth ain't no good.' But you wouldn't listen."

"Can me and Sonny stay here?" Mama asks.

"Where else can y'all go?" Gran'mon says. "I'm your mon, ain't I? You think I can put you out in the cold like he did?"

"He didn't put me out, Mama, I left," Mama says.

"You finally getting some sense in your head," Gran'mon says. "You ought to been left that nigger years ago."

Uncle Al comes in the front room and looks at the bundle of clothes on the floor. Uncle Al's got on his overalls and got just one strap hooked. The other strap's hanging down his back.

"Fix that thing on you," Gran'mon says. "You not in a stable."

Uncle Al fixes his clothes and looks at me and Mama at the fire.

"Y'all had a round?" he asks Mama.

"Eddie and that car again," Mama says.

"That's all they want these days," Gran'mon says. "Cars. Why don't they marry them cars? No. When they got their troubles, they come running to the women-folks. When they ain't got no troubles and when their pockets full of money they run jump in the car. I told you that when you was working to help him get that car."

Uncle Al stands 'side me at the fireplace, and I lean against him and look at the steam coming out a piece of wood. Lord knows I get tired of Gran'mon fussing all the time.

"Y'all moving in with us?" Uncle Al asks.

"For a few days," Mama says. "Then I'll try to find another place somewhere in the quarter."

"We got plenty room here," Uncle Al says. "This old man here can sleep with me."

Uncle Al gets a little stick out of the corner and hands it to me so I can light it for him. I hold it to the fire till it's lit, and I hand it back to Uncle Al. Uncle Al turns the pipe upside down in his mouth and holds the fire to it. When the pipe's good and lit, Uncle Al gives me the little stick and I throw it back in the fire.

"Y'all ate anything?" Gran'mon asks.

"Sonny ate," Mama says. "I'm not hungry."

"I reckon you go'n start looking for work now?" Gran'mon says.

"There's plenty cane to cut," Mama says. "I'll get me a cane knife and go out tomorrow morning."

"Out in all that cold?" Gran'mon says.

"They got plenty women cutting cane," Mama says. "I don't mind. I done it before."

"You used to be such a pretty little thing, Amy," Gran'mon says. "Long silky curls. Prettiest little face on this whole plantation. You could've married somebody worth something. But, no, you had to throw yourself away to that yellow nigger who don't care for nobody, 'cluding himself."

"I loved Eddie," Mama says.

"Poot," Gran'mon says.

"He wasn't like this when we married," Mama says.

"Every nigger from Bayonne like this now, then, and forever," Gran'mon says.

"Not then," Mama says. "He was the sweetest person . . ."

"And you fell for him?" Gran'mon says.

" . . . He changed after he got that car," Mama says. "He changed overnight."

"Well, you learned your lesson," Gran'mon says. "We all get teached something no matter how old we get. 'Live and learn,' what they say."

"Eddie's all right," Uncle Al says. "He—"

"You keep out of this, Albert," Gran'mon says. "It don't concern you."

Uncle Al don't say no more, and I can feel his hand on my shoulder. I like Uncle Al because he's good, and he never talk bad about Daddy. But Gran'mon's always talking bad about Daddy.

"Freddie's still there," Gran'mon says.

"Mama, please," Mama says.

"Why not?" Gran'mon says. "He always loved you."

"Not in front of him," Mama says.

Mama leaves the fireplace and goes to the bundle of clothes. I can hear her untying the bundle.

"Ain't it 'bout time you was leaving for school?" Uncle Al asks.

"I don't want go," I say. "It's too cold."

"It's never too cold for school," Mama says. "Warm up good and let Uncle Al button your coat for you."

I get closer to the fire and I feel the fire hot on my pants. I turn around and warm my back. I turn again, and Uncle Al leans over and buttons up my coat. Uncle Al's pipe almost gets in my face, and it don't smell good.

"Now," Uncle Al says. "You all ready to go. You want take a potato with you?"

"Uh-huh."

Uncle Al leans over and gets me a potato out of the ashes. He knocks all the ashes off and puts the potato in my pocket.

"Wait," Mama says. "Mama, don't you have a little paper bag?"

Gran'mon looks on the mantelpiece and gets a paper bag. There's something in the bag, and she takes it out and hands the bag to Mama. Mama puts the potato in the bag and puts it in my pocket. Then she goes and gets my book and tucks it under my arm.

"Now you ready," she says. "And remember, when you get out for dinner come back here. Don't you forget and go up home now. You hear, Sonny?"

"Uh-huh."

"Come on," Uncle Al says. "I'll open the gate for you."

"'Bye, Mama," I say.

"Be a good boy," Mama says. "Eat your potato at recess. Don't eat it in class now."

Me and Uncle Al go out on the gallery. The sun is shining but it's still cold out there. Spot follows me and Uncle Al down the walk. Uncle Al opens the gate for me and I go out in the road. I hate to leave Uncle Al and Spot. And I hate to leave Mama—and I have to leave the fire. But I got to, because they want me to learn.

"See you at twelve," Uncle Al says.

I go up the quarter and Uncle Al and Spot go back to the house. I see all the children going to school. But I don't see Lucy. When I get to her house I'm go'n stop at the gate and call her. She must be don't want go to school, cold as it is.

It still got some ice in the water. I better not walk in the water. I'll get my feet wet and Mama'll whip me.

When I get closer I look and see Lucy and her mama on the gallery. Lucy's mama ties her bonnet for her, and Lucy comes down the steps. She runs down the walk toward the gate. Lucy's bonnet is red and her coat is red.

"Hi," I say.

"Hi," she says.

"It's some cold," I say.

"Unnn-hunnnn," Lucy says.

Me and Lucy walk side by side up the quarter. Lucy's got her book in her book sack.

"We moved," I say. "We staying with Gran'mon now."

"Y'all moved?" Lucy asks.

"Uh-huh."

"Y'all didn't move," Lucy says. "When y'all moved?"

"This morning."

"Who moved y'all?" Lucy asks.

"Me and Mama," I say. "I'm go'n sleep with Uncle Al."

"My legs getting cold," Lucy says.

"I got a potato," I say. "In my pocket."

"You go'n eat it and give me piece?" Lucy says.

"Uh-huh," I say. "At recess."

Me and Lucy walk up the quarter, and Lucy stops and touches the ice with her shoe.

"You go'n get your foot wet," I say.

"No, I'm not," Lucy says.

Lucy breaks the ice with her shoe and laughs. I laugh and I break a piece of ice with my shoe. Me and Lucy laugh and I see the smoke coming out of Lucy's mouth. I open my mouth and go, "Haaaa," and plenty smoke comes out of my mouth. Lucy laughs and points at the smoke.

Me and Lucy go on up the quarter to the schoolhouse. Billy Joe Martin and Ju-Ju and them's playing marbles right by the gate. Over 'side the schoolhouse Shirley and Dottie and Katie's jumping rope. On the other side of the schoolhouse some more children playing "Patty-cake, patty-cake, baker-man" to keep warm. Lucy goes where Shirley and them's jumping rope and asks them to play. I stop where Billy Joe Martin and them's at and watch them shoot marbles.

2

It's warm inside the schoolhouse. Bill made a big fire in the heater, and I can hear it roaring up the pipes. I look out the window and I can see the smoke flying across the yard. Bill sure knows how to make a good fire. Bill's the biggest boy in school, and he always makes the fire for us.

Everybody's studying their lesson, but I don't know mine. I wish I knowed it, but I don't. Mama didn't teach me my lesson last night, and she didn't teach it to me this morning, and I don't know it.

"Bob and Rex in the yard. Rex is barking at the cow." I don't know what all this other reading is. I see "Rex" again, and I see "cow" again—but I don't know what all the rest of it is.

Bill comes up to the heater and I look up and see him putting another piece of wood in the fire. He goes back to his seat and sits down 'side Juanita. Miss Hebert looks at Bill when he goes back to his seat. I look in my book at Bob and Rex. Bob's got on a white shirt and blue pants. Rex is a German police dog. He's white and brown. Mr. Bouie's got a dog just like Rex. He don't bite though. He's a good dog. But Mr. Guerin's old dog'll bite you for sure. I seen him this morning when me and Mama was going down to Gran'mon's house.

I ain't go'n eat dinner at us house because me and Mama don't stay there no more. I'm go'n eat at Gran'mon's house. I don't know where Daddy go'n eat dinner. He must be go'n cook his own dinner.

I can hear Bill and Juanita back of me. They whispering to each other, but I can hear them. Juanita's some pretty. I hope I was big so I could love her. But I better look at my lesson and don't think about other things.

"First grade," Miss Hebert says.

We go up to the front and sit down on the bench. Miss Hebert looks at us and make a mark in her roll book. She puts the roll book down and comes over to the bench where we at.

"Does everyone know his lesson today?" she asks.

"Yes, Ma'am," Lucy says, louder than anybody else in the whole schoolhouse.

"Good," Miss Hebert says. "And I'll start with you today, Lucy. Hold your book in one hand and begin."

"'Bob and Rex are in the yard,'" Lucy reads. "'Rex is barking at the cow. The cow is watching Rex.'"

"Good," Miss Hebert says. "Point to barking."

Lucy points.

"Good. Now point to watching."

Lucy points again.

"Good," Miss Hebert says. "Shirley Ann, let's see how well you can read."

I look in the book at Bob and Rex. "Rex is barking at the cow. The cow is looking at Rex."

"William Joseph," Miss Hebert says.

I'm next, I'm scared. I don't know my lesson and Miss Hebert go'n whip me. Miss Hebert don't like you when you don't know your lesson. I can see her strap over there on the table. I can see the clock and the little bell, too. Bill split the end of the strap, and them little ends sting some. Soon's Billy Joe Martin finishes, then it's me. I don't know . . . Mama ought to been . . . "Bob and Rex" . . .

"Eddie," Miss Hebert says.

I don't know my lesson. I don't know my lesson. I don't know my lesson. I feel warm. I'm wet. I hear the wee-wee dripping on the floor. I'm crying. I'm crying because I wee-wee on myself. My clothes's wet. Lucy and them go'n laugh at me. Billy Joe Martin and them go'n tease me. I don't know my lesson. I don't know my lesson. I don't know my lesson.

"Oh, Eddie, look what you've done," I think I hear Miss Hebert saying. I don't know if she's saying this, but I think I hear her say it. My eye's shut and I'm crying. I don't want look at none of them, because I know they laughing at me.

"It's running under that bench there now," Billy Joe Martin says. "Look out for your feet back there, it's moving fast."

"William Joseph," Miss Hebert says. "Go over there and stand in that corner. Turn your face to the wall and stay there until I tell you to move."

I hear Billy Joe Martin leaving the bench, and then it's quiet. But I don't open my eyes.

"Eddie," Miss Hebert says, "go stand by the heater."

I don't move, because I'll see them, and I don't want see them.

"Eddie?" Miss Hebert says.

But I don't answer her, and I don't move.

"Bill?" Miss Hebert says.

I hear Bill coming up to the front and then I feel him taking me by the hand and leading me away. I walk with my eyes shut. Me and Bill stop at the heater, because I can feel the fire. Then Bill takes my book and leaves me standing there.

"Juanita," Miss Hebert says, "get a mop, will you please."

I hear Juanita going to the back, and then I hear her coming back to the front. The fire pops in the heater, but I don't open my eyes. Nobody's saying anything, but I know they all watching me.

When Juanita gets through mopping up the wee-wee she carries the mop back to the closet, and I hear Miss Hebert going on with the lesson. When she gets through with the first graders, she calls the second graders up there.

Bill comes up to the heater and puts another piece of wood in the fire.

"Want turn around?" he asks me.

I don't answer him, but I got my eyes open now and I'm looking down at the floor. Bill turns me round so I can dry the back of my pants. He pats me on the shoulder and goes back to his seat.

After Miss Hebert gets through with the second graders, she tells the children they can go out for recess. I can hear them getting their coats and hats. When they all leave I raise my head. I still see Bill and Juanita and Veta sitting there. Bill smiles at me, but I don't smile back. My clothes's dry now, and I feel better. I know the rest of the children go'n tease me, though.

"Bill, why don't you and the rest of the seventh graders put your arithmetic problems on the board," Miss Hebert says. "We'll look at them after recess."

Bill and them stand up, and I watch them go to the blackboard in the back.

"Eddie?" Miss Hebert says.

I turn and I see her sitting behind her desk. And I see Billy Joe Martin standing in the corner with his face to the wall.

"Come up to the front," Miss Hebert says.

I go up there looking down at the floor, because I know she go'n whip me now.

"William Joseph, you may leave," Miss Hebert says.

Billy Joe Martin runs over and gets his coat, and then he runs outside to shoot marbles. I stand in front of Miss Hebert's desk with my head down.

"Look up," she says.

I raise my head and look at Miss Hebert. She's smiling, and she don't look mad.

"Now," she says. "Did you study your lesson last night?"

"Yes, ma'am," I say.

"I want the truth, now," she says. "Did you?"

It's a sin to story in the churchhouse, but I'm scared Miss Hebert go'n whip me.

"Yes, ma'am," I say.

"Did you study it this morning?" she asks.

"Yes, ma'am," I say.

"Then why didn't you know it?" she asks.

I feel a big knot coming up in my throat and I feel like I'm go'n cry again. I'm scared Miss Hebert go'n whip me, that's why I story to her.

"You didn't study your lesson, did you?" she says.

I shake my head. "No, ma'am."

"You didn't study it last night either, did you?"

"No ma'am," I say. "Mama didn't have time to help me. Daddy wasn't home. Mama didn't have time to help me."

"Where is your father?" Miss Hebert asks.

"Cutting cane."

"Here on this place?"

"Yes ma'am," I say.

Miss Hebert looks at me, and then she gets out a pencil and starts writing on a piece of paper. I look at her writing and I look at the clock and the strap. I can hear the clock. I can hear Billy Joe Martin and them shooting marbles outside. I can hear Lucy and them jumping rope, and some more children playing "Patty-cake."

"I want you to give this to your mother or your father when you get home," Miss Hebert says. "This is only a little note saying I would like to see them sometime when they aren't too busy."

"We don't live home no more," I say.

"Oh?" Miss Hebert says. "Did you move?"

"Me and Mama," I say. "But Daddy didn't."

Miss Hebert looks at me, and then she writes some more on the note. She puts her pencil down and folds the note up.

"Be sure to give this to your mother," she says. "Put it in your pocket and don't lose it."

I take the note from Miss Hebert, but I don't leave the desk.

"Do you want to go outside?" she asks.

"Yes, ma'am."

"You may leave," she says.

I go over and get my coat and cap, and then I go out in the yard. I see Billy Joe Martin and Charles and them shooting marbles over by the gate. I don't go over there because they'll tease me. I go 'side the schoolhouse and look at Lucy and them jumping rope. Lucy ain't jumping right now.

"Hi, Lucy," I say.

Lucy looks over at Shirley and they laugh. They look at my pants and laugh.

"You want a piece of potato?" I ask Lucy.

"No," Lucy says. "And you not my boyfriend no more, either."

I look at Lucy and I go stand 'side the wall in the sun. I peel my potato and eat it. And look like soon 's I get through, Miss Hebert comes to the front and says recess is over.

We go back inside, and I go to the back and take off my coat and cap. Bill comes back there and hang the things up for us. I go over to Miss Hebert's desk and Miss Hebert gives me my book. I go back to my seat and sit down 'side Lucy.

"Hi, Lucy," I say.

Lucy looks at Shirley and Shirley puts her hand over her mouth and laughs. I feel like getting up from there and socking Shirley in the mouth, but I know Miss Hebert'll whip me. Because I got no business socking people after I done wee-wee on myself. I open my book and look at my lesson so I don't have to look at none of them.

3

It's almost dinner time, and when I get home I ain't coming back here either, now. I'm go'n stay there. I'm go'n stay right there and sit by the fire. Lucy and them don't want play with me, and I ain't coming back up here. Miss Hebert go'n touch that little bell in a little while. She getting ready to touch it right now.

Soon 's Miss Hebert touches the bell all the children run go get their hats and coats. I unhook my coat and drop it on the bench till I put my cap on. Then I put my coat on, and I get my book and leave.

I see Bill and Juanita going out the schoolyard, and I run and catch up with them. Time I get there I hear Billy Joe Martin and them coming up behind us.

"Look at that baby," Billy Joe Martin says.

"Piss on himself," Ju-Ju says.

"Y'all leave him alone," Bill says.

"Baby, baby, piss on himself," Billy Joe Martin sings.

"What did I say now?" Bill says.

"Piss on himself," Billy Joe Martin says.

"Wait," Bill says. "Let me take off my belt."

"Good-bye, piss pot," Billy Joe Martin says. Him and Ju-Ju run down the road. They spank their hind parts with their hands and run like horses.

"They just bad," Juanita says.

"Don't pay them no mind," Bill says. "They'll leave you alone.

We go on down the quarter and Bill and Juanita hold hands. I go to Gran'mon's gate and open it. I look at Bill and Juanita going down the quarter. They walking close together, and Juanita done put her head on Bill's shoulder. I like to see Bill and Juanita like that. It makes me feel good. But I go in the yard and I don't feel good any more. I know old Gran'mon go'n start her fussing. Lord in Heaven knows I get tired of all this fussing, day and night. Spot runs down the walk to meet me. I put my hand on his head and me and him go back to the gallery. I make him stay on the gallery, because Gran'mon don't want him inside. I pull the door open and I see Gran'mon and Uncle Al sitting by the fire. I look for my mama, but I don't see her.

"Where Mama?" I ask Uncle Al.

"In the kitchen," Gran'mon says. "But she talking to somebody."

I go back to the kitchen.

"Come back here," Gran'mon says.

"I want see my mama," I say.

"You'll see her when she come out," Gran'mon says.

"I want see my mama now," I say.

"Don't you hear me talking to you, boy?" Gran'mon hollers.

"What's the matter?" Mama asks. Mama comes out of the kitchen and Mr. Freddie Jackson comes out of there, too. I hate Mr. Freddie Jackson. I never did like him. He always want to be round my mama.

"That boy don't listen to nobody," Gran'mon says.

"Hi, Sonny," Mr. Freddie Jackson says.

I look at him standing there, but I don't speak to him. I take the note out of my pocket and hand it to my mama.

"What's this?" Mama says.

"Miss Hebert sent it."

Mama unfolds the note and take it to the fireplace to read it. I can see her mouth working. When she gets through reading, she folds the note up again.

"She want see me or Eddie sometime when we free," Mama says. "Sonny been doing pretty bad in his class."

"I can just see that nigger husband of yours in a schoolhouse," Gran'mon says. "I doubt if he ever went to one."

"Mama, please," Mama says.

Mama helps me off with my coat and I go to the fireplace and stand 'side Uncle Al. Uncle Al pulls me between his legs and he holds my hand out to the fire.

"Well?" I hear Gran'mon saying.

"You know how I feel 'bout her," Mr. Freddie Jackson says. "My house opened to her and Sonny any time she want come there."

"Well?" Gran'mon says.

"Mama, I'm still married to Eddie," Mama says.

"You mean you still love that yellow thing," Gran'mon says. "That's what you mean, ain't it?"

"I didn't say that," Mama says. "What would people say, out one house and in another one the same day?"

"Who care what people say?" Gran'mon says. "Let people say what they big enough to say. You looking out for yourself, not what people say."

"You understand, don't you, Freddie?" Mama says.

"I think I do," he says. "But like I say, Amy, any time—you know that."

"And there ain't no time like right now," Gran'mon says. "You can take that bundle of clothes down there for her."

"Let her make up her own mind, Rachel," Uncle Al says. "She can make up her own mind."

"If you know what's good for you you better keep out of this," Gran'mon says. "She my daughter and if she ain't got sense enough to look out for herself, I have. What you want to do, go out in that field cutting cane in the morning?"

"I don't mind it," Mama says.

"You done forgot how hard cutting cane is?" Gran'mon says. "You must be done forgot."

"I ain't forgot," Mama says. "But if the other women can do it, I suppose I can do it, too."

"Now you talking back," Gran'mon says.

"I'm not talking back, Mama," Mama says. "I just feel it ain't right to leave one house and go to another house the same day. That ain't right in nobody's book."

"Maybe she's right, Mrs. Rachel," Mr. Freddie Jackson says.

"Her trouble is she's still in love with that mariny," Gran'mon says. "That's what your trouble is. You ain't satisfied 'less he got you doing all the work while he rip and run up and down the road with his other nigger friends. No, you ain't satisfied."

Gran'mon goes back in the kitchen fussing. After she leaves the fire, everything gets quiet. Everything stays quiet a minute, and then Gran'mon starts singing back in the kitchen.

"Why did you bring your book home?" Mama says.

"Miss Hebert say I can stay home if I want," I say. "We had us lesson already."

"You sure she said that?" Mama says.

"Uh-huh."

"I'm go'n ask her, you know."

"She said it," I say.

Mama don't say no more, but I know she still looking at me, but I don't look at her. Then Spot starts barking outside and everybody look that way. But nobody don't move. Spot keeps on barking, and I go to the door to see what he's barking at. I see Daddy coming up the walk. I pull the door and go back to the fireplace.

"Daddy coming, Mama," I say.

"Wait," Gran'mon says, coming out the kitchen. "Let me talk to that nigger. I'll give him a piece of my mind."

Gran'mon goes to the door and pushes it open. She stands in the door and I hear Daddy talking to Spot. Then Daddy comes up to the gallery.

"Amy in there, Mama?" Daddy says.

"She is," Gran'mon says.

I hear Daddy coming up the steps.

"And where you think you going?" Gran'mon asks.

"I want speak to her," Daddy says.

"Well, she don't want speak to you," Gran'mon says. "So you might 's well go right on back down them steps and march right straight out of my yard."

"I want speak to my wife," Daddy says.

"She ain't your wife no more," Gran'mon says. "She left you."

"What you mean she left me?" Daddy says.

"She ain't up at your house no more, is she?" Gran'mon says. "That look like a good enough sign to me that she done left."

"Amy?" Daddy calls.

Mama don't answer him. She's looking down in the fire. I don't feel good when Mama's looking like that.

"Amy?" Daddy calls.

Mama still don't answer him.

"You satisfied?" Gran'mon says.

"You the one trying to make Amy leave me," Daddy says. "You ain't never liked me—from the starting."

"That's right, I never did," Gran'mon says. "You yellow, you got a gap 'tween your teeth, and you ain't no good. You want me to say more?"

"You always wanted her to marry somebody else," Daddy says.

"You right again," Gran'mon says.

"Amy?" Daddy calls. "Can you hear me, honey?"

"She can hear you," Gran'mon says. "She's standing right there by that fireplace. She can hear you good 's I can hear you, and nigger, I can hear you too good for comfort."

"I'm going in there, Daddy says. "She got somebody in there and I'm going in there and see."

"You just take one more step toward my door," Gran'mon says, "and it'll take a' undertaker to get you out of here. So help me, God, I'll get that butcher knife out of that kitchen and chop on your tail till I can't see tail to chop on. You the kind of nigger like to rip and run up and down the road in your car long 's you got a dime, but when you get broke and your belly get empty you run to your wife and cry on her shoulder. You just take one more step toward this door, and I bet you somebody'll be crying at your funeral. If you know anybody who care that much for you, you old yellow dog."

Daddy is quiet a while, and then I hear him crying. I don't feel good, because I don't like to hear Daddy and Mama crying. I look at Mama, but she's looking down in the fire.

"You never liked me," Daddy says.

"You said that before," Gran'mon says. "And I repeat, no, I never liked you, don't like you, and never will like you. Now, get out my yard 'fore I put the dog on you."

"I want see my boy," Daddy says, "I got a right to see my boy."

"In the first place, you ain't got no right in my yard," Gran'mon says.

"I want see my boy," Daddy says. "You might be able to keep me from seeing my wife, but you and nobody else can keep me from seeing my son. Half of him is me and I want see my—I want see him."

"You ain't leaving?" Gran'mon asks Daddy.

"I want see my boy," Daddy says. "And I'm go'n see my boy."

"Wait," Gran'mon says. "Your head hard. Wait till I come back. You go'n see all kind of boys."

Gran'mon comes back inside and goes to Uncle Al's room. I look toward the wall and I can hear Daddy moving on the gallery. I hear Mama crying and I look at her. I don't want see my mama crying, and I lay my head on Uncle Al's knee and I want cry, too.

"Amy, honey," Daddy calls, "ain't you coming up home and cook me something to eat? It's lonely up there without you, honey. You don't know how lonely it is without you. I can't stay up there without you, honey. Please come home. . . ."

I hear Gran'mon coming out of Uncle Al's room and I look at her. Gran'mon's got Uncle Al's shotgun and she's putting a shell in it.

"Mama?" Mama screams.

"Don't worry," Gran'mon says. "I'm just go'n shoot over his head. I ain't go'n have them sending me to the pen for a good-for-nothing nigger like that."

"Mama, don't," Mama says. "He might hurt himself."

"Good," Gran'mon says. "Save me the trouble of doing it for him."

Mama runs to the wall. "Eddie, run," she screams. "Mama got the shotgun."

I hear Daddy going down the steps. I hear Spot running after him barking. Gran'mon knocks the door open with the gun barrel and shoot. I hear Daddy hollering.

"Mama, you didn't?" Mama says.

"I shot two miles over that nigger's head," Gran'mon says. "Long-legged coward."

We all run out on the gallery, and I see Daddy out in the road crying. I can see the people coming out on the galleries. They looking at us and they looking at Daddy. Daddy's standing out in the road crying.

"Boy, I would've like to seen old Eddie getting out of this yard," Uncle Al says.

Daddy's walking up and down the road in front of the house, and he's crying.

"Let's go back inside," Gran'mon says. "We won't be bothered with him for a while."

It's cold, and me and Uncle Al and Gran'mon go back inside. Mr. Freddie Jackson and Mama don't come back in right now, but after a little while they come in, too.

"Oh, Lord," Mama says.

Mama starts crying and Mr. Freddie Jackson takes her in his old arms. Mama lays her head on his old shoulder, but she just stays there a little while and then she moves.

"Can I go lay 'cross your bed, Uncle Al?" Mama asks.

"Sure," Uncle Al says.

I watch Mama going to Uncle Al's room.

"Well, I better be going," Mr. Freddie Jackson says.

"Freddie?" Gran'mon calls him, from the kitchen.

"Yes, ma'am?" he says.

"Come here a minute," Gran'mon says.

Mr. Freddie Jackson goes back in the kitchen where Gran'mon is. I get between Uncle Al's legs and look at the fire. Uncle Al rubs my head with his hand. Mr. Freddie Jackson comes out of the kitchen and goes in Uncle Al's room where Mama is. He must be sitting down on the bed because I can hear the springs.

"Gran'mon shot Daddy?" I ask.

Uncle Al rubs my head with his hand.

"She just scared him," he says. "You like your daddy?"

"Uh-huh."

"Your daddy's a good man," Uncle Al says. "A little foolish, but he's okay."

"I don't like Mr. Freddie Jackson," I say.

"How come?" Uncle Al says.

"I just don't like him," I say. "I just don't like him. I don't like him to hold my mama, neither. My daddy suppose to hold my mama. He ain't suppose to hold my mama."

"You want go back home?" Uncle Al asks.

"Uh-huh," I say. "But me and Mama go'n stay here now. I'm go'n sleep with you."

"But you rather go home and sleep in your own bed, huh?"

"Yes," I say. "I pull the cover 'way over my head. I like to sleep under the cover."

"You sleep like that all the time?" Uncle Al asks.

"Uh-huh."

"Even in the summertime, too?" Uncle Al says.

"Uh-huh," I say.

"Don't you ever get too warm?" Uncle Al says.

"Uh-uh," I say. "I feel good 'way under there."

Uncle Al rubs my head and I look down in the fire.

"Y'all come on in the kitchen and eat," Gran'mon calls.

Me and Uncle Al go back in the kitchen and sit down at the table. Gran'mon already got us food dished up. Uncle Al bows his head and I bow my head.

"Thank Thee, Father, for this food Thou has given us," Uncle Al says.

I raise my head and start eating. We having spaghetti for dinner. I pick up a string of spaghetti and suck it up in my mouth. I make it go *loo-loo-loo-loo-loo-loo-loop.* Uncle Al looks at me and laugh. I do it again, and Uncle Al laughs again.

"Don't play with my food," Gran'mon says. "Eat it right."

Gran'mon is standing 'side the stove looking at me. I don't like old Gran'mon. Shooting at my daddy—I don't like her.

"Taste good?" Uncle Al asks.

"Uh-huh," I say.

Uncle Al winks at me and wraps his spaghetti on his fork and sticks it in his mouth. I try to wrap mine on my fork, but it keeps falling off. I can just pick up one at a time.

Gran'mon starts singing her song again. She fools round the stove a little while, and then she goes in the front room. I get a string of spaghetti and suck it up in my mouth. When I hear her coming back I stop and eat right.

"Still out there," she says. "Sitting on that ditch bank crying like a baby. Let him cry. But he better not come back in this yard."

Gran'mon goes over to the stove and sticks a piece of wood in the fire. She starts singing again:

> *Oh, I'll be there,*
> *I'll be there,*
> *When the roll is called in Heaven, I'll be there.*

Uncle Al finishes his dinner and waits for me. When I finish eating, me and him go in the front room and sit at the fire.

"I want go to the toilet, Uncle Al," I say.

I get my coat and cap and bring them to the fireplace, and Uncle Al helps me get in them. Uncle Al buttons up my coat for me, and I go out on the gallery. I look out in the road and I see Daddy sitting out on the ditch bank. I go round the house and go back to the toilet. The grass is dry like hay. There ain't no leaves on the trees. I see some birds in the tree. The wind's moving the birds's feathers. I bet you them little birds's some cold. I'm glad I'm not a bird. No daddy, no mamma—I'm glad I'm not a bird.

I open the door and go in the toilet. I get up on the seat and pull down my pants. I squat over the hole—but I better not slip and fall in there. I'll get all that poo-poo on my feet, and Gran'mon'll kill me if I tramp all that poo-poo in her house.

I try hard and my poo-poo come. It's long. I like to poo-poo. Sometimes I poo-poo on my pot at night. Mama don't like for me to go back to the toilet when it's late. Scared a snake might bite me.

I finish poo-poo-ing and I jump down from the seat and pull up my pants. I look in the hole and I see my poo-poo. I look in the top of the toilet, but I don't see any spiders. We got spiders in us toilet. Gran'mon must be done killed all her spiders with some Flit.

I push the door open and I go back to the front of the house. I go round the gallery and I see Daddy standing at the gate looking in the yard. He sees me.

"Sonny?" he calls.

"Hanh?"

"Come here, baby," he says.

I look toward the door, but I don't see nobody and I go to the gate where Daddy is. Daddy pushes the gate open and grabs me and hugs me to him.

"You still love your daddy, Sonny?" he asks.

"Uh-huh," I say.

Daddy hugs me and kisses me on the face.

"I love my baby," he says. "I love my baby. Where your mama?"

"Laying 'cross Uncle Al's bed in his room," I say. "And Mr. Freddie Jackson in there, too."

Daddy pushes me away real quickly and looks in my face.

"Who else in there?" he asks. "Who?"

"Just them," I say. "Uncle Al's in Gran'mon's room by the fire, and Gran'mon's in the kitchen."

Daddy looks toward the house.

"This is the last straw," he says. "I'm turning your Gran'mon in this minute. And you go'n be my witness. Come on."

"Where we going?" I ask.

"To that preacher's house," Daddy says. "And if he can't help me, I'm going back in the field to Madame Toussaint."

Daddy grabs my hand and me and him go up the quarter. I can see all the children going back to school.

" . . . Lock her own daughter in a room with another man and got her little grandson there looking all the time," Daddy says. "She ain't so much Christian as she put out to be. Singing round that house every time you bat your eyes and doing something like that in broad daylight. Step it up, Sonny."

"I'm coming fast as I can," I say.

"I'll see about that," Daddy says. "I'll see about that."

When me and Daddy get to Reverend Simmons's house, we go up on the gallery and Daddy knocks on the door. Mrs. Carey comes to the door to see what we want.

"Mrs. Carey, is the Reverend in?" Daddy asks.

"Yes," Mrs. Carey says. "Come on in."

Me and Daddy go inside and I see Reverend Simmons sitting at the fireplace. Reverend Simmons got on his eyeglasses and he's reading the Bible. He turns and looks at us when we come in. He takes off his glasses like he can't see us too good with them on, and he looks at us again. Mrs. Carey goes back in the kitchen and me and Daddy go over to the fireplace.

"Good evening, Reverend," Daddy says.

"Good evening," Reverend Simmons says. "Hi, Sonny."

"Hi," I say.

"Reverend, I hate busting in on you like this, but I need your help," Daddy says. "Reverend, Amy done left me and her mama got her down at her house with another man and—"

"Now, calm down a second," Reverend Simmons says. He looks toward the kitchen. "Carey, bring Mr. Howard and Sonny a chair."

Mrs. Carey brings the chairs and goes right on back in the kitchen again. Daddy turns his chair so he can be facing Reverend Simmons.

"I come in pretty late last night 'cause my car broke down on me and I had to walk all the way—from the other side of Morgan up there," Daddy says. "When I get home me and Amy get in a little squabble. This morning we squabble again, but I don't think too much of it. You know a man and a woman go'n have their little squabbles every once in a while. I go to work in the field. Work like a dog. Cutting cane right and left—trying to make up lost time I spent at the house this morning. When I come home for dinner—hungry 's a dog—my wife, neither my boy is there. No dinner—and I'm hungry 's a dog. I go in the front room and all their clothes gone. Lord, I almost go crazy. I don't know what to do. I run out the house because I think she still mad at me and done gone down to her mama. I go down there and ask for her, and first thing I know here come Mama Rachel shooting at me with Uncle Al's shotgun."

"I can't believe that," Reverend Simmons says.

"If I'm telling a lie I hope to never rise from this chair," Daddy says. "And I reckon she would've got me if I wasn't moving fast."

"That don't sound like Sister Rachel," Reverend Simmons says.

"Sound like her or don't sound like her, she did it," Daddy says. "Sonny right over there. He seen every bit of it. Ask him."

Reverend Simmons looks at me but he don't ask me nothing. He just clicks his tongue and shakes his head.

"That don't sound like Sister Rachel," he says. "But if you say that's what she did, I'll go down there and talk to her."

"And that ain't all," Daddy says.

Reverend Simmons waits for Daddy to go on.

"She got Freddie Jackson locked up in a room with Amy," Daddy says.

Reverend Simmons looks at me and Daddy, then he goes over and gets his coat and hat from against the wall. Reverend Simmons's coat is long and black. His hat is big like a cowboy's hat.

"I'll be down the quarter, Carey," he tells Mrs. Simmons. "Be back quick as I can."

We go out of the house and Daddy holds my hand. Me and him and Reverend Simmons go out in the road and head on back down the quarter.

"Reverend Simmons, I want my wife back," Daddy says. "A man can't live by himself in this world. It too cold and cruel."

Reverend Simmons don't say nothing to Daddy. He starts humming a little song to himself. Reverend Simmons is big and he can walk fast. He takes big old long steps and me and Daddy got to walk fast to keep up with him. I got to run because Daddy's got my hand.

We get to Gran'mon's house and Reverend Simmons pushes the gate open and goes in the yard.

"Me and Sonny'll stay out here," Daddy says.

"I'm cold, Daddy," I say.

"I'll build a fire," Daddy says. "You want me build me and you a little fire?"

"Uh-huh."

"Help me get some sticks, then," Daddy says.

Me and Daddy get some grass and weeds and Daddy finds a big chunk of dry wood. We pile it all up and Daddy gets a match out of his pocket and lights the fire.

"Feel better?" he says.

"Uh-huh."

"How come you not in school this evening?" Daddy asks.

"I wee-weed on myself," I say.

I tell Daddy because I know Daddy ain't go'n whip me.

"You peed on yourself at school?" Daddy asks. "Sonny, I thought you was a big boy. That's something little babies do."

"Miss Hebert want see you and Mama," I say.

"I don't have time to see nobody now," Daddy says. "I got my own troubles. I just hope that preacher in there can do something."

I look up at Daddy, but he's looking down in the fire.

"Sonny?" I hear Mama calling me.

I turn and I see Mama and all of them standing out there on the gallery.

"Hanh?" I answer.

"Come in here before you catch a death of cold," Mama says.

Daddy goes to the fence and looks across the pickets at Mama.

"Amy," he says, "please come home. I swear I ain't go'n do it no more."

"Sonny, you hear me talking to you?" Mama calls.

"I ain't go'n catch cold," I say. "We got a fire. I'm warm."

"Amy, please come home," Daddy says. "Please, honey. I forgive you. I forgive Mama. I forgive everybody. Just come home."

I look at Mama and Reverend Simmons talking on the gallery. The others ain't talking; they just standing there looking out in the road at me and Daddy. Reverend Simmons comes out the yard and over to the fire. Daddy comes to the fire where me and Reverend Simmons is. He looks at Reverend Simmons but Reverend Simmons won't look back at him.

"Well, Reverend?" Daddy says.

"She say she tired of you and that car," Reverend Simmons says.

Daddy falls down on the ground and cries.

"A man just can't live by himself in this cold, cruel world," he says. "He got to have a woman to stand by him. He just can't make it by himself. God, help me."

"Be strong, man," Reverend Simmons says.

"I can't be strong with my wife in there and me out here," Daddy says. "I need my wife."

"Well, you go'n have to straighten that out the best way you can," Reverend Simmons says. "And I talked to Sister Rachel. She said she didn't shoot to hurt you. She just shot to kind of scare you away."

"She didn't shoot to hurt me?" Daddy says."And I reckon them things was jelly beans I heard zooming just three inches over my head?"

"She said she didn't shoot to hurt you," Reverend Simmons says. He holds his hands over the fire. "This fire's good, but I got to get on back up the quarter. Got to get my wood for tonight. I'll see you people later. And I hope everything comes out all right."

"Reverend, you sure you can't do nothing?" Daddy asks.

"I tried, son," Reverend Simmons says. "Now we'll leave it in God's hand."

"But I want my wife back now," Daddy says. "God take so long to—"

"Mr. Howard, that's blasphemous," Reverend Simmons says.

"I don't want blaspheme Him," Daddy says. "But I'm in a mess. I'm in a big mess. I want my wife."

"I'd suggest you kneel down sometime," Reverend Simmons says. "That always helps in a family."

Reverend Simmons looks at me like he's feeling sorry for me, then he goes on back up the quarter. I can see his coattail hitting him round the knees.

"You coming in this yard, Sonny?" Mama calls.

"I'm with Daddy," I say.

Mama goes back in the house and Gran'mon and them follow her.

"When you want one of them preachers to do something for you, they can't do a doggone thing," Daddy says. "Nothing but stand up in that churchhouse and preach 'bout Heaven. I hate to go to that old hoo-doo woman, but I reckon there ain't nothing else I can do. You want go back there with me, Sonny?"

"Uh-huh."

"Come on," Daddy says.

Daddy takes my hand and me and him leave the fire. When I get 'way down the quarter I look back and see the fire still burning. We cross the railroad tracks and I can see the people cutting cane. They got plenty cane all on the ground.

"Get me piece of cane, Daddy," I say.

"Sonny, please," Daddy says. "I'm thinking."

"I want piece of two-ninety," I say.

Daddy turns my hand loose and jumps over the ditch. He finds a piece of two-ninety and jumps back over. Daddy takes out a little pocketknife and peels the cane. He gives me a round and he cut him off a round and chew it. I like two-ninety cane because it's soft and sweet and got plenty juice in it.

"I want another piece," I say.

Daddy cuts me off another round and hands it to me.

"I'll be glad when you big enough to peel your own cane," he says.

"I can peel my own cane now," I say.

Daddy breaks me off three joints and hands it to me. I peel the cane with my teeth. Two-ninety cane is soft and it's easy to peel.

Me and Daddy go round the bend, and then I can see Madame Toussaint's house. Madame Toussaint's got a' old house, and look like it want to fall down any minute. I'm scared of Madame Toussaint. Billy Joe Martin say Madame Toussaint's a witch, and he say one time he seen Madame Toussaint riding a broom.

Daddy pulls Madame Toussaint's little old broken-down gate open and we go in the yard. Me and Daddy go far as the steps, but we don't go up on the gallery. Madame Toussaint's got plenty trees round her house, little trees and big trees. And she got plenty moss hanging on every tree. I see a pecan over there on the ground but I'm scared to go and pick it up. Madame Toussaint'll put bad mark on me and I'll turn to a frog or something. I let Madame Toussaint's little old pecan stay right where it is. And I go up to Daddy and let him hold my hand.

"Madame Toussaint?" Daddy calls.

Madame Toussaint don't answer. Like she ain't there.

"Madame Toussaint?" Daddy calls again.

"Who that?" Madame Toussaint answers.

"Me," Daddy says. "Eddie Howard and his little boy Sonny."

"What you want, Eddie Howard?" Madame Toussaint calls from in her house.

"I want talk to you," Daddy says. "I need little advice on something."

I hear a dog bark three times in the house. He must be a big old dog because he's sure got a heavy voice. Madame Toussaint comes to the door and cracks it open.

"Can I come in?" Daddy says.

"Come in, Eddie Howard," Madame Toussaint says.

Me and Daddy go up the steps and Madame Toussaint opens the door for us. Madame Toussaint's a little bitty little old woman and her face is brown like cowhide. I look at Madame Toussaint and I walk close 'side Daddy. Me and Daddy go in the house and Madame Toussaint shuts the door and comes back to her fireplace. She sits down in her big old rocking chair and looks at me and Daddy. I look round Daddy's leg at Madame Toussaint, but I let Daddy hold me hand. Madame Toussaint's house don't smell good. It's too dark in there. It don't smell good at all. Madame Toussaint ought to have a window or something open in her house.

"I need some advice, Madame Toussaint," Daddy says.

"Your wife left you," Madame Toussaint says.

"How you know?" Daddy asks.

"That's all you men come back here for," Madame Toussaint says. "That's how I know."

Daddy nods his head. "Yes," he says. "She done left me and staying with another man."

"She left," Madame Toussaint says. "But she's not staying with another man."

"Yes, she is," Daddy says.

"She's not," Madame Toussaint says. "You trying to tell me my business?"

"No, ma'am," Daddy says.

"I should hope not," Madame Toussaint says.

Madame Toussaint ain't got but three old rotten teeth in her mouth. I bet you she can't peel no cane with them old rotten teeth. I bet you they'd break off in a hard piece of cane.

"I need advice, Madame Toussaint," Daddy says.

"You got money?" Madame Toussaint asks.

"I got some," Daddy says.

"How much?" she asks Daddy. She's looking up at Daddy like she don't believe him.

Daddy turns my hand loose and sticks his hand down in his pocket. He gets all his money out his pocket and leans over the fire to see how much he's got. I see some matches and piece of string and some nails in Daddy's hand. I reach for the piece of string and Daddy taps me on the hand with his other hand.

"I got about seventy-five cents," Daddy says. "Counting them pennies."

"My price is three dollars," Madame Toussaint says.

"I can cut you a load of wood," Daddy says. "Or make grocery for you. I'll do anything in the world if you can help me, Madame Toussaint."

"Three dollars," Madame Toussaint says. "I got all the wood I'll need this winter. Enough grocery to last me till summer."

"But this all I got," Daddy says.

"When you get more, come back," Madame Toussaint says.

"But I want my wife back now," Daddy says. "I can't wait till I get more money."

"Three dollars is my price," Madame Toussaint says. "No more, no less."

"But can't you give me just a little advice for seventy-five cents?" Daddy says. "Seventy-five cents worth? Maybe I can start from there and figure something out."

Madame Toussaint looks at me and looks at Daddy again.

"You say that's your boy?" she says.

"Yes, ma'am," Daddy says.

"Nice-looking boy," Madame Toussaint says.

"His name's Sonny," Daddy says.

"Hi, Sonny," Madame Toussaint says.

"Say 'Hi' to Madame Toussaint," Daddy says. "Go on."

"Hi," I say, sticking close to Daddy.

"Well, Madame Toussaint?" Daddy says.

"Give me the money," Madame Toussaint says. "Don't complain to me if you not satisfied."

"Don't worry," Daddy says. "I won't complain. Anything to get her back home."

Daddy leans over the fire again and picks the money out of his hand. Then he reaches it to Madame Toussaint.

"Give me that little piece of string," Madame Toussaint says. "It might come in handy sometime in the future. Wait," she says. "Run it 'cross the left side of the boy's face three times, then pass it to me behind your back."

"What's that for?" Daddy asks.

"Just do like I say," Madame Toussaint says.

"Yes, ma'am," Daddy says. Daddy turns to me. "Hold still, Sonny," he says. He rubs the little old dirty piece of cord over my face, and then he sticks his hand behind his back.

Madame Toussaint reaches in her pocket and takes out her pocketbook. She opens it and puts the money in. She opens another little compartment and stuffs the string down in it. Then she snaps the pocketbook and puts it back in her pocket. She picks up three little green sticks she got tied together and starts poking in the fire with them.

"What's the advice?" Daddy asks.

Madame Toussaint don't say nothing.

"Madame Toussaint?" Daddy says.

Madame Toussaint still don't answer him, she just looks down in the fire. Her face is red from the fire. I get scared of Madame Toussaint. She can ride all over the plantation on her broom. Billy Joe Martin say he seen her one night riding 'cross the houses. She was whipping her broom with three switches.

Madame Toussaint raises her head and looks at Daddy. Her eyes's big and white, and I get scared of her. I hide my face 'side Daddy's leg.

"Give it up," I hear her say.

"Give what up?" Daddy says.

"Give it up," she says.

"What?" Daddy says.

"Give it up," she says.

"I don't even know what you talking 'bout," Daddy says. "How can I give up something and I don't even know what it is?"

"I said it three times," Madame Toussaint says. "No more, no less. Up to you now to follow it through from there."

"Follow what from where?" Daddy says. "You said three little old words: 'Give it up.' I don't know no more now than I knowed 'fore I got here."

"I told you you wasn't go'n be satisfied," Madame Toussaint says.

"Satisfied?" Daddy says. "Satisfied for what? You gived me just three little old words and you want me to be satisfied?"

"You can leave," Madame Toussaint says.

"Leave?" Daddy says. "You mean I give you seventy-five cents for three words? A quarter a word? And I'm leaving? No, Lord."

"Rollo?" Madame Toussaint says.

I see Madame Toussaint's big old black dog get up out of the corner and come where she is. Madame Toussaint pats the dog on the head with her hand.

"Two dollars and twenty-five cents more and you get all the advice you need," Madame Toussaint says.

"Can't I get you a load of wood and fix your house for you or something?" Daddy says.

"I don't want my house fixed and I don't need no more wood," Madame Toussaint says. "I got three loads of wood just three days ago from a man who didn't have money. Before I know it I'll have wood piled up all over my yard."

"Can't I do anything?" Daddy says.

"You can leave," Madame Toussaint says. "I ought to have somebody else dropping round pretty soon. Lately I've been having men dropping in three times a day. All of them just like you. What they can do to make their wives love them more. What they can do to keep their wives from running round with some other man. What they can do to make their wives give in. What they can do to make their wives scratch their backs. What they can do to make their wives look at them when they talking to her. Get out my house before I put the dog on you. You been here too long for seventy-five cents."

Madame Toussaint's big old jet-black dog gives three loud barks that makes my head hurt. Madame Toussaint pats him on the back to calm him down.

"Come on, Sonny," Daddy says.

I let Daddy take my hand and we go over to the door.

"I still don't feel like you helped me very much, though," Daddy says.

Madame Toussaint pats her big old jet-black dog on the head and she don't answer Daddy. Daddy pushes the door open and we go outside. It's some cold outside. Me and Daddy go down Madame Toussaint's old broken-down steps.

"What was them words?" Daddy asks me.

"Hanh?"

"What she said when she looked up out of that fire?"

"I was scared," I say. "Her face was red and her eyes got big and white. I was scared. I had to hide my face."

"Didn't you hear what she told me?" Daddy asks.

"She told you three dollars," I say.

"I mean when she looked up," Daddy says.

"She say, 'Give it up,'" I say.

"Yes," Daddy says. "'Give it up.' Give what up? I don't even know what she's talking 'bout. I hope she don't mean give you and Amy up. She ain't that crazy. I don't know nothing else she can be talking 'bout. You don't know, do you?"

"Uh-uh," I say.

"'Give it up,'" Daddy says. "I don't even know what she's talking 'bout. I wonder who them other men was she was speaking of. Johnny and his wife had a fight the other week. It might be him. Frank Armstrong and his wife had a round couple weeks back. Could be him. I wish I knowed what she told them."

"I want another piece of cane," I say.

"No," Daddy says. "You'll be pee-ing in bed all night tonight."

"I'm go'n sleep with Uncle Al," I say. "Me and him go'n sleep in his bed."

"Please, be quiet, Sonny," Daddy says. "I got enough troubles on my mind. Don't add more to it."

Me and Daddy walk in the middle of the road, Daddy holds my hand. I can hear a tractor—I see it across the field. The people loading cane on the trailer back of the tractor.

"Come on," Daddy says. "We going over to Frank Armstrong."

Daddy totes me 'cross the ditch on his back. I ride on Daddy's back and I look at the stubbles where the people done cut the cane. Them rows some long. Plenty cane's laying on the ground. I can see cane all over the field. Me and Daddy go over where the people cutting cane.

"How come you ain't working this evening?" a man asks Daddy. The man's shucking a big armful of cane with his cane knife.

"Frank Armstrong round anywhere?" Daddy asks the man.

"Farther over," the man says. "Hi, youngster."

"Hi," I say.

Me and Daddy go 'cross the field. I look at the people cutting cane. That cane is some tall. I want another piece, but I might wee-wee in Uncle Al's bed.

Me and Daddy go over where Mr. Frank Armstrong and Mrs. Julie's cutting cane. Mrs. Julie got overalls on just like Mr. Frank got. She's even wearing one of Mr. Frank's old hats.

"How y'all?" Daddy says.

"So-so, and yourself?" Mrs. Julie says.

"I'm trying to make it," Daddy says. "Can I borrow your husband there a minute?"

"Sure," Mrs. Julie says. "But don't keep him too long. We trying to reach the end 'fore dark."

"It won't take long," Daddy says.

Mr. Frank and them got a little fire burning in one of the middles. Me and him and Daddy go over there. Daddy squats down and let me slide off his back.

"What's the trouble?" Mr. Frank asks Daddy.

"Amy left me, Frank," Daddy says.

Mr. Frank holds his hands over the fire.

"She left you?" he says.

"Yes," Daddy says. "And I want her back, Frank."

"What can I do?" Mr. Frank says. "She's no kin to me. I can't go and make her come back."

"I thought maybe you could tell me what you and Madame Toussaint talked about," Daddy says. "That's if you don't mind, Frank."

"What?" Mr. Frank says. "Who told you I talked with Madame Toussaint?"

"Nobody," Daddy says. "But I heard you and Julie had a fight, and I thought maybe you went back to her for advice."

"For what?" Mr. Frank says.

"So you and Julie could make up," Daddy says.

"Well, I'll be damned," Mr. Frank says. "I done heard everything. Excuse me, Sonny. But your daddy's enough to make anybody cuss."

I look up at Daddy, and I look back in the fire again.

"Please, Frank," Daddy says. "I'm desperate. I'm ready to try anything. I'll do anything to get her back in my house."

"Why don't you just go and get her?" Mr. Frank says. "That makes sense."

"I can't," Daddy says. "Mama won't let me come in the yard. She even took a shot at me once today."

"What?" Mr. Frank says. He looks at Daddy, and then he just bust out laughing. Daddy laughs little bit, too.

"What y'all talked about, Frank?" Daddy asks. "Maybe if I try the same thing, maybe I'll be able to get her back, too."

Mr. Frank laughs at Daddy, then he stops and just looks at Daddy.

"No," he says. "I'm afraid my advice won't help your case. You got to first get close to your wife. And your mother-in-law won't let you do that. No, mine won't help you."

"It might," Daddy says.

"No, it won't," Mr. Frank says.

"It might," Daddy says. "What was it?"

"All right," Mr. Frank says. "She told me I wasn't petting Julie enough."

"Petting her?" Daddy says.

"You think he knows what we talking 'bout?" Mr. Frank asks Daddy.

"I'll get him piece of cane," Daddy says.

They got a big pile of cane right behind Daddy's back, and he crosses the row and gets me a stalk of two-ninety. He breaks off three joints and hands it to me. He throws the rest of the stalk back.

"So I start petting her," Mr. Frank says.

"What you mean 'petting her'?" Daddy says. "I don't even know what you mean now."

"Eddie, I swear," Mr. Frank says. "Stroking her. You know. Like you stroke a colt. A little horse."

"Oh," Daddy says. "Did it work?"

"What you think?" Mr. Frank says, grinning. "Every night, a little bit. Turn your head, Sonny."

"Hanh?"

"Look the other way," Daddy says.

I look down the row toward the other end. I don't see nothing but cane all over the ground.

"Stroke her a little back here," Mr. Frank says. I hear him hitting on his pants. "Works every time. Get along now like two peas in one pod. Every night when we get in the bed—" I hear him hitting again. "—couple little strokes. Now everything's all right."

"You was right," Daddy says. "That won't help me none."

"My face getting cold," I say.

"You can turn round and warm," Daddy says.

I turn and look at Mr. Frank. I bite off piece of cane and chew it.

"I told you it wouldn't," Mr. Frank says. "Well, I got to get back to work. What you go'n do now?"

"I don't know," Daddy says. "If I had three dollars she'd give me some advice. But I don't have a red copper. You wouldn't have three dollars you could spare till payday, huh?"

"I don't have a dime," Mr. Frank says. "Since we made up, Julie keeps most of the money."

"You think she'd lend me three dollars till Saturday?"

"I don't know if she got that much on her," Mr. Frank says. "I'll go over and ask her."

I watch Mr. Frank going 'cross the rows where Mrs. Julie's cutting cane. They start talking, and then I hear them laughing.

"You warm?" Daddy asks.

"Uh-huh."

I see Mr. Frank coming back to the fire.

"She don't have it on her but she got it at the house," Mr. Frank says. "If you can wait till we knock off."

"No," Daddy says. "I can't wait till night. I got to try to borrow it from somebody now."

"Why don't you go 'cross the field and try Johnny Green," Mr. Frank says. "He's always got some money. Maybe he'll lend it to you."

"I'll ask him," Daddy says. "Get on, Sonny."

Me and Daddy go back 'cross the field. I can hear Mr. Johnny Green singing, and Daddy turns that way and we go down where Mr. Johnny is. Mr. Johnny stops his singing when he sees me and Daddy. He chops the top off a' armful of cane and throws it 'cross the row. Mr. Johnny's cutting cane all by himself.

"Hi, Brother Howard," Mr. Johnny says.

"Hi," Daddy says. Daddy squats down and let me slide off.

"Hi there, little Brother Sonny," Mr. Johnny says.

"Hi," I say.

"How you?" Mr. Johnny asks.

"I'm all right," I say.

"That's good," Mr. Johnny says. "And how you this beautiful, God-sent day, Brother Howard?"

"I'm fine," Daddy says. "Johnny, I want know if you can spare me 'bout three dollars till Saturday?"

"Sure, Brother Howard," Mr. Johnny says. "You mind telling me just why you need it? I don't mind lending a good brother anything, long 's I know he ain't wasting it on women or drink."

"I want pay Madame Toussaint for some advice," Daddy says.

"Little trouble, Brother?" Mr. Johnny asks.

"Amy done left me, Johnny," Daddy says. "I need some advice. I just got to get her back."

"I know what you mean, Brother," Mr. Johnny says. "I had to visit Madame—you won't carry this no farther, huh?"

"No," Daddy says.

"Couple months ago I had to take a little trip back there to see her," Mr. Johnny says.

"What was wrong?" Daddy asks.

"Little misunderstanding between me and Sister Laura," Mr. Johnny says.

"She helped?" Daddy asks.

"Told me to stop spending so much time in church and little more time at home," Mr. Johnny says. "I couldn't see that. You know, far back as I can go in my family my people been good church members."

"I know that," Daddy says.

"My pappy was a deacon and my mammy didn't miss a Sunday long as I can remember," Mr. Johnny says. "And that's how I was raised. To fear God. I just couldn't see it when she first told me that. But I thought it over. I went for a long walk back in the field. I got down on my knees and looked up at the sky. I asked God to show me the way—to tell me what to do. And He did, He surely did. He told me to do just like Madame Toussaint said. Slack up going to church. Go twice a week, but spend the rest of the time with her. Just like that He told me. And I'm doing exactly what He said. Twice a week. And, Brother Howard, don't spread this round, but the way Sister Laura been acting here lately, there might be a little Johnny next summer sometime."

"No?" Daddy says.

"Uhnnnn-hunh," Mr. Johnny says.

"I'll be doggone," Daddy says. "I'm glad to hear that."

"I'll be the happiest man on this whole plantation," Mr. Johnny says.

"I know how you feel," Daddy says. "Yes, I know how you feel. But that three, can you lend it to me?"

"Sure, Brother," Mr. Johnny says. "Anything to bring a family back together. Nothing more important in this world than family love. Yes, indeed."

Mr. Johnny unbuttons his top overalls pocket and takes out a dollar.

"Only thing I got is five, Brother Howard," he says. "You wouldn't happen to have some change, would you?"

"I don't have a red copper," Daddy says. "But I'll be more than happy if you can let me have that five. I need some grocery in the house, too."

"Sure, Brother," Mr. Johnny says. He hands Daddy the dollar. "Nothing looks more beautiful than a family at a table eating something the little woman just cooked. But you did say Saturday didn't you, Brother?"

"Yes," Daddy says. "I'll pay you back soon 's I get paid. You can't ever guess how much this means to me, Johnny."

"Glad I can help, Brother," Mr. Johnny says. "Hope she can do likewise."

"I hope so too," Daddy says. "Anyhow, this a start."

"See you Saturday, Brother," Mr. Johnny says.

"Soon 's I get paid," Daddy says. "Hop on, Sonny, and hold tight. We going back."

4

Daddy walks up on Madame Toussaint's gallery and knocks on the door.

"Who that?" Madame Toussaint asks.

"Me. Eddie Howard," Daddy says. He squats down so I can slide off his back. I slide down and let Daddy hold my hand.

"What you want, Eddie Howard?" Madame Toussaint asks.

"I got three dollars," Daddy says. "I still want that advice."

Madame Toussaint's big old jet-black dog barks three times, and then I hear Madame Toussaint coming to the door. She peeps through the keyhole at me and Daddy. She opens the door and let me and Daddy come in. We go to the fireplace and warm. Madame Toussaint comes to the fireplace and sits down in her big old rocking chair. She looks up at Daddy. I look for big old Rollo, but I don't see him. He must be under the bed or hiding somewhere in the corner.

"You got three dollars?" Madame Toussaint asks Daddy.

"Yes," Daddy says. He takes out the dollar and shows it to Madame Toussaint. Madame Toussaint holds her hand up for it.

"This is five," Daddy says. "I want two back."

"You go'n get your two," Madame Toussaint says.

"Come to think of it," Daddy says, "I ought to just owe you two and a quarter, since I done already gived you seventy-five cents."

"You want advice?" Madame Toussaint asks Daddy. Madame Toussaint looks like she's getting mad with Daddy now.

"Sure," Daddy says. "But since—"

"Then shut up and hand me your money," Madame Toussaint says.

"But I done already—" Daddy says.

"Get out my house, nigger," Madame Toussaint says. "And don't come back till you learn how to act."

"All right," Daddy says, "I'll give you three more dollars."

He hands Madame Toussaint the dollar.

Madame Toussaint gets her pocketbook out her pocket. Then she leans close to the fire so she can look down in it. She sticks her hand in the pocketbook and gets two dollars. She looks at the two dollars a long time. She stands up and gets her eyeglasses off the mantelpiece and puts them on her eyes. She looks at the two dollars a long time, then she hands them to Daddy. She sticks the dollar bill Daddy gived her in the pocketbook, then she takes her eyeglasses off and puts them back on the mantelpiece. Madame Toussaint sits in her big old rocking chair and starts poking in the fire with the three sticks again. Her face gets red from the fire, her eyes get big and white. I turn my head and hide behind Daddy's leg.

"Go set fire to your car," Madame Toussaint says.

"What?" Daddy says.

"Go set fire to your car," Madame Toussaint says.

"You talking to me?" Daddy says.

"Go set fire to your car," Madame Toussaint says.

"Now, just a minute," Daddy says. "I didn't give you my hard-earned three dollars for that kind of foolishness. I dismiss that seventy-five cents you took from me, but not my three dollars that easy."

"You want your wife back?" Madame Toussaint asks Daddy.

"That's what I'm paying you for," Daddy says.

"Then go set fire to your car," Madame Toussaint says. "You can't have both."

"You must be fooling," Daddy says.

"I don't fool," Madame Toussaint says. "You paid for advice and I'm giving you advice."

"You mean that?" Daddy says. "You mean I got to go burn up my car for Amy to come back home?"

"If you want her back there," Madame Toussaint says. "Do you?"

"I wouldn't be standing here if I didn't," Daddy says.

"Then go and burn it up," Madame Toussaint says. "A gallon of coal oil and a penny box of match ought to do the trick. You got any gas in it?"

"A little bit—if nobody ain't drained it," Daddy says.

"Then you can use that," Madame Toussaint says. "But if you want her back there you got to burn it up. That's my advice to you. And if I was you I'd do it right away. You can never tell."

"Tell about what?" Daddy asks.

"She might be sleeping in another man's bed a week from now," Madame Toussaint says. "This man loves her and he's kind. And that's what a woman wants. That's what they need. You men don't know this, but you better learn it before it's too late."

"What's that other man's name?" Daddy asks. "Can it be Freddie Jackson?"

"It can," Madame Toussaint says. "But it don't have to be. Any man that'd give her love and kindness."

"I love her," Daddy says. "I give her kindness. I'm always giving her love and kindnesss."

"When you home, you mean," Madame Toussaint says. "How about when you running up and down the road in your car? How do you think she feels then?"

Daddy don't say nothing.

"You men better learn," Madame Toussaint says. "Now, if you want her, go and burn it. If you don't want her, go and get drunk off them two dollars and sleep in a cold bed tonight."

"You mean she'll come back tonight?" Daddy asks.

"She's ready to come back right now," Madame Toussaint says. "Poor little thing."

I look round Daddy's leg at Madame Toussaint. Madame Toussaint's looking in the fire. Her face ain't red no more; her eyes ain't big and white, either.

"She's not happy where she is," Madame Toussaint says.

"She's with her mama," Daddy says.

"You don't have to tell me my business," Madame Toussaint says. "I know where she is. And I still say she's not happy. She much rather be back in her own house. Women like to be in their own house. That's their world. You men done messed up the outside world so bad that they feel lost and out of place in it. Her house is her world. Only there she can do what she want. She can't do that in anybody else house—mama or nobody else. But you men don't know any of this. Y'all never know how a woman feels, because you never ask how she feels. Long's she there when you get there you satisfied. Long's you give her two or three dollars every weekend you think she ought to be satisfied. But keep on. One day all of you'll find out."

"Couldn't I sell the car or something?" Daddy asks.

"You got to burn it," Madame Toussaint says. "How come your head so hard?"

"But I paid good money for that car," Daddy says. "It wouldn't look right if I just jumped up and put fire to it."

"You, get out my house," Madame Toussaint says, pointing her finger at Daddy. "Go do what you want with your car. It's yours. But just don't come back here bothering me for no more advice."

"I don't know," Daddy says.

"I'm through talking," Madame Toussaint says. "Rollo? Come here, baby."

Big old jet-black Rollo comes up and puts his head in Madame Toussaint's lap. Madame Toussaint pats him on the head.

"That's what I got to do, hanh?" Daddy says.

Madame Toussaint don't answer Daddy. She starts singing a song to Rollo:

> *Mama's little baby,*
> *Mama's little baby.*

"He bad?" Daddy asks.

> *Mama's little baby,*
> *Mama's little baby.*

"Do he bite?" Daddy asks.

Madame Toussaint keeps on singing:

Mama's little baby,
Mama's little baby.

"Come on," Daddy says. "I reckon we better be going."

Daddy squats down and I climb up on his back. I look down at Madame Toussaint patting big old jet-black Rollo on his head.

Daddy pushes the door open and we go outside. It's cold outside. Daddy goes down Madame Toussaint's three old broken-down steps and we go out in the road.

"I don't know," Daddy says.

"Hanh?"

"I'm talking to myself," Daddy says. "I don't know about burning up my car."

"You go'n burn up your car?" I ask.

"That's what Madame Toussaint say to do," Daddy says.

"You ain't go'n have no more car?"

"I reckon not," Daddy says. "You want me and Mama to stay together?"

"Uh-huh."

"Then I reckon I got to burn it up," Daddy says. "But I sure hope there was another way out. I put better than three hundred dollars in that car."

Daddy walks fast and I bounce on his back.

"God, I wish there was another way out," Daddy says. "Don't look like that's right for a man to just jump up and set fire to something like that. What you think I ought to do?"

"Hanh?"

"Go back to sleep," Daddy says. "I don't know what I'm educating you for."

"I ain't sleeping," I say.

"I don't know," Daddy says. "That don't look right. All Frank Armstrong had to do was pop Julie on the butt little bit every night 'fore she went to sleep. All Johnny had to do was stop going to church so much. Neither one of them had to burn down anything. Johnny didn't have to burn down the church; Frank didn't have to burn down the bed—nothing. But me, I got to burn up my car. She charged all us the same thing—no, she even charged me seventy-five cents more, and I got to burn up a car I can still get some use out. Now, that don't sound right, do it?"

"Hanh?"

"I can't figure it," Daddy says. "Look like I ought to be able to sell it for little something. Get some of my money back. Burning it, I don't get a red copper. That just don't sound right to me. I wonder if she was fooling. No. She say she wasn't. But maybe that wasn't my advice she seen in that fireplace. Maybe that was somebody else advice. Maybe she gived me the wrong one. Maybe it belongs to the man coming back there after me. They go there three times a day, she can get them mixed up."

"I'm scared of Madame Toussaint, Daddy," I say.

"Must've been somebody else," Daddy says. "I bet it was. I bet you anything it was."

I bounce on Daddy's back and I close my eyes. I open them and I see me and Daddy going 'cross the railroad tracks. We go up the quarter to Gran'mon's house. Daddy squats down and I slide off his back.

"Run in the house to the fire," Daddy says. "Tell your mama come to the door."

Soon 's I come in the yard, Spot runs down the walk and starts barking. Mama and all of them come out on the gallery.

"My baby," Mama says. Mama comes down the steps and hugs me to her. "My baby," she says.

"Look at that old yellow thing standing out in that road," Gran'mon says. "What you ought to been done was got the sheriff on him for kidnap."

Me and Mama go back on the gallery.

"I been to Madame Toussaint's house," I say.

Mama looks at me and looks at Daddy out in the road. Daddy comes to the gate and looks at us on the gallery.

"Amy?" Daddy calls. 'Can I speak to you a minute? Just one minute?"

"You don't get away from my gate, I'm go'n make that shotgun speak to you," Gran'mon says. "I didn't get you at twelve o'clock, but I won't miss you now."

"Amy, honey," Daddy calls. "Please."

"Come on, Sonny," Mama says.

"Where you going?" Gran'mon asks.

"Far as the gate," Mama says. "I'll talk to him. I reckon I owe him that much."

"You leave this house with that nigger, don't ever come back here again," Gran'-mon says.

"You oughtn't talk like that, Rachel," Uncle Al says.

"I talk like I want," Gran'mon says. "She's my daughter; not yours, neither his."

Me and Mama go out to the gate where Daddy is. Daddy stands outside the gate and me and Mama stand inside.

"Lord, you look good, Amy," Daddy says. "Honey, didn't you miss me? Go on and say it. Go on and say how bad you missed me."

"That's all you want say to me?" Mama says.

"Honey, please," Daddy says. "Say you missed me. I been grieving all day like a dog."

"Come on, Sonny," Mama says. "Let's go back inside."

"Honey," Daddy says. "Please don't turn your back on me and go back to Freddie Jackson. Honey, I love you. I swear 'fore God I love you. Honey, you listening?"

"Come on, Sonny," Mama says.

"Honey," Daddy says, "if I burn the car like Madame Toussaint say, you'll come back home?"

"What?" Mama says.

"She say for Daddy—"

"Be still, Sonny," Mama says.

"She told me to set fire to it and you'll come back home," Daddy says. "You'll come back, honey?"

"She told you to burn up your car?" Mama says.

"If I want you to come back," Daddy says. "If I do it, you'll come back?"

"If you burn it up," Mama says. "If you burn it up, yes, I'll come back."

"Tonight?" Daddy says.

"Yes; tonight," Mama says.

"If I sold it?" Daddy says.

"Burn it," Mama says.

"I can get about fifty for it," Daddy says. "You could get couple dresses out of that."

"Burn it," Mama says. "You know what burn is?"

Daddy looks across the gate at Mama, and Mama looks right back at him. Daddy nods his head.

"I can't argue with you, honey," he says. "I'll go and burn it right now. You can come see if you want."

"No," Mama says, "I'll be here when you come back."

"Couldn't you go up home and start cooking some supper?" Daddy asks. "I'm just 's hungry as a dog."

"I'll cook when that car is burnt," Mama says. "Come on, Sonny."

"Can I go see Daddy burn his car, Mama?" I ask.

"No," Mama says. "You been in that cold long enough."

"I want see Daddy burn his car," I say. I start crying and stomping so Mama'll let me go.

"Let him go, honey," Daddy says. "I'll keep him warm."

"You can go," Mama says. "But don't come to me if you start that coughing tonight, you hear?"

"Uh-huh," I say.

Mama makes sure all my clothes's buttoned good, then she let me go. I run out in the road where Daddy is.

"I'll be back soon 's I can, honey," Daddy says. "And we'll straighten out everything, hear?"

"Just make sure you burn it," Mama says. "I'll find out."

"Honey, I'm go'n burn every bit of it," Daddy says.

"I'll be here when you come back," Mama says. "How you figuring on getting up there?"

"I'll go over and see if George Williams can't take me," Daddy says.

"I don't want Sonny in that cold too long," Mama says. "And you keep your hands in your pockets, Sonny."

"I ain't go'n take them out," I say.

Mama goes back up the walk toward the house. Daddy stands there just watching her.

"Lord, that's a sweet little woman," he says, shaking his head. "That's a sweet little woman you see going back to that house."

"Come on, Daddy," I say. "Let's go burn up the car."

Me and Daddy walk away from the fence.

"Let me get on your back and ride," I say.

"Can't you walk sometime," Daddy says. "What you think I'm educating you for—to treat me like a horse?"

5

Mr. George Williams drives his car to the side of the road, then we get out.

"Look like we got company," Mr. George Williams says.

Me and Daddy and Mr. George Williams go over where the people is. The people got a little fire burning, and some of them's sitting on the car fender. But most of them's standing round the little fire.

"Welcome," somebody says.

"Thanks," Daddy says. "Since this is my car you sitting on."

"Oh," the man says. He jumps up and the other two men jump up, too. They go over to the little fire and stand round it.

"We didn't mean no harm," one of them say.

Daddy goes over and peeps in the car. Then he opens the door and gets in. I go over to the car where he is.

"Go stand 'side the fire," Daddy says.

"I want to get in with you," I say.

"Do what I tell you," Daddy says.

I go back to the fire, and I turn and look at Daddy in the car. Daddy passes his hand all over the car; then he just sit there quiet-like. All the people round the fire look at Daddy in the car. I can hear them talking real low.

After a little while, Daddy opens the door and gets out. He comes over to the fire.

"Well," he says, "I guess that's it. You got a rope?"

"In the trunk," Mr. George Williams says. "What you go'n do, drag it off the highway?"

"We can't burn it out here," Daddy says.

"He say he go'n burn it," somebody at the fire says.

"I'm go'n burn it," Daddy says. "It's mine, ain't it?"

"Easy, Eddie," Mr. George Williams says.

Daddy is mad but he don't say any more. Mr. George Williams looks at Daddy, then he goes over to his car and gets the rope.

"Ought to be strong enough," Mr. George Williams says.

He hands Daddy the rope, then he goes and turns his car around. Everybody at the fire looks at Mr. George Williams backing up his car.

Daddy gets between the cars and ties them together. Some of the people come over and watch him.

"Y'all got a side road anywhere round here?" he asks.

"Right over there," the man says. "Leads off back in the field. You ain't go'n burn up that good car for real, is you?"

"Who field this is?" Daddy asks.

"Mr. Roger Medlow," the man says.

"Any colored people got fields round here anywhere?" Daddy asks.

"Old man Ned Johnson 'bout two miles farther down the road," another man says.

"Why don't we just take it on back to the plantation?" Mr. George Williams says. "I doubt if Mr. Claude'll mind if we burnt it there."

"All right," Daddy says. "Might as well."

Me and Daddy get in his car. Some of the people from the fire run up to Mr. George Williams's car. Mr. George Williams tells them something, and I see three of them jumping in. Mr. George Williams taps on the horn, then we get going. I sit 'way back in the seat and look at Daddy. Daddy's quiet. He's sorry because he got to burn up his car.

We go 'way down the road, then we turn and go down the quarter. Soon 's we get down there, I hear two of the men in Mr. George Williams's car calling to the people. I sit up in the seat and look out at them. They standing on the fenders, calling to the people.

"Come on," they saying. "Come on to the car-burning party. Free. Everybody welcome. Free."

We go farther down the quarter, and the two men keep on calling.

"Come on, everybody," one of them says.

"We having a car-burning party tonight," the other one says. "No charges."

The people start coming out on the galleries to see what all the racket is. I look back and I see some out in the yard, and some already out in the road. Mr. George Williams stops in front of Gran'mon's house.

"You go'n tell Amy?" he calls to Daddy. "Maybe she like to go, since you doing it all for her."

"Go tell your mama come on," Daddy says.

I jump out the car and run in the yard.

"Come on, everybody," one of the men says.

"We having a car-burning party tonight," the other one says. "Everybody invited. No charges."

I pull Gran'mon's door open and go in. Mama and Uncle Al and Gran'mon's sitting at the fireplace.

"Mama, Daddy say come on if you want see the burning," I say.

"See what burning?" Gran'mon asks. "Now don't tell me that crazy nigger going through with that."

"Come on, Mama," I say.

Mama and Uncle Al get up from the fireplace and go to the door.

"He sure got it out there," Uncle Al says.

"Come on, Mama," I say. "Come on, Uncle Al."

"Wait till I get my coat," Mama says. "Mama, you going?"

"I ain't missing this for the world," Gran'mon says. "I still think he's bluffing."

Gran'mon gets her coat and Uncle Al gets his coat; then we go on outside. Plenty people standing round Daddy's car now. I can see more people opening doors and coming out on the galleries.

"Get in," Daddy says. "Sorry I can't take but two. Mama, you want ride?"

"No, thanks," Gran'mon says. "You might just get it in your head to run off in that canal with me in there. Let your wife and child ride. I'll walk with the rest of the people."

"Get in, honey," Daddy says. "It's getting cold out there."

Mama takes my arm and helps me in; then she gets in and shuts the door.

"How far down you going?" Uncle Al asks.

"Near the sugar house," Daddy says. He taps on the horn and Mr. George Williams drives away.

"Come on, everybody," one of the men says.

"We having a car-burning party tonight," the other one says. "Everybody invited."

Mr. George Williams drives his car over the railroad tracks. I look back and I see plenty people following Daddy's car. I can't see Uncle Al and Gran'mon, but I know they back there, too.

We keep going. We get almost to the sugar house, then we turn down another road. The other road is bumpy and I have to bounce on the seat.

"Well, I reckon this's it," Daddy says.

Mama don't say nothing to Daddy.

"You know it ain't too late to change your mind," Daddy says. "All I got to do is stop George and untie the car."

"You brought matches?" Mama asks.

"All right," Daddy says. "All right. Don't start fussing."

We go a little farther and Daddy taps on the horn. Mr. George Williams stops his car. Daddy gets out his car and go and talk with Mr. George Williams. Little bit later I see Daddy coming back.

"Y'all better get out here," he says. "We go'n take it down the field a piece."

Me and Mama get out. I look down the headland and I see Uncle Al and Gran'-mon and all the other people coming. Some of them even got flashlights because it's getting dark now. They come where me and Mama's standing. I look down the field and I see the cars going down the row. It's dark, but Mr. George Williams got bright lights on his car. The cars stop and Daddy get out his car and go and untie the rope. Mr. George Williams goes and turns around and come back to the head-land where all the people standing. Then he turns his lights on Daddy's car so every-body can see the burning. I see Daddy getting some gas out the tank.

"Give me a hand down here," Daddy calls. But that don't even sound like Daddy's voice.

Plenty people run down the field to help Daddy. They get round the car and start shaking it. I see the car leaning; then it tips over.

"Well," Gran'mon says. "I never would've thought it."

I see Daddy going all round the car with the can, then I see him splashing some inside the car. All the other people back back to give him room. I see Daddy scratch-ing a match and throwing it in the car. He scratches another one and throw that one in the car, too. I see little bit fire, then I see plenty.

"I just do declare," Gran'mon says. "I must be dreaming. He's a man after all."

Gran'mon the only person talking; everybody else is quiet. We stay there a long time and look at the fire. The fire burns down and Daddy and them go and look at the car again. Daddy picks up the can and pours some more gas on the fire. The fire gets big. We look at the fire some more.

"Never thought that was in Eddie," somebody says real low.

"You not the only one," somebody else says.

"He loved that car more than he loved anything."

"No, he must love her more," another person says.

The fire burns down again. Daddy and them go and look at the car. They stay there a good while, then they come out to the headland where we standing.

"What's that, George?" Mama asks.

"The pump," Mr. George Williams says. "Eddie gave it to me for driving him to get his car."

"Hand it here," Mama says.

Mr. George Williams looks at Daddy, but he hands the pump to Mama. Mama goes on down the field with the pump and throws it in the fire. I watch Mama coming back.

"When Eddie gets paid Saturday he'll pay you," Mama says. "You ready to go home, Eddie?"

Daddy nods his head.

"Sonny," Mama says.

I go where Mama is and Mama takes my hand. Daddy raises his head and looks at the people standing round looking at us.

"Thank y'all," he says.

Me and Mama go in Gran'mon's house and pull the big bundle out on the gallery. Daddy picks the bundle up and puts it on his head, then we go up the quarter to us house. Mama opens the gate and me and Daddy go in. We go inside and Mama lights the lamp.

"You hungry?" Mama asks Daddy.

"How can you ask that?" Daddy says. "I'm starving."

"You want eat now or after you whip me?" Mama says.

"Whip you?" Daddy asks. "What I'm go'n be whipping you for?"

Mama goes back in the kitchen. She don't find what she's looking for, and I hear her going outside.

"Where Mama going, Daddy?"

"Don't ask me," Daddy says. "I don't know no more than you."

Daddy gets some kindling out of the corner and puts it in the fireplace. Then he pours some coal oil on the kindling and lights a match to it. Me and Daddy squat down on the fireplace and watch the fire burning.

I hear the back door shut, then I see Mama coming in the front room. Mama's got a great big old switch.

"Here," she says.

"What's that for?" Daddy says.

"Here. Take it," Mama says.

"I ain't got nothing to beat you for, Amy," Daddy says.

"You whip me," Mama says, "or I turn right round and walk on out that door."

Daddy stands up and looks at Mama.

"You must be crazy," Daddy says. "Stop all that foolishness, Amy, and go cook me some food."

"Get your pot, Sonny," Mama says.

"Shucks," I say. "Now where we going? I'm getting tired walking in all that cold. 'Fore you know it I'm go'n have whooping cough."

"Get your pot and stop answering me back, boy," Mama says.

I go to my bed and pick up the pot again.

"Shucks," I say.

"You ain't leaving here," Daddy says.

"You better stop me," Mama says, going to the bundle.

"All right," Daddy says. "I'll beat you if that's what you want."

Daddy gets the switch off the floor and I start crying.

"Lord, have mercy," Daddy says. "Now what?"

"Whip me," Mama says.

"Amy, whip you for what?" Daddy says. "Amy, please, just go back there and cook me something to eat."

"Come on, Sonny," Mama says. "Let's get out of this house."

"All right," Daddy says. Daddy hits Mama two times on the legs. "That's enough," he says.

"Beat me," Mama says.

I cry some more. "Don't beat my mama," I say. "I don't want you to beat my mama."

"Sonny, please," Daddy says. "What y'all trying to do to me—run me crazy? I burnt up the car—ain't that enough?"

"I'm just go'n tell you one more time," Mama says.

"All right," Daddy says. "I'm go'n beat you if that's what you want."

Daddy starts beating Mama, and I cry some more; but Daddy don't stop beating her.

"Beat me harder," Mama says. "I mean it. I mean it."

"Honey, please," Daddy says.

"You better do it," Mama says. "I mean it."

Daddy keeps on beating Mama, and Mama cries and goes down on her knees.

"Leave my mama alone, you old yellow dog," I say. "You leave my mama alone." I throw the pot at him but I miss him, and the pot go bouncing 'cross the floor.

Daddy throws the switch away and runs to Mama and picks her up. He takes Mama to the bed and begs her to stop crying. I get on my own bed and cry in the cover.

I feel somebody shaking me, and I must've been sleeping.

"Wake up," I hear Daddy saying.

I'm tired and I don't feel like getting up. I feel like sleeping some more.

"You want some supper?" Daddy asks.

"Uh-huh."

"Get up then," Daddy says.

I get up. I got all my clothes on and my shoes on.

"It's morning?" I ask.

"No," Daddy says. "Still night. Come on back in the kitchen and eat supper."

I follow Daddy in the kitchen and me and him sit down at the table. Mama brings the food to the table and she sits down, too.

"Bless this food, Father, which we're about to receive, the nurse of our bodies, for Christ sake, amen," Mama says.

I raise my head and look at Mama. I can see where she's been crying. Her face is all swole. I look at Daddy and he's eating. Mama and Daddy don't talk, and I don't say nothing, either. I eat my food. We eating sweet potatoes and bread. I'm having a glass of clabber, too.

"What a day," Daddy says.

Mama don't say nothing. She's just picking over her food.

"Mad?" Daddy says.

"No," Mama says.

"Honey?" Daddy says.

Mama looks at him.

"I didn't beat you because you did us thing with Freddie Jackson, did I?" Daddy says.

"No," Mama says.

"Well, why then?" Daddy says.

"Because I don't want you to be the laughingstock of the plantation," Mama says.

"Who go'n laugh at me?" Daddy says.

"Everybody," Mama says. "Mama and all. Now they don't have nothing to laugh about."

"Honey, I don't mind if they laugh at me," Daddy says.

"I do mind," Mama says.

"Did I hurt you?"

"I'm all right," she says.

"You ain't mad no more?" Daddy says.

"No," Mama says. "I'm not mad."

Mama picks up a little bit of food and puts it in her mouth.

"Finish eating your supper, Sonny," she says.

"I got enough," I say.

"Drink your clabber," Mama says.

I drink all my clabber and show Mama the glass.

"Go get your book," Mama says. "It's on the dresser."

I go in the front room to get my book.

"One of us got to go to school with him tomorrow," I hear Mama saying. I see her handing Daddy the note. Daddy waves it back. "Here," she says.

"Honey, you know I don't know how to act in no place like that," Daddy says.

"Time to learn," Mama says. She gives Daddy the note. "What page your lesson on, Sonny?"

I turn to the page, and I lean on Mama's leg and let her carry me over my lesson. Mama holds the book in her hand. She carries me over my lesson two times, then she makes me point to some words and spell some words.

"He knows it," Daddy says.

"I'll take you over it again tomorrow morning," Mama says. "Don't let me forget it now."

"Uh-uh."

"Your daddy'll carry you over it tomorrow night," Mama says. "One night me, one night you."

"With no car," Daddy says, "I reckon I'll be round plenty now. You think we'll ever get another one, honey?"

Daddy's picking in his teeth with a broom straw.

"When you learn how to act with one," Mama says. "I ain't got nothing against cars."

"I guess you right, honey," Daddy says. "I was going little too far."

"It's time for bed, Sonny," Mama says. "Go in the front room and say your prayers to your daddy."

Me and Daddy leave Mama back there in the kitchen. I put my book on the dresser and I go to the fireplace where Daddy is. Daddy puts another piece of wood on the fire and plenty sparks shoot up in the chimley. Daddy helps me to take off my clothes. I kneel down and lean against his leg.

"Start off," Daddy says. "I'll catch you if you miss something."

"Lay me down to sleep," I say. "I pray the Lord my soul to keep. If I should die before I wake, I pray the Lord my soul to take. God bless Mama and Daddy. God bless Gran'mon and Uncle Al. God bless the church. God bless Miss Hebert. God bless Bill and Juanita." I hear Daddy gaping. "God bless everybody else. Amen."

I jump up off my knees. Them bricks on the fireplace make my knees hurt.

"Did you tell God to bless Johnny Green and Madame Toussaint?" Daddy says.

"No," I say.

"Get down there and tell Him to bless them, too," Daddy says.

"Old Rollo, too?"

"That's up to you and Him for that," Daddy says. "Get back down there."

I get back on my knees. I don't get on the bricks because they make my knees hurt. I get on the floor and lean against the chair.

"And God bless Mr. Johnny Green and Madame Toussaint," I say.

"All right," Daddy says. "Warm up good."

Daddy goes over to my bed and pulls the cover back.

"Come on," he says. "Jump in."

I run and jump in the bed. Daddy pulls the cover up to my neck.

"Good night, Daddy."

"Good night," Daddy says.

"Good night, Mama."

"Good night, Sonny," Mama says.

I turn on my side and look at Daddy at the fireplace. Mama comes out of the kitchen and goes to the fireplace. Mama warms up good and goes to the bundle.

"Leave it alone," Daddy says. "We'll get up early tomorrow and get it."

"I'm going to bed," Mama says. "You coming now?"

"Uhhunnnnn," Daddy says.

Mama comes to my bed and tucks the cover under me good. She leans over and kisses me and tucks the cover some more. She goes over to the bundle and gets her nightgown, then she goes in the kitchen and puts it on. She comes back and puts her clothes she took off on a chair 'side the wall. Mama kneels down and says her prayers, then she gets in the bed and covers up. Daddy stands up and takes off his clothes. I see Daddy in his big old long white BVD's. Daddy blows out the lamp, and I hear the spring when Daddy gets in the bed. Daddy never says his prayers.

"Sleepy?" Daddy says.

"Uh-uhnnn," Mama says.

I hear the spring. I hear Mama and Daddy talking low, but I don't know what they saying. I go to sleep some, but I open my eyes again. It's some dark in the room. I hear Mama and Daddy talking low. I like Mama and Daddy. I like Uncle Al, but I don't like old Gran'mon too much. Gran'mon's always talking bad about Daddy. I don't like old Mr. Freddie Jackson, either. Mama say she didn't do her and Daddy's thing with Mr. Freddie Jackson. I like Mr. George Williams. We went riding 'way up the road with Mr. George Williams. We got Daddy's car and brought it all the way back here. Daddy and them turned the car over and Daddy poured some gas on it and set it on fire. Daddy ain't got no more car now. . . . I know my lesson. I ain't go'n wee-wee on myself no more. Daddy's going to school with me tomorrow. I'm go'n show him I can beat Billy Joe Martin shooting marbles. I can shoot all over Billy Joe Martin. And I can beat him running, too. He thinks he can run fast. I'm go'n show Daddy I can beat him running. . . . I don't know why I had to say, "God bless Madame Toussaint." I don't like her. And I don't like old Rollo, either. Rollo can bark some loud. He made my head hurt with all that loud barking. Madame Toussaint's old house don't smell good. Us house smell good. I hear the spring on Mama and Daddy's bed. I get 'way under the cover. I go to sleep little bit, but I wake up. I go to sleep some more. I hear the spring on Mama and Daddy's bed. I hear it plenty now. It's some dark under here. It's warm. I feel good 'way under here.

The King of Slack

LOUIS GALLO

It would never occur to Mona to dismount our Exercycle before the timer rings. She could not bear it, not if the house were burning. It's the prescribed twenty minutes or nothing with her. I always set the timer slightly over twenty so I can finish before I'm supposed to yet still pump for optimal aerobic benefits. Mona takes it personally. My cheating a bell will somehow injure the cosmos.

The timer ticks away as I climb the stairs to the den where she waits in ambush. She has never understood my rejection of principle on principle.

I'm breathing roughly. Sweat from my forehead drips onto the oak floorboards Mona has just doused with Murphy's Oil. I'd like her to congratulate me on a fine workout, but her eyes remain riveted to the television screen.

"You think nobody notices, but they do," she sighs. Does she mean the clicking downstairs or my sweat?

I let it go because she's always right. I did cheat on the Exercycle in a way, yet my violation was a far cry from genuine slack. Cutting corners is the real thing, and I cut them wherever I can. Last summer, for instance, I used only three of the four screws provided by Sears to install a window unit. Mona, who has a passion for direction manuals, spotted the empty gaping hole which should have contained the fourth screw and roused me from my nap in protest.

"Three screws are all right," I mumbled. "Jiggle it. See if it shifts." I covered my head with pillows so I wouldn't hear the jiggling. When I got up I found the fourth screw inserted exactly where it belonged, and I commended her on a fine job.

"It's the way you do everything," she said, dashing out a cigarette. "You just pour soap into the washer. You're supposed to measure it out. You use one tea bag for two cups of tea. You never rinse the hairs out of the tub—"

I reminded her I am nearsighted and cannot *see* hairs.

"Well, they're there. You put air filters in backwards. You leave two or three coffee grounds in the sink. If you dump them, why not dump them all? Why the two or three? I don't understand. Fungus grows in the coffee cups on your desk."

She compiles endless lists of my indiscretions. I approve. It does her good, and me too. When she doesn't complain, I worry.

She cannot see that slack is a philosophic option. It gives me great pleasure to sabotage directions and not see hairs and use three screws instead of four. "Slack," I have tried to explain to Mona, "is a form of hope, the prisoner's puny gesture of freedom."

Do I believe I am a prisoner? Yes and no.

The other day I was having trouble with the buttons on our new Mitsubishi. I always press the channel button when I mean to lower the volume, which triggers a sort of cathode ray catastrophe. Static and wave patterns flicker and hiss across the screen. Mona likes buttons because she thinks they're more advanced and precise than dials, but pressing a button for volume makes no sense to me. We have nearly come to blows over it.

I finally pressed the right one and beheld the image of a woman form on the screen. I upped the volume by fingering another button about twenty times. The woman wore leather culottes and a white cowgirl vest with magenta spangles, the color of her lipstick. She looked forty-five or so and verged on obesity. She gazed straight into the camera and wept, mascara streaking down her doughy cheeks. The word "Bluefield" and an 800 phone number flashed brightly at the bottom of the screen.

"I just can't help it," the cowgirl choked. "Jesus loves me so much He died for me so I could live with Him in paradise all the time. It makes me so happy I want to cry."

What ho, I thought, Hookers for Christ—a new twist. Not so new, on second thought.

I flipped to CNN and caught the weather. Snow flurries in the Northeast. Humid and hot in the Deep South. A balmy paradise in San Francisco. Dry in the plains with promises of drought. An ominous front moving in from Canada.

I have no interest in weather and make plans without giving it a second thought. The idea is to cut out variables. If we took every variable into account, we would never crawl out of our beds. Best to live without forecasts and barometric pressures. We have done ourselves a massive disservice in elevating the weather to prime time. There is something amiss when millions of people watch a spiffy young model point her baton at a map depicting grids of portentous fronts. I have even heard that in the TV studio the map doesn't exist, that the announcers point at a blank wall—as if the weather itself didn't exist.

When I lived on the Gulf Coast I once heeded the forecast of an impending hurricane and boarded up every window in the house. I bought candles and batteries and canned soup and waited in endless lines at 7-11 and Jiffy Mart. My family and I huddled in a spasm of fear, confessing things to each other that still embarrass us.

The hurricane never materialized. No one could explain why. Shades of Kahoutek, I suppose. Yet we had all acted accordingly and I could not help but notice a surge in the moral climate. Nature had shafted us, true, but we ripped the boards from our windows with cheerful conviction. The ozone itself rejoiced as we sucked its delicious ions into our lungs. We would go to heaven.

"Why are you staring at the weather?" Mona asked from the kitchen, her arms laden with groceries. The truth was that I was at once both staring at CNN and not staring at CNN. A moment of pure nothingness. I was being recharged and felt wonderful. It has always amazed me how we can slip out of ourselves for a fraction of a second and then return, our neural circuitry intact, our atomic structure unravaged.

"Any goodies?" I asked, full of love and good cheer.

Mona stared the way she stares when she's on the prowl for slack. She got out the vacuum and efficiently sucked up debris and bits of misplaced matter and stray molecules. I dug into the Kroger bag, tore at the cellophane encasing the Oreos and dumped them out onto the kitchen counter, gobbling them up with both hands. She disapproved silently, afraid I will not put the remaining cookies in the jar where they belong.

"I thought sugar raised your triglycerides."

"I never appreciated sugar before triglycerides," I mumbled as crumbs exploded from my lips. "Don't worry, I'll clean up."

Triglycerides are fatty lipids that have not yet hardened into cholesterol. They thicken the blood and foreshadow cardiovascular problems. I may die, after all.

Soon I was busy pushing our Dustbuster across the cold, eerie linoleum of our perfect kitchen.

My four-year-old daughter has lost interest in the gerbil Mona brought home from the pre-school this weekend. He resists cuddling and scampers away when we approach him. This makes him worthless to Karen, a born cuddler. The gerbil, Sam, dumps in his food and treads his wheel maniacally. Seeing her mistake, Mona eyes Sam with loathing. She fears his seeds and sawdust will find their way onto the dining room table, where she has stationed his cage. She'll scrub it with Lysol when he's gone.

The cage is an aquarium with two plastic tubes issuing out of its lid. They connect with another horizontal tube about a foot above the top. The tubes are fluted so Sam can make the rounds. The two vertical tubes end with little square cubicles, in each of which Sam spends a lot of time. We call them "penthouses." A plastic treadmill takes up most of the middle of the aquarium, and there is also a water dispenser at one end. I've noticed Sam does not drink very much.

On Friday night when Mona and Karen were asleep I heard him racing on his wheel. The spin makes a grating, harsh sound, and it distracted me from my book. I drifted into the dining room and pulled a chair up beside the aquarium. Sam interests me. His life seems futile and without purpose, his movements jerky and erratic. He has no plan for eating or excreting. He runs on the wheel with great determination, and when he stops he sits up on his hind legs, jerks his head about and freezes for a few seconds to stare at me. Then it's back to the wheel. Sam has obviously not checked the weather.

He zipped up one of the tubes into a penthouse and burrowed in the sawdust and shredded paper and came out with a green nut, which he chewed thoughtfully. I studied him but discerned no order in or purpose to his frantic pace. He never relaxes, accomplishes nothing. He is a ludicrous packet of DNA, all vector and spring, a perpetual anxiety machine. Did Jesus die to redeem Sam? I will have to call that cowgirl in Appalachia and ask.

I should explain that I am punctual, systematic and efficient at my job. I work as a high level executive in the insurance empire. Policies and sales seem as distant from my realm as the stars; I handle mergers, investments and long-range planning, and the empire rewards me handsomely. My family is massively covered against all disaster. Catastrophe for us would mean financial paradise. We all know it, even Karen who asked me if she could set her room on fire so she could make enough money to buy Disneyworld. It is as if we are marooned in some mad, actuarial dream, and await a holocaust with both dread and secret longing. There is no room for slack in the empire, which may explain why I go out of my way to engineer it on the outskirts.

"Sam bothers me," I tell Mona the next morning. I have overslept and feel groggy as I fix my coffee. My eyes have grown fuzz.

"He bothers me too."

"I know why he bothers you, but I'm talking about something else. He has no purpose. How would Spinoza explain Sam?"

Mona has no interest in Spinoza. She fixes a peanut butter-and-jelly sandwich for Karen, who is mesmerized by a new video of Bugs Bunny cartoons I dubbed for her.

"Everything has a purpose," Mona says.

"Owl food," I cough. I am coughing lately. Why? I take every symptom seriously. Slack of the flesh.

Mona pours Karen's apple juice into a Star Wars cup. "It's the ragweed. I have headaches every day. There's mildew in the air."

Mona has headaches, I cough, Karen watches Bugs, Sam stores nuts in his penthouse and the cowgirl weeps.

I watch my wife pluck a bag of Fritos from the cupboard. Our cupboards bulge with artificial blessings.

"I thought we weren't letting her have chips anymore."

Mona passes the package to me, for it is impossible to tear open. I am good at tearing open the impossible. I pull on the two ends, the bag rips and Frito chips splatter all over the floor. Mona gives me her look. I unlock the Dustbuster from its casing on the wall and proceed to clean up. When Mona steps out of the room with Karen's sandwich, chips and juice, I pop a few stray Fritos into my mouth. Once food hits the floor Mona considers it contaminated and out it goes with the trash, as I agree it should. But sometimes I feel compelled to eat the contaminated food that would otherwise be tossed, especially hard, simple things like cookies, chips or candy. Sometimes I actually hope a bit of food does fall on the floor. I feel a surge of leniency, tolerance, even transcendence when dirty food treks its way into my stomach.

Mona returns to the kitchen, lugging the big vacuum cleaner behind her. We are in for some serious cleaning. She inserts the AC prong into a socket and the vacuum's roar drowns out any further speculations upon owls and gerbils.

On Sunday I find myself catching up with some business and domestic transactions I'd missed during the week because of unauthorized stretches of slack here and there. The secret of slack is accumulation. One drop of water is nothing, but a tidal wave can wipe out entire cities. One atomic particle can hardly be said to exist, but add them up and you've got a universe. Statistics is all that is the case. Conglomerates. Mergers. The ultimate Lego structure or primal sac. Which? Or both?

I need to change a washer in the basin faucet of the upstairs bathroom. It has leaked for the last six months, eroding some of the enamel. Mona and Karen have gone to get the white pound puppy at Hardee's. I unscrew the screw holding the handle of the cold water spigot to its stem, remove the valve assembly and pry off the old corroded washer. Then I hear Sam on the wheel. The grating seems louder than ever, and for a moment I fear the wheel itself has somehow worked its way loose, and Sam is spinning to freedom across the living room floor. I throw aside my tools and rush down only to find Sam rummaging about one of the penthouses.

Again, I pull up the chair and watch him. He looks at me and thrusts his splayed fingers onto the plastic as if beseeching me to respond in a way meaningful to gerbils.

I must have spent quite some time observing his antics because next thing Mona and Karen are back.

"Look, Daddy," Karen cries, "my new puppy! It's white!"

She crawls onto my lap and batters the pound puppy's head against one of Sam's walls. Mona hustles in with a bagful of fast food.

"I thought we gave up that stuff."

She picks out some French fries and inserts them into her mouth. "I couldn't resist. I'm starving. Did you do the faucet?"

"I have only begun to fix the faucet," I say, coveting her French fries. My stomach suddenly lurches with appetite.

"Jesus," Mona replies.

Does she say Jesus because of the sink or my rumbling stomach? I feel too sheepish to ask.

It is late Sunday night. We are all in bed, but as usual I am wide awake. The moment Mona's head touches a pillow, she's out. Her luck has irritated me for years. She can just shut off and then bounce back the next day. I am always groggy the next day because it takes me hours to get to sleep. I suspect Mona's luck is not luck at all; more likely it has something to do with her intolerance of slack. Perhaps there is an inverse ratio between the slack in a person's life and the ability to sleep. Because she functions smoothly, like a pristine machine, there are no loose ends to dread, no leftover hysteria, no incompleted tasks—the very substance of insomnia. I have all sorts of leftover anxieties and I complete nothing, except at work. When I close my eyes, it gets brighter. I listen to my heart beat in the pillow and slowly panic. Sometimes when I drift off, my entire body jerks violently, as if to remind me that sleep is a forbidden pleasure. The only time I sleep is at three o'clock in the afternoon, when everyone else is out mowing lawns or shopping or pouring oil into a crankcase.

At first I dream I am on the Exercycle. Then I'm in Sam's cage. I am both myself and Sam at once. A dozen or so official faces peer in at me as I root for nuts in the sawdust of Penthouse A. One face seems more official than the others, distinguished as it is by a neatly trimmed beard and moustache streaked with handsome strands of gray. It wears thick, frameless lenses. I hear the others refer to him as Dr. something or the other. I cannot concentrate for more than a few seconds at a time. The doctor intrigues me at first, then bores me. Things happen fast in the mind of a gerbil.

The doctor's face moves in closer, distorted grotesquely by ripples in the plastic wall. We behold each other, and he smiles.

"Ehhhh, what's up Doc?" I ask, surprised at the nasality of my own voice. I speak with a sprightly, rodent-like zeal.

"Hello, Sam," he asks, "how are you today?"

I scamper down a tube and station myself by the water dispenser. "How 'bout some Perrier, Doc. This tap shit cramps my style. And what's with the slammer anyway? What'd I do?"

"Well, Sam," he says, "we're here to observe your behavior. We'd like to know what makes you you. Sorry about all the plastic. It can't be helped."

I take a spin on my wheel, then rise on my hind quarters and stare him down. "Ehhhh, like, I'm lonely, Doc. Can't we arrange, you know, a little company. I'm talking romance, Doc, a nice dollface to help me get by. The French Riviera this ain't. I'm not complaining, don't get me wrong, but, you know, I've always relied on the kindness of strangers. They don't call me the King of Slack for nothing."

The doctor consults with his colleagues for a moment. His face returns, and I notice little rodent-like hairs growing out of his nose.

I miss part of the question he asks because once more I'm turning on the wheel, getting nowhere and everywhere, doing my thing and putting my all into it. "Hi Ho Siiiiilver," I cry. Then I'm sucking wildly on the water tube. Next it's burrowing through sawdust in Penthouse B. Another nut, another turn on the wheel. Everything stops and suddenly the doctor and I are connected by our eyes.

I awake from deep sleep with a total body spasm, my face and palms feverish. Our house is dry and sealed against humidity, extreme temperatures, fog, weather itself. We often arise with parched throats and dried blood caked in our nasal passages. We're always thirsty. I tear off my T-shirt and lie still on my back, a position for meditation, not sleeping. Sleep for me is a foetal enterprise all the way. I'm thinking about the thing I forgot to do. I'd meant to pay the property tax bill on our Nissan wagon. I see hands outstretched around me. Give us your money, cry the hands in unison. I reach into my pockets and clutch a small furry thing, not the wad of cash I usually carry. Sam squirms a little but soon yields. The hands close in on him.

I awake once more, this time because of the grating downstairs. I tiptoe into Karen's room, suspecting she is awake since she has inherited my insomnia. As I fix her covers her eyes pop open. "Hi," I say, but she seems still unconscious. "That dinosaur ate me," she mumbles, rolling over onto her side, smacking her lips like her mother. We have just learned that Karen is allergic to stuffed animals yet haven't the heart to remove all of them from the room. Rabbits are her favorite. The dinosaur intrigues her because it frightens her. I place a finger kiss on her puffy little lips. That the world should be a place where children are afraid enrages me. I would not have designed such a world.

The grating intensifies. Sam does not respond when I grope for the light in the room. He seems to be washing his face or scratching his whiskers. I pull up my chair. A toilet flushes upstairs. Sam's ears perk up, then quickly flatten. He eyes me suspiciously. I feel disoriented but get the distinct impression that Sam is on to something. Has he been faking it all along?

Monday is so gruesome I call in sick. I'm awake at ten which means I've had about four hours sleep. Mona and Karen are busy in the bathroom, or brafroom, as Karen says—which Mona despises. I love baby talk and secretly collect Karen's best in a company notebook. Once when I was pruning ivy off the front steps, Karen asked me what I was doing. I told her I was cutting the ivy away. "Oooh," she said, "you better not touch ivy, you might catch a radish."

Mona is chastising Karen for not standing still while she combs her hair. Karen whimpers. From what I can gather, Karen has a temperature. They drift down the stairs and into the kitchen. Mona pours out a bowlful of Cheerios and Karen picks at them until Mona threatens her. Karen becomes absorbed in her Punky Brewster cartoon and forgets to eat or drink her apple juice, which is the only juice she can stand. I appear shortly, hair tussled, bags under my eyes, wrapped in a filthy old robe. I dump my coffee directly into the perculator without measuring out the five correct tablespoons. I look for a banana—bananas are easy—and plop down next to Karen and stare at Punky.

Mona is changing the garbage bags because I forgot to change them last night. It's one of my official duties. She hates coffee grounds. I hear Sam running. I passed him on the way to the kitchen but didn't notice. "Sam," I whisper.

"What?" Karen asks, her eyes focused on the TV.

"Nothing," I say. "How are you today?"

She will say *fine* in an adorable cartoon voice.

"Fine," she says in an adorable cartoon voice.

"She's not fine," Mona calls from somewhere. "She has one-hundred-and-two degrees."

Disease too, Lord. Fears and Disease. Why the children? I don't understand, but worse, I accuse. I might, like Zeus, transform myself into a swan and take the pudgy cowgirl for a loop, but why suffer the little children? I do not grasp your rationale. Don't tell me about Jesus.

"Let me feel your head." I reach over and place my palm squarely on Karen's forehead. She is blazing, and I feel my stomach turn. I take all symptoms seriously.

"OK, little girl, after Punky, it's up to bed."

The shower revives my sagging spirit and flesh. I could stand under a hot shower all morning. I like long hot baths too, much longer than the norm, which I understand is 8.7 minutes. There is nothing like a steamy bath flowered with herbs and kelp, but the secret is timing: you must loll without distraction and always stay put longer than you should so time stops and you simply float away.

Mona interrupts my reveries with a knock on the door. She wants to know if I think a handicapped doll is a good idea for Karen's birthday.

"What sort of handicap did you have in mind?" I ask.

"Well, the blind doll comes with a cane, but the crippled one comes with a wheelchair. It's a toss up."

"I'm for blind. If the aim here is to teach Karen the fundaments of tragedy, blind is worse."

"Why is blind the worse?"

"Because eyes are more useful than legs. Would you rather see or walk?"

I expect an argument, but she is gone. I question the value of handicapped dolls but want to avoid an argument. I have an even more questionable tendency to want to shield Karen from reality.

Why do we never see blind or crippled gerbils?

What is Sam to me?

I've been in the water so long my fingers have wilted. A good sign—now I can emerge without holding a grudge against whatever it is that compels me to emerge. Vaguely, I hear the Sam-noise issuing out of the heating vent. This is nice; I'll get nothing done today.

There is a sudden commotion outside, and I am still drying myself when Mona screams and pounds at the door. I fling it open and stand dripping on the transom. Mona looks possessed, crazy.

"What is it?" I cry. "What's wrong?"

She can hardly speak. Her face has turned white as the brafroom tiles.

I'm in my clothes in no time and rush down the stairs. Karen shifts on the sofa, her eyes rolling behind the lids. A light froth bubbles at the corners of her lips, "Baby! Baby!" I wail, scooping her up in my arms and carrying her out to the car.

I must calm myself, or I will kill us all on this dismal interstate. Mona, in the back seat with Karen, is out of her head. "We'll get you that doll, honey," she murmurs. "We'll get you the crippled one, OK?" She rubs a rag wrapped around ice cubes along Karen's forehead. In the rear view I see I have not combed my hair. Mona has not only combed her hair, but Karen's as well.

The doctors in the emergency room keep her behind a screen while we wait in two aluminum chairs stationed along a wall made of construction blocks. The walls are parrot green and flawless. Fluorescent tubes in the light fixtures hum madly, like insects. My feet are cold. Mona sobs softly, and my arm does not console her. A young intern finally comes out and tells us that the convulsions have stopped. They suspect Reye's syndrome.

"But we don't give her aspirin," Mona protests.

He consults his chart. "It could be a virus. We'll probably know soon. We're running tests."

"How is she?" Mona asks.

"How will she be?" I ask.

The intern shuffles uncomfortably. "We'll have to do a scan, of course. In most cases like this, everything turns out all right. Children are very susceptible to convulsions. If you or I had one, well, that's a different story. I think your little girl will be fine."

Fine. What a superb word, the ultimate consolation. I can feel Mona and me shifting back to reality. Now it's all wait and hope, the horrible slack time after which lives are broken or repaired.

Within the week Karen is up and about, and no damage seems to have been done. We love her more than ever, shower her with presents—including the crippled doll, which she cuddles gently; we hug her passionately and cater to her every whim.

On Saturday night she sits on my lap and watches the new "Rainbow Bright" cartoon. My hand rests on her chest and I feel her heart beating. Her heart, I think, must look like a little red valentine. Rainbow is busy restoring color to a land turned arid by evil agents, so I allow my mind to drift off into the black and white zone of Forms 1040, 2106, Schedule A and Miscellaneous Deductions.

There is no real evil in "Rainbow Bright." Evil is simple ignorance, mistakes, soured personalities, lost hope. The Phantom of the Opera may have his face eaten away by acid, but Clearasil helps him swagger to the prom with confidence and élan.

Karen's body suddenly twitches in my arms. I am used to such spasms, of course, and suspect she has fallen asleep. But no—she becomes rigid, almost rocklike. Rainbow's horse Starbright gallops across the sky at the speed of light. Karen's head flings back over my arm, and once again I am seized with alarm. These are the only moments we ever really remember. I see only the whites of her eyes.

A second trip to the hospital reveals nothing new about Karen's condition. A young intern in soiled scrubs uses the word *etiology* in a tone I find ominous. Earlier in the night he had sewn up the abdomen of a man whose wife had ripped him open with a barbecue skewer.

Mona and I lean against the hard cold wall sipping coffee from styrofoam cups. I ask her if she is hungry. No, she says.

"Karen," I cry softly.

Mona tells me to stop. I am making a scene.

The hospital is awash with hums, clicks, static, rumblings, buzzes and human murmurs. People come and go with efficiency. Everyone knows what to do.

My wrist is swollen and itchy and I tear at it with my fingernails. "What's wrong now?" Mona asks.

It dawns on me that I have caught a radish.

As the days pass we notice that Karen seems to forget things too easily, her speech is a bit slurred, weird glazes subdue her eyes, which do not focus properly. Batteries of tests do indeed reveal some malfunction in the brain, enough, according to the neurosurgeon we consult, to make long-term therapy and special education mandatory. "Of course, we'll just have to wait and see," he says. "Sometimes they just outgrow these things."

They still don't know what caused my daughter's problem. A simple and elegant catastrophe had struck. One specialist believes it was a rare brain virus but no one knows for sure. As the weeks pass I watch Karen sink into an eerie lethargy; her limbs seem limp and lifeless; she tends to make some gurgling noises that leave me horrified. Mona has adjusted admirably and is busy reading shelves of literature on children with brain damage. She will devote her life to comforting the child and making her world as normal as possible. I have not adjusted. I succumb to profound depressions and erupt in violent rages when I don't have my work to distract me. I am, of course, guilty.

Slack has become a thing of the past.

Instead of heading toward my office one Friday morning, I find myself driving to the Presbyterian Church where Karen went to preschool. I park the car in front and walk steadily up the sidewalk, then turn onto the mud path that leads to an auxiliary building behind the church. All seems dream-like and destined, and I feel I am no longer in control of my actions. If I have a purpose I am no longer sure what it is. Through the window I see Karen's old class playing with stuffed animals, toy kitchen sets, Lego blocks, balls and crayons. The children look beautiful but are frightened when I fling open the door and stand gawking like a madman. Their teacher, a young girl from the neighborhood, looks equally terrified. She wears faded blue jeans and a Mickey sweat shirt, and reminds me of a girl I knew once in my distant youth, a girl I languished over for an entire summer.

"Oh, hi," she stammers. " How is Karen?"

I am obviously not supposed to be here. We stash our afflicted and are done with them.

"Where is Sam?" I demand, pushing her aside.

She recoils, screeches, but I ignore her because I spot the plastic aquarium set atop a small table and rush for it. The girl is going berserk in the background. I hear her howl in some far off place.

Neither she nor the children exist for me now. I rip off the lid of Sam's cage and reach in. He tries to scamper away, but I promptly grasp him. A chorus of wailing children engulfs me as I apply steady pressure to my grip. Sam sputters, his taut body convulses in my hand.

The girl, now a frenzied blur, tears at my arm. "Stop, stop! Sam *died*. That's Willie! I'm calling the police!"

I drop the stunned rodent onto the table; he cannot move. His eyes look dim and cold and contain nothing even remotely loveable in them. My hand feels gigantic, rock-like, and as I raise it slowly into the air, my fingers curl into a tight fist. I gaze back at the children and smile. I would like to scoop them into my arms and embrace them, protect them from all that is random, spurious and foreign. They can only try to cover their eyes when my fist comes down hard upon the beast.

Welding with Children

TIM GAUTREAUX

Tuesday was about typical. My four daughters, not a one of them married, you understand, brought over their kids, one each, and explained to my wife how much fun she was going to have looking after them again. But Tuesday was her day to go to the casino, so guess who got to tend the four babies? My oldest daughter also brought over a bed rail that the end broke off of. She wanted me to weld it. Now, what the hell you can do in a bed that'll cause the end of a iron rail to break off is beyond me, but she can't afford another one on her burger-flipping salary, she said, so I got to fix it with four little kids hanging on my coveralls. Her kid is seven months, nicknamed Nu-Nu, a big-head baby with a bubbling tongue always hanging out his mouth. My second-oldest, a flight attendant on some propeller airline out of Alexandria, has a little six-year-old girl named Moonbean, and that ain't no nickname. My third-oldest, who is still dating, dropped off Tammynette, also six, and last to come was Freddie, my favorite because he looks like those old photographs of me when I was seven, a round head with copper bristle for hair, cut about as short as Velcro. He's got that kind of papery skin like me, too, except splashed with a handful of freckles.

When everybody was on deck, I put the three oldest in front the TV and rocked Nu-Nu off and dropped him in the Portacrib. Then I dragged the bed rail and the three awake kids out through the trees, back to my tin workshop. I tried to get something done, but Tammynette got the big grinder turned on and jammed a file against the stone just to laugh at the sparks. I got the thing unplugged and then started to work, but when I was setting the bed rail in the vise and clamping on the ground wire from the welding machine, I leaned against the iron and Moonbean picked the electric rod holder off the cracker box and struck a blue arc on the zipper of my coveralls, low. I jumped back like I was hit with religion and tore those coveralls off and shook the sparks out of my drawers. Moonbean opened her goat eyes wide and sang, "Whoo. Grendaddy can bust a move." I decided I better hold off trying to weld with little kids around.

I herded them into the yard to play, but even though I got three acres, there ain't much for them to do at my place, so I sat down and watched Freddie climb on a Oldsmobile engine I got hanging from a willow oak on a long chain. Tammynette and Moonbean pushed him like he was on a swing, and I yelled at them to stop, but they wouldn't listen. It was a sad sight, I guess. I shouldn't have that old greasy engine hanging from that Kmart chain in my side yard. I know better. Even in this central Louisiana town of Gumwood, which is just like any other red-dirt place in the South, trash in the yard is trash in the yard. I make decent money as a now-and-then welder.

I think sometimes about how I even went to college once. I went a whole semester to LSU. Worked overtime at a sawmill for a year to afford the tuition and showed up in my work boots to be taught English 101 by a black guy from Pakistan who couldn't understand one word we said, much less us him. He didn't teach me a damn thing and would sit on the desk with his legs crossed and tell us to write nonstop in what he called our "portfolios," which he never read. For all I know, he sent our tablets back to Pakistan for his relatives to use as stove wood.

The algebra teacher talked to us with his eyes rolled up like his lecture was printed out on the ceiling. He didn't even know we were in the room, most of the time, and for a month I thought the poor bastard was stone-blind. I never once solved for X.

The chemistry professor was a fat drunk who heated Campbell's soup on one of those little burners and ate it out the can while he talked. There was about a million of us in that classroom, and I couldn't get the hang of what he wanted us to do with the numbers and names. I sat way in the back next to some fraternity boys who called me "Uncle Jed." Time or two, when I could see the blackboard off on the horizon, I almost got the hang of something, and I was glad of that.

I kind of liked the history professor and learned to write down a lot of what he said, but he dropped dead one hot afternoon in the middle of the pyramids and was replaced by a little porch lizard that looked down his nose at me where I sat in the front row. He bit on me pretty good because I guess I didn't look like nobody else in that class, with my short red hair and blue jeans that were blue. I flunked out that semester, but I got my money's worth learning about people that don't have hearts no bigger than bird shot.

Tammynette and Moonbean gave the engine a long shove, got distracted by a yellow butterfly playing in a clump of pigweed, and that nine-hundred-pound V-8 kind of ironed them out on the backswing. So I picked the squalling girls up and got everybody inside, where I cleaned them good with Go-Jo.

"I want a Icee," Tammynette yelled while I was getting the motor oil from between her fingers. "I ain't had a Icee all day."

"You don't need one every day, little miss," I told her.

"Don't you got some money?" She pulled a hand away and flipped her hair with it like a model on TV.

"Those things cost most of a dollar. When I was a kid, I used to get a nickel for candy, and that once twice a week."

"Icee," she yelled in my face, Moonbean taking up the cry and calling out from the kitchen in her dull little voice. She wasn't dull in the head; she just talked low, like a bad cowboy actor. Nu-Nu sat up in the Portacrib and gargled something, so I gathered everyone up, put them in the Caprice, and drove them down to the Gumwood Pak-a-Sak. The baby was in my lap when I pulled up, Freddie tuning in some rock music that sounded like hail on a tin roof. Two guys I know, older than me, watched us roll to the curb. When I turned the engine off, I could barely hear one of them say, "Here comes Bruton and his bastardmobile." I grabbed the steering wheel hard and looked down on the top of Nu-Nu's head, feeling like someone just told me my house burned down. I'm naturally tanned, so the old men couldn't see the shame rising in my face. I got out, pretending I didn't hear anything. Nu-Nu in the crook of my arm like a loaf of bread. I wanted to punch the older guy and break his upper plate, but I could see the article in the local paper. I could imagine the memories the kids would have of their grandfather whaling away at two snuff-dripping geezers. I looked them in the eye and smiled, surprising even myself. Bastardmobile. Man.

"Hey, Bruton," the younger one said, a Mr. Fordlyson, maybe sixty-five. "All them kids yours? You start over?"

"Grandkids," I said, holding Nu-Nu over his shoes so maybe he'd drool on them.

The older one wore a straw fedora and was nicked up in twenty places with skin cancer operations. He snorted. "Maybe you can do better with this batch," he told me. I remembered then that he was also a Mr. Fordlyson, the other guy's uncle. He used to run the hardwood sawmill north of town, was a deacon in the Baptist church, and owned about 1 percent of the pissant bank down next to the gin. He thought he was king of Gumwood, but then, every old man in town who had five dollars in his pocket and an opinion on the tip of his tongue thought the same.

I pushed past him and went into the Pak-a-Sak. The kids saw the candy rack and cried out for Mars Bars and Zeroes. Even Nu-Nu put out a slobbery hand toward the Gummy Worms, but I ignored their whining and drew them each a small Coke Icee. Tammynette and Moonbean grabbed theirs and headed for the door. Freddie took his carefully when I offered it. Nu-Nu might be kind of wobbleheaded and plain as a melon, but he sure knew what an Icee was and how to go after a straw. And what a smile when that Coke syrup hit those bald gums of his.

Right then, Freddie looked up at me with his green eyes in that speckled face and said, "What's a bastardmobile?"

I guess my mouth dropped open. "I don't know what you're talking about."

"I thought we was in a Chevrolet," he said.

"We are."

"Well, that man said we was in a—"

"Never mind what he said. You must have misheard him." I nudged him toward the door and we went out. The older Mr. Fordlyson was watching us like we were a parade. I was trying to look straight ahead. In my mind, the newspaper bore the headline, LOCAL MAN ARRESTED WITH GRANDCHILDREN FOR ASSAULT. I got into the car with the kids and looked back out at the Fordlysons where they sat on a bumper rail, sweating through their white shirts and staring at us all. Their kids owned sawmills, ran fast-food franchises, were on the school board. They were all married. I guess the young Fordlysons were smart, though looking at that pair, you'd never know where they got their brains. I started my car and backed out onto the highway, trying not to think, but to me the word was spelled out in chrome script on my fenders: BASTARDMOBILE.

On the way home, Tammynette stole a suck on Freddie's straw, and he jerked it away and called her something I'd only heard the younger workers at the plywood mill say. The words hit me in the back of the head like a brick, and I pulled off the road onto the gravel shoulder. "What'd you say, boy?"

"Nothing." But he reddened. I saw he cared what I thought.

"Kids your age don't use language like that."

Tammynette flipped her hair and raised her chin. "How old you got to be?"

I gave her a look. "Don't you care what he said to you?"

"It's what they say on the comedy program," Freddie said. "Everybody says that."

"What comedy program?"

"It comes on after the nighttime news."

"What you doing up late at night?"

He just stared at me, and I saw that he had no idea of what *late* was. Glendine, his mama, probably lets him fall asleep in front of the set every night. I pictured him crumpled up on that smelly shag rug his mamma keeps in front of the TV to catch the spills and crumbs.

When I got home, I took them all out on our covered side porch. The girls began to struggle with jacks, their little ball bouncing crooked on the slanted floor, Freddie played tunes on his Icee straw, and Nu-Nu fell asleep in my lap. I stared at my car and wondered if its name had spread throughout the community, if everywhere I drove people would call out, "Here comes the bastardmobile." Gumwood is one of those towns where everybody looks at everything that moves. I do it myself. If my neighbor Miss Hanchy pulls out of her lane, I wonder, Now, where is the old bat off to? It's two-thirty, so her soap opera must be over. I figure her route to the store and then somebody different will drive by and catch my attention, and I'll think after them. This is not all bad. It makes you watch how you behave, and besides, what's the alternative? Nobody giving a flip about whether you live or die? I've heard those stories from the big cities about how people will sit in an apartment window six stories up, watch somebody take ten minutes to kill you with a stick, and not even reach for the phone.

I started thinking about my four daughters. None of them has any religion to speak of. I thought they'd pick it up from their mamma, like I did from mine, but LaNelle always worked so much, she just had time to cook, clean, transport, and fuss. The girls grew up watching cable and videos every night, and that's where they got their view of the world, and that's why four dirty blondes with weak chins from St. Helena Parish thought they lived in a Hollywood soap opera. They also thought the married pulpwood truck drivers and garage mechanics they dated were movie stars. I guess a lot of what's wrong with my girls is my fault, but I don't know what I could've done different.

Moonbean raked in a gaggle of jacks, and a splinter from the porch floor ran up under her nail. "Shit dog," she said, wagging her hand like it was on fire and coming to me on her knees.

"Don't say that."

"My finger hurts. Fix it, Paw-Paw."

"I will if you stop talking like white trash."

Tammynette picked up on fivesies. "Mamma's boyfriend, Melvin, says *shit dog.*"

"Would you do everything your mamma's boyfriend does?"

"Melvin can drive," Tammynette said. "I'd like to drive."

I got out my penknife and worked the splinter from under Moonbean's nail while she jabbered to Tammynette about how her mamma's Toyota cost more than Melvin's teeny Dodge truck. I swear I don't know how these kids got so complicated. When I was their age, all I wanted to do was make mud pies or play in the creek. I didn't want anything but a twice-a-week nickel to bring to the store. These kids ain't eight years old and already know enough to run a casino. When I finished, I looked down at Moonbean's brown eyes, at Nu-Nu's pulsing head. "Does your mammas ever talk to y'all about, you know, God?"

"My mamma says *God* when she's cussing Melvin," Tammynette said.

"That's not what I mean. Do they read Bible stories to y'all at bedtime?"

Freddie's face brightened. "She rented *Conan the Barbarian* for us once. That movie kicked ass."

"That's not a Bible movie," I told him.

"It ain't? It's got swords and snakes in it."

"What's that got to do with anything?"

Tammynette came close and grabbed Nu-Nu's hand and played the fingers like they were piano keys. "Ain't the Bible full of swords and snakes?"

Nu-Nu woke up and peed on himself, so I had to go for a plastic diaper. On the way back from the bathroom, I saw our little book rack out the corner of my eye. I found my old Bible stories hardback and brought it out on the porch. It was time somebody taught them something about something.

They gathered round, sitting on the floor, and I got down amongst them. I started into Genesis and how God made the earth, and how he made us and gave us a soul that would live forever. Moonbean reached into the book and put her hand on God's beard. "If he shaved, he'd look just like that old man down at the Pak-a-Sak," she said.

My mouth dropped a bit. "You mean Mr. Fordlyson? That man don't look like God."

Tammynette yawned. "You just said God made us to look like him."

"Never mind," I told them, going on into Adam and Eve and the Garden. Soon as I turned the page, they saw the snake and began to squeal.

"Look at the size of that sucker," Freddie said.

Tammynette wiggled closer. "I knew they was a snake in this book."

"He's a bad one," I told them. "He lied to Adam and Eve and said not to do what God told them to do."

Moonbean looked up at me slow. "This snake can talk?"

"Yes."

"How about that. Just like on cartoons. I thought they was making that up."

"Well, a real snake can't talk, nowadays," I explained.

"Ain't this garden snake a real snake?" Freddie asked.

"It's the devil in disguise," I told them.

Tammynette flipped her hair. "Aw, that's just a old song. I heard it on the reddio."

"That Elvis Presley tune's got nothing to do with the devil making himself into a snake in the Garden of Eden."

"Who's Elvis Presley?" Moonbean sat back in the dust by the weatherboard wall and stared out at my overgrown lawn.

"He's some old singer died a million years ago," Tammynette told her.

"Was he in the Bible, too?"

I beat the book on the floor. "No, he ain't. Now pay attention. This is important." I read the section about Adam and Eve disobeying God, turned the page, and all hell broke loose. An angel was holding a long sword over Adam and Eve's downturned heads as he ran them out of the Garden. Even Nu-Nu got excited and pointed a finger at the angel.

"What's that guy doing?" Tammynette asked.

"Chasing them out of Paradise. Adam and Eve did a bad thing, and when you do bad, you get punished for it." I looked down at their faces and it seemed that they were all thinking about something at the same time. It was scary, the little sparks I saw flying in their eyes. Whatever you tell them at this age stays forever. You got to be careful. Freddie looked up at me and asked, "Did they ever get to go back?"

"Nope. Eve started worrying about everything and Adam had to work every day like a beaver just to get by."

"Was that angel really gonna stick Adam with that sword?" Moonbean asked.

"Forget about that darned sword, will you?"

"Well, that's just mean" is what she said.

"No it ain't," I said. "They got what was coming to them." Then I went into Noah and the Flood, and in the middle of things, Freddie piped up.

"You mean all the bad people got drownded at once? All right!"

I looked down at him hard and saw that the Bible was turning into one big adventure film for him. Freddie had already watched so many movies that any religion he would hear about would nest in his brain on top of *Tanga the Cave Woman* and *Bikini Death Squad*. I got everybody a cold drink and jelly sandwiches, and after that I turned on a window unit, handed out Popsicles, and we sat inside on the couch because the heat had waked up the yellow flies outside. I tore into how Abraham almost stabbed Isaac, and the kids' eyes got big when they saw the knife. I hoped that they got a sense of obedience to God out of it, but when I asked Freddie what the point of the story was, he just shrugged and looked glum. Tammynette, however, had an opinion. "He's just like O. J. Simpson!"

Freddie shook his head. "Naw. God told Abraham to do it just as a test."

"Maybe God told O. J. to do what he did," Tammynette sang.

"Naw. O. J. did it on his own," Freddie told her. "He didn't like his wife no more."

"Well, maybe Abraham didn't like his son no more neither, so he was gonna kill him dead and God stopped him." Tammynette's voice was starting to rise the way her mother's did when she'd been drinking.

"Daddies don't kill their sons when they don't like them," Freddie told her. "They just pack up and leave." He broke apart the two halves of his Popsicle and bit one, then the other.

Real quick, I started in on Sodom and Gomorrah and the burning of the towns full of wicked people. Moonbean was struck with Lot's wife. "I saw this movie once where Martians shot a gun at you and turned you into a statue. You reckon it was Martians burnt down those towns?"

"The Bible is not a movie," I told her.

"I think I seen it down at Blockbuster," Tammynette said.

I didn't stop to argue, just pushed on through Moses and the Ten Commandments, spending a lot of time on number six, since that one give their mammas so much trouble. Then Nu-Nu began to rub his nose with the backs of his hands and started to tune up, so I knew it was time to put the book down and wash faces and get snacks and play crawl-around. I was determined not to turn on TV again, but Freddie hit the button when I was in the kitchen. When Nu-Nu and me came into the living room, they were in a half circle around a talk show. On the set were several overweight, tattooed, frowning, slouching individuals who, the announcer told us, had tricked their parents into signing over ownership of their houses, and then evicted them. The kids watched like they were looking at cartoons, which is to say, they gobbled it all up. At a commercial, I asked Moonbean, who has the softest heart, what she thought of kids that threw their parents in the street. She put a finger in an ear and said through a long yawn that if the parents did mean things, then the kids could do what they wanted to them. I shook my head, went in the kitchen, found the Christmas vodka, and poured myself a long drink. I stared out in the yard to where my last pickup truck lay dead and rusting in a pile of wisteria at the edge of the lot. I formed a little fantasy about gathering all these kids into my Caprice and heading out northwest to start over, away from their mammas, TVs, mildew, their casino-mad grandmother, and Louisiana in general. I could get a job, raise them right, send them to college so they could own sawmills and run car dealerships. A drop of sweat rolled off the glass and hit my right shoe, and I looked down at it. The leather lace-ups I was wearing were paint-spattered and twenty years old. They told me I hadn't held a steady job in a long time, that whatever bad was gonna happen was partly my fault. I wondered then if my wife had had the same fantasy: leaving her scruffy, sunburned, failed-welder husband home and moving away with these kids, maybe taking a course in clerical skills and getting a job in Utah, raising them right, sending them off to college. Maybe even each of their mammas had the same fantasy, pulling their kids out of their parents' gassy-smelling old house and heading away from the heat and humidity. I took another long swallow and wondered why one of us didn't do it. I looked out to my Caprice sitting in the shade of a pecan tree, shadows of leaves moving on it, making it wiggle like a dark green flame, and I realized we couldn't drive away from ourselves. We couldn't escape in the bastardmobile.

In the pantry, I opened the house's circuit panel and rotated out a fuse until I heard a cry from the living room. I went in and pulled down a storybook, something about a dog chasing a train. My wife bought it twenty years ago for one of our daughters but never read it to her. I sat in front of the dark television.

"What's wrong with the TV, Paw-Paw?" Moonbean rasped.

"It died," I said, opening the book. They squirmed and complained, but after a few pages they were hooked. It was a good book, one I'd read myself one afternoon during a thunderstorm. But while I was reading, this blue feeling got me. I was thinking, What's the use? I'm just one old man with a little brown book of Bible stories and a doggy-hero book. How can that compete with daily MTV, kids' programs that make big people look like fools, the Playboy Channel, the shiny magazines their mammas and their boyfriends leave around the house, magazines like *Me,* and *Self,* and *Love Guides,* and rental movies where people kill one another with no more thought than it would take to swat a fly, nothing at all like what Abraham suffered before he raised that knife? But I read on for a half hour, and when that dog stopped the locomotive before it pulled the passenger train over the collapsed bridge, even Tammynette clapped her sticky hands.

The next day, I didn't have much on the welding schedule, so after one or two little jobs, including the bed rail that my daughter called and ragged me about, I went out to pick up a window grate the town marshal wanted me to fix. It was hot right after lunch, and Gumwood was wiggling with heat. Across from the cypress railroad station was our little redbrick city hall with a green copper dome on it, and on the grass in front of that was a pecan tree with a wooden bench next to its trunk. Old men sometimes gathered under the cool branches and told one another how to fix tractors that hadn't been made in fifty years, or how to make grits out of a strain of corn that didn't exist anymore. That big pecan was a landmark, and locals called it the "Tree of Knowledge." When I walked by going to the marshal's office, I saw the older Mr. Fordlyson seated in the middle of the long bench, blinking at the street like a chicken. He called out to me.

"Bruton," he said. "Too hot to weld?" I didn't think it was a friendly comment, though he waved for me to come over.

"Something like that." I was tempted to walk on, but he motioned for me to sit next to him, which I did. I looked across the street for a long time. "The other day at the store," I began, "you said my car was a bastardmobile."

Fordlyson blinked twice but didn't change his expression. Most local men would be embarrassed at being called down for a lack of politeness, but he sat there with his face as hard as a plowshare. "Is that not what it is?" he said at last.

I should have been mad, and I was mad, but I kept on. "It was a mean thing to let me hear." I looked down and wagged my head. "I need help with those kids, not your meanness."

He looked at me with his little nickel-colored eyes glinting under that straw fedora with the black silk hatband. "What kind of help you need?"

I picked up a pecan that was still in its green pod. "I'd like to fix it so those grandkids do right. I'm thinking of talking to their mammas and—"

"Too late for their mammas." He put up a hand and let it fall like an ax. "They'll have to decide to straighten out on their own or not at all. Nothing you can tell those girls now will change them a whit." He said this in a tone that hinted I was stupid for not seeing this. Dumb as a post. He looked off to the left for half a second, then back. "You got to deal directly with those kids."

"I'm trying." I cracked the nut open on the edge of the bench.

"Tryin' won't do shit. You got to bring them to Sunday school every week. You go to church?"

"Yeah."

"Don't eat that green pecan—it'll make you sick. Which church you go to?"

"Bonner Straight Gospel."

He flew back as though he'd just fired a twelve-gauge at the dog sleeping under the station platform across the street. "Bruton, your wild-man preacher is one step away from taking up serpents. I've heard he lets the kids come to the main service and yells at them about frying in hell like chicken parts. You got to keep them away from that man. Why don't you come to First Baptist?"

I looked at the ground. "I don't know."

The old man bobbed his head once. "I know damned well why not. You won't tithe."

That hurt deep. "Hey, I don't have a lot of extra money. I know the Baptists got good Sunday-school programs, but . . ."

Fordlyson waved a finger in the air like a little sword. "Well, join the Methodists. The Presbyterians." He pointed up the street. "Join those Catholics. Some of them don't put more than a dollar a week in the plate, but there's so many of them, and the church has so many services a weekend, the priests can run the place on volume like Wal-Mart."

I knew several good mechanics who were Methodists. "How's the Methodists' children's programs?"

The old man spoke out of the side of his mouth. "Better'n you got now."

"I'll think about it," I told him.

"Yeah, bullshit. You'll go home and weld together a log truck, and tomorrow you'll go fishing, and you'll never do nothing for them kids, and they'll all wind up serving time in Angola or on their backs in New Orleans."

It got me hot the way he thought he had all the answers, and I turned on him quick. "Okay, wise man. I came to the Tree of Knowledge. Tell me what to do."

He pulled down one finger on his right hand with the forefinger of the left. "Go join the Methodists." Another finger went down and he told me, "Every Sunday, bring them children to church." A third finger, and he said, "And keep 'em with you as much as you can."

I shook my head. "I already raised my kids."

Fordlyson looked at me hard and didn't have to say what he was thinking. He glanced down at the ground between his smooth-toe lace-ups. "And clean up your yard."

"What's that got to do with anything?"

"It's got everything to do with everything."

"Why?"

"If you don't know, I can't tell you." Here he stood up, and I saw his daughter at the curb in her Lincoln. One leg wouldn't straighten all the way out, and I could see the pain in his face. I grabbed his arm, and he smiled a mean little smile and leaned in to me for a second and said, "Bruton, everything worth doing hurts like hell." He toddled off and left me with his sour breath on my face and a thought forming in my head like a rain cloud.

After a session with the Methodist preacher, I went home and stared at the yard, then stared at the telephone until I got up the strength to call Famous Amos Salvage. The next morning, a wrecker and a gondola came down my road, and before noon, Amos loaded up four derelict cars, six engines, four washing machines, ten broken lawn mowers, and two and one-quarter tons of scrap iron. I begged and borrowed Miss Hanchy's Super-A and bush-hogged the three acres I own and then some. I cut the grass and picked up around the workshop. With the money I got from the scrap, I bought some aluminum paint for the shop and some first-class stuff for the outside of the house. The next morning, I was up at seven replacing screens on the little porch, and on the big porch on the side, I began putting down a heavy coat of glossy green deck enamel. At lunch, my wife stuck her head through the porch door to watch me work. "The kids are coming over again. How you gonna keep 'em off of all this wet paint?"

My knees were killing me, and I couldn't figure how to keep Nu-Nu from crawling where he shouldn't. "I don't know."

She looked around at the wet glare. "What's got into you, changing our religion and all?"

"Time for a change, I guess." I loaded up my brush.

She thought about this a moment, then pointed. "Careful you don't paint yourself in a corner."

"I'm doing the best I can."

"It's about time," she said under her breath, walking away.

I backed off the porch and down the steps, then stood in the pine straw next to the house, painting the ends of the porch boards. I heard a car come down the road and watched my oldest daughter drive up and get out with Nu-Nu over her shoulder. When she came close, I looked at her dyed hair, which was the color and texture of fiberglass insulation, the dark mascara, and the olive skin under her eyes. She smelled of cigarette smoke, stale smoke, like she hadn't had a bath in three days. Her tan blouse was tight and tied in a knot above her navel, which was a lardy hole. She passed Nu-Nu to me like he was a ham. "Can he stay the night?" she asked. "I want to go hear some music."

"Why not?"

She looked around slowly. "Looks like a bomb hit this place and blew everything away." The door to her dusty compact creaked open, and a freckled hand came out. "I forgot to mention that I picked up Freddie on the way in. Hope you don't mind." She didn't look at him as she mumbled this, hands on her cocked hips. Freddie, who had been sleeping, I guess, sat on the edge of the car seat and rubbed his eyes like a drunk.

"He'll be all right here," I said.

She took in a deep, slow breath, so deathly bored that I felt sorry for her. "Well, guess I better be heading on down the road." She turned, then whipped around on me. "Hey, guess what?"

"What?"

"Nu-Nu finally said his first word yesterday." She was biting the inside of her cheek. I could tell.

I looked at the baby, who was going after my shirt buttons. "What'd he say?"

"Da-da." And her eyes started to get red, so she broke and ran for her car.

"Wait," I called, but it was too late. In a flash, she was gone in a cloud of gravel dust, racing toward the most cigarette smoke, music, and beer she could find in one place.

I took Freddie and the baby around to the back steps by the little screen porch and sat down. We tickled and goo-gooed at Nu-Nu until finally he let out a "Da-da"—real loud, like a call.

Freddie looked back toward the woods, at all the nice trees in the yard, which looked like what they were now that the trash had been carried off. "What happened to all the stuff?"

"Gone," I said. "We gonna put a tire swing on that tall willow oak there, first off."

"All right. Can you cut a drain hole in the bottom so the rainwater won't stay in it?" He came close and put a hand on top of the baby's head.

"Yep."

"A big steel-belt tire?"

"Sounds like a plan." Nu-Nu looked at me and yelled, "Da-da," and I thought how he'll be saying that in one way or another for the rest of his life and never be able to face that fact that Da-da had skipped town, whoever Da-da was. The baby brought me in focus, somebody's blue eyes looking at me hard. He blew spit over his tongue and cried out, "Da-da," and I put him on my knee, facing away toward the cool green branches of my biggest willow oak.

"Even Nu-Nu can ride the tire," Freddie said.

"He can fit the circle in the middle," I told him.

Sportfishing with Cameron

NORMAN GERMAN

for Steve German

"Man, oh, man, what I wouldn't do to have one of *those* on the end of my line."

His son Randall standing beside him, Cameron gazed through the thick glass of the Gulf of Mexico tank at a school of thirty-pound redfish.

Sweeping by him with a push broom, the night custodian at the Aquarium of the Americas glanced at the cruising fish. On his next pass, he stopped and spoke in a low voice over the man's left shoulder.

"I might be able to he'p you with that."

Cameron turned. "What's that?"

"I said, I might be able to he'p you with that."

"Help me with what?"

"Catch one of those," he said, pointing with his chin.

Cameron turned to the fish, then back. "You some kind of a guide or something?"

"You might say that."

The small brown man was a mixture Cameron had never seen—Cajun, Creole, Mexican, and something else. Hindu. Or Mediterranean.

Cameron looked at the tag on his shirt. "Mr. Thales."

"Yep," the man said, touching his name with an index finger missing the last joint, "that's the way it's spelt, but it's pronounced thay-leez. Like that. thay-leez."

Cameron pulled him aside when Randall turned to watch the sawfish gliding by.

"I'll have to run my boy home first. What time should I meet you?"

"Ten-thirty," Thales said. "By that door right ch'onder." He pointed and shuffled off, trailing his broom. Then, barely audible, "And don't be late. We don't like nobody bein' late."

Cameron's wife had left him six months before. Too much drinking and too much fishing. If he had only picked one or the other, Carlee could have lived with it. But she was jealous of the neighboring women who had lost their husbands to sports like sailing or golf—the rolling fairways, the carpet-neat greens, the right to say "yacht club."

She was the only reason Cameron lived in Hammond, so he moved back to New Orleans near his cousin Steve, a fisherman and taxidermist with a weekly television show.

Since earliest boyhood, Cameron had fished with Steve all over the toe of Louisiana: Lake Ponchartrain, Golden Meadow, Delacroix, Pointe-aux-Chenes, and dozens of little slackwater, no-name bayous. But he had never caught a 30-pound redfish. His biggest was 18, and in the circles Steve ran in that barely counted as a "bull" red.

Pulling his Bondo-gray Camaro onto the parking lot, Cameron realized they had not discussed money. *As soon as he opens the door,* Cameron thought, *he'll have his hand out.*

Walking to the entrance, Cameron separated out a twenty, a ten, and some ones and stashed them in his shirt pocket. "That's all I've got," he'd tell the little man when he asked for fifty or a hundred.

But he didn't ask for a fee, didn't even speak until the two had climbed to the second-floor eye, a thick, five-foot diameter circle of glass that watched over the marine life weaving around the barnacle-encrusted legs of the fake oil derrick below.

Cameron and Thales stood over the lens. Reef sharks, manta rays, and tarpon peacefully criss-crossed at various depths in the after-hours, blue-green glow of the tank.

Pointing, Cameron said, "How much will that gar go?"

"Oh, three, fo' hundred pounds. But that ain't why we got him. That's the oldest garfish on record. Been in a tank somewheres North or South for a hundred and fifty years, since right after the Silver War."

All of the fish swam lazily about until Thales unlocked the door to the storage room, then another that gave onto an iron-grate catwalk painted caution yellow. Hearing the sound of his brogans on the footbridge spanning two crosspieces of the oil platform, the larger fish rushed to the surface, agitating the water.

Thales ladled cut and whole mullet from an orange bucket, slinging the chum out over the water. Trained to the routine, the fish went about their business with a patient ferocity.

Cameron was anxious to fish. "I imagine those reds'll need at least 25-pound test, huh?"

"My little rub-a-dub tub, as I call it, is twenty foot deep and holds half a million gallons of high-salinity H_2O." The shriveled man's bloodshot eyes looked at Cameron for the first time. "That's scientific talk for regular old seawater." Thales turned wearily and walked to the supply room like he had done it a thousand times too many.

In a corner by the life preservers stood two fishing rods Cameron had not seen on their first pass through. Thales grabbed the smaller rod as if he had never handled fishing tackle. "This one oughta be about right for tonight," he said, holding it out to Cameron.

Cameron pushed the spool-release button and let the weight spin off a few feet of line, then engaged the reel and wrapped the monofilament around his palm a couple of turns. As he pulled hard to check the drag, he watched Thales bend over the orange bucket and use his hand to chase a finger mullet around in the bloody water.

"Come on now, little friend," he chuckled, "you know it ain't no use trying to get away from old T'ales." A corner of Cameron's mind wondered why he had mispronounced his own name. When Thales jerked the hook through the mullet's back, Cameron thought, *If it were up to me, I would have punched the barb through his bottom lip, then threaded it up through a nostril.*

As if reading Cameron's mind, Thales said, "Gotta take some spunk out of the little rascal. He *too* lively, a tarpon liable to get to him 'fore a red. Now, stay here while I go downstairs and give you directions."

While he was waiting, Cameron watched the larger fish moving near the surface. The reef sharks had white tips on their dorsal fins and moved with a slow, sinister undulation. He remembered something about a shark having to constantly move water through its gills, even while sleeping, or it would drown. He wondered if these sharks were sleeping, or if the tale was even true.

"Okay," Thales said. "Lower it down to the bottom." Cameron hit the release and let the line spin off the reel while keeping slight contact with his thumb. "Now, stop it there," Thales called. "Heah they come. 'Bout ten feet away and a foot off the bottom. Lift up a bit." Cameron raised the rod tip. "Right there. Now hold steady."

Cameron felt a dull thump, and the line moved slowly away. He was used to fishing in shallow marshes, so the strike was more subtle than he expected. "Now!" Thales cried. "Drive it home!" Cameron lowered the rod while turning the handle a few rounds, then grabbed the rod just above the reel and set the hook hard.

It felt like he hooked a slow-moving boulder. Then the boulder stopped, as if asking a question, surged once, twice, and headed for home, stripping line off the reel like it was a top. Cameron laughed. The redfish made a long looping arc to the far side of the tank, then ran straight for Cameron. He reeled as fast as he could to take up the slack. When it was directly below him, Cameron saw the distorted shape of the fish heading for one of the derrick's pylons. He walked in the opposite direction down the footbridge, pulling the rod to the breaking point. Under his feet, the catwalk gave a slight shudder, and he knew the redfish had rammed the leg to cut loose on a barnacle.

A queasy feeling rushed through his stomach, like the time a nine-pound bass threw his Devil's Horse. Then the redfish turned away and the line started hissing as it sliced the surface of the water. Cameron saw it rising so he backed off the drag and gave the fish its head, knowing he could leverage him better when he reached the top.

In a couple of minutes the fish was wallowing on the surface toward Cameron, waggling his head as if to say "no, this can't be possible." Cameron pulled the rod tip up to keep the fish's head above the surface and winched him in. Ten feet away, the fish turned on its side and Cameron surfed it the rest of the way to the platform. There, Cameron's heart surged once, hard. When it struck him that he had no idea how to lift the fish the four feet onto the bridge, Thales suddenly appeared with a homemade gaff, a large hook strapped to the end of a broom handle, and expertly lipped the giant fish and hoisted him onto the grating.

"Would you look at that hump on his back," Cameron said. "Looks like a Brahma bull." The burnished bronze fish worked its mouth and lifted his tail once in slow motion.

They admired the trophy for a while. Pointing at the black sun on its tail, Thales said, "Eclipse must be the size of a silver dollar. That eye keeps the fish after it from knowing which way he's headed, you see."

Thales pulled a large white garbage bag from his back pocket like a magician producing an endless stream of handkerchiefs from his fist. He held the bag while Cameron fed the redfish into the opening headfirst. He wanted it to be in perfect shape for Steve, so he squeegeed all the air bubbles out of the bag, making it conform tightly to the fish. Then he rolled the fish over several times to wrap the remaining flag of material around its body.

Cameron stood. "Mr. Thales," he said, "I'm mighty glad I met you." Smiling big, he patted his shirt pocket. "I guess that just leaves us with your fee. How much do I owe you?"

Thales looked at him with sleepy eyes. "Whatever you think it's worth."

Cameron thought, *Well, if he's going to be that stupid.* He plucked a ten carefully from the shirt and handed it to Thales, who stuffed the bill in his back pocket without checking it. Then he turned away, almost sad, and waved a dry, leathery hand. "See you next time."

"Okay," Cameron said.

Walking to his car with the fish tucked under his arm like a huge loaf of French bread, Cameron wondered why Thales had said that, because he had no intention of returning.

Early the next morning Cameron kicked open the screen door to his cousin's taxidermy shop and walked in, cradling the white-bagged fish against his chest. There was always a small crowd in the shop, hangers-on and droppers-by drinking black coffee or straight whiskey and telling about the ones that didn't get away. Cameron knew them all. Saying nothing, Tim, a hunter with a scarred cheek from falling on a broadhead arrow, stepped aside to let him pass.

Seated behind a heavy-planked worktable, Steve, in a blood spattered white-canvas apron, was airbrushing the large caudal eye on a 40-inch redfish. Steve glanced over the top of his reading glasses. His practiced eyes scanned the white bag and guessed 44 inches. Affecting boredom, he said, "Looks like you done caught the world record boudin link."

"Ha!" Cameron said. "Boudin, my ass. Try a 30-pound red." He set the fish on the worktable with a heavy thump.

"Where'd you catch him?"

"In the water."

Nobody laughed at the old answer.

Cameron tried to outwait them, then said, "South of Lake Pontchartrain."

One of the regulars, Larry, a lanky, bearded man with a hawk nose, said, "That narrows it down to half the earth."

Finally, thinking the crew would be amazed by his exotic adventure, he said proudly, pausing at the key spot, "In the Gulf of Mexico . . . *tank* at the Aquarium of the Americas."

Steve threw his hands up and backed away like he'd heard a rattlesnake. "Are you crazy? Get that thing outa here. I could lose my license for doing that fish."

Larry eyed the fish with scorn. "Might as well be a hardhead cat for all the good it'll do you now." He spit into the clear-plastic cup he was holding. "Can't eat a redfish that size. Taste like shad."

Tim winked at Steve. "Say, I know where there's some penned-up deer you could shoot."

Dwayne, a river rat of the plaid-wearing, pot-bellied variety, threw in his two. "Hell, why go all the way to Africa for a safari when we got the Audubon Zoo right down the street? Last week me and the kids saw a lion and a . . ."

By that point, Cameron had picked up his treasure, stepped through the screen door, and slammed it on Dwayne's ridicule.

Cameron opened the door of the icebox, bent over, and squinted at the middle shelf dedicated to Busch beer. His fingers wiggled past the first three rows and grabbed a cold one. Turning the 12-ounce can in his hand, he inspected the label to make sure it wasn't one of the non-alcoholic brews he stocked for Randall.

He popped the top and slugged half of it back, then walked to the living room and fell back in the lumpy recliner covered with a dingy yellow bedspread. Staring at the blank television screen, he took a few more swallows. He pulled the TV tray closer and set his beer on it. A worn, red photo album lay open on the coffee table.

Cameron leaned forward and retrieved the book. He flipped slowly through the pages: dove, squirrel, largemouth bass and striped bass, long stringers of bluegill, two Canadian geese from his trip to Minnesota, deer, quail, redfish, limits of speckled trout, a beautiful brace of drake widgeons, woodcock, doormat-sized flounder gigged off the beaches of Grand Isle, ring-necked pheasant from his Kansas trip with Steve, an eleven-pound bass taken from Mexico's Lake Guerrero. On and on the pages went. Hundreds of pictures, thousands of stories.

Cameron closed the album and dropped it on the wobbly tray. He picked his beer up and shook it. Empty. His eyes wandered to the aquarium he and Randall had set up last summer. The 30-gallon tank held three bass—two yearlings and a three-pounder. Their gills pumped and their pectoral fins fanned as bream of assorted sizes darted around them.

It was illegal to keep game fish, but everybody did it. He had seen game wardens in bait shops and restaurants pass tanks filled with bass and white perch without batting an eye.

Cameron finished a second and carried a third beer outside to the backyard patio. He had taken the redfish from the trash bag and put it in the big white Igloo ice chest to show Randall, but he was off somewhere on his bike. The lid was still open. He looked down at his trophy. The fish was already gathering flies. Cameron shooed them away and clamped the lid down. He skidded a lounge chair across the cement into the rectangle of shade by the house. He sat and drank and thought about his fight with the big fish.

Walking into the house for number four, Cameron noticed how dark it was. There was only one working bulb in most of the ceiling fixtures. He reached in the icebox and retrieved a beer and walked back to the living room. The faint green glow of the aquarium drew him to the tank. The sediment was roiled from recent activity. The largest bass seemed agitated. As Cameron absently popped the top on his beer, the three-pounder lunged for a bluegill.

Cameron leaned over for a closer look. He laughed at the tail fluttering between the clamped lips of the bass. He shook his head and was about to take a swallow from the can. Then he thought of something. He smiled and addressed the tank. "Life's a bitch at the bottom of the food chain, huh?" He lifted his beer in salute and took a slug.

The taste was so foul he wanted it out of his mouth as fast as possible but he didn't want to blow it across the living room. His cheeks puffed out, he looked quickly back at the door, decided the aquarium was closer, and spewed the non-alcoholic brew on the face of the water.

He ran to the kitchen sink and gargled with tap water, then opened a real beer, swished the fizzing liquid around his mouth and swallowed.

Outside, the shade had receded toward the house, exposing the lounge chair to the sun. Cameron nudged it back in the shade with his shin, dropped his cap on the cement, then sank into the white and tan rubber straps. He took a few more swallows and looked into the blue and white label on the can. He tried to imagine himself on the sunny slope of the snow-capped mountains.

He leaned forward in the lounge chair, ratcheted the headrest down, and eased back, placing the cool bottom of the can on his forehead and holding it there. He imagined hunting bighorn sheep high on the mountain. He was tracking one with the biggest rack he had ever seen. He had never hunted bighorns, but it was the biggest rack he had ever seen. Each time he put the crosshairs on him, the ram ducked behind a boulder. He walked and aimed, walked and aimed, and the sun was getting hot and melting all the snow off the side of the can he was hunting on. He could see himself, very small, a moving speck on the side of the can. Then he trapped the ram on the edge of a ravine. It was an easy shot and he squeezed off three rounds. His shoulder jerked three times, and the ram fell and rolled over the edge. He heard Randall calling from down in the ravine. "Dad." It was like a question. "Dad, Dad."

"Dad, wake up," Randall repeated, poking his shoulder. "Look at this, Dad."

As Cameron awakened with a jolt, the beer slid off his forehead and hit the patio. Pouring foamy beer, the can rolled almost a full turn before Cameron was able to reach down and rescue it.

"Dad, look at this." It was bright and hot, and Cameron realized his shade had ebbed and he had fallen asleep in the sun. Through an alcoholic haze that was almost a sound, high-pitched and buzzing like locusts in the noon heat, Cameron tried to focus on the fluffy pigeon lying on its back in his son's hands. "I shot it *in the air*. I put some bread crumbs down and had a bead on him sitting on a fire hydrant and when he took off I figured what-the-heck, so I pulled the trigger and, bam, he dropped like a stone."

Cameron looked sleepily at the fat bird.

"Hell, that ain't nothing, boy. Take a look at this." He worked himself up from the lounge chair, staggered to the ice chest, and lifted the lid with a flourish. Randall stepped over and peered inside. A stale-plastic, warm-fish smell rose from the ice chest.

A white, syrupy film enveloped the once-bronze body of the redfish. A single fly was parked on the dull, exposed eye. The black eyespot on his tail was already gray.

"Wow," Randall said, "where'd you catch him?"

"Down in Eden Isles with Uncle Steve."

Randall stomped his foot. "Why didn't you take me with you?"

"I tried, but you wouldn't wake up." Cameron paused. "As usual." He knocked the lid down with a pop. "Well, maybe next time, sport." Cameron clapped his son on the back.

Randall tried again to share his own triumph. "Have *you* ever shot a flying bird with a pellet gun?"

His father looked at the pigeon. It was a splendid bird, cream-and-fuchsia with white chevrons on its wings. Its feet and dainty legs were flamingo pink.

Randall looked at the bird proudly, then looked up at his father looking at it in disgust.

"Boy, are you crazy?" he said. "What you shoot that thang for?"

The way his father said "thing" gave Randall a sick feeling in his heart.

"Well, you were the one told me flying pigeons look just like dove. Remember? That first week when we saw a flock circling the mall?"

"Yes, but I didn't say shoot 'em."

"Why can't you? They're way bigger than dove."

"Because you don't shoot pigeons," Cameron said.

"But why not?"

Cameron thought for a second. "Because that's just the way it is, that's all." The image of tourists feeding pigeons in Jackson Square popped into his mind. "They're scavengers," he said. "They ain't nothing but flying rats." He smiled drunkenly at the inspired thought and took a swig of the warm beer.

"But, Dad, it was such a great shot," the boy pleaded.

"A great shot on a rat and a great shot on a dove are two different things. Nobody cares about the rat. There's no sport to it."

Cameron told Randall to put the redfish back in the white bag and throw it in the blue trash bin at the Exxon station down the street. Then he shuffled into the house to sleep off his hangover.

In the bathroom he washed and rinsed his hands, then soaped them again and washed his face. Toweling off, he palmed his closed eyes and tried to rub away the drugged feeling. He gave out a satisfied sound and looked in the mirror. The sun had branded a white circle on his forehead where the can had rested.

Randall tore off a section of the white bag and wrapped his pigeon in it. His thinking was to store it in the freezer until his Uncle Steve visited, then sneak it to him as he was leaving so he could mount it for him.

He shoved aside some Mexican TV dinners, pulled out a quart of frozen fish, gently positioned the bird so it wouldn't lose its shape, and carefully replaced the frozen quart.

Outside, the day was humid, bright, and yellow-hot. Randall kicked the side of the ice chest, then opened the lid. As he reached for the fish, the full force of the stench hit him.

"Gah!" he said, dropping the lid as he backed away. Randall planted his hands on his hips and looked at the ice chest. He thought of gloves, but he had been around fish long enough to know that the best way to do the job was barehanded. He pressed his lips tight and shook his head and looked off toward the gas station.

To fortify himself against the sweltering, stinking task, he walked inside. He opened the icebox and closed his fingers around a can of non-alcoholic Busch, then paused. He looked over his shoulder at his father's bedroom down the darkened hall, then moved his hand over to a real Busch. He pulled the tab and took a small sip and swished it around in his mouth to get used to the taste. It reminded him of the juice from a jar of green olives. He took a larger swallow and closed his eyes against the pleasantly painful sting, then said, "Ahh!"

Randall moved his drinking into the living room. He sat on the arm of the green vinyl couch next to the aquarium and watched the fish. Half a beer later, the idea descended on him. He walked to the hall closet and moved a bass rod so he could reach his bream pole with the Zebco 33. It was already rigged with a black and red jig resembling a crawfish.

In the center of the living room, he punched the reel button, released it, and punched it again when two feet of line had played out. He rocked the lure back and forth to feel the rhythm, then pitched it underhand toward the aquarium. It hit the side of the tank and bounced on the hardwood floor. He smiled and took another swig of beer before trying again.

Cameron awoke with a dry mouth and burning thirst. When he swung his legs over the edge of the bed and sat up, it felt like a Russian weightlifter was pressing his palms against his temples. He broke into a sweat and remembered the sunburn.

Walking down the hall, he heard movement in the living room. He would get a drink of water, then see if Randall had dumped the redfish. The jug was almost to his lips when he changed his mind. He replaced the jug and picked up a beer. Double-checking the label before popping the top, he turned toward the living room. "Hair of the dog," he said, and raised the can to his lips. Over the top of the can, he saw Randall backpedal into view and set the hook. There was a loud splash, followed by some thrashing.

Cameron padded quickly down the hall. He turned the corner into the living room just in time to see Randall reach over the rim of the tank, expertly lip the three-pound bass, and lift him out.

"Son," he said as if it were an indictment. "Have you lost your mind?"

Randall looked over his shoulder. "Just a second," he said. "I gotta get him back in the tank." He draped the bass over his knee, then worked the hook loose.

A thought of self-recognition sputtered briefly in Cameron's mind. He saw the similarity, but the difference was a great one. Less water, no sharks.

When Randall dropped the fish into the aquarium, it bounded off the glass panels a few times, then settled on the bottom with its nose in a back corner.

"Now," Cameron said. "Tell me. What the hell would possess you to do such a thing?"

Randall knew he was supposed to feel bad, but he didn't. He felt anger. He thought for a moment and looked at his father.

"Boredom," he said. "There's nobody my age on this crummy block, and I wanna go fishing and you won't take me. I might as well be living with Mom."

Cameron looked at his son. "Boy, a three-pound bass ain't even picture-worthy." He lifted the photo album from the TV tray and tossed it on the couch, where it bounced once and opened. "Look in that picture book. You ain't gonna find a single shot of no bass under four pounds."

A lump grew in Randall's throat. It felt uncomfortable, a blend of anger and shame about to find release in crying and he didn't want to cry, so he defended himself carefully, hoping for his father's sympathy. "It's not like I was gonna keep him. I've caught the two yearlings four or five times and the big one twice."

Cameron looked at his boy, trying to get inside his mind and understand what would make him do something like this, but he could not penetrate that deep, so he just shook his head. "How stupid can you get."

"At least I'm smart enough to throw 'em back so I can catch 'em again." It was the beer talking now. "You, you wasted that big redfish for nothing."

In no condition to reason, Cameron spoke slowly so his son would catch the meaning of each word. "Don't fish. In the god-damned tank. Those fish are for looks, understand?"

Randall put his hands on his hips and thrust his head forward. "Well, I wouldn't have to fish in the *got*-damn tank if you'd take me with you once in a while."

Cameron flicked a backhand at his son's face, swift but not hard, and stung him on the cheek with the ends of his fingers.

"And don't curse me," he said. "Ever again. You got that, you little shit?"

Driving to the Aquarium that night, Cameron had tarpon on his mind. Aloud, he said, "That biggest one had silver scales the size of pancakes. I can't wait to see the look on their faces when I haul *that* son-of-a-bitch into the shop."

"Been expecting you," Thales said as he unlocked the door.

Cameron was anxious to get down to business. "How much?"

"'Pends on what you after tonight."

"Tarpon."

"He-*hee*." Thales rubbed his hands together. "Tarpons don't always bite at night. Let's see if you ketch one first, then talk."

In the supply room, a single large rod leaned in the corner. It was already rigged with a heavy yellow and red popper with a white feather streamer. On the footbridge Cameron cast out and retrieved. He was used to bass lures and its bulk felt awkward in the water.

"Ever caught a tarpon before?" Thales asked.

"No," Cameron said. "No, I haven't."

Thales giggled. "Keep castin', son, keep castin'. I got to finish sweeping up."

In five minutes of casting Cameron saw only one tarpon track the bait with half interest. He called down to Thales, "What am I doing wrong?"

Thales stopped his broom and watched Cameron chug the popper across the surface.

"Wait a minute, then try again," he called. "Don't jerk it, pull it. And don't wait so long between pulls." Then he went back to his work.

A minute later, Thales heard the explosion like a wave crashing against a rock, then a holler from Cameron. He paused in his cleaning to watch the action.

The tarpon made short, frantic runs, shaking his head to throw the hook. Several smaller tarpon excitedly trailed him, looking for other prey. Cameron's tarpon rose and broke the surface with half his length, shaking his gaping mouth. He fell back and drove down, then rushed the surface and breached with a glorious leap, flipping over at the peak just before his body slapped the ceiling.

Thales knew the battle was just beginning, and he had work to do, so he returned to his sweeping.

Stunned, the tarpon sank, angling down and away from the straining rod. The driving force of the tarpon, added to Cameron's weight, sagged the footbridge, but he held tight. Then there was a metallic bang and the panels of the bridge dropped like a trapdoor, spilling Cameron into the water.

He held onto the rod as the tarpon dragged him across the surface of the water, shoving saltwater up his nostrils. Then the tarpon sounded, pulling Cameron under, but he would not turn loose. The tarpon shot to the surface and jumped again in a series of spectacular, tail-walking leaps, then wrapped around a leg of the oil rig and broke loose.

Thales looked up from his broom in time to see the rod butt hit the bottom and kick up a spurt of gray chips. Then the length of the rod settled gently against the floor as if it were falling asleep.

Cameron swam and kicked toward the surface, struggling hard not to breathe. He felt the salt stinging a cut on his forearm. When he came clear, he treaded water and tried to cough out the seawater. He swiveled around to get his bearings. Twenty yards away, the broken catwalk formed two ladders leading out of the water. Cameron took the first strokes toward the bridge, then noticed a fast, gray shadow gliding beneath him. He froze. Looking down, he saw blood leaking from his wound. Then he glanced around.

Exposed above the surface of the water, the white tip on the dorsal fin sizzled toward him. Cameron couldn't remember what to do if a shark attacked—thrash the water? sit still? hit him on the nose? Or was it bear you did that to?

It would be a stupid way to die, he thought, to be eaten by a scavenger. Or were they predators? *I'll try to punch his nose. A good hit should repel him.*

But the strike was more swiftly violent than he thought it would be, like a star fullback hitting a tackling dummy. He felt his body tossed to the side like a ragdoll, then a hit in the back, followed by one from below.

Several streams of blood blossomed into a red cloud that suspended in the middle of the tank. In less than a minute, nothing was left, not even a shred of clothing. The cloud expanded in the tank, thinning to a pink fog that finally disappeared completely.

Looking on as if it were a work of art, Thales smiled, made a mental note to retrieve the rod by morning, and moved on, pushing ahead of his broom the scraps of the day.

Rich

ELLEN GILCHRIST

Tom and Letty Wilson were rich in everything. They were rich in friends because Tom was a vice-president of the Whitney Bank of New Orleans and liked doing business with his friends, and because Letty was vice-president of the Junior League of New Orleans and had her picture in *Town and Country* every year at the Symphony Ball.

The Wilsons were rich in knowing exactly who they were because every year from Epiphany to Fat Tuesday they flew the beautiful green and gold and purple flag outside their house that meant that Letty had been queen of the Mardi Gras the year she was a debutante. Not that Letty was foolish enough to take the flag seriously.

Sometimes she was even embarrassed to call the yardman and ask him to come over and bring his high ladder.

"Preacher, can you come around on Tuesday and put up my flag?" she would ask.

"You know I can," the giant black man would answer. "I been saving time to put up your flag. I won't forget what a beautiful queen you made that year."

"Oh, hush, Preacher. I was a skinny little scared girl. It's a wonder I didn't fall off the balcony I was so scared. I'll see you on Monday." And Letty would think to herself what a big phony Preacher was and wonder when he was going to try to borrow some more money from them.

Tom Wilson considered himself a natural as a banker because he loved to gamble and wheel and deal. From the time he was a boy in a small Baptist town in Tennessee he had loved to play cards and match nickels and lay bets.

In high school he read *The Nashville Banner* avidly and kept an eye out for useful situations such as the lingering and suspenseful illnesses of Pope Pius.

"Let's get up a pool on the day the Pope will die," he would say to the football team, "I'll hold the bank." And because the Pope took a very long time to die with many close calls there were times when Tom was the richest left tackle in Franklin, Tennessee.

Tom had a favorite saying about money. He had read it in the *Reader's Digest* and attributed it to Andrew Carnegie. "Money," Tom would say, "is what you keep score with. Andrew Carnegie."

Another way Tom made money in high school was performing as an amateur magician at local birthday parties and civic events. He could pull a silver dollar or a Lucky Strike cigarette from an astonished six-year-old's ear or from his own left palm extract a seemingly endless stream of multicolored silk chiffon or cause an ordinary piece of clothesline to behave like an Indian cobra.

He got interested in magic during a convalescence from German measles in the sixth grade. He sent off for books of magic tricks and practiced for hours before his bedroom mirror, his quick clever smile flashing and his long fingers curling and uncurling from the sleeves of a black dinner jacket his mother had bought at a church bazaar and remade to fit him.

Tom's personality was too flamboyant for the conservative Whitney Bank, but he was cheerful and cooperative and when he made a mistake he had the ability to turn it into an anecdote.

"Hey, Fred," he would call to one of his bosses. "Come have lunch on me and I'll tell you a good one."

They would walk down St. Charles Avenue to where it crosses Canal and turns into Royal Street as it enters the French Quarter. They would walk into the crowded, humid excitement of the quarter, admiring the girls and watching the Yankee tourists sweat in their absurd spun-glass leisure suits, and turn into the side door of Antoine's or breeze past the maitre d' at Galatoire's or Brennan's.

When a red-faced waiter in funereal black had seated them at a choice table, Tom would loosen his Brooks Brothers' tie, turn his handsome brown eyes on his guest, and begin.

"That bunch of promoters from Dallas talked me into backing an idea to video-tape all the historic sights in the quarter and rent the tapes to hotels to show on closed-circuit television. Goddamit, Fred, I could just see those fucking tourists sitting around their hotel rooms on rainy days ordering from room service and taking in the Cabildo and the Presbytere on T.V." Tom laughed delightedly and waved his glass of vermouth at an elegantly dressed couple walking by the table.

"Well, they're barely breaking even on that one, and now they want to buy up a lot of soft porn movies and sell them to motels in Jefferson Parish. What do you think? Can we stay with them for a few more months?"

Then the waiter would bring them cold oysters on the half shell and steaming pompano *en papillote* and a wine steward would serve them a fine Meursault or a Piesporter, and Tom would listen to whatever advice he was given as though it were the most intelligent thing he had ever heard in his life.

Of course he would be thinking, "You stupid, impotent son of a bitch. You scrawny little frog bastard, I'll buy and sell you before it's over. I've got more brains in my balls than the whole snotty bunch of you."

"Tom, you always throw me off my diet," his friend would say, "dammed if you don't."

"I told Letty the other day," Tom replied, "that she could just go right ahead and spend her life worrying about being buried in her wedding dress, but I didn't hustle my way to New Orleans all the way from north Tennessee to eat salads and melba toast. Pass me the French bread."

Letty fell in love with Tom the first time she laid eyes on him. He came to Tulane on a football scholarship and charmed his way into a fraternity of wealthy New Orleans boys famed for its drunkenness and its wild practical jokes. It was the same old story. Even the second, third, and fourth generation blue bloods of New Orleans need an infusion of new genes now and then.

The afternoon after Tom was initiated he arrived at the fraternity house with two Negro painters and sat in the low-hanging branches of a live oak tree overlooking Henry Clay Avenue directing them in painting an official-looking yellow-and-white-striped pattern on the street in front of the property. "D-R-U-N-K," he yelled to his painters, holding on to the enormous limb with one hand and pushing his black hair out of his eyes with the other. "Paint it to say D-R-U-N-K Z-O-N-E."

Letty stood near the tree with a group of friends watching him. He was wearing a blue shirt with the sleeves rolled up above his elbows, and a freshman beanie several sizes too small was perched on his head like a tipsy sparrow.

"I'm wearing this goddamn beanie forever," Tom yelled. "I'm wearing this beanie until someone brings me a beer," and Letty took the one she was holding and walked over to the tree and handed it to him.

One day a few weeks later, he commandeered a Bunny Bread truck while it was parked outside the fraternity house making a delivery. He picked up two friends and drove the truck madly around the Irish Channel, throwing fresh loaves of white and whole-wheat and rye bread to the astonished housewives.

"Steal from the rich, give to the poor," Tom yelled, and his companions gave up trying to reason with him and helped him yell.

"Free bread, free cake," they yelled, handing out powdered doughnuts and sweet rolls to a gang of kids playing baseball on a weed-covered vacant lot.

They stopped off at Darby's, an Irish bar where Tom made bets on races and football games, and took on some beer and left off some cinnamon rolls.

"Tom, you better go turn that truck in before they catch you," Darby advised, and Tom's friends agreed, so they drove the truck to the second-precinct police headquarters and turned themselves in. Tom used up half a year's allowance paying the damages, but it made his reputation.

In Tom's last year at Tulane a freshman drowned during a hazing accident at the Southern Yacht Club, and the event frightened Tom. He had never liked the boy and had suspected him of being involved with the queers and nigger lovers who hung around the philosophy department and the school newspaper. The boy had gone to prep school in the East and brought weird-looking girls to rush parties. Tom had resisted the temptation to blackball him as he was well connected in uptown society.

After the accident, Tom spent less time at the fraternity house and more time with Letty, whose plain sweet looks and expensive clothes excited him.

"I can't go in the house without thinking about it," he said to Letty. "All we were doing was making them swim from pier to pier carrying martinis. I did it fifteen times the year I pledged."

"He should have told someone he couldn't swim very well," Letty answered. "It was an accident. Everyone knows it was an accident. It wasn't your fault." And Letty cuddled up close to him on the couch, breathing as softly as a cat.

Tom had long serious talks with Letty's mild, alcoholic father, who held a seat on the New York Stock Exchange, and in the spring of the year Tom and Letty were married in the Cathedral of Saint Paul with twelve bridesmaids, four flower girls, and seven hundred guests. It was pronounced a marriage made in heaven, and Letty's mother ordered masses said in Rome for their happiness.

They flew to New York on the way to Bermuda and spent their wedding night at the Sherry Netherland Hotel on Fifth Avenue. At least half a dozen of Letty's friends had lost their virginity at the same address, but the trip didn't seem prosaic to Letty.

She stayed in the bathroom a long time gazing at her plain face in the oval mirror and tugging at the white lace nightgown from the Lylian Shop, arranging it now to cover, now to reveal her small breasts. She crossed herself in the mirror, suddenly giggled, then walked out into the blue and gold bedroom as though she had been going to bed with men every night of her life. She had been up until three the night before reading a book on sexual intercourse. She offered her small unpainted mouth to Tom. Her pale hair smelled of Shalimar and carnations and candles. Now she was safe. Now life would begin.

"Oh, I love you. I love, I love, I love you," she whispered over and over. Tom's hands touching her seemed a strange and exciting passage that would carry her simple dreamy existence to a reality she had never encountered. She had never dreamed anyone so interesting would marry her.

Letty's enthusiasm and her frail body excited him, and he made love to her several times before he asked her to remove her gown.

The next day they breakfasted late and walked for a while along the avenue. In the afternoon Tom explained to his wife what her clitoris was and showed her some of the interesting things it was capable of generating, and before the day was out Letty became the first girl in her crowd to break the laws of God and the Napoleonic Code by indulging in oral intercourse.

Fourteen years went by and the Wilsons' luck held. Fourteen years is a long time to stay lucky even for rich people who don't cause trouble for anyone.

Of course, even among the rich there are endless challenges, unyielding limits, rivalry, envy, quirks of fortune. Letty's father grew increasingly incompetent and sold his seat on the exchange, and Letty's irresponsible brothers went to work throwing away the money in Las Vegas and L.A. and Zurich and Johannesburg and Paris and anywhere they could think of to fly to with their interminable strings of mistresses.

Tom envied them their careless, thoughtless lives and he was annoyed that they controlled their own money while Letty's was tied up in some mysterious trust, but he kept his thoughts to himself as he did his obsessive irritation over his growing obesity.

"Looks like you're putting on a little weight there," a friend would observe.

"Good, good," Tom would say, "makes me look like a man. I got a wife to look at if I want to see someone who's skinny."

He stayed busy gambling and hunting and fishing and being the life of the party at the endless round of dinners and cocktail parties and benefits and Mardi Gras functions that consume the lives of the Roman Catholic hierarchy that dominates the life of the city that care forgot.

Letty was preoccupied with the details of their domestic life and her work in the community. She took her committees seriously and actually believed that the work she did made a difference in the lives of other people.

The Wilsons grew rich in houses. They lived in a large Victorian house in the Garden District, and across Lake Ponchartrain they had another Victorian house to stay in on the weekends, with a private beach surrounded by old moss-hung oak trees. Tom bought a duck camp in Plaquemines Parish and kept an apartment in the French Quarter in case one of his business friends fell in love with his secretary and needed someplace to be alone with her. Tom almost never used the apartment himself. He was rich in being satisfied to sleep with his own wife.

The Wilsons were rich in common sense. When five years of a good Catholic marriage went by and Letty inexplicably never became pregnant, they threw away their thermometers and ovulation charts and litmus paper and went down to the Catholic adoption agency and adopted a baby girl with curly black hair and hazel eyes. Everyone declared she looked exactly like Tom. The Wilsons named the little girl Helen and, as the months went by, everyone swore she even walked and talked like Tom.

About the same time Helen came to be the Wilsons' little girl, Tom grew interested in raising Labrador retrievers. He had large wire runs with concrete floors built in the side yard for the dogs to stay in when he wasn't training them on the levee or at the park lagoon. He used all the latest methods of training Labs, including an electric cattle prod given to him by Chalin Perez himself and live ducks supplied by a friend on the Audubon Park Zoo Association Committee.

"Watch this, Helen," he would call to the little girl in the stroller, "watch this." And he would throw a duck into the lagoon with its secondary feathers neatly clipped on the left side and its feet tied loosely together, and one of the Labs would swim out into the water and carry it safely back and lay it at his feet.

As so often happens when childless couples are rich in common sense, before long Letty gave birth to a little boy, and then to twin boys, and finally to another little Wilson girl. The Wilsons became so rich in children the neighbors all lost count.

"Tom," Letty said, curling up close to him in the big walnut bed, "Tom, I want to talk to you about something important." The new baby girl was three months old. "Tom I want to talk to Father Delahoussaye and ask him if we can use some birth control. I think we have all the children we need for now."

Tom put his arms around her and squeezed her until he wrinkled her new green linen B. H. Wragge, and she screamed for mercy.

"Stop it," she said, "be serious. Do you think it's all right to do that?"

Then Tom agreed with her that they had had all the luck with children they needed for the present, and Letty made up her mind to call the cathedral and make an appointment. All her friends were getting dispensations so they would have time to do their work at the Symphony League and the Thrift Shop and the New Orleans Museum Association and the PTAs of the private schools.

All the Wilson children were in good health except Helen. The pediatricians and psychiatrists weren't certain what was wrong with Helen. Helen couldn't concentrate on anything. She didn't like to share and she went through stages of biting other children at the Academy of the Sacred Heart of Jesus.

The doctors decided it was a combination of prenatal brain damage and dyslexia, a complicated learning disability that is a fashionable problem with children in New Orleans.

Letty felt like she spent half her life sitting in offices talking to people about Helen. The office she sat in most often belonged to Dr. Zander. She sat there twisting her rings and avoiding looking at the box of Kleenex on Dr. Zander's desk. It made her feel like she was sleeping in a dirty bed even to think of plucking a Kleenex from Dr. Zander's container and crying in a place where strangers cried. She imagined his chair was filled all day with women weeping over terrible and sordid things like their husbands running off with their secretaries or their children not getting into the right clubs and colleges.

"I don't know what we're going to do with her next," Letty said. "If we let them hold her back a grade it's just going to make her more self-conscious than ever."

"I wish we knew about her genetic background. You people have pull with the sisters. Can't you find out?"

"Tom doesn't want to find out. He says we'll just be opening a can of worms. He gets embarrassed even talking about Helen's problem."

"Well," said Dr. Zander, crossing his short legs and settling his steel-rimmed glasses on his nose like a tiny bicycle stuck on a hill, "let's start her on Dexedrine."

So Letty and Dr. Zander and Dr. Mullins and Dr. Pickett and Dr. Smith decided to try an experiment. They decided to give Helen five milligrams of Dexedrine every day for twenty days each month, taking her off the drug for ten days in between.

"Children with dyslexia react to drugs strangely," Dr. Zander said. "If you give them tranquilizers it peps them up, but if you give them Ritalin or Dexedrine it calms them down and makes them able to think straight."

"You may have to keep her home and have her tutored on the days she is off the drug," he continued, "but the rest of the time she should be easier to live with." And he reached over and patted Letty on the leg and for a moment she thought it might all turn out all right after all.

Helen stood by herself on the playground of the beautiful old pink-brick convent with its drooping wrought-iron balconies covered with ficus. She was watching the girl she liked talking with some other girls who were playing jacks. All the little girls wore blue-and-red-plaid skirts and navy blazers or sweaters. They looked like a disorderly marching band. Helen was waiting for the girl, whose name was Lisa, to decide if she wanted to go home with her after school and spend the afternoon. Lisa's mother was divorced and worked downtown in a department store, so Lisa rode the streetcar back and forth from school and could go anywhere she liked until 5:30 in the afternoon. Sometimes she went home with Helen so she wouldn't have to ride the streetcar. Then Helen would be so excited the hours until school let out would seem to last forever.

Sometimes Lisa liked her and wanted to go home with her and other times she didn't but she was always nice to Helen and let her stand next to her in lines.

Helen watched Lisa walking toward her. Lisa's skirt was two inches shorter than those of any of the other girls, and she wore high white socks that made her look like a skater. She wore a silver identification bracelet and Revlon nail polish.

"I'll go home with you if you get your mother to take us to get an Icee," Lisa said. "I was going last night but my mother's boyfriend didn't show up until after the place closed so I was going to walk to Manny's after school. Is that O.K.?"

"I think she will," Helen said, her eyes shining. "I'll go call her up and see."

"Naw, let's just go swing. We can ask her when she comes." Then Helen walked with her friend over to the swings and tried to be patient waiting for her turn.

The Dexedrine helped Helen concentrate and it helped her get along better with other people, but it seemed to have an unusual side effect. Helen was chubby and Dr. Zander had led the Wilsons to believe the drug would help her lose weight, but instead she grew even fatter. The Wilsons were afraid to force her to stop eating for fear they would make her nervous, so they tried to reason with her.

"Why can't I have any ice cream?" she would say. "Daddy is fat and he eats all the ice cream he wants." She was leaning up against Letty, stroking her arm and petting the baby with her other hand. They were in an upstairs sitting room with the afternoon sun streaming in through the French windows. Everything in the room was decorated with different shades of blue, and the curtains were white and old-fashioned blue-and-white-checked ruffles.

"You can have ice cream this evening after dinner," Letty said, "I just want you to wait a few hours before you have it. Won't you do that for me?"

"Can I hold the baby for a while?" Helen asked, and Letty allowed her to sit in the rocker and hold the baby and rock it furiously back and forth crooning to it.

"Is Jennifer beautiful, Mother?" Helen asked.

"She's O.K., but she doesn't have curly black hair like you. She just has plain brown hair. Don't you see, Helen, that's why we want you stop eating between meals, because you're so pretty and we don't want you to get too fat. Why don't you go outside and play with Tim and try not to think about ice cream so much?"

"I don't care," Helen said, "I'm only nine years old and I'm hungry. I want you to tell the maids to give me some ice cream now," and she handed the baby to her mother and ran out of the room.

The Wilsons were rich in maids, and that was a good thing because there were all those children to be taken care of and cooked for and cleaned up after. The maids didn't mind taking care of the Wilson children all day. The Wilsons' house was much more comfortable than the ones they lived in, and no one cared whether they worked very hard or not as long as they showed up on time so Letty could get to her meetings. The maids left their own children with relatives or at home watching television, and when they went home at night they liked them much better than if they had spent the whole day with them.

The Wilson house had a wide white porch across the front and down both sides. It was shaded by enormous oak trees and furnished with swings and wicker rockers. In the afternoons the maids would sit on the porch and other maids from around the neighborhood would come up pushing prams and strollers and the children would all play together on the porch and in the yard. Sometimes the maids fixed lemonade and the children would sell it to passersby from a little stand.

The maids hated Helen. They didn't care whether she had dyslexia or not. All they knew was that she was a lot of trouble to take care of. One minute she would be as sweet as pie and cuddle up to them and say she loved them and the next minute she wouldn't do anything they told her.

"You're a nigger, nigger, nigger, and my mother said I could cross St. Charles Avenue if I wanted to," Helen would say, and the maids would hold their lips together and look into each other's eyes.

One afternoon the Wilson children and their maids were sitting on the porch after school with some of the neighbors' children and maids. The baby was on the porch in a bassinet on wheels and a new maid was looking out for her. Helen was in the biggest swing and was swinging as high as she could go so that none of the other children could get in the swing with her.

"Helen," the new maid said, "it's Tim's turn in the swing. You been swinging for fifteen minutes while Tim's been waiting. You be a good girl now and let Tim have a turn. You too big to act like that."

"You're just a high yeller nigger," Helen called, "and you can't make me do anything." And she swung up higher and higher.

This maid had never had Helen call her names before and she had a quick temper and didn't put up with children calling her a nigger. She walked over to the swing and grabbed the chain and stopped it from moving.

"You say you're sorry for that, little fat honky white girl," she said, and made as if to grab Helen by the arms, but Helen got away and started running, calling over her shoulder, "nigger, can't make me do anything."

She was running and looking over her shoulder and she hit the bassinet and it went rolling down the brick stairs so fast none of the maids or children could stop it. It rolled down the stairs and threw the baby onto the sidewalk and the blood from the baby's head began to move all over the concrete like a little ruby lake.

The Wilsons' house was on Philip Street, a street so rich it even had its own drugstore. Not some tacky chain drugstore with everything on special all the time, but a cute drugstore made out of a frame bungalow with gingerbread trim. Everything inside cost twice as much as it did in a regular drugstore, and the grown people could order any kind of drugs they needed and a green Mazda pickup would bring them right over. The children had to get their drugs from a fourteen-year-old pusher in Audubon Park named Leroi, but they could get all the ice cream and candy and chewing gum they wanted from the drugstore and charge it to their parents.

No white adults were at home in the houses where the maids worked so they sent the children running to the drugstore to bring the druggist to help with the baby. They called the hospital and ordered an ambulance and they called several doctors and they called Tom's bank. All the children who were old enough ran to the drugstore except Helen. Helen sat on the porch steps staring down at the baby with the maids hovering over it like swans, and she was crying and screaming and beating her hands against her head. She was in one of the periods when she couldn't have Dexedrine. She screamed and screamed, but none of the maids had time to help her. They were too busy with the baby.

"Shut up, Helen," one of the maids called. "Shut up that goddamn screaming. This baby is about to die."

A police car and the local patrol service drove up. An ambulance arrived and the yard filled with people. The druggist and one of the maids rode off in the ambulance with the baby. The crowd in the yard swarmed and milled and swam before Helen's eyes like a parade.

Finally they stopped looking like people and just looked like spots of color on the yard. Helen ran up the stairs and climbed under her cherry four-poster bed and pulled her pillows and her eiderdown comforter under it with her. There were cereal boxes and an empty ice cream carton and half a tin of English cookies under the headboard. Helen was soaked with sweat and her little Lily playsuit was tight under the arms and cut into her flesh. Helen rolled up in the comforter and began to dream the dream of the heavy clouds. She dreamed she was praying, but the beads of the rosary slipped through her fingers so quickly she couldn't catch them and it was cold in the church and beautiful and fragrant, then dark, then light, and Helen was rolling in the heavy clouds that rolled her like biscuit dough. Just as she was about to suffocate they rolled her face up to the blue air above the clouds. Then Helen was a pink kite floating above the houses at evening. In the yards children were playing and fathers were driving up and baseball games were beginning and the sky turned gray and closed upon the city like a lid.

And now the baby is alone with Helen in her room and the door is locked and Helen ties the baby to the table so it won't fall off.

"Hold still, Baby, this will just be a little shot. This won't hurt much. This won't take a minute." And the baby is still and Helen begins to work on it.

Letty knelt down beside the bed. "Helen, please come out from under there. No one is mad at you. Please come out and help me, Helen. I need you to help me."

Helen held on tighter to the slats of the bed and squeezed her eyes shut and refused to look at Letty.

Letty climbed under the bed to touch the child. Letty was crying and her heart had an anchor in it that kept digging in and sinking deeper and deeper.

Dr. Zander came into the bedroom and knelt beside the bed and began to talk to Helen. Finally he gave up being reasonable and wiggled his small gray-suited body under the bed and Helen was lost in the area of arms that tried to hold her.

Tom was sitting in the bank president's office trying not to let Mr. Saunders know how much he despised him or how much it hurt and mattered to him to be listening to a lecture. Tom thought he was too old to have to listen to lectures. He was tired and he wanted a drink and he wanted to punch the bastard in the face.

"I know, I know," he answered, "I can take care of it. Just give me a month or two. You're right. I'll take care of it."

And he smoothed the pants of his cord suit and waited for the rest of the lecture.

A man came into the room without knocking. Tom's secretary was behind him.

"Tom, I think your baby has had an accident. I don't know any details. Look, I've called for a car. Let me go with you."

Tom ran up the steps of his house and into the hallway full of neighbors and relatives. A girl in a tennis dress touched him on the arm, someone handed him a drink. He ran up the winding stairs to Helen's room. He stood in the doorway. He could see Letty's shoes sticking out from under the bed. He could hear Dr. Zander talking. He couldn't go near them.

"Letty," he called, "Letty, come here, my god, come out from there."

No one came to the funeral but the family. Letty wore a plain dress she would wear any day and the children all wore their school clothes.

The funeral was terrible for the Wilsons, but afterward they went home and all the people from the Garden District and from all over town started coming over to cheer them up. It looked like the biggest cocktail party ever held in New Orleans. It took four rented butlers just to serve the drinks. Everyone wanted to get in on the Wilsons' tragedy.

In the months that followed the funeral Tom began to have sinus headaches for the first time in years. He was drinking a lot and smoking again. He was allergic to whiskey, and when he woke up in the morning his nose and head were so full of phlegm he had to vomit before he could think straight.

He began to have trouble with his vision.

One November day the high yellow windows of the Shell Oil Building all turned their eyes upon him as he stopped at the corner of Poydras and Carondelet to wait for a streetlight, and he had to pull the car over to a curb and talk to himself for several minutes before he could drive on.

He got back all the keys to his apartment so he could go there and be alone and think. One afternoon he left work at two o'clock and drove around Jefferson Parish all afternoon drinking Scotch and eating potato chips.

Not as many people at the bank wanted to go out to lunch with him anymore. They were sick and tired of pretending his expensive mistakes were jokes.

One night Tom was gambling at the Pickwick Club with a poker group and a man jokingly accused him of cheating. Tom jumped up from the table, grabbed the man and began hitting him with his fists. He hit the man in the mouth and knocked out his new gold inlays.

"You dirty little goddamn bond peddler, you son of a bitch! I'll kill you for that," Tom yelled, and it took four waiters to hold him while the terrified man made his escape. The next morning Tom resigned from the club.

He started riding the streetcar downtown to work so he wouldn't have to worry about driving his car home if he got drunk. He was worrying about money and he was worrying about his gambling debts, but most of the time he was thinking about Helen. She looked so much like him that he believed people would think she was his illegitimate child. The more he tried to talk himself into believing the baby's death was an accident, the more obstinate his mind became.

The Wilson children were forbidden to take the Labs out of the kennels without permission. One afternoon Tom came home earlier than usual and found Helen sitting in the open door of one of the kennels playing with a half-grown litter of puppies. She was holding one of the puppies and the others were climbing all around her and spilling out onto the grass. She held the puppy by its forelegs, making it dance in the air, then letting it drop. Then she would gather it in her arms and hold it tight and sing to it.

Tom walked over to the kennel and grabbed her by an arm and began to paddle her as hard as he could.

"Goddamn you, what are you trying to do? You know you aren't supposed to touch those dogs. What in the hell do you think you're doing?"

Helen was too terrified to scream. The Wilsons never spanked their children for anything.

"I didn't do anything to it. I was playing with it," she sobbed.

Letty and the twins came running out of the house and when Tom saw Letty he stopped hitting Helen and walked in through the kitchen door and up the stairs to the bedroom. Letty gave the children to the cook and followed him.

Tom stood by the bedroom window trying to think of something to say to Letty. He kept his back turned to her and he was making a nickel disappear with his left hand. He thought of himself at Tommie Keenen's birthday party wearing his black coat and hat and doing his famous rope trick. Mr. Keenen had given him fifteen dollars. He remembered sticking the money in his billfold.

"My god, Letty, I'm sorry. I don't know what the shit's going on. I thought she was hurting the dog. I know I shouldn't have hit her and there's something I need to tell you about the bank. Kennington is getting sacked. I may be part of the house-cleaning."

"Why didn't you tell me before? Can't Daddy do anything?"

"I don't want him to do anything. Even if it happens it doesn't have anything to do with me. It's just bank politics. We'll say I quit. I want to get out of there anyway. That fucking place is driving me crazy."

Tom put the nickel in his pocket and closed the bedroom door. He could hear the maid down the hall comforting Helen. He didn't give a fuck if she cried all night. He walked over to Letty and put his arms around her. He smelled like he'd been drinking for a week. He reached under her dress and pulled down her pantyhose and her underpants and began kissing her face and hair while she stood awkwardly with the pants and hose around her feet like a halter. She was trying to cooperate.

She forgot that Tom smelled like sweat and whiskey. She was thinking about the night they were married. Every time they made love Letty pretended it was as that night. She had spent thousands of nights in a bridal suite at the Sherry Netherland Hotel in New York.

Letty lay on the walnut bed leaning into a pile of satin pillows and twisting a gold bracelet around her wrist. She could hear the children playing outside. She had a headache and her stomach was queasy, but she was afraid to take a Valium or an aspirin. She was waiting for the doctor to call her back and tell her if she was pregnant. She already knew what he was going to say.

Tom came into the room and sat by her on the bed.

"What's wrong?"

"Nothing's wrong. Please don't do that. I'm tired."

"Something's wrong."

"Nothing's wrong. Tom, please leave me alone."

Tom walked out through the French windows and onto a little balcony that overlooked the play yard and the dog runs. Sunshine flooded Philip Street, covering the houses and trees and dogs and children with a million volts a minute. It flowed down to hide in the roots of trees, glistening on the cars, baking the street, and lighting Helen's rumpled hair where she stooped over the puppy. She was singing a little song. She had made up the song she was singing.

"The baby's dead. The baby's dead. The baby's gone to heaven."

"Jesus God," Tom muttered. All up and down Philip Street fathers were returning home from work. A jeep filled with teenagers came tearing past and threw a beer can against the curb.

Six or seven pieces of Tom's mind sailed out across the street and stationed themselves along the power line that zigzagged back and forth along Philip Street between the live oak trees.

The pieces of his mind sat upon the power line like a row of black starlings. They looked him over.

Helen took the dog out of the buggy and dragged it over to the kennel.

"Jesus Christ," Tom said, and the pieces of his mind flew back to him as swiftly as they had flown away and entered his eyes and ears and nostrils and arranged themselves in their proper places like parts of a phrenological head.

Tom looked at his watch. It said 6:15. He stepped back into the bedroom and closed the French windows. A vase of huge roses from the garden hid Letty's reflection in the mirror.

"I'm going to the camp for the night. I need to get away. Besides, the season's almost over."

"All right," Letty answered. "Who are you going with?"

"I think I'll take Helen with me. I haven't paid any attention to her for weeks."

"That's good," Letty said, "I really think I'm getting a cold. I'll have a tray up for supper and try to get some sleep."

Tom moved around the room, opening drawers and closets and throwing some gear into a canvas duffel bag. He changed into his hunting clothes.

He removed the guns he needed from a shelf in the upstairs den and cleaned them neatly and thoroughly and zipped them into their carriers.

"Helen," he called from the downstairs porch. "Bring the dog in the house and come get on some play clothes. I'm going to take you to the duck camp with me. You can take the dog."

"Can we stop and get beignets?" Helen called back, coming running at the invitation.

"Sure we can, honey. Whatever you like. Go get packed. We'll leave as soon as dinner is over."

It was past 9:00 at night. They crossed the Mississippi River from the New Orleans side on the last ferry going to Algier's Point. There was an offshore breeze and a light rain fell on the old brown river. The Mississippi River smelled like the inside of a nigger cabin, powerful and fecund. The smell came in Tom's mouth until he felt he could chew it.

He leaned over the railing and vomited. He felt better and walked back to the red Chevrolet pickup he had given himself for a birthday present. He thought it was chic for a banker to own a pickup.

Helen was playing with the dog, pushing him off the seat and laughing when he climbed back on her lap. She had a paper bag of doughnuts from the French Market and was eating them and licking the powdered sugar from her fingers and knocking the dog off the seat.

She wasn't the least bit sleepy.

"I'm glad Tim didn't get to go. Tim was bad at school, that's why he had to stay home, isn't it? The sisters called Momma. I don't like Tim. I'm glad I got to go by myself." She stuck her fat arms out the window and rubbed Tom's canvas hunting jacket. "This coat feels hard. It's all dirty. Can we go up in the cabin and talk to the pilot?"

"Sit still, Helen."

"Put the dog in the back, he's bothering me." She bounced up and down on the seat. "We're going to the duck camp. We're going to the duck camp."

The ferry docked. Tom drove the pickup onto the blacktop road past the city dump and on into Plaquemines Parish.

They drove into the brackish marshes that fringe the Gulf of Mexico where it extends in ragged fingers along the coast below and to the east of New Orleans. As they drove closer to the sea the hardwoods turned to palmetto and water oak and willow.

The marshes were silent. Tom could smell the glasswort and black mangrove, the oyster and shrimp boats.

He wondered if it were true that children and dogs could penetrate a man's concealment, could know him utterly.

Helen leaned against his coat and prattled on.

In the Wilson house on Philip Street Tim and the twins were cuddled up by Letty, hearing one last story before they went to bed.

A blue wicker tray held the remains of the children's hot chocolate. The china cups were a confirmation present sent to Letty from Limoges, France.

Now she was finishing reading a wonderful story by Ludwig Bemelmans about a little convent girl in Paris named Madeline who reforms the son of the Spanish ambassador, putting an end to his terrible habit of beheading chickens on a miniature guillotine.

Letty was feeling better. She had decided God was just trying to make up to her for Jennifer.

The camp was a three-room wooden shack built on pilings out over Bayou Lafouche, which runs through the middle of the parish.

The inside of the camp was casually furnished with old leather office furniture, hand-me-down tables and lamps, and a walnut poker table from Neiman-Marcus. Photographs of hunts and parties were tacked around the walls. Over the poker table were pictures of racehorses and their owners and an assortment of ribbons won in races.

Tom laid the guns down on the bar and opened a cabinet over the sink in the part of the room that served as a kitchen. The nigger hadn't come to clean up after the last party and the sink was piled with half-washed dishes. He found a clean glass and a bottle of Tanqueray gin and sat down behind the bar.

Helen was across the room on the floor finishing the beignets and trying to coax the dog to come closer. He was considering it. No one had remembered to feed him.

Tom pulled a new deck of cards out of a drawer, broke the seal, and began to shuffle them.

Helen came and stood by the bar. "Show me a trick, Daddy. Make the queen disappear. Show me how to do it."

"Do you promise not to tell anyone the secret? A magician never tells his secrets."

"I won't tell, Daddy, please show me, show me now."

Tom spread out the cards. He began to explain the trick.

"All right, you go here and here, then here. Then pick up these in just the right order, but look at the people while you do it, not at the cards."

"I'm going to do it for Lisa."

"She's going to beg you to tell the secret. What will you do then?"

"I'll tell her a magician never tells his secrets."

Tom drank the gin and poured some more.

"Now let me do it to you, Daddy."

"Not yet, Helen. Go sit over there with the dog and practice it where I can't see what you're doing. I'll pretend I'm Lisa and don't know what's going on."

Tom picked up the Kliengunther 7 mm. Magnum rifle and shot the dog first, splattering its brains all over the door and walls. Without pausing, without giving her time to raise her eyes from the red and gray and black rainbow of the dog, he shot the little girl.

The bullet entered her head from the back. Her thick body rolled across the hardwood floor and lodged against a hat rack from Jody Mellon's old office in the Hibernia Bank Building. One of her arms landed on a pile of old *Penthouse* magazines and her disordered brain flung its roses north and east and south and west and rejoined the order from which it casually arose.

Tom put down the rifle, took a drink of the thick gin, and, carrying the pistol, walked out onto the pier through the kitchen door. Without removing his glasses or his hunting cap he stuck the .38 Smith and Wesson revolver against his palate and splattered his own head all over the new pier and the canvas covering of the Boston Whaler. His body struck the boat going down and landed in eight feet of water beside a broken crab trap left over from the summer.

A pair of deputies from the Plaquemines Parish sheriff's office found the bodies.

Everyone believed it was some terrible inexplicable mistake or accident.

No one believed that much bad luck could happen to a nice lady like Letty Dufrechou Wilson, who never hurt a flea or gave anyone a minute's trouble in her life.

No one believed that much bad luck could get together between the fifteenth week after Pentecost and the third week in Advent.

No one believed a man would kill his own little illegitimate dyslexic daughter just because she was crazy.

And no one, not even the district attorney of New Orleans, wanted to believe a man would shoot a $3,000 Labrador retriever sired by Super Chief out of Prestidigitation.

Mink

JOAN ARBOUR GRANT

Gloria's husband, Earl, had spent seven thousand five hundred and forty-three dollars on a coat that Gloria was refusing to wear. Not that she didn't like the coat. She'd looked everywhere, been looking for years, waiting for the right moment, the right coat. It was one thing after the other—an addition on the house, college for Josephine and then her wedding, new cars, taxes, Earl's mother, the list went on and on. But Earl's mother was gone, Josephine settled, Earl's practice doing better than ever (he was senior partner, he worked hard), and they had a fat retirement fund. In short, they could finally afford it. So what was to stop them? It was natural ranch mink, almost black. It had Joan Crawford shoulders, the way she'd pictured, and reached almost to the ground in panels of dense, dark mink. Except that it was a bit too long, and that could be fixed, it was perfect. Earl paid by check and the coat was theirs.

On Wednesday, the day she was to pick up the coat, Gloria woke up feeling energetic, exhilarated. Her voice in the shower (she often sang in the shower), was clear, pure, right on key. She sang a song her mother used to sing.

He'll come for me when I am blue.

It was a cool, bright morning, about 45 degrees when she left the house, but the afternoon was expected to be warmer. Too warm for fur, but there would be other days. Gloria listened for the weather as she drove up River Road on her way to the mall. Colder temperatures for the weekend. Wonderful. She'd wear the coat to Catherine's party at the club on Friday night.

She made her way through home furnishings, the children's department, ladies' lingerie and then over to furs, feeling prosperous, pleased. They hadn't bought the coat on credit, they'd paid in full and she took pride in that. Brenda, the saleslady whom she'd gotten to know, brought out the coat draped over her arms, and Gloria thought she detected envy there. Envy was something she'd have to deal with when wearing a coat like this. There were the haves and have nots in this world, it was as simple as that. She slid into the coat in front of the three-way mirror to check the length. It was perfect. These people were experts. It looked even better than she'd hoped. Gloria drew the front panel closer to her face and remarked that the pelts were flawlessly matched. The lush fur gleamed in the fluorescent lighting. Gloria's green eyes shone and her dark hair, drawn up in a fashionable twist, seemed to match the color of the coat exactly. Brenda said it was uncanny, she'd never seen a coat look so good on a customer. Brenda worked on commission but still there was truth in what she said.

That evening Gloria greeted Earl at the door, draped in the fur. Earl laughed and held her in his arms, his fingers laced in the soft rich majesty. There'd been moments like this when they were first married—capricious, carefree moments. That evening it remained hanging on the door-frame in the bedroom so that Gloria and Earl could watch TV and view it simultaneously. They sat very close on the velvet love seat across from the TV, holding hands, something they hadn't done for years. A couple of times, during commercials, Gloria got up, slipped into the coat, and paraded back and forth in front of Earl as she'd seen professional models do on the runway. Once, she hung the coat on the door, then sauntered over and sat on the floor at Earl's feet, her head resting on his knee. He stroked her thick, dark hair that looked like the fur on the coat, while she massaged his ankles, thighs. In the old days, Gloria's arthritis would have bothered her too much to sit on the floor. A coat that restored youth. That was how she thought about it that night in bed with Earl, her head resting on his chest contentedly, before she drifted off.

The next morning, after sending Earl off with a passionate kiss on the lips instead of the usual peck on the cheek, Gloria stood at the sink rinsing the breakfast dishes. She watched her hands moving the soapy yellow sponge efficiently over the pots and dishes. Gloria had never wanted to be conceited, the most despicable of human emotions to her mind, but she couldn't help feeling a tinge of pride in herself for going through with the purchase of the coat. She remembered how timid she'd been with other major purchases in her life. Just two short years ago, the acquisition of her Volvo, the expensive four-door model, had proven too much for her; it had had to be a gift from Earl. Did she feel unworthy of such a costly car? She didn't know; but in the end she had not been able to commit to that "inordinate sum" for what she referred to as a "hunk of metal." Earl had been forced to buy it on his own, even picking out the color—a conservative silver grey—alone. He'd driven it home from the dealership by himself (something they could have enjoyed doing together, he'd said), and left the keys on the kitchen table with a note: "Enjoy this car. Life is short."

Gloria drove the Volvo because it was a gift (her name was nowhere on the note) and therefore, she didn't have to feel guilty. Gloria was forever feeling guilty, a gnawing dark feeling that would wash over her at odd moments—in parking lots, or the drugstore—causing her to reach out in outbursts of protectiveness. "Do you think his feet are cold?" Gloria would say to the mother of a crying barefoot infant in Eckerd's, or, "Can I drive you home?" to old ladies at bus stops. Earl detested Gloria's negative attitude, her "black cloud," he called it. Gloria sympathized with Earl, understood how he felt, but she couldn't seem to control the downward spiral she would sometimes find herself in.

The fur coat was different.

Gloria felt she would be able to wear the coat and enjoy it. She did not see it as extravagant. People had been wearing fur since the beginning of time. Fur was functional. Gloria was too old for a thin wool coat, even if it was cashmere. She did not want to catch cold and get laid up and be useless, be a burden. Gloria had dealt with enough helpless people in her life to ever want to end up that way herself. After Gloria's father had left her mother and her when she was a child, "deserted them" was what people said, her mother had been nothing but a burden, a burden that Gloria remembered only too well.

She looked at the thermometer attached to the kitchen window outside and smiled. Thirty-three degrees. Mink coat weather, no doubt about it. Gloria knew some people might think it gauche to wear a mink to the grocery, but she hadn't waited all this time to be timid. She dressed with extra care, spending a little more time than usual on her make-up and being very particular with her hair. She stepped into the deep warmth of the coat and admired her reflection in the full length mirror. Fifty-two years old. Not bad, not bad at all. And the coat felt marvelous. Wasn't warmth the primary function of a coat? It was 33 degrees outside and Gloria was wearing a warm coat that happened to be fur, happened to be mink.

She swept into the Fresh Market with her head held high, but the truth was she didn't feel the exhilaration she'd felt when modeling the coat for Earl the night before. Martha at the check-out was working the register when she walked in; Gloria could see her shabby green wool sweater. Gloria had known Martha for years.

Martha had been with the old Hill Street grocery they'd torn down to build the Fresh Market. Gloria was familiar with Martha's expressions, knew her children's names. Martha glanced over, said good morning, nothing else, and gave Gloria an odd look. It wasn't envy like Brenda in the fur department, she'd been expecting a little of that, but that was not what the look was about. She pushed her cart down the first aisle past the cheese and yogurt and eggs, wishing she'd worn her old black cashmere. She considered going home and changing, but that would be so obvious. She stopped at the deli for some sliced turkey and, Melinda, the cold cuts girl— something about the tilt of her head, the firm set of her mouth—she gave Gloria a look much like Martha's at the check-out. What was going on?

Her head throbbed as she pushed her cart quickly through the rest of the grocery, ignoring her list. She hoped she wasn't getting sick because she did not want to miss Catherine's party. Catherine gave fabulous parties. She could picture her regal entrance in the coat—heads turning, people making comments. Her headache was feeling slightly better until it was her turn to check out. No, it was not Gloria's imagination, Martha was not acting the way she usually did. It was almost as if, crazy as it seemed, as if Martha didn't approve.

She drove the half mile home slowly, clutching the wheel, feeling angry, confused. It couldn't be the money. Martha had no idea of her financial situation. Maybe it was the minks. She remembered Martha's "Save the Whales" T-shirt. Of course it was the minks. Well, she thought, to each his own, and anyway, who was Martha to approve or disapprove?

She placed the coat in its special paper covering marked "Mink" with the sign of a crown, hung it in the back of the hall closet and walked into the kitchen. Gloria stood, leaning against the sink, gazing out at the enclosed patio on the side of the house. She was thinking she'd better sweep the patio and gather the branches and twigs that blew in with the cold front last night. She watched a squirrel scamper across the bricks and stop by one of the dwarf azaleas that lined the patio. She saw him raise himself up holding something in his paws, and she noticed his full sweep of a tail. Gloria had never seen a tail like that on a squirrel. She leaned over the sink and put her face closer to the glass to get a better look. She thought maybe it was the color, maybe the shape. It was unusual, not brown, but long white fur surrounded by an auburn color on the edges. Two-toned. She watched him twitching his tail in the sunlight, accentuating the unusual white color of the fur. What a coat that would make! Then she saw another squirrel, a little brown one, scurry over and stop next to the first one, as if they were meeting.

Gloria stood there a moment, watching the squirrels, feeling odd and uncomfortable; her head still ached and now her ear was ringing, the way it did when she was overtired or under stress. She was frowning, her arms were crossed. Earl would scold her for ruining this day with negative thoughts, but she couldn't seem to keep them out. She was wondering about squirrels, about their relationships, about whether they formed attachments. Did they mate for life? As a child, Gloria had found it shocking that certain animals formed lifelong commitments. Her parents had not had the wherewithal to make a life together, but some animals did instinctively. She knew Canadian geese did, but she didn't know much about squirrels. She'd have to ask Earl. He was full of information like that. She began putting the groceries away, stopped and looked out again. Then it hit her.

What about minks, did *they* mate for life?

Gloria closed her eyes. She was calculating the number of years she'd been living with Earl, that she'd been Earl's wife. She knew it was more than twenty-five, it had to have been. Earl had never cared much for anniversaries, "not necessary," he'd said, and somewhere along the way, Gloria had quit counting. Was it twenty-seven, or twenty-eight years? She had to stop and think. More than half her life at any rate. She sat in a kitchen chair with her shoulders sagging forward, her eyes following the pattern of the grain in the top of their country pine breakfast table. She sighed deeply and when she looked out again, the squirrels were gone. Thank God, Gloria thought. As she finished up with the last of the groceries, she realized she was avoiding the window. Oh come on, she said to herself, squirrels were a dime a dozen. So where was the high she'd been on since she bought the coat? How could it have vanished so fast?

She made herself some herb tea, the kind that was good for her nerves, and sat with her back to the window, waiting for it to cool. Gloria didn't know much about minks except that maybe they were cousins of the weasel. She had a vague notion that weasels were menaces to society. Maybe minks were too. Maybe minks did awful things like prey on sheep or pet ducks and baby chicks. Gloria sipped from her mug then stood up and glanced outside. No squirrels. She walked with a determined gait into the den and sat in Earl's reading chair in front of the encyclopedias. . . . K . . . L . . . M, she grabbed the dark red leather volume marked "M," with gold binding that was peeling away. These had been her encyclopedias in high school. She remembered the idealistic girl of those days, an Albert Schweitzer fan. Would *she* have worn a fur? She opened the book and located m-i-n-k. She saw, "weasel-like species," that was what she'd thought. She read, "nocturnal and semi-aquatic," and then she stopped—"a litter of ten kits." She read the last phrase over slowly. She slammed the book shut, pushed herself up from the chair and slid the volume back into place.

She walked out of the den and down the hall to what used to be Josephine's bathroom. She opened the medicine closet, got out a couple of Tylenols and swallowed them without water. She could see her granddaughter Marybelle's sweet, innocent face with those puffy cheeks of hers. A wave of pity overtook her for all those baby minks.

Carefully, Gloria took the coat from the back of the hall closet. It was neatly arranged in its custom paper covering. "Keep it in this," Brenda had said, "never plastic. The pelts need to breathe." She shook her head. She'd done some thoughtless things in her life, but buying this coat was probably the most thoughtless of them all. She laid the coat on Earl's side of the bed and began searching for the receipt in the top drawer of her bureau. What would she tell Earl? Should she tell him about the squirrel with the beautiful tail, about what the encyclopedia said? She located the receipt at the bottom of the pile where she'd put it yesterday, remembering how she'd felt then, remembering last night with Earl. She decided that when Earl had his money in hand, his seven thousand five hundred and forty-three dollars, he wouldn't feel so bad. He'd say she was impetuous, unpredictable, sentimental, but he'd have his money and that would please him more than any coat.

By the time Gloria got back to the store it was almost five. She was wearing her black cashmere, her hair tied back with a black and white striped scarf. She looked sensible, modern, at least that was what she thought, glancing in the mirror as she walked through housewares. In the fur department a stiff woman dressed in a dark suit told her that Brenda was off. She took the coat from Gloria without smiling and hurried to find the manager. Gloria assumed a firm, matter-of-fact air. This was business. She was returning merchandise for her money back, her reasons were her reasons.

Mr. Salassi, the manager, was all smiles. His job, he said, was to keep the customer happy, but he could not break the rules. "The problem is, Mrs. Price," Mr.

Salassi's voice was controlled, "that is, if we hadn't altered the coat, custom fit it to you, there would be no problem." Gloria, feeling slightly faint, sat in one of the three upholstered French chairs next to the mirror with her purse in her lap and looked up at the manager. She'd forgotten about the hem. She felt foolish, flushed. Mr. Salassi was holding up the hem showing her the workmanship, pointing it out with his long, tapered fingers, explaining to her the process. Mr. Salassi was clean-cut, earnest. "Mr. Gerhardt in alterations is our fur specialist. He takes great care. . . ." Gloria wasn't listening. She was staring across the room at the rack of furs, all kinds, that lined the wall, picturing bloody scenes of animals in mass slaughterings.

Gloria pulled into the driveway behind Earl who was just getting home. She waited as he waved in his rear view mirror, then carefully parked his car in the carport— Earl was careful about everything. He was an uncomplicated man, easy to please. It was Gloria who shot for the stars, the coat had been her idea. What was she going to tell Earl?

"I tried to return the coat," she blurted through the window without thinking.

"You what?" Earl looked stunned. "Is that what that is in the back seat?" He thrust his head in the window to get a better look. Earl was an attorney. His practice had its ups and downs but they were nothing compared to Gloria. Second guessing her had been a life-long impossibility.

"Mr. Salassi wouldn't take it back. I felt so stupid. I forgot about the hem." Gloria was sitting behind the wheel, tears mixed with black mascara running down her cheeks.

"Who's Mr. Salassi? You loved that coat! What the hell are you saying?" Earl held on to the car door for support. He was a man who had counted on drawing strength from his wife. When she was off, he was worse. His handsome face was turning red.

"It's the little minks, Earl." Her voice choked. "I've been thinking all day about the baby minks—mink families." Gloria looked up at Earl. *He'll come for me when I am blue, He'll take me far away.* She felt weak, fear was creeping up her legs. She hated to fight with Earl. She wished someone would come for her now. Earl's panicked expression had changed to one of disgust. He looked fed up. "I can't wear the coat and they won't take it back," she sobbed.

"Little minks is it?" Earl was shouting. "Little minks?" Earl was shouting louder. There was nothing she could do when he got like this.

"Okay, Earl. Okay," she said. "I understand how you feel." She collected her purse, dropped in the keys. "Don't worry about it. Just forget it." Gloria had fought many losing battles. She recognized the signs.

"Don't worry about it?" Earl's face was almost purple but he'd lowered his tone. He was speaking through clenched teeth. "What the hell did you expect?" He hesitated, shook his head. "Why?" he said. "Why do you do these things? Why do you?" Earl fumbled through his pockets for his pressure medicine.

"I'm sorry, Earl. I . . ."

"What the hell did you expect?"

Gloria watched Earl swallow a pill, take a deep breath and walk off toward the house, watched his feet in his brown loafers as they carried him toward the back door. She noticed his head was bent slightly forward from fatigue or maybe disgust, how the afternoon sun hit his hair, washing out the color, making him look older than he was, making him look like an old man. Gloria remembered her father walking away like that, the sight of his tan gabardine trousers from the back, his brown hair tinged with grey, his strong neck. It seemed her father had always been walking away. One day he walked out the door and kept on going, and her mother had been left to grow old alone. Gloria could picture her mother's face, her pale blue eyes staring out into the yard and beyond, the way she did when she thought no one was looking.

Gloria heard Earl slam the back door shut. She kept her fists clenched, her eyes on the quiet door with the pale afternoon light sliding down off it onto the carport floor.

On Friday evening, the evening of Catherine's party, Gloria and Earl were expecting guests for drinks and hors d'oeuvres. She showered and did her hair, then dressed in her green velvet evening suit, Earl's favorite because it matched her eyes. When she was all done, she went into the kitchen and stood by the window. The mink was hanging on the back of one of the dining room chairs. She would wear it to the party as she had originally planned. Earl was setting up a bar in the solarium, the way he always did for company. He'd just walked through with his sterling ice bucket mumbling something about dull blades; his cheek was cut and he'd stuck a small piece of toilet tissue near his jawbone to stop the bleeding. They didn't speak. He didn't say she looked well, he didn't say she didn't.

The Forresters and the Simpsons were due a little before seven—Bill and Sadie, Ruth and Paul. Sadie would be in her sealskin jacket, Ruth's was full length pony she'd picked up in Seattle when the bar met there spring before last. Gloria would greet them at the door with her party smile, her voice gay. They'd want to see the coat. They'd heard all about it, she'd have to put it on. "You don't look like our Gloria without your black cashmere," Sadie would say. "It's positively ravishing," she'd continue. "We approve, Earl, we approve of Gloria's new look." And they would be right, she was no longer "their" Gloria. But why explain? Why waste her breath? Why look foolish?

Catherine's party would be like the others—in truth, far from sensational— the same boring faces, the same hollow chatter. When they got home, Earl would put on his red pajamas, then say something about Ruth and Sadie, about how good they looked in their furs, about how well they handle things. Gloria could see his face, she was familiar with those implications, with the tone he'd use. Then he'd fall asleep and grind his teeth, as always. She would spend another sleepless night.

She continued standing at the kitchen sink, looking out the window at the patio, waiting. It was dusk, but there was enough light, that soft grey evening light, to see the spot clearly. The seed she'd sprinkled on the bricks, the kind the man at the hardware said the squirrels liked best, lay untouched. Gloria opened the window, felt the chilly air, heard the soft tinkling of the wind chimes hanging from the carport. She had roughly seven more minutes to stand by the window and wait before the guests came. If the squirrels didn't come this evening, they would come another evening or another day. Sooner or later they would come. When they did, she would be there and she would explain herself, tell them what had happened, tell them that she wasn't the same. She would tell them that the way she saw it (they would have to understand), the way she saw it, she'd say, it was their skin or hers.

Letting Go

SHIRLEY ANN GRAU

As Freezing persons, recollect the Snow—
First—Chill—then Stupor—then the letting go—
—EMILY DICKINSON

Except for a couple of cruising sea gulls, the entire north shore of the bay was empty and still—the tumbled concrete blocks of the erosion barriers, the wide mud flats, ripple-covered now by high tide. Far offshore, a mile or so, the silver gray water darkened into the slate gray of the deep buoy-marked ship channel where oil tankers passed in slow procession against an always hazy horizon.

Mary Margaret knew every line and shadow out there. She'd grown up watching—sitting on the front porch in summer, and in winter rubbing a little frost-free spot on the windowpane. She'd wished for a ship to come sailing right up to the shore, a pirate ship with blood red sails and a big black flag. Or a white and gold yacht, its crew dressed in navy and braid. But this part of the bay was only a few feet deep, and good for nothing but summer fishermen. Their outboards left shimmering oil stains on the quiet surface and their beer cans drifted to the beach and caught in the breakwater.

She sniffed the familiar decaying smell of salt shore as she parked in front of her parents' house and checked her watch. Right on time. They were expecting her, they knew she was always prompt. But no front curtain moved, no front door opened. The house looked as it always did—small, gray, like a nun with folded hands, waiting or sleeping.

She thought: Just once they might be looking for me. I come every Wednesday for supper and the novena. Perpetual novena. That was how I learned what eternity was—like the novena, it goes on and on without end.

She climbed the narrow concrete driveway, barely wide enough for a car, cut deep into the slope, terraced carefully and secured by creeping greenery, perfectly clipped. All as neat as an ironed handkerchief.

Now three concrete steps up to the walk. The lawn was still green, there'd been no frosts, and the yellow mums were full and glowing in their beds. There were even a few dozen pink roses on the climber against the house.

It was a marvel, this garden. Her parents' pride. Since his retirement, her father spent his days out here, working until the hard winter freezes forced him inside and returning with the first feel of spring in the air, brushing aside the last melting patches of snow.

They take more care of the garden, she thought, than they ever did of me.

That goddamned garden, Edward called it. In the first months of their marriage, when Edward tried very hard to be friendly with her parents, he'd sent them a present, a special lightweight battery-powered weed trimmer. "It's for their goddamn garden," he said. "Even if they can't stand me, they got to like this." He'd been wrong.

Her parents had never used the trimmer. They hadn't even given it to one of the parish fairs at St. Joseph's Church. They had simply thrown it out. When Mary Margaret and Edward came for dinner the following Wednesday, they found the trimmer, unopened in its bright red and yellow carton, lying across the trash cans at curbside.

Collection wasn't until Monday, Mary Margaret thought dully. Her parents weren't just throwing away an unwanted present. They had intended only one thing—for Edward to see it. . . . He picked up the trimmer, holding it delicately as china, turning it, examining it carefully. He brushed off a few bits of grass before putting it in the trunk of their car.

"I am not going in there," he said quietly to Mary Margaret. "Will you come home with me or will you go on?"

She didn't answer. She couldn't. She fumbled for words and found none.

He nodded. "I've had enough. I am not going into that house again, and I am not going to see them again, not even at their funerals. I will come back and pick you up whatever time you say. Next week you can have the car and come by yourself."

So it was settled. If her parents noticed his absence, they never mentioned it. It was as if he had never existed.

Now on another Wednesday evening, she bent to examine the dahlias, their heavy burgundy heads staked against the wind. Her father had a hand with dahlias, they

were always magnificent. The red and yellow combination—dahlias and mums—
was her mother's choice, repeated year after year.

And that was another thing, a strange thing. Her parents always agreed.

Everything was settled with a flick of an eye, a shrug of the shoulder—never an
argument. Together they moved smoothly and silently through their days, as if they
had taken a train and knew precisely where the track led.

Mary Margaret pushed open the door (her parents kept it unlocked until they
went to bed) and stepped into the dim living room.

It had been brighter when she was a child, when the print curtains and the chair
covers were new. Over the years darkening wood-paneled walls had absorbed their
colors and turned everything into a very dense forest shade.

She'd thought of that image, years ago, when she was in high school. It still
pleased her: forest shade. Not gloomy. But the regal dimness of a great forest . . .

As always her parents sat at the table by the window. Cards were neatly stacked
in the very center of the table, but they weren't playing. They never played this time
of day—only in the evenings for an hour or so before bed. (Her mother always used
the bathroom first, while her father riffled the cards through a game of solitaire.)

Her mother was sewing—a long white piece of cloth stretched across her lap
to fall in soft folds on the floor. The Altar Society. Again. How many altar cloths
had her mother made over the years? And how could a church wear out so many
linens?

Pencil in hand, her father was studying the *Daily Racing Form.* Soon he would
carefully reconsider his findings, write down his conclusions, and phone his
bookie. He was a good handicapper and a very lucky one; he won forty or fifty
dollars a week. Steadily, week after week. He rarely went to the track. He didn't like
crowds, he said, and all those mutuel windows were a temptation to bet too much.
He liked things just the way they were. His winnings took them to dinner and a
movie once a week. Which was more than his pension would ever have done.

"Hello," Mary Margaret said.

"You're here," her mother said.

Her father waved the tip of his pencil at her and went on reading.

"You didn't need that," her mother said. "It's not cold yet."

"It might be by the time I drive home."

"Not this time of year."

She folded the coat carefully on the corner of the couch. She put her purse on the coffee table, next to her father's World War II helmet with the gaping hole in its top. *Looks like some kind of can opener, huh?* he'd say now and then. *Never even parted my hair, can you believe it?* The same blast left a load of shrapnel in his back. *They missed killing me, but they sure fixed my ass,* he'd say.

For years little metal pieces worked their way out, and he'd been in the Veterans Hospital half a dozen times. There hadn't been any trouble for years now; the bits of metal and dirt must be gone at last. Still, whenever the weather was warm, he'd scratch at the long bluish-purple scars criss-crossing the backs of his thighs. They'd never quite healed.

Mary Margaret picked up the shattered helmet, now rusting ever so faintly, and fingered the ragged edges, thinking: Funny thing, luck and the difference between living and dying.

Her mother's first husband was in that same infantry company. His name was George Maley; his picture, smiling, uniformed, cap at an angle, hung on the dining room wall, all that was left of his life wrapped around by a fancy gold frame. PFC Maley had been standing next to PFC Borges when German shells began falling. . . . George Patrick Maley died (atomized, blown into dust, returned to earth with a speed greater than the grave's), and Alwyn Peter Borges lived and married his buddy's widow and sired a child.

If he'd lived, I'd be Mary Margaret Maley. I'd have different blood but the same name because my mother always planned to call her daughter Mary Margaret after her own mother.

When she was very little, long before she went to school, she used to imagine herself Mary Margaret Maley. And that the man in the picture, tall, thin, dark-haired, wide-eyed, handsome, eternally young, was her real father. Even though she knew it wasn't so.

Her father stood up very slowly, belt buckle catching the edge of the table and shaking it. He made a final check of the *Racing Form*, nodded to himself, and went to phone the bookie. The floorboards creaked under his feet.

Mary Margaret sat down next to her mother. "Another altar cloth?"

Her mother nodded. "There's only twenty members in the Altar Society and most of them don't do anything."

"People have a lot to do, they don't have the extra time."

"Last Sunday there wasn't a single bunch of flowers on the altar, not one on the main altar."

"Ma, you could have brought flowers. The garden's full of them."

Her mother stopped the methodical drawing and tying of threads. "I don't bring flowers," she said flatly.

In the long silence that followed, Mary Margaret thought: That is perfectly true. You sew, you have for years, you will sew your way into heaven, faithful servant of Jesus. But you have a limit. God can have the linen, but the garden belongs to you and my father.

"I don't even have flowers in the house," her mother said, head bent to the drawnwork again.

That was also true. The flowers stayed on bush or vine or plant, stayed through their cycle of days and development, withered and died. And were immediately clipped and carried away.

Her father came back, floor timbers groaning again. "I got to put another support in that cellar," he said.

"Or go on a diet."

"Two forty. Not all that much."

"Wait till you can't bend over in the garden any more."

"I can bend over plenty good." He showed her. He could touch his ankles with ease. "Not too bad for an old man." He sat down again, scratching at the scars on the backs of his thighs.

"You want some tea?" her mother asked.

"Sure," she said. "What have you got. Iced or hot?"

"Iced this time of year. It's nowhere near cold yet."

"And I didn't have to wear my coat, huh?" Mary Margaret called after her.

"She don't like to think winter's coming," her father said. "She stands out in the yard and she don't see any signs in the leaves."

"I don't much like it either."

"My luck's better in winter," he said. "A lot better. Why do you suppose that is?"

There were long pauses now. Mary Margaret could feel herself slowing down, fitting into the pace of this house. At work she was efficient and quick and bustling, heels rattling on the office floors. She drove the highways like a racer, changing lanes, brake lights flashing, impatient, restless. In this house, she found silences appearing between her words, comfortable silences, like soft beds to rest your thoughts on.

"Florida," he said. "I do great at Calder. And Louisiana."

"I don't know why, Pa."

Her mother came back with three glasses of iced tea rattling on the metal tray. "No lemon this week. Said it was the truck strike or something like that."

"It's okay, Ma. I don't really care about the lemon."

"You always take lemon." Her mother picked up her work again.

Her father twirled the ice in his glass. His nails were dirt-rimmed, he never was able to scrub them clean. "Yeah," he said. "All my luck's in the south. Like the day at Gulfstream when they disqualify the winner and they hand me thirty-eight dollars and forty cents. You remember that, honey?"

Her mother's name was Christine, but he never called her that. Always honey. Maybe it had something to do with the long dead husband and friend, George Maley.

Her mother nodded absentmindedly, counting her threads. A faint odor of cooking drifted into the room. She had turned on the oven while making the tea. Tuna fish casserole. They always had tuna fish casserole before the novena on Wednesdays.

"I like those southern tracks. None of that skidding around on the ice like at Aqueduct."

She drank her iced tea slowly. Her mother had added orange juice in place of the missing lemon.

"Sometimes my luck's rotten though. Like Amato turning mule on me."

That caught her attention. "I didn't know that, Pa."

"He muled. Owed me a hundred and ninety-four dollars."

She clucked with surprise. "You don't bet that much."

He shook his head, sadly. "My best week ever, Jesus, the prices. I don't even want to think about it."

"What happened to him? Amato?"

"I don't know. I don't have nothing to do with him any more."

He is not even curious, Mary Margaret thought. The bookie he used for twenty years doesn't pay off, and he doesn't wonder what happened to him.

"When was that?" Mary Margaret said. "You didn't tell me about it."

He drank his iced tea, wiped his mouth with one finger. "Years ago. The Slob was still coming here then."

"Him," her mother echoed.

She felt the usual anger grow and turn to sharp stomachache. Him. Or the Slob. They never used his name, as if he didn't have one. Edward MacIntyre. Her husband by the rites of the Catholic Church.

"I guess there wouldn't have been time to tell me," she said, keeping her voice perfectly even. "Not when every Wednesday was a fight."

She was the one arguing, defending, pleading. Edward said nothing, only played with the food on his plate until it was time for the novena and the silence it brought.

Evenings driving home they hardly said a word, each fearful of the other's misery.

Mary Margaret said: "He came because you were my parents and I wanted him to come."

Her mother smiled patiently at her. Her father drank the last of his tea.

"You want some more tea, Al?" her mother asked.

They hadn't even come to her wedding. She'd hoped they would, until the last minute she'd hoped, right up to the minute Father Robichaux began the ceremony. Edward's parents were there, and his two brothers and their wives, and his sister and her husband and their grown son, and his unmarried sister who'd flown from Milwaukee especially for the ceremony.

In the rectory parlor that afternoon there hadn't been a single person of her blood.

I minded that most, she thought.

Stirring restlessly in her chair, Mary Margaret said, "You know, I never knew why you called him the Slob."

(She felt disloyal saying the word aloud.)

Her father laughed, her mother chuckled. Her father said, "The way he just sat there, mealy-mouthed, like he was ready to cry. He just plain looked like a slob."

Oh, she thought wearily, oh oh oh oh.

"We didn't care about him one way or the other," her mother said. Which was a very long speech for her.

And me, Mary Margaret thought, did you care nothing for me? You're my parents and you raised me and you sent me to school and you bought my clothes and took me to catechism classes. But there's got to be more than that.

"You want to watch the evening news?" she asked, abruptly changing the subject.

"Enough news in the paper," her father said.

So she crossed the room and watched by herself.

"If you gotta watch, keep it low," her father said.

She watched the flickering images, conscious now of something happening within her, of a pain that was not quite that, of a loneliness that was near to happiness.

She was not used to thinking about her feelings. They were just there, they were part of things. No more to be studied than the sky when it rained or the wind when it blew. If you worked hard and were good, there'd be nothing to trouble your thoughts.

But that didn't seem to be so.

Lately she'd started thinking about herself, she could even see so clearly. . . . The small child: black plaits down her back and skinny legs covered with half-healed scabs. The older child: the plaits crisscrossed on top her head, the scarred knees covered by longer skirts. Her Communion: white dress and veil and a crown of white flowers on the thick coil of hair. Then her hair was short and curly and there were boys and movies and high school and her first paycheck and the first clothes she had ever bought without her mother's help. Then she was nineteen and finished business school and a full-time employee of the Consolidated Service Company. She was neat and reliable and worked very hard to increase the speed and accuracy of her typing and shorthand. (She practiced every evening at home, after supper, dating only on Friday and Saturday.) She was careful to learn everybody's name and to be smiling and deferential and never never gossip. By the time she was twenty-three she was secretary to the senior vice-president. Soon she would have a fancy title like Executive Assistant and a very nice salary and she would really be somebody. When she was twenty-four she married Edward MacIntyre. He was twenty-eight, a CPA who worked in the same building. They met in line at the building's cafeteria, and they married a few months later.

They drove to work together and parted in the elevator with a kiss. In a few years they'd buy a house and later she'd take leave for a child or two and maybe even give up full-time work. For now they had a two-room apartment that was all yellow and white and green with heavy curtains to pull tight across the windows at night. She vacuumed twice a week and polished the furniture so often that the rooms always smelled of wax. She even washed the windows once a month. It was a way of quieting the restlessness that surged up in her now and then.

On Saturdays she and Edward shopped and went to a late afternoon movie, had supper at a fast-food place, and came home to bed. On Sundays in summer they went to the beach, though they didn't swim. In winter they drove out into the country where the snow was white and untouched. They never skied or skated. They were content to look at the immense shivering whiteness. And once every couple of months they got up in time to go to mass. Neither of them liked the English service, so they looked for a church where mass was still in Latin, but they found only a small group of Charismatics, and after that they'd stopped looking.

Five years.

Then two months ago, on a Thursday, Edward went home early, saying he had a headache.

She thought nothing of it. He'd looked a bit tired that morning, and there was absolutely no sense trying to work if you weren't able to do a good job.

When she got home, he was sitting in the living room. There were no lights, no lights at all, and evening dark filled the room, obscuring the leaf patterns on the chairs, dulling the white walls.

"Are you all right?" With the first jolt of alarm, she switched on one lamp. "Are you sick?"

"No," he said, "I wanted to think."

She hung up her coat, brushed it quickly, put it away neatly.

"About what?"

His dark brown eyes were flecked with yellow, they glittered like fancy marbles. Huge eyes with dark circles under them. "The way it is with us, I've been thinking, is that all there is?"

She stared at him, not answering.

LETTING GO | 265

"You've been feeling it too, Mary Margaret. I know that."

Carefully, levelly, without a shade of anger or fear—words to meet his words, thoughts to be born of them. No midwife here, take care. "Maybe I do wonder. Sometimes. And I don't know why."

He sat down, then got right up again. "It's hard to talk about it sensibly, you know. People go to psychiatrists for this, to find out how to put feelings into words."

"I don't think—it's nothing to do with you, Edward. And not with me either."

"You know, the books you read, they say it's sex."

So he'd been reading books; she hadn't known. Maybe he read them at lunchtime, and kept them locked in his office desk.

"This one book by a New York psychiatrist, he says that if the sex adjustment is all right, everything else in the marriage will be fine."

"There's nothing wrong with sex," she said, "not for me."

"Not me either."

They were both silent for a moment, remembering. She felt the familiar flood of blood and heat—only a ghost now, faint and barely recognizable.

"It's something else," she said.

Because his eyes were glittering as bright as if there were Christmas tree lights behind them, she reached out and touched his cheek, bristly and blue-shadowed. He was sweating heavily, the stubble was slippery with moisture. He smelled sweaty too, heavy and musky.

They made love there on the couch, quick and uncomfortable. Then in bed, comfortable and insatiable. They both overslept and were late for work in the morning.

But the words remained. They hung in the living room air; they hung, muted, over the bed. The words had been heard, had danced through ears and rattled in heads: More than this?

Mary Margaret shook herself back to the present, turned off the TV. To say something, anything, she asked: "Pa, isn't that a new road sign out front? The curve sign?"

"No," her father said.

"Looks new to me."

"No," her father said. "They put that sign there three, four years ago."

"You ready for dinner?" her mother said.

That meant the casserole was already on the table.

"Wait a minute, Ma. I've got to tell you something, something important. Edward and I are going to get a divorce."

They stared at her blankly.

"It's not that there's anything wrong between us." (How could she explain when she was so uncertain herself?) "We just thought it would be better this way." (But maybe it wouldn't.) "Edward got a big promotion and a transfer to the Houston office. He'll leave in a couple of weeks, they want him right away. And I'm not going with him."

Not seeming to hear, her father walked out the front door, slowly, putting his feet down in the manner of very heavy men. He crossed the lawn to check the date stenciled on the sign, then came back to the house. "Seventy-eight." The climb had left him puffing slightly. "Like I said, 8–22–78, three years ago. Clear as can be."

The sound of the closing front door, muted by thick weather stripping, set echoes bouncing in Mary Margaret's head: *More than this. There must be more than this.*

"Did you listen, Pa? Did you hear what I said?"

"He's got to do one thing at a time," her mother said. "You asked him about the sign."

Always on his side, Mary Margaret thought. You're alike as twins.

"Edward and I are still friends, but we want a divorce and that's what we're going to get."

"Catholic people don't get divorced," her mother said.

Her father said, "The Slob walked out on you."

I have honored these people, she thought, I have honored them for all my twenty-nine years, and I am not about to stop now.

"His name is Edward, and he didn't leave me. We agreed to separate, both of us."

"You want to eat dinner?" her mother said to her father.

They heaved themselves out of their chairs and went to the table.

The words were still echoing. Hers? Or Edward's? *More than this.*

Her parents ate steadily, she only pushed the noodles across her plate, separating the bits of tuna, the peas.

"You don't want to eat?" her mother said. "You got to eat to keep your strength up."

"I'm not hungry."

Her father said, "You're not going to keep that apartment?"

"Just for a couple of weeks," she said.

"You got to think of where to live."

Mary Margaret pushed a red fleck of pimiento to the rim of her plate. "Yes."

Her mother folded her hands. With her heavy sloping shoulders and small head topped by a cone of black hair she was a perfect pyramid. "Her room's still here."

"How would it look," her father said. "Her living here, married and without a husband and divorced."

"How it looks?" her mother repeated hesitantly.

"Who'd care," Mary Margaret said. "Who'd know. Who ever comes here?"

Only their blood, their cousins, on special holidays and saint's days and Communion days, when white-dressed children went from house to house, bringing with them innocence and spiritual grace. And good luck. Her father said he always brought in his longest shots on Communion days.

Now they were telling her she wasn't welcome back. That her parents' house was closed. . . . Except for Wednesday supper and perpetual novena.

I must tell Edward that, she thought, as soon as I get home. He'll love that and we'll have a good laugh.

He'd be waiting for her—she was certain. Sex was now a hunger for them, demanding, painful, then satisfied and comfortable. They were so happy together, they were friends. In two weeks they would separate, with a kiss.

Maybe, she thought, that's all there is.

Her mother was saying with unusual emphasis, "She can come back here, Al. I want her to come back here." She wiped the perspiration from her fat cheeks with her paper napkin. "I don't care what you or anybody says."

Well, Mary Margaret thought wryly, scratch one, but the old mare came through. . . . And aloud she said, "I didn't know you thought so much about appearances, Pa."

"It's her room." Her mother was shivering—anger or nervousness—her pudgy shoulders shook and a sharp smell of old woman's sweat came from her.

"Wait, Ma," Mary Margaret said, "you didn't let me finish. I'm changing jobs too and I'm moving. To Oklahoma City."

Slowly her father got up and took the paperbound *Texaco Atlas of the United*

States from the corner bookshelf. (They'd gotten it years before, when they drove to Florida. It was their first and only vacation, they hated every minute.) He unfolded the largest map and put it on the table.

Mary Margaret pointed. "There. Right there."

Everything had happened at once. The evening they decided on divorce, the very same evening Edward told her he'd be moving to Houston, they went out to dinner. It was an Italian restaurant—checkered tablecloths and candles in wine bottles and the heavy greasy pasta they both liked. They finished a bottle of wine and became giggly and secretive, heads together, holding hands and touching knees.

We must look like lovers, she thought, and we are. In a way.

"Look." Edward was playing with her hand, twirling the silver and amethyst ring he'd given her for Christmas. "Are you really going to stay here? Won't it be a little rough for you, I mean?"

"I've got my parents," she said.

They both smiled warmly at the joke.

He insisted: "My boss, you know him, Hank Cavendish, he's being transferred, it's a big step up for him. He wanted his secretary to go with him, but she won't leave. I bet anything he'd jump at the chance to hire you if you'd relocate right away."

"Why not?" she said, giggling, the wine still singing in her ears. "Why not. Where?"

"Oklahoma City."

"Where's that?"

"I don't know," he said. "I do know it'll be a good move for you. They're expecting that office to grow pretty fast. Wherever it is."

She told her parents: "I get a twenty per cent raise, plus medical and dental coverage, plus they are paying my moving expenses."

They nodded. Figures were something they had no difficulty understanding.

"Will you be coming next Wednesday?" her mother said.

"Next Wednesday. But not the one after that."

Her mother nodded, the twisted knot of gray and black hair moved up and down slowly.

Don't you want to ask when I will be back? If I will come back? If I'll be here at Christmas? If I'll come back for your funerals? Do you never worry about anything?

"Time to go." Her father pushed himself up from the table. The atlas lay open, one page soaking in the vinegar of his salad plate.

Go? Where would they go, who never went anywhere? The novena. The Wednesday perpetual novena.

Her mother smoothed back her hair in the sideboard mirror, her father went to put on his leather shoes.

If I stay any longer, I am going to break every dish on the table, or I am going to throw a chair through that window, or I am going to scream and keep on screaming. I am going to dishonor my father and my mother. If I don't get out of here.

Her chair, pushed too hard, slid back into the wall. The picture of her mother's first husband shivered and slipped sidewise."

"I'm not going," she said. Then louder, for her father who was still in the bedroom: "I'm not going to the novena."

"You always go," her mother said.

Her father came to the doorway, one shoe still in his hand.

Four eyes, surprised, accusing, puzzled, shocked.

Don't look at me. You are my parents but don't look at me that way. You've had all you can have from me. One novena more is too much.

"I'll go next week," she said. "For the last time, next week."

They both nodded to her, pyramids of flesh with tiny heads perched on top, like kindergarten drawings.

She hurried through the living room, snatching her coat and purse as she went. Running with fear from something she didn't know, something that might not have been there, something that might even have loved her.

She drove off, tires squealing, leaving the thing that had chased her growling emptily at the end of the driveway.

By the time she got to the crowded highway, she felt better, the soft singing of the engine comforted her. She opened the window and familiar exhaust-laden air curled across her face and shoulders.

It was a very warm night, she thought. As her mother had said, she hadn't really needed to bring her coat.

Wide Awake in Baton Rouge

DINTY W. MOORE

Warren knows that the world is a strange and dangerous place, that anything can happen at any time. Often as not, this keeps him awake when he'd rather be asleep, or thinking about one thing when he'd rather be thinking about another. Tonight, however, a Friday night in July, Warren is sleeping just fine until his wife Karen plants her left elbow in the center of his back.

"Warren?"

"What?"

"Can you smell it?"

"What?"

"That smell."

"It's a car door," Warren says, burrowing his face in a blue pillow. "Or maybe one of the Peterson's dogs."

"I didn't hear something, Warren, I smell something, and it's making me sick."

Warren picks his head out of the pillow and inhales a quantity of air loudly through his nose, but all he smells is Karen's aloe vera skin lotion. Karen is sitting up in bed wearing a pink nightgown and a look Warren last remembers seeing the time an overfed nutria found its way into their laundry room. She is also inhaling, and when she does this the few odd-shaped freckles across the bridge of her nose squeeze into a tight ball. Warren watches her and thinks she seems paler than usual.

"You look sick," he says. "Maybe you shouldn't drink so much coffee at night."

"I can't believe you don't smell it."

"I have allergies." He sits up, trying to look sleepy so Karen will feel bad. "What's it smell like?"

"It smells like oil."

Karen is a puzzle to Warren. When he asks her a simple question like "What should we have for dinner?" she is vague and noncommittal. But her complaints are specific as a bank statement. Karen never has a backache, it's always one of six distinct sections of the back that's in pain, and she can invariably tell Warren if it's caused by a muscle or tendon. Karen never has an upset stomach, it's always a particular food item that can't be digested, as if that food item were sitting whole in her stomach, as if a doctor could x-ray and get a sharply outlined head of broccoli smothered in Swiss cheese or baked chicken breast with too many cloves of garlic. Tonight, Karen smells oil.

"Thirty weight or 40 weight?" Warren asks.

"What?"

"Never mind." He lifts his legs off the side of the platform bed, finds his glasses and checks the floor for his green shorts. They're next to the bedside table, so he grabs them, cinches the elastic about midway up his 35-year-old waist, and says to Karen: "I'll look around and make sure everything's okay. You go back to sleep."

Karen switches on her lamp and sits further up in bed. "I feel sick," she says. "I might vomit."

When the light hits Warren's eyes, he notices that a small headache is beginning to form behind his right pupil. He winces, snatches a New Orleans Saints t-shirt off a doorknob, checks Karen's expression again, and guesses she is somewhere between twenty minutes and an hour away from sleep, barring complications. The muscles in her cheeks are rigid, holding the eyes open, the eyes themselves are puffy but alert, and the mouth is quietly trying to turn itself inside out. Warren knows from past experience that it will primarily be a matter of getting the facial muscles to relax before anyone in the house can ever think of sleeping again.

He pulls the t-shirt over his head and walks into the main section of their one-story Acadian style home. The hall light burns all night, so Warren has no trouble finding the kitchen. He pours himself some apple juice, sits at the butcher block table and shuts his eyes. The headache is starting to assert itself—he feels like someone has taken a pair of needlenose pliers, stuck them through his ear, and begun rewiring his brain.

Warren's body has been doing things to hurt him lately. First it was an inguinal hernia, then it was the left knee that stopped him from jogging around the lakes, and now he's overweight and nothing works right. Sometimes at night, when he can't sleep, Warren listens to his heart—he thinks it might be missing occasional beats. Warren's second-cousin Leonard died from a heart attack six years back. And how old was Leonard? Thirty-seven? What bothers Warren most about his body is that there's nowhere to go now but down. He knows he has thirty or so good years left, if he cuts back on the salt, but the end is coming and Warren can see it—he envisions himself a slalom skier descending the last long hill toward the finish line, the distant crowd waving their flags wildly overhead and cheering him in. But the flags are black and the people in the crowd look suspiciously dead.

Warren remembers that Karen is worrying herself sick, so he gets up and wanders around the kitchen, investigating. He checks the pilot light on the stove and sniffs the air above the trash can, but everything seems to smell exactly like it should. He stares into the empty laundry room, walks through the living room, dining room and extra bedroom, and finds nothing out of place. He goes back to the main bedroom and looks at Karen. "There's nothing here," he says. She doesn't answer, so he adds, "Want me to check outside?" She doesn't answer again, which usually means yes, so Warren goes to the front door, unlocks it and steps onto the lawn.

Standing outside, Warren sees nothing but long, flat houses and grey sky; the grey sky because it is three in the morning and the flat houses because Warren's neighbors don't have basements or second floors. The ground in Warren's subdivision barely supports single-level dwellings, and Warren sometimes worries that his own house is gradually sinking into the ground.

He looks under the streetlight and debates whether or not the night air is mistier than usual. Since moving south from Ohio, Warren has grown fond of Louisiana's natural wonders, but he can't quite come to appreciate flying roaches, stinging caterpillars and humidity that you can see. Tonight he can see the humidity better than other nights, but he knows he won't tell this to Karen. She was born in a small Pennsylvania mountain town where underground coal deposits have been burning out of control for years. Karen's grandmother had to abandon the family home when the earth opened in her backyard and smoke came pouring through her vegetable garden, and Warren knows this has affected how Karen views her environment.

But Warren also knows that there are no coal deposits burning under Baton Rouge, so he steps back through his front door, wipes his feet and walks through the living room and long hallway to the bedroom. Karen is twisting a long strand of hair rapidly back and forth in her fingers when he enters.

"Ow," he says, cupping a hand over his eyes, "the light."

Karen doesn't turn it off or acknowledge his comment, so he sits down at the end of the bed, facing away. "Whatever it was," he says, "I think it's gone."

"Check the stove?"

"Twice." He removes his Saints t-shirt, wads and drops his shorts on the hardwood floor, and reaches behind himself to pat Karen on the side of her leg. "Going to sleep?"

"I can't."

"Going to turn off the light?"

"Warren, I still smell it."

He makes a yawning sound, places his shoulder down on the bed, pulls up his knees and closes his eyes. "Goodnight," he says. "Hope you can sleep." He counts under his breath, waiting for Karen to say something, and reaches ninety before beginning to doze.

Warren is on the front lawn, wearing only his tennis shorts and watching water seep up from the ground below. The grass is puddled and squishy and Warren is in mud up to his ankles, sinking. The neighbors are standing on the asphalt road about twenty feet away, asking Warren tough questions about homeowners' insurance. Just inside the open door is Karen, wearing a shimmering pink nightgown, one that Warren has always liked because in a certain light it's nearly transparent. Warren is thinking: "Go back inside. They can see everything." But he can't form the words. He notices that the doorframe in which Karen is standing is not level. The right side of the house is sinking, faster than the left. Warren is reminded of a movie he saw where it took the Titanic 45 minutes to finally go under. Karen is trying to stand straight, but the tilting house makes her wobble like a drunk. Smoke begins pouring up from underneath the outer walls, making the mud bubble and pop. Warren realizes he has sunk nearly knee-deep in the lawn, so he turns to the neighbors and asks for help. They don't understand, but silver-haired Mrs. Lewis, the widow from across the street, remarks on how fat and white Warren looks with his shirt off. Warren turns back to the house and suddenly can't see it; he can't tell, though, if the air is just too thick with smoke or if the house is finally gone. He remembers the money he spent remodeling the kitchen and regrets it. "Warren?" He can hear Karen calling and he wants desperately to have her but he can't lift his legs out of the sucking ooze that is now up to waist-level. He feels a sharp stab in his brain, right above the eye, and thinks, "Oh my God, I'm dying." He looks back and the neighbors are receding into the distance, slowly waving goodbye. He sees Karen with the group, her nightgown soaking wet and clear as cellophane. He admires his wife for one last time and then there is blackness. Then Karen's voice again. "Warren! Wake up, Warren? I think we're being gassed."

Karen is still sitting up in bed, fanning herself with a *Glamour* magazine. "Can you smell it now? Can you smell that? Don't you realize we could be in danger?"

Warren sits up, dazed. "Cripes, Karen."

"Call the police, Warren."

"What's wrong now?"

"We could be getting something toxic and not know it. Call the police."

Warren blinks his eyes open and sees that Karen is panicking. He sees it in her expression, in the way her eyes don't move in the sockets but stay still while her head rocks back and forth. "If it were anything," he says, "the Petersons would have called the police by now. The Petersons always call the police."

"The Petersons could be dead."

"Karen."

"I'm going to call."

"You'll wake them."

"The police? The police are awake."

"No, the Petersons," Warren says. Then he gives up. He's seen Karen in this state before and he knows there is no use arguing. "Okay. Call Trudy. See what she smells."

Karen reaches over, picks the princess touch tone off the table near the bed and looks at it strangely, then turns and holds it straight out to Warren. "You call. Tell them you're sorry to wake them," she says. "Tell Trudy it smells like oil."

Warren takes the phone and stares blankly at the twelve buttons. He knows he's going to do exactly as Karen asks, but first he ponders what Bob Peterson is dreaming about and whether Bob will appreciate being awakened. Warren sometimes dreams about Trudy Peterson in the tight shorts she wore at the Boudreaux's crawfish boil, and he often wonders whether Bob ever dreams the same way about Karen. He might ask sometime, but not tonight. For now he first dials and sits with his eyes clenched shut while the phone next door rings six times. Then the machine answers:

"This is the Peterson residence. No one can come to the phone right now. If you have a message, please . . ."

Warren hangs up.

"What?" Karen asks. "Aren't they there?"

"I got the machine."

"They could be dead. Like Bhopal."

"Karen!" Warren turns, opens his eyes and takes his wife by the shoulders. "No one's dead. The Petersons are sleeping. It's very late and everybody in the world is sleeping. Get a grip on yourself."

Karen looks at Warren like she doesn't recognize him. "You have a headache, don't you?"

"Yes," he answers, crawling back into bed.

"Is it nerves? Is it your tension level?"

"Karen, let's sleep. If I go to sleep, I won't feel it." He does feel it, though—it feels like an invisible hand has hold of the front of his brain and is squeezing it like a sponge.

"You really can't smell it?" Karen asks.

Warren inhales about a pint of air, then exhales like a snorting, angry bull on a Bugs Bunny cartoon.

"What's wrong?" Karen asks. "You sound mad."

He inhales again, snorts a second time, and smells something. It smells vaguely like turpentine. It's slightly nauseating, and Warren knows what it is. He jumps up out of bed and lands on two feet. "It's your nail polish remover," he cries. "You forgot the lid." He heads into the bathroom at a trot with Karen calling after him, but he can't hear what she says. He's convinced that all he has to do is find the nail polish remover and put the lid back on so Karen will go to sleep and he can go to sleep and in the morning the headache will be history and all will be well.

Without turning on the bathroom light, he opens the medicine chest and searches for the smell, sniffing like a bloodhound. But it isn't there. Utterly frustrated, he sits on the edge of the toilet. He decides to get the Lysol from under the bathroom sink and spray the bedroom, hoping perhaps this will calm his wife. He gets down on the cold floor, opens the door of the wood cabinet and fishes around among the cans and jars. His hand finds the plunger, then something with a plastic lid that he hopes isn't the drain cleaner because he has it all over his fingers, then just when he touches what he thinks is the Lysol, Karen turns on the light and says something and he slams his head on the bottom of the sink.

"Aaaaaw!"

Karen's voice leaps up. "What? What? Are you okay?"

"My head!" He slams the cabinet door shut and hits his knee on the toilet getting up.

"Aaaaaw, Jeeez! My bad knee."

He rushes past Karen, limping, and dives into the bed for the final time. Karen follows, turns off the bedroom light, gets into bed and puts her right hand on his forehead. For a moment, Warren thinks it might be worth it to have hit his head, because now the lights are out and Karen is saying "go to sleep, go to sleep." But he worries that he has ripped his hernia scar, his heart seems to be pumping faster than normal, maybe missing a beat now and then, and he feels fatter than he did the day before. So maybe this is it, he thinks, maybe this is how it all ends. Maybe the big heart attack isn't going to come, like it did for cousin Leonard, but maybe the little things will finally do him in.

"You know," he says, speaking in a pain-minimizing whisper. "You know, younger men than me have died suddenly."

"Don't even say it, Warren. What are you talking about?" She continues rubbing his forehead slowly.

"I bought some insurance. If anything should happen, I'm worth more than the house. Just have me cremated and use the money to have fun."

"Warren, please. You're scaring me. Come on, go to sleep."

She pulls her body up against his back, tangles her feet up in his feet, and begins to breathe slowly and evenly, catching the rhythm of Warren's breath. She massages his head some more, then his stomach, and it occurs to Warren that he'd rather not die real soon, because he would miss Karen.

"Warren, you're not going to die."

"How can you tell? How do you know?"

"Just don't, okay?"

"How can I help it? When my number's up, my number's up."

"Come on now, calm down. There's nothing wrong with you." She pulls closer into her husband's back and Warren remembers what exactly it is that he likes about the shimmery pink nightgown she's wearing. He turns, slowly slides the gown over her head and kisses her on the mouth. Eventually, he makes love to her in a way that, if he should die anytime soon, he hopes she'll remember making love with him to have been. Finally, they fall asleep.

In the morning, Warren wakes up early, pulls on his t-shirt and sneakers and walks out onto the front lawn. Everything is intact—his house hasn't sunk, nor have those of the neighbors, and there are no poisoned corpses littering the landscape. The lawn is moist, but the air is pleasantly dry for mid-summer. Two lizards are basking on the leaves of a caladium and Bob Peterson is standing next door in his thick white terrycloth robe and brown slippers, waving.

"Hey, Warren!" Bob begins to stroll across the lawn, cradling a fat cup of coffee in his right hand. "Hear about the chemical spill? Sent a cloud of crap down through here. Said on the radio it wasn't dangerous, but whatta you expect 'em to say?"

Warren lifts his right eyebrow, the dull echo of the headache just barely there, and says nothing.

"You'd think the idiots'd learn how not to spill the stuff by now," Bob continues. "But, hey, not my problem. Anyway, Trudy didn't seem to mind." He gives Warren a large, suggestive wink.

Warren looks across the street and notices Mrs. Lewis coming out of the house with her fox terrier, the dog acting like it had never been outside in its life.

"You know, I heard it made a bunch a folks sick up in Baker," Bob says. "Headaches and nausea. You and Karen smell anything?"

Warren looks back at Bob, remembers the three a.m. phone call, and says: "No, we had a quiet night."

"Well, no use getting in a fuss, right? I mean, that cloud's halfway to New Orleans by now. What the heck." Bob reaches over and gives Warren a neighborly slap on the side of the arm and the two men stare thoughtfully at Mrs. Lewis and her dog before turning back to their respective homes.

As Warren's feet squish across his damp lawn, he looks at his house and worries one more time that it seems to be slipping lower into the ground. He and Karen are happy in that house, he thinks, and he'd hate to see that happen. Then it occurs to him that the house isn't really sinking, that he's been wrong all along. The grass is just getting higher.

It Pours

TIM PARRISH

The rain dripped crazy time on our walkway as I watched Mr. Ramos emerge from his house across the street. He tilted his head back to study the sky, ran his hand down his throat and peered into the orange bucket beside his porch, a bucket he called his "flood gauge." After he jotted a figure on a pad, he walked to his garage and carefully uncovered his car, a powder blue, '57 Chevy, folding the tarp from one side to the other, then from front to rear. Even in the shade of the garage, the car's pristine paint gleamed. Our mantle clock read 5:42.

Behind me my mother wrote a letter to my brother, Bob, while the news played on TV. Before Bob had left for Vietnam, my father was the one who always watched the news, but now he never did. My father came into the living room and stood next to me.

"Rain finally let up?" he asked. I nodded. Mr. Ramos slid into the driver's seat. Our mantle clock read 5:44. "This keeps on we're all gon wash away," my father said.

The second hand swept on, reached five forty-five and twelve seconds. That morning Mr. Ramos had driven his oldest son, Tootie, to the parish prison to begin serving time for a marijuana bust, and my father had told me to wait a day before I went to see my friend Donny. Donny was nine, two years younger than I was. He and Tootie were the only brothers I knew separated by more than the eight years that separated me from Bob. Now both of our brothers were gone.

The Chevy roared alive. "Jeb, close that door," my mother said, the thick, green air bringing the noise inside our living room, but I glanced at the mantle clock and said, "It ain't gonna be loud in a couple of seconds." Mr. Ramos's engine idled. He stepped out of the car and opened the hood.

"Ramos shoulda kept a firm hand on that boy," my father said. "Shouldn't of let him move out."

"Tootie's Bob's age, Harlan," my mother said.

"Bob didn't move out before he went in the army, did he? He didn't get mixed up with drugs."

Donny came out of the house and put his hands behind his head the way I'd seen prisoners on TV do. The day before, Donny had yelled at Tootie for pouring beer into their father's flood gauge and this was the first time I had seen him since. He stared toward his father, still under the hood, then called out, "Daddy," twice, much louder the second time. Mr. Ramos banged closed the hood and went back behind the wheel. Our clock's second hand glided past the minute forty-five mark. Mr. Ramos revved the car one last long time. "Now," I said, and the engine fell silent. Donny spun, went inside and slammed the door behind him.

"How'd you know that?" my father asked me.

"It's always two minutes," I said.

"Always? What you mean?"

"He starts it four times a day. You ain't noticed?"

My father rubbed the dark bristles on the side of his face. "Four times a day? What for?" he asked. I shrugged. He glanced at my mother. "If Ramos'd paid attention to that boy the way he does that car, he wouldn't be in jail."

A reporter's frantic voice blurted from the TV. On the screen, soldiers crouched in water behind a dirt wall. "Damnit," my father said. "Why you watch that, Winona? They only show you what they want." My mother ignored him. Every time my father was home during the news, he said the same thing. He frowned at the TV. "I'm going out and clear the drain. Water's starting to back up into the yard."

For the last several days, my father had prodded and picked at the street drain with his shovel, even though it never made the water drain any faster. I followed him out and stood with my bare feet in a cool puddle as he poked at the dark hole. After a minute he gazed toward Mr. Ramos, who was back at the flood gauge. "Ramos ever drive that car?" my father asked. I shook my head. My father stabbed with the shovel several more times. "Your momma thinks that news is gon tell her something. Only gon tell her what it wants." He tossed the shovel away and knelt.

"Daddy, you think Bob gets shot at?" I asked.

He reached into the water and searched as if trying to catch something. "Bob's on a big base, Jeb. Ain't nobody gets shot there."

The following morning after the rain let up, I rode my bike over to the Ramoses' where Donny was oiling the chain on his bicycle. "Mine rusted, too," I said. He didn't look at me. In the garage the Chevy's hood was raised. "He's here?" I asked.

"I can't go anywhere," Donny said.

"Ain't he gonna get a job this summer?" Mr. Ramos was a high school math teacher who always worked summer jobs.

"Momma got one. Daddy said he wants to work on his car. He wants me to go get a fuel pump with him."

"A fuel pump? He never drives it."

Donny's brown eyes met mine. He raised up, lifted the rear of his bike and gave his pedal a hard push, setting his back tire spinning. Mr. Ramos stuck his head out of the door.

"Donny, you ready to go?"

Donny lowered the tire so that it scuffed to a stop. "I ain't going," he said.

Mr. Ramos shifted his black-framed glasses. "Yes you are. Come in and clean your hands." Donny walked to the hose at the corner of the house and turned it on. "How's your family?" Mr. Ramos asked me, using the formal voice he'd adopted in the last few months.

"They're okay," I said.

"Your brother seeing any fighting?"

I hesitated, not sure how to answer such a strange question. "He ain't been in any fights."

"That's what I thought." Mr. Ramos pointed at his flood gauge. "You know we got over two inches yesterday? That's over four inches this week. Has your father said anything about how soaked the ground is?"

"He said his tomatoes died."

"The Amite River's already backed up into neighborhoods. Donny, hurry with that." Donny slowly scrubbed his fingers, looking at his father through the tops of his eyes. He turned the faucet up, then aimed the hose into the air, creating a small downpour. "Stop that," Mr. Ramos said. Donny smiled and pointed the nozzle's hard spray into Mr. Ramos's bucket. Mr. Ramos bounded toward him, but Donny toppled the bucket, jumped on his bike and hurried away. "Damn," Mr. Ramos said, "I almost had the whole week." He turned off the water and righted the bucket, then bent and touched his fingers to the wet grass. He pressed his hand to the soggy ground. "Go keep an eye on him," he said to me. "No telling what he could do."

Donny was waiting at the end of the street. "Fuck that bucket," he said, and pedalled off. Large puddles lay in the asphalt street's potholes and on its shoulders and

Donny hit as many as he could, his fenderless tire throwing muddy water onto his back. He went through every shallow ditch, and I pedalled hard to match his pace. When he headed into a little bamboo thicket, I knew he was going to Hurricane Creek, the deep drainage ditch that snaked across the city. My bike bumped over the narrow, rooted path through the shoots and over the wooden bridge, and there sat Donny on his bike, staring at the black water rushing by only five feet below the canal's lip.

"Jesus, I never seen it so fast," I said.

"And deep," Donny said.

The torrent carried sticks and paper trash. Downstream, a snagged limb created a whirlpool. Donny pedalled toward it, his bike tightroping the edge, and I followed, nervous that the muddy ground might give way and send him in. Near the whirlpool he stopped. I pulled up next to him, plucked mud from my chain, flung it from my fingers, then wiped oil on my sock. "You're flipped," I said. With my tongue I tried to catch a few of the rain drops starting to fall. "I wish we had a bateau."

"We could swim across," Donny said.

"Bullshit. That water's gross anyway."

"I could still do it."

"Your daddy told me to keep you from doing something stupid."

"You think you could?"

I shrugged. Donny toed the ground. "I ain't crazy enough to swim in that shit," he said. We both spat into the water.

"Why you think your daddy does his car like that?" I asked. "You know, starting it and all at the same time?"

"I don't know. Ask him." Donny spat again, arching a white glob into the swirling water where it circled and went down.

"Didn't he start after Tootie got busted?" I asked.

"Maybe. Why's your old man keep shovelling the drain?" Donny pointed. "Look."

An island of debris nearly the width of the canal floated toward us, a shapeless form defying the speed of the current. I took a step back as it came on, branches bristling and adorned with pieces of ripped plastic and cloth hanging like banners. In the midst of the island's tangle, a kitchen chair's legs stuck straight up, a car tire cut a black arc, and a dead bird's wing fluttered. Donny and I threw handfuls of mud at it. "Keep it from the whirlpool," I said, but the mass snagged on the limb anyway. Donny searched the ground, worked from the mud a chunk of concrete as big as his head. Together we lifted it and heaved. The chunk crashed through but the island closed its own hole and went on slowly turning. We gathered rocks and moved to the edge of the ditch hurling at the thing. Donny slipped, his feet flying from under him, but he scrambled up and threw again, moving as close as he could to the water. He cursed at it, flinging rocks, and I was reaching to grab his shirt, sure he was about to leap out toward the island, when it broke away and moved off.

"Let's split," I said. The rain was getting harder, large drops exploding on my head. I mounted my bike and turned around, but Donny stood and stared into the water. "Donny!" I yelled, but he didn't respond. Instead he took another step down the bank, the mud sliding beneath him until his feet were almost in the water. He turned and pinched his nose, held a hand in the air.

The rain kept on, not just a thundershower an afternoon like most summers, but often all day until the water never drained from the edges of our street. The ground squished and oozed beneath my feet, trees drooped under the weight of water, mosquitoes swarmed and the air grew greener as if the plants and rain had mixed to form a hovering stew. In the gulf a tropical depression formed and broke apart. My mother watched it so closely I almost believed her eyes made it dissipate. I began to wake up at 5:45 a.m., to stay awake until 11:45 p.m., in order to hear Mr. Ramos start his Chevy. If I missed it, I felt irritable, especially if I hadn't received a letter or cassette from Bob. Once my whole day was ruined because Bob's letter was soaked so badly that the ink had run.

One evening Brother Thomas, the preacher of our Baptist church, arrived unexpectedly at our house. He had only been our pastor a year and was boisterous and irreverent and theologically contentious in ways that made my father mad, but that night he was solemn as he took a seat in the living room. "Bob's been sending me tapes," Brother Thomas said, and smoothed a hand over his bald head. "He said not to let you all hear what's on them. Still, I think you should have a listen."

My father looked at my mother. "If Bob said not to listen, I don't think we ought to."

"I want to hear," she said. "Jeb, get the cassette player."

When I came back in, my father was standing with his arms crossed, looking sideways at Brother Thomas. "Bob didn't send us this for a reason," my father said. "We best respect that."

My mother took the player from me and inserted the tape. "If you don't want to hear it, Harlan, just leave the room."

"You think you old enough to hear this?" my father asked me.

"Yes, sir," I said.

"You ain't gon like it," my father said. He went to the picture window and stared into the night.

I barely recognized Bob's voice, so halting and without energy. He told in detail about his job, not only how he drove wounded and dead from the helipads and landing field, but also how he bagged body parts and corpses, how their weight made them seem filled with sand. A particular incident, though, an accident, had spurred him to send this tape. A sergeant, who Bob said was the closest thing he had to a father over there, had been checking a rocket tube on a grounded helicopter when the pilot pushed the wrong button. The rocket disintegrated the sergeant's head, then careened through offices and hootches, not exploding but fragmenting, each piece hurtling on, until one struck the arm of a friend of Bob's who was getting up from sleeping late. Bob had been the first to come on him, had put out the fire burning in the man's flesh, then helped carry him to surgery. The man had lost his arm.

"You can't say why shit happens here," Bob said. "Everybody's scared or wasted or totally whacked just trying to get through. I try to be brave, you know, but I stay stoned half the time. I want to prove I did right to join, prove I'm brave, but I got no idea what brave is. I'm barely keeping it together."

When the tape ended, my father hit the eject button, removed the cassette and placed it in his pocket. My mother said my father's name, but my father levelled his eyes on Brother Thomas.

"You best leave," my father said.

The preacher's head colored pink. "I thought you all should know."

"If Bob would've wanted his mother to hear this, he would've sent it to our house. I'd appreciate you not telling anybody about this, especially not in a sermon." The preacher nodded. "That son of a bitch," my father said when the preacher was gone. "Ain't got a lick of sense."

"I'm glad I heard," my mother said. "We need to know."

"I already knew," my father said. "I tried to tell him before he signed up."

"You did not. You never told him."

"I tried. He wouldn't listen. He was set on going. Now he's got to face it like a man."

"A man. He's just a boy." My mother spun and headed to their bedroom. I heard her start crying behind the closed door. My father frowned.

"You don't say nothing about that tape to nobody," he said to me. "I won't have Bob's secrets spread." He walked past me, through the kitchen and into the garage. Through the picture window, I saw him head toward the drain. He jabbed the shovel into the dark slit a couple of times, then reached into his pocket. He flicked the tape down the hole.

The following afternoon, my father called Donny and me to the trunk of his car. "Y'all help me unload this," he said, and started handing us brushes, buckets, and jugs that smelled like a swimming pool. "We gon scrub the mildew off the house. Line them jugs up neat in the garage so we can see what we got." When everything was out of the trunk, my father put his hands on his hips. "Your daddy ain't working this summer?" he asked Donny.

He says he's got stuff around the house to do."

My father raised his eyebrows and nodded. "Jeb, get on some old clothes. We about to do battle."

"Why don't we start tomorrow?" I said.

"Cause we starting now."

I changed into old jeans and a tattered T-shirt and when I came back out, my father had two buckets, two jugs, and two scrub brushes laid out. He filled a quarter of each bucket with bleach, the fumes burning my eyes. "Bottom half of the house is yours, top half's mine," he said.

Faint gray streaks of mildew lay here and there on the white siding tiles, but my father scrubbed every inch as if rubbing out a fire. Donny got an old brush from our garage and helped until at 5:45 the Chevy cranked and revved across the street. Donny stood erect, dropped his brush and walked home as if in a trance. My father didn't seem to notice, nor did he notice that we worked through supper time since my mother was at work and not there to remind him. Around dark it started raining, cold and hard, but still he didn't slow down. When all our light was gone, we moved to the front where the porch light illuminated the house.

About nine-thirty my mother's ride brought her home from J.C. Penney's. She walked up under her umbrella. "What on earth are y'all doing?" she asked.

"Taking back our house," my father said from his ladder.

My mother looked at me like I might be able to explain, then asked if we'd eaten yet. "Harlan, do you know what time it is?" They didn't speak to each other again the rest of the night.

After supper I went straight to bed, my muscles waterlogged, and blew air from my nose, trying to expel the odor of chlorine. I wanted to stay awake until I heard Mr. Ramos's car, so I opened my window to the damp night and sat on the edge of the bed. The breeze brought a tinge of seared metal, bauxite, from the aluminum plant by the river. In the distance, flares from Esso and Ethyl blazed against the low sky. Water dripped from the eave of the house into puddles in our back-yard. I thought of a letter I'd gotten from Bob early on, a letter that joked about boredom and told how he'd thrown an army brownie against a truck 438 times before it broke. I imagined Bob helping us wash the house, my father criticizing Bob and Bob joking until Daddy stormed away. But then the images from the tape seeped into my mind—a man with no head, an arm on fire, Bob lowering a human leg into a sack. I stared at the white wall near the baseboard, trying to reconcile the images of my laughing brother with the voice I'd heard on tape. It was if the old Bob had died and spoken to me from a horrible other side.

After a while Mr. Ramos's car spoke through the night air. I lay on my stomach, staring at the baseboard and hoping the peaceful sound of the rain would bring the old Bob back into my head. Then I saw them on the white wall, several tiny spots like pox. I swung out of bed and touched the spots with my fingers. Mildew blooming in the dampness. I tried to smear them, but they wouldn't smudge. I pressed my palm against them. For a moment I thought I could feel them growing.

My father stayed home from work at the chemical plant so we could finish cleaning the house. My mother reminded him that a new tropical depression was heading inland, but he didn't answer. All morning the clouds thickened, the humid heat surrounding us like a membrane. My father kept examining my work, sometimes pointing to a spot I had missed, although I never saw what he was pointing at.

Donny came over and he and I moved away from my father to the opposite side of the house where I told him about Bob's tape. Then Donny told me that he'd gotten a letter from Tootie telling how the others in prison on possession charges had taken him in and helped protect him from the dangerous convicts. We wondered why Tootie and Bob had never been friends, wondered if things would have been different for them if they had.

At 11:45 when his father started the Chevy, Donny tried to act nonchalant, but his face blanched as if it and not my hands had been in the bucket. "I got to go with him to get new spark plugs," Donny said.

I watched Donny walk away, then went to my father's ladder.

"Why we cleaning the house before a storm?" I asked.

"When you have something you take care of it," he said.

"It ain't dirty."

"It's dirty, even if you can't see it. Now get on it."

He sloshed bleach onto the tiles and went on without looking at me. I remembered the time Bob, on his own, had cleaned the garage, putting away the scramble of tools on my father's work bench, straightening the scrap lumber heaped in the corners, scrubbing the oil stains on the floor. When my father came home from a double shift, he studied the garage, a scowl on his face. "You piled all my tools in them boxes?" he asked Bob. "I'll never find nothing now." He shook his head and walked off.

"You could've stopped him from going," I said to him up on his ladder. He knew immediately what I meant. His eyes widened with hurt in a way I had never seen before, then they darkened.

"He made his own mind up," he said.

That afternoon the storm drove us inside. My mother said she'd told him so but my father didn't look at her. Near 5:45 I opened the door to listen for Mr. Ramos's car. "Close that," my father said.

"In a minute," I said.

"I said now. I'm tired of you listening to that silliness." I slammed the door. "Boy, you want a whipping?" He went toward their bedroom where my mother was lying down. I heard the Chevy start. For some reason, it made me want to scream at my father. I walked down the hall and stopped outside the door.

"It ain't my fault, Winona," I heard him say.

"He wanted to make you happy," she said. "If you don't know that, you should." No sound came from the room for several seconds, then the door opened. My father walked past me as if I weren't there.

In my room, I smoothed my hand over my bed, the spread damp beneath my fingers even though the house had been closed all day. Above the baseboard the spots of mildew were larger. I turned off the light and opened my curtain so I could see the pine needles just outside my window moving beneath the rain, could see reflections shimmering off the puddles in the backyard. It was out there that Bob had thrown me the football after rainstorms, taught me how to plant and cut on wet ground. Afterward we would slide and tear ruts in the grass, infuriating our father when he came home from work. I knew if Bob were home now, he'd be doing something about the rising water, even if only taking me out to walk in it.

I joined my mother at the picture window in the living room. Gray sheets of rain, illuminated by flashes of lightning, whipped the water standing in the road and edging into our yard. Flood warnings rolled across the TV screen. Weather radar showed even heavier rains moving through New Orleans on their way to us. My father came in and watched the screen, his hands on the back of my mother's chair, then went through the kitchen into the garage. I found him there, staring at the damp floor near the wall, his arms hanging at his sides. "Is it coming in?" I asked.

He jerked as though he hadn't heard me come out behind him. "Go back inside," he said, his voice sharp. From the kitchen, I heard him sliding scrap lumber into the rafters of the garage ceiling, heard the garage door being raised. "What's he doing out there?" my mother asked. She walked to the door, touched the knob, then shook her head and returned to the living room. Through the door window, I saw him sitting on an overturned bucket, watching the street.

At 11:45 I walked onto the porch to listen for Mr. Ramos's car and found my father standing calf-deep in the street near the drain. He scanned our yard and the yards nearest us where the water had moved halfway up to the houses. I waded out to him. "Ground just can't take no more," he said, rain pouring off the brim of his aluminum hard hat. Mr. Ramos's garage light was on, but I didn't see him.

"What we gonna do?" I asked.

My father shook his head. "Might as well get some sleep." His listless voice reminded me of Bob's on the tape. I wanted him to grab his shovel and go to the drain, to tell me to get a bucket and bleach, to do something. Instead, he turned to go inside. My mother stepped out onto the porch. He sat near her feet and pulled off his boots.

"You think it'll get in the house?" my mother asked him.

"Never has before," he said.

With his right hand, he pulled against the fingers of his left. "One of y'all think you can stop it from raining, be my guest," he said, and went in the house.

I stayed where I was, my feet covered by water. Across the street Mr. Ramos hustled outside and bent over his bucket, watching it fill, I guessed, faster than he'd imagined it could. Their yard was lower than ours and the water had already reached their house. Donny's face peered through the back door window. "I'm going in," my mother said. I followed her, expecting her to argue or at least talk to my father, but both of them silently retired.

In the darkness of our living room, I sat in my father's chair and listened to the downpour, impossibly hard after so many hours. I pictured our house going under, all of us standing there, doing nothing.

Someone pounding on the door awakened me, but before I could move, my father opened it. "You gotta come," Donny Ramos said, his clothes laden with water, his hair wetted flat against his head. "Momma said to get you."

"Wait here," my father said, and surprised me by not asking Donny what was happening. I slipped on my shoes and my raincoat and joined Donny outside where a quarter inch of water covered our porch. The rain, though not as fierce as before, was still falling. "It's in our house," Donny said to me. "Daddy's in the garage."

When my father came out, we waded in, the water deepening to my waist as we descended to the street. Donny hurried ahead of us, the water, black as oil and smelling of gasoline and sewage, even deeper on him. Grass and leaves floated on the surface. "Be careful where you step," my father said, directing us away from the drain, but Donny plowed ahead.

As soon as we reached their driveway, I saw Mr. Ramos jacking the Chevy, the car leaning at a precarious angle toward the driver's side. The water covered the car's bumper even though the car itself was completely off the ground. Mrs. Ramos stood at the back door next to a dam of towels as high as her knees. "He won't leave that car," she said. "I'm raising what I can. I didn't know what to do but call."

"How much water you got in the house?" my father asked.

"A couple of inches, but it's still coming up."

My father pushed a fist against his mouth, then walked toward the garage. Mr. Ramos, drenched, glanced at us and continued jacking.

"You getting water in your house, Ramos," my father said.

"You came over to tell me that? I can see that."

Mr. Ramos stopped jacking, took a deep breath and ducked into the water. After several seconds his head came up next to the car. He inhaled and went under again.

"He keeps raising them standing jacks," Donny said.

Mr. Ramos popped up, leaned with his hands on his knees and took a deep breath. He flicked the directional switch on the jack, lowered it until the car rested on the submerged stand, then took the jack to the other side of the car.

"If you got some bricks, we can lift your furniture," my father said.

"There's a pile in the backyard," Mr. Ramos said. "Have at it." He locked the jack against the back bumper. My father took a step toward Mr. Ramos, then examined the Chevy. The space between the side wall of the garage and the car was much closer in the rear than in the front.

"Them jacks ain't high enough to get this car out of the water, Ramos. You can't even see if you're getting them firm under the supports."

"I don't have to see. I can feel."

Donny walked to the car and laid his hands on the hood while Mr. Ramos pumped the jack handle once more, the tilted car creaking. Donny lifted his hands and gaped at the car as if it were being magically levitated.

"Stay here," my father said to me. He started through the narrow space between the car and the wall.

"I didn't ask you to come over here," Mr. Ramos said. "I can take care of this myself."

"You got to come with me. We got to help your wife get the furniture up off the floor.

Mr. Ramos looked beyond my father as if he suddenly remembered his wife. "Go help your mother, Donny," he said.

"Stop acting crazy," my father said.

Mr. Ramos jerked as though stung, then stepped toward my father. "Crazy. Who you calling crazy?" He shook the jack handle. "You think I'm crazy?"

"Your house is going under. It's too dangerous messing around under this car." My father reached out and tried to grab Mr. Ramos's arm, but Ramos jerked away and pointed the jack handle like a sword.

"Who you think you are? You think you're better than I am?" He shook his head. "I've got something right here. I'm not letting it get ruined."

Mr. Ramos jabbed the bar into the jack and pumped double-time. The car wavered. He knelt, then went under again. My father made a move toward him, but the jack let out a shriek. The car lurched to the side, sending a wave against the wall. My father rushed the length of the car, his hand on the Chevy as if he could stop another shift, and reached underwater. Donny tried to get past me, but I grabbed him. He thrashed against me but I held on. In the narrow space, my father pulled Mr. Ramos from the water, my father's arms on Mr. Ramos's, and tried to move him out of the garage. They struggled a moment, a slow-motion dance, then Mr. Ramos threw off my father's grip. Mr. Ramos sloshed past the car and kept going on into the house. My father hesitated, then hurried through where Mr. Ramos had gone.

Donny stared at the house for a long moment, then he spun on the car, hit the hood with his fist and began pushing against it. I froze, believing for a second that the car was going to topple, believing that Donny could do that. My father hugged Donny from the rear, hugged him until Donny stopped resisting. "We got to help your momma," my father said, his voice quiet. "We got to go in and help her." Donny gazed toward the house, his expression disconnected and furious. Then he nodded and headed toward the bricks.

Once inside the Ramoses' house, I tried not to hear Mr. Ramos talking to himself in his room, Tootie's name a wail. Donny, Mrs. Ramos, my father, and I lifted the furniture onto bricks without speaking or even looking at one another. I wanted my father to speak, to at least break the silence and shame, and when he didn't I knew that he was scared, too.

After we finished, my father and I waded into the street again. Lights burned in all the houses now, people scrabbling to find whatever they could to elevate their belongings. My father walked ahead, not speaking, and even though I knew better, I said, "Mr. Ramos is nuts." He slapped me on the side of the head, not hard, but unexpectedly.

"Don't ever say that again," he said, and walked on.

I stopped in the street, the dark water to my waist. The low sky pulsed salmon from the plant flares burning even in the rain. My father's back moved away from me, the water sloshing before him. And at that moment I hated him, for hitting me, for making Bob go to war, for being an adult in a place that made no sense. But mostly I hated him for being weak in the way a child sees weakness, hated him for being unable to solve complexity with a simple gesture, hated him because when he'd held Mr. Ramos I had seen the limitations of strength.

"You coming?" he asked, holding upon the screen door. I forced my legs to move through the water.

When we entered the house, my mother was mopping the quarter inch of water on the living room floor. It seemed impossible that it could be there. My father scratched his head and scanned the room, walked over and peered the length of the hall. "How long?" he asked.

"A half hour," my mother said. My father nodded, shoved his hands in his pockets and took in the scene as if he had to see every inch of the floor under water before he could comprehend any of it. He took his hands out and rubbed them together, then arched an eyebrow at my mother. "When it rains, huh?" he said. My mother and I glanced at each other. My father looked at me, his face breaking into a weird smile. He stomped his foot, making a small splash. "Y'all know. When it rains it pours. Can't argue that, can we?"

He slapped his hands together, the laughter taking him until he held his stomach. I moved away from him and looked at my mother. I had never heard him laugh like this, in an abandoned way that recalled Mr. Ramos wailing for Tootie. My father stepped toward me, grabbed me and pulled me to him. I pushed against him, but he held me, his body shaking against mine. He started to dance, water splashing onto the walls and furniture, my mother holding out her palms to tell him to stop. Then he pirouetted with me, lifted my feet off the ground, as the floor warped right there beneath us.

Brownsville

TOM PIAZZA

I've been trying to get to Brownsville, Texas, for weeks. Right now it's a hundred degrees in New Orleans and the gays are running down Chartres Street with no shirts on, trying to stay young. I'm not running anymore. When I get to Brownsville I'm going to sit down in the middle of the street, and that will be the end of the line.

Ten in the morning and they're playing a Schubert piano trio on the tape and the breeze is blowing in from the street and I'm sobbing into a napkin. "L. G.," she used to say, "you think I'm a mess? You're a mess, too, L. G." That was a consolation to her.

The walls in this café have been stained by patches of seeping water that will never dry, and the plaster has fallen away in swatches that look like silhouettes of countries nobody's ever heard of. Pictures of Napoleon are all over the place: Napoleon blowing it at Waterloo, Napoleon holding his dick on St. Helena, Napoleon sitting in some subtropical café thinking about the past, getting drunk, plotting revenge.

I picture Brownsville as a place under a merciless sun, where one-eyed dogs stand in the middle of dusty, empty streets staring at you and hot breeze blows inside your shirt and there's nowhere to go. It's always noon, and there are no explanations required. I'm going to Brownsville exactly because I've got no reason to go there. Anybody asks me why Brownsville—there's no fucking answer. That's why I'm going there.

Last night I slept with a woman who had hair down to her ankles and a shotgun in her bathtub and all the mirrors in her room rattled when she laughed. She was good to me; I'll never say a bad word about her. There's always a history, though; her daughter was sleeping on a blanket in the dining room. It would have been perfect except for that.

The past keeps rising up here; the water table is too high. All around the Quarter groups of tourists float like clumps of sewage. The black carriage drivers pull their fringed carts full of white people from nowhere up to the corner outside and tell them how Jean Lafitte and Andrew Jackson plotted things out, as if the driver knew them personally. The conventioneers sit under the carriage awning, looking around with the crazed, vacant stare of babies, shaded by history, then move on.

The sun is getting higher, the shadows are shortening, the moisture is steaming off the sidewalks. The Schubert, or Debussy, or whatever it is, has turned into an oboe rhapsody, with French horns and bassoons quacking and palmetto bugs crawling across the tile floor, making clicking sounds that I can't hear because the music is too loud. If she didn't love me, why didn't she just tell me so? I asked her why she lied to me and she said she was afraid to tell me the truth. In other words it was my fault. She doesn't even have a friend named Debbie.

I keep trying to look at what's right in front of me. I want to stop trying to mess with the past. The last thing she said to me was, "I have to get this other call." But I'm not going to think about her.

One cloth napkin.

One butter knife.

One fork.

One frosted glass containing partly melted ice and a slice of cucumber. Another frosted glass with similar contents. Where's the waiter? A small menu, marked with coffee along one edge. Breeze from a ceiling fan. Three Germans at the next table. The pictures of Napoleon must make them nervous. A waiter on a stool, leaning back against the wall by the ice chest, hair already pasted to his forehead with sweat.

A white Cadillac just backed into a car parked right outside, making a loud noise and partly caving in the wooden column supporting the balcony above the sidewalk. People are getting up and walking to the door, looking. The driver is black and is wearing a full Indian costume, plumes mushrooming as he gets out to look. He is about seventy years old; a five-year-old boy waits in the front seat. The driver gets back into the Cadillac and drives off.

One coffee mug at the next table. One crumpled pack of Winstons.

Hopeless.

I saw a sign once, on a building outside Albuquerque, that read ALL AMERICAN SELF-STORAGE. If you could just pay a fee somewhere and put yourself in a warehouse, just for a night.

Brownsville.

I picture a little booth at the edge of town, with a bored-looking woman sitting in it. You pay fifty cents and leave everything you can remember in a box with her. You walk down Main Street at high noon, wearing a leather vest, on the balls of your feet. The one-eyed dogs bark and shy away, walking sideways, eyeing you. You walk into the saloon, which is cool and dark, and order a bourbon. You look in the mirror behind the bar and talk to yourself in the second person. Maybe it would be better to stay outside in the sun.

Here is what morning is like in New Orleans. Just before the sky starts getting light, the last freight train inches its way through Ville Platte and the stars have drifted off to sleep. Slowly, the sky exhales its darkness and the trees look black against the deep blue over Gentilly. The houses along Felicity Street, and farther out toward Audubon Park, are cool to the touch, and dew covers the flower beds. A taxi pulls up to a traffic light, looks, goes through. The smell of buttered toast disappears around the corner and televisions are going in the kitchens of the black section. The St. Charles trolley, as unbelievable as it was yesterday, shuttles its first serious load toward the business district. Later, the men will have taken their jackets off and folded them in their laps, staring out the streetcar windows, caught in that dream. Already the first shoeshine boys are out hustling on Bourbon Street, and the first dixieland band is playing for the after-breakfast tourists, and the first conventioneers are climbing into carriages at Jackson Square, and the Vietnamese waitresses at the Cafe du Monde are getting off their all-night shifts, and luggage is lined up on the sidewalk outside the Hyatt.

If there was just some way to stay in it, to be there and see it without starting in. If there was just some way to wipe the slate clean. As soon as I can, I'm going to pay my tab and step outside. I'm closing my accounts and going to Brownsville. I'll leave everything at the edge of town. I'm going to walk in and take it from there.

What You Do Next

NANCY RICHARD

The summer they turned seventeen Emma Terrebonne and Billy Badeaux sneaked out every night to the pecan grove behind St. Basil's Cemetery. At first it was to smoke the cigarettes Emma stole from Theriot's Grocery, then to drink the beer Billy swiped from his grandfather's stash. Emma will remember that Billy smelled of the earth he tilled on the family farm and the dogs he played with. And she will remember that he kissed her for the first time on the Fourth of July, in the pecan grove, while the hot night buzzed with mosquitoes, the moon smiled, and the Maringouin Knights of Columbus fireworks whistled and rained and dazzled overhead.

But now it is late winter, and Emma is no longer seventeen. Billy is dead, and her husband has left her. For the first week, Emma paced at night and watched a late snow curl in drifts around the mailbox at the corner and the lamppost beneath her window. When she slept Emma dreamed of her grandmother's old house, sitting empty and abandoned on the bayou. Feral cats now inhabited her sleeping; from her grandmother's barn they moved into the house and lounged on the beds, sprawled rangy bodies across the kitchen table, and dozed on the porches. They mated yowling beneath the house in spring and left bits of mouse fur and bone and batwings in the barn. A child who was both Emma and not Emma played in the yard and hid in the hayloft. When she woke to bone-chilling cold and a still and pale landscape, she climbed from her dreaming life into the waking one, where she met her classes and moved through her duties each day as if by rote.

In late spring Robert began to call. He was having second thoughts. Perhaps they could talk. Emma stopped answering her phone and, when she heard his voice, erased his messages. At the end of the school year, Emma submitted her resignation at the high school, wrote her mother in New Orleans, and settled with the landlord to break the lease.

She made an appointment with her hairdresser. "Get rid of it," she said. "It's too cold here. I'm moving to a warmer climate." Emma listened to the metallic snip, snip and stared into the mirror as her hair left the scissors, dropped to her shoulders, slid to the floor. The woman who stared back at her looked frightened, as though she had been asked a question whose answer she could not know. "Okay," her own eyes begged, "okay, what now?"

That afternoon Emma called Goodwill and donated all the furniture, some of it Robert's. Three days later, just after the Goodwill truck had lumbered up the street, Emma packed her car and drove all one day and all night, chasing the moon south and west, winding down through red dirt hills toward the landscape of heat and water she often visited in her dreams. For the whole of her first day in her grandmother's old house, Emma swept cobwebs from the ceilings and dusted furniture and washed walls and floors. At nightfall she stood before the kitchen sink, where the window gave a view of the yard, and beyond it, the angel trumpet tree. Emma saw a movement there, hardly more than a sliding of one shadow into another. When she stepped onto the porch for a closer look, Emma saw the girl, standing before the tree, in a pool of light beneath the bright eye of the waxing moon. When Emma stepped from the porch into the yard, the girl slipped away into the darkness.

That night Emma lay awake for hours, conscious of the weight of the night air upon her skin. Later, dreaming, she saw the tree covered in snow, a young girl standing on its crown. When she woke, her sheets were damp and tangled, her hair wet against her neck. The smell of the bayou had drifted through her windows and clung to the walls. She had lived in the city too long, Emma thought, and open windows and wild, chirping night songs had made her delirious. She woke on the edge of vague memory and imagined she emanated a white heat.

In the winter of the year that Emma loved Billy, her grandmother—her mother was too upset—took her to old Dr. Melançon, but she already knew, of course, that Emma was pregnant. Billy had dropped out of school by then and was working somewhere on the coast on an uncle's shrimp boat. Her mother began to cry and did not stop; her grandmother, more pragmatic than hysterical, asked her every day, "What will you do, chère? What you decide makes that baby's life: you will give that baby a chance or not?" Every day Mémé took her hand and whispered a prayer. If Emma tried to avoid her by neglecting her daily visit, her grandmother phoned or drove into town herself. What will you do next? What? She ignored Emma's answers, "I don't know, Mémé, I don't know."

On her second morning Emma walked the outside of the house, examined the front porch supports and rails, the back porch and window screens, the condition of the eaves. The house needed paint, most of the screens wanted replacing, and all around her were twenty acres in need of bush hogging. She made a list of supplies and groceries and stared at the balance in her checkbook. With no rent to pay, she would have enough money to last a few months; when fall came she'd need a job.

For dinner Emma finished the last of the bread and cheese she'd brought with her and the last orange. She turned off all the lights in the house and took a cup of coffee to the back porch. There she watched the sky, where an occasional cloud drifted across the rising moon, and the yard filled with dancing shadows. Presently the girl appeared. Within moments the bats came, too, flying within feet of her head, a swooping, circling, and banking in the patchy moonlight. Emma watched the girl watch the bats feed, their bodies hovering before one pale trumpet and the next, until the colony moved together toward the tree line and beyond. When the bats had disappeared, so had the girl, but Emma had seen enough of her to know she was Lily. She went inside and poured another cup of coffee. It was strong and black and would keep her awake, but she didn't care. Her nights brought dreams that flirted with memory, leaving her exhausted, her heart racing, and abandoned her to days of frenzied work.

It all happened in her senior year, but of course Emma could not stay in school, not in her condition. It just wasn't done. Her teachers had expected her to win scholarships, but now they looked at her the same way her mother did, with profound disappointment. They sent work to her at home, and she studied fiercely, but when her diploma arrived in the mail, she'd refused to open the envelope. Her back hurt, and the heat made her faint, so she slept away the long hot afternoons and dreamed of swimming.

On Saturday morning Emma stood before her empty refrigerator. She stared at the bare shelves of the pantry. She had avoided it long enough. She would have to go to town. She would have to walk into Touchet's Grocery and face T-Boy; she had come home, and she needed groceries. It had been three days, and of course everyone knew she'd been moving about in her grandmother's house like some dark and lonely ghost. She drove into town past St. Basil's and the bakery where her mother had worked, and the apartment over the bakery where they had lived. T-Boy's house was still there, next door to the rectory. Cats sat on the porch rails and steps. Emma stopped at the highway, crossed to T-Boy's store, and parked in the clamshell lot. At first she merely sat for long moments, listening to her own heart, her own breathing.

On Emma's eighteenth birthday Mémé brought Father Mike to visit again, and this time Emma did not send him away. The family, they have to be Catholic, her grandmother explained. We can't go through the state agency, have that baby's Catholic soul in a house full of—What's that new religion I just heard about, it was on the news?—Unitarians. Mon Dieu, we can't have that. If Emma wished, Father Mike would make some phone calls. Yes, Emma said, her mother crying still, yes. The priest blessed her and patted her hand. "Okey doke," he said. It was June. She was eight months pregnant, and the baby's movement frightened her. When it kicked at night and woke her, Emma spread her fingertips over the foreign swell that was her own body and imagined the baby spoke to her in a secret, atonal humming. She knew her baby was a girl; she could not have explained how she knew this, but as Emma felt her baby's elbow in her ribs, a tiny knee in her back, the rolling tumble of weightless floating, she heard a girl-child singing her own name. Father Mike returned in three days with T-Boy and Grace.

A cat startled her when it leapt onto the hood of her car. She got out, picked up the cat and put it down. The inside of the store still smelled the same, a combination of detergent and apples, and everything was in exactly the same place it had always been. Emma could have gone through the store with her eyes closed, moving aisle to aisle through perfect memory. She looked about for T-Boy but saw only an old woman examining the tomatoes. Emma pushed a basket through the store, choosing what she wanted, as if she had a job. As she rounded the corner from the cleaning supplies to the dairy case, she saw him.

When she'd tagged along after him as a child, T-Boy's face had worn a look of patient amusement. Today he looked neither patient nor amused.

He crossed his arms and took one measured breath. "Tell me you came to sell the house."

"If I don't find a job," Emma said, "I might have to."

"There's nothing here," he said, "unless you want to work the fields."

"There are teachers here, too," she said, "and I applied to some schools in Baton Rouge."

"That's a long way to drive," he said.

"I guess I'd better be willing to drive an hour if I want porch paint and paper towels," Emma said.

"We got paper towels," T-Boy said. "They on special. For porch paint you got to go to Maringouin."

"I guess Lily told you," Emma said, "that I was back, that she saw me in the house."

"That's right," T-Boy said. "And your mama was here to get the utilities turned on. Seems like you could have called or something. Seems like we should have known ahead of time, from *you*." His face had reddened, and now he uncrossed his arms and thrust his hands into his pockets.

"Yes," she said. "I know. I didn't plan things well." Emma imagined her mother's explanation, which of course would have been another apology. *My daughter, behaving badly again. I'm sorry. She won't listen. She has never listened.* "I guess I'll finish my shopping," she said.

"That college teacher you married—"

"Robert."

"He ran away with a famous French actress?"

"She's a poet," Emma said, "visiting the college. She's from Romania."

"Same thing," he said. He just looked at her. When Emma was a child he'd looked at her that way, as though he expected an explanation for some unacceptable behavior. But she'd never had a satisfactory one.

"I need my phone turned on," Emma said. "May I use yours?"

"They closed on Saturday," T-Boy said. "My cousin works there. Her son, too. I'll call for you Monday morning. You in a hurry?"

"Yes," she said, "I need a job."

"She'll send somebody Monday." T-Boy gave her a dark look. "Don't need a phone if you not staying. Somebody gets a phone, looks for a job, that means they staying."

"I won't interfere," she said. "I promised, and I meant it."

"Like the last promise you made," he muttered. He shrugged and turned away. "I got to go back to work. I got to pull the bad lettuce." T-Boy looked at her once more. "What you did to your hair?" But he didn't wait for an answer.

Emma returned to her car, where the cat, a small calico, now lay on the back seat. She picked it up and set it down, but it shot beneath the car to the other side and leapt through the open window onto the front passenger seat.

"Go away," Emma said. "Shoo." She waved her hand at the cat, but it merely turned its back and washed its face. Emma raised all the windows, picked up the cat, and removed her from the car again. She set the groceries into the trunk. When she opened her door, the cat appeared from beneath the car and jumped inside. She made her way to the passenger seat, curled up, and tucked her nose beneath her tail. Emma went back into the store and found T-Boy at the lettuce display.

"Is the calico in the parking lot one of yours?"

"No, indeed," he said. "It's prob'ly related to one of mine, though."

"She's decided to go home with me. I'll need some cat food."

T-Boy dropped a head of lettuce into the box at his feet. "Somebody gets a cat," he said, "that means they staying."

Next, Emma drove to Maringouin while the cat dozed beside her. When she arrived at the hardware store, she left the windows down, and when she returned to her car with the porch paint, the cat was still there.

In her kitchen that afternoon Emma read her mail: a letter from her mother—*Are you eating?*—and two letters from schools where she'd applied for a job. There were no openings, but they thanked her for her interest. There was also a letter from Robert. He would like to call sometime and talk. Perhaps now that there was some distance from the unhappy events of last spring . . . He would always wish her the best, he closed, and did not mention the furniture. Emma took Robert's crisp, typed and blocked letter to the stove, turned on a burner, and set it on fire. She held the letter over the sink, dropping it when the flames licked at her fingertips. Later, she scooped up the cold ashes and tossed them into the waste can.

That night the cat refused to come into the kitchen, choosing to remain on the back porch, where Emma set out food and water. She watched the cat eat. "Always leave your options open," Emma said. "Always know where the back door is." That night Emma's dream could have been an old movie, one she'd seen before.

T-Boy and Grace agreed to take Emma's baby. They would care for the baby as their own, they promised. When she moved away to college they would send pictures if she liked. Emma felt her baby turn beneath her heart. Once I leave, she thought, I will never come back. At eighteen Emma knew, or thought she knew, that her life would have to play itself out somewhere—anywhere—else. Yes, she said to Father Mike later.

Yes, as her mother cried and her grandmother told her beads with silent prayers, bring me the paperwork. And, no pictures, she said. Please. No pictures.

On Monday, T-Boy's cousin, the phone installer, came at noon. He gave her the number of his brother, who owned a bush hogging business. Emma called the two school board offices she had not yet heard from and gave them her phone number. That afternoon she scraped old paint from the front porch and drew smooth gray strokes of fresh paint across thirsty planks. She was cleaning her brush when the phone rang.

It was Robert. "So you've been busy, I guess, fixing up the old house?"

"Yes," she said, "there's a lot to be done."

He cleared his throat. "It's good to hear your voice again," he said.

"How did you know where to find me?" The sun had dropped to the roofline of the barn, throwing the side yard into shadow. Soon the bats would emerge from the hayloft, and perhaps Lily would appear.

"Where else would you go?"

Emma said nothing. He was right, of course. She had nowhere else to go.

"You're not making this any easier," he said, and laughed a little.

She regarded the paint splatters on her shoes. "Robert," she said, "my paintbrush is drying. I should go now."

For a week Emma's nights were dreamless. She woke slowly, climbing toward the light as from a cave. On those days she moved through her work without thinking. She swept cobwebs from all the windows and shutters. On the pitched and gabled roof she swept debris from the channels of the corrugated tin. One evening when Emma had not seen Lily for three nights, she heard a noise on her back porch. Expecting to see the cat, she found Lily. The girl stood in the far corner, still and alone in the dark.

"Is something wrong?" Emma asked. "Are you all right?"

Lily took a deep breath before she spoke. "It took you a long time to ask that." She watched Emma from the shadowed corner where she stood. "Besides," Lily said, "I wanted to see what you look like."

"So," Emma said, "what do I look like?"

"Like someone who wished I hadn't shown up on her back porch." Lily crossed and uncrossed her arms.

"You've always known," Emma said, "haven't you?" She remained in the doorway. Lily might have been some frightened wild creature, and if Emma moved suddenly, the girl would disappear.

"They tell me the truth," Lily said. "Everybody in the town has always known. There's no way I couldn't. Is it true, the reason you came back?"

"I have nowhere else to go," Emma said. She searched the darkening yard, but saw only the calico making her way toward the porch.

"In case you were wondering," the girl began, "they take good care of me."

"I knew they would," Emma said. "So did Father Mike."

Lily turned for the door. "I ought to go," she said. "They'll worry."

Emma followed her into the yard. "Aren't you afraid of the bats? That you'll get bitten?"

Lily stooped to call to the cat, but the calico ran beneath the porch. "They don't attack," she said, "and they don't fly into your hair, either. That's a myth." She stood and turned to go. "They always know where they're going," Lily called over her shoulder. "Echolocation. It never fails." And she began to run.

Emma called to her, but Lily did not turn. "Do you ever watch them return in the morning? I could make breakfast." But the girl had slipped into the woods, into the midst of a chorus of singing tree frogs and cicadas.

Later Emma would recall her labor and delivery as a fog of delirium, the baby turned and resisting, as if she knew her arrival would bring a disorder no wisdom would correct. Emma held her, a near weightless ghost-baby she seemed, with hair pale as light and a body fine-boned and still. She thought then of the bird Billy once rescued from a barn cat. She'd held its entire body in the palm of her hand, felt its racing heart and knew the terror alone could cause it to die. To Emma it seemed her baby might have been the body of that terrified bird. After the wail at her birth, Emma's baby did not cry, not once during the first week of her life, while Emma held her and watched her and fed her, until she gained enough weight to go home, to a place not Emma's. Mémé said she was a child waiting to leave them, as if she knew, tiny brand-new thing that she was, her stay was temporary, and she would not trouble them with the waiting.

Emma sat in her kitchen the next morning and drank coffee. When the phone rang it startled her; she took a deep breath before she answered. A job, she thought. Let it be a job.

It was Robert again. "What?" she said. "What?"

"Did I wake you? I thought you'd be up, but I guess, you're busy," he said.

"You're right," Emma said. "I was up and I am busy. What is it?"

"No particular reason," Robert said. "I mean, I wanted to let you know, if you ever want to talk, I'm ready."

In the background, Emma recognized the sounds of a daily news program. They had never owned a television. She saw the two of them, Robert and the poet, shopping at Sears for a television.

"If I ever want to talk," she said, "I'll let you know." From beneath Emma's house, directly under her kitchen, came a thud and the sound of a voice. "I should go," she said to Robert. "I'm expecting a call."

Alongside her back porch, Emma stooped toward the darkness. The noise returned, but this time the voice was clear. It was Lily, and she was calling to the cat. Soon Emma caught sight of the girl, pulling herself along in the dirt on her stomach. She crawled out, stood, and brushed herself off. There were cobwebs in her hair.

"She almost let me pick her up," Lily said, "but she ran off."

Emma led her inside and handed her a damp towel. Lily wiped her face and arms and washed her hands at the sink.

"She jumped right into my car," Emma said, "when I was in town. She can't be too wild. She'll warm up to us in time."

"What's her name?" Lily stood in the center of the room and studied everything in it.

"We're not that close," Emma said.

"So who's the famous French actress?" Lily strolled about Emma's kitchen, fingering the curtains, pausing to gaze from each window. "Anybody we heard of?"

"She's a poet," Emma said. "Romanian. And not famous at all."

"Same thing," Lily said. "What kind of poetry does she write?"

"The sad kind." Emma thought of Lily as a baby, fragile as a glass bird, but now she stood here, brown and lean and straight. "She writes about the dying in her homeland, about losing mothers and children and lovers."

"Is that what men like?" Lily was studying the kitchen, one wall at a time.

"I think it had little to do with the poetry," Emma said. "I was about to have breakfast. Are you hungry?"

Lily shrugged, and Emma set out the eggs and milk and bread for French toast.

She watched as Lily broke eggs into a bowl and fished out pieces of shell with her fingers. When the phone rang Emma was setting soggy bread into sizzling butter; she directed Lily to answer.

"I'm fine, Daddy," Lily said. She listened a moment. "Making French toast. Yes, she knows how."

When the tops of the two slices in the skillet were set, Emma turned them.

"It was a Romanian poet," Lily said into the phone, "not a French actress." She smiled a little at something he said. "That's what I told her," she answered. Lily returned the receiver to its cradle. "He's coming in his truck. But we can eat first." She stood beside Emma at the stove. "The old ladies at mass this morning," she began, "they said I look just like you did at twelve."

Emma moved the cooked slices to a plate, sprinkled them with cinnamon sugar, and dropped more butter into the pan. She waited while it melted. "Do you think we look alike?" She slid more egg-and-milk-soaked bread into the skillet, lowered the flame a little, and listened to her daughter's breathing. Once their shoulders touched.

"Sometimes when Daddy looks at me, I can tell it isn't me he sees. Once he even called me by your name. It was the hair, he said." Lily slipped the spatula beneath one slice, flipped it, and did the same with the other.

"The day before I moved back," Emma said, "I was thinking about the air here—how heavy it is—and the heat, and I had it all cut off. I have a picture." She went to her bedroom closet, where she found the box marked PHOTOS. She searched through it until she found the one her mother had taken at T-Boy and Grace's wedding. All of them—T-Boy and Grace in the middle, surrounded by family, friends, the priest—stood before St. Basil's squinting in the noonday sun. Emma returned to the kitchen and laid the photo on the table.

Lily turned off the burner and lifted the two slices onto a plate. She took the photo into her hands and stood at the window over the sink. She held it there, in the morning light, and stared. "How old were you then?"

"They were married the month before I turned seventeen," Emma said.

Lily looked up from the photo and directly at Emma for the first time. "You needn't look like that," she said.

Emma stepped toward her and, with her fingertips, lifted the silvery cobwebs from Lily's hair. "Like what? What do I look like?"

Lily stared through the window. She might have been talking to herself. "Like you're about to cry, except you won't. I don't cry."

"You're right," Emma said, "I don't. And I wasn't about to. I was thinking about when I asked T-Boy and Grace not to send pictures of you. I thought if I didn't look at you, even in a photograph, I'd be able to think of you as a stranger. Someone else's child."

"I guess that seemed easier." Lily poured herself a glass of milk and Emma a cup of coffee.

"That's what I thought," Emma said.

They ate without talking. From time to time when Lily speared a piece of French toast, she tapped her fork on the edge of her plate to shake loose the extra sugar.

"Maybe I should have called ahead, to let your father know I was coming," Emma said at last. "I should have let him know before I just showed up in his store like that. I'm afraid my life, my thinking, has been a bit disorderly."

"Daddy says disorder is what happens when people do as they please and forget about everybody else." Lily ran a fingertip along the edge of her plate, licked off the sugar, and resumed eating.

"I think he said that to me a time or two, when I was about your age," Emma said. "I always did as I pleased, and I always managed to make a mess of things."

Lily set her fork down and finished her milk. "Did he know? Your husband. Did he know about me?"

"Robert knew everything." Emma cleared the table. "He always knew everything." She broke more eggs and soaked more bread. "For your father," she said to Lily. "We'll keep it warm until he gets here."

Emma covered T-Boy's plate and put it into the oven, over the pilot flame. She and Lily sat on the back porch to wait. The calico had come out of hiding and sat beside Lily's feet. Lily leaned forward and rubbed her ears. "We have that wedding picture—" Lily began, and did not look up, "my parents, you, Father Mike—everybody is looking at the camera except for one person. In the picture, there's a boy, and he's looking at you. He's the only one not looking at the camera. Daddy says he's the one."

"Yes," Emma said. "Yes, that would be Billy."

"Daddy says he died in an accident." Lily was concentrating on the cat. She stroked her from head to tail, again and again.

306 | **NANCY RICHARD**

"Yes, a fishing accident in the Gulf. While I was at college." Emma watched Lily's hands, her fine long fingers, and the familiar way she handled the cat. "Billy came from Baton Rouge every summer to work on his grandfather's farm and on holidays for visits. He always seemed to find something to rescue: a raccoon one summer, a squirrel the next. He was the only one the feral barn cats would allow to touch their kittens."

Lily had moved to the floor and was coaxing the cat into her lap. "You've got that look again."

Emma stood and looked toward the road. "It's temporary," she said.

When T-Boy arrived, he was carrying a cardboard box. "I brought you some food from the store and some paper towels. Just this time. Don't expect it all the time. I had extras. Grace sent some vegetables from the garden, too." He set the box down and looked around. Emma could hear the faint, familiar wheezing from his chest. "Looks like somebody moved in for good," he said.

Emma poured a glass of milk at the place she'd set for him at the table. "I've been keeping it warm. We expected you sooner."

T-Boy sat at the table and cut into the first slice. He ate one bite, then another, and drank some milk before he spoke. "You got a job yet?"

Emma took a sip of her coffee, which was now cold, and swallowed. "I have prospects," she said.

"Prospects don't sound like a job to me," he said. "Can't pay bills with prospects."

"You wouldn't happen to have any cousins on the school board in Baton Rouge, would you?" Emma got up and poured her coffee into the sink.

"No," he said, and looked somewhere over Emma's head as he chewed. "Just in Lafayette. My cousin—she's a nun, her mama's my godmother—she's the principal at the big Catholic high school. But she's the only one. We don't have a lot of teachers in our family."

Emma waited.

T-Boy looked to the porch where Lily was playing with the cat. "I guess you want me to call her."

Emma refilled his milk glass. "That would be nice," she said.

"That fellow—Robert?—he came in the store." T-Boy cut into the French toast and speared another piece. "That's why I'm late. I was by myself."

"That's not possible," Emma said. "It must have been someone else. Why would he be here?"

T-Boy looked at her. "How many people you know would pretend to be somebody like that? Said maybe he shouldn't just show up at your door. I said depends how lucky he's feeling. He decided he'd go back to Baton Rouge, already got him a motel room."

"I guess he needed directions," Emma said, "back to the Interstate."

"No, he didn't need no directions." T-Boy continued to eat. "He found his way here, a man with all that education, I guess he can find his way back." He swallowed. "He says to me, 'What kind of coffee Emma buys?' I said, 'How come? You want something else? Only other kind I got,' I told him, 'ain't no good. That nasty instant. But buy what you want.'" He paused. "You got some cane syrup?"

Emma shook her head and looked into the box he'd brought. She found a jar of figs and handed it to him. She watched as he added a heaping spoonful to his second slice. "Well? That's it? He went in to get advice about coffee?"

T-Boy chewed slowly. He licked the sugar off the corner of his mouth. "That's about it," he said. "He paid for the coffee and said pleased to meet you and was talking to himself on the way out." He moved a piece of French toast around on his plate, cleaning up the extra sugar that had mingled with the dark syrup from the figs. "And that's the one you picked," he murmured.

Emma pulled his plate away. "If you don't get to the end of this, I'm picking up your food. What was he saying, on the way out?"

"He won't hurry," Lily called from the porch. "You can't make him hurry." She was holding the cat, which seemed to have fallen asleep in her arms.

T-Boy waved his fork in Lily's direction. "No more cats," he said. "You can't have no more cats." He turned to Emma. "And you, you still mean as sin, you know that? He said looked like he better get used to the kind of coffee you can stand a spoon in. May as well start drinking it now. He said don't say nothing to you, but me, I don't owe him nothing. Give me back my food."

When he had finished, T-Boy and Lily got into his truck. "You can make gumbo?"

"I'll work on it," Emma said.

"It's too hot for gumbo now," T-Boy said, throwing his leg into the clutch. The truck shuddered and lurched forward. "In the fall and winter, that's when you eat gumbo."

"I know," Emma said. "I grew up here."

"How about that?" T-Boy said. "I keep forgetting. Grace, she'll send you some okra if you want. Okra's good in a gumbo, long as you don't cook it slimy." T-Boy leaned through his window. "He came to take you back," he said. "Only reason he's here. It's sure not to drink our coffee. Do what you want. But he's not even Catholic. How come you don't have more sense than you did at seven?" The truck rolled forward before Emma could answer. Lily's face appeared in the rear window, but she did not wave.

The phone was ringing when Emma returned to the kitchen. "I'm in Baton Rouge," Robert said. "The phone calls weren't working out."

"You came a long way to chat," Emma said.

"I set out yesterday to pick up some dry cleaning," he said. "But instead of going home, I just kept driving until I got to the airport. I waited for hours for the next flight that would get me here."

"You went to a lot of trouble," Emma said, "and I'm not sure I have much to say." She thought about his dry cleaning, still hanging in his car at the airport parking garage.

"You don't sound surprised."

"T-Boy told me," she said.

"I asked him not to," he said, "but I guess I shouldn't expect any favors from him."

Emma picked up the phone and walked to her back door. There were holes in the screens of the porch. Once she had a job, she'd have them replaced, except for the one the cat used. "That's what he said," Emma replied, "in so many words." The calico crossed the porch to where Emma stood. She brushed against Emma's leg, purring.

"Emma," Robert said, "are you there?"

"Yes, Robert," she said. "I'm here. I have a phone and a cat. I think I'll be here awhile."

"I'm going to quit my job," he said.

Emma said, "What are you doing, Robert?"

He said, "I can't make this right from a thousand miles away, so I'm here."

Emma watched the cat return to her chair, stretch, yawn, and roll onto her back. "You shouldn't do anything rash." That chair should have a cushion, she thought.

Robert cleared his throat. "I think I've already done that," he said.

Emma waited. "Lily thinks you were swept off your feet by the pathos."

"She sounds like you," Robert said.

"No," Emma said, "she's smarter and kinder."

"I'll go home to pack—" he went on, "—there isn't much—and I'll drive back in a week or so. I'm going to look for a job here and get an apartment."

Emma went into the kitchen, where sticky plates and bowls and a messy skillet waited. "What if I told you not to bother?" she said. "I mean to stay here."

"I'm moving here anyway," Robert said. "I'm not here to talk you into leaving. I'm going to work at convincing you to let me stay."

"You have your work cut out for you," she said, and began to clear the table. "And Robert," she added, "you'll need a furnished apartment."

When her kitchen was clean again, Emma walked out into the yard. She followed the cat into the barn, where the light was dim and the cool air smelled of hay and things wild hanging from rafters and hiding in corners. She moved the ladder from where it led to the loft and laid it on the floor. The cat watched her from atop the old tractor.

"None of this is simple," Emma said to the cat. "Now I'll have to take you to a veterinarian. I wonder if T-Boy has a cousin in the business." She gathered up a rusty shovel and a pair of rakes and leaned them against a corner. "Did I mention Robert's allergic to cats?" The calico followed her from the barn and onto the back porch where she allowed Emma to pick her up. Emma stroked her throat, until she purred. "Well," Emma said, "I guess he'll have to work that out."

The phone rang, and she meant to ignore it. It rang four times, five. When Emma answered, there was quiet for a few moments.

Lily said, "Next month is my birthday."

Emma said, "I know."

"Can I name her?" Lily asked.

"What did you have in mind?" Emma set the cat onto the floor and watched her move through the kitchen, checking every cabinet door, before she found her way to the hall and the bedrooms.

"I'm working on it," Lily said. "I'll make a list and get back to you." And she hung up.

Emma stood in her kitchen, where the scent of cinnamon lingered, and with it the memory of cane fields burning in the fall, the sharp bite in the air of sweet black smoke drifting with the autumn fog. She heard, too, in the voices of her students, their anxious need to have answers, to know the why and how and when of their lives.

"Why do we hurt each other?" the plain girl in the back row will ask.

"How can we allow suffering in the world?" the bright young man who seldom attends will ask.

And the student who is lost, the one who will never ask for help, will only think about asking, "When will we be old enough to understand what we are meant to do next?"

Emma will tell them the truth, though it is not the answer they want. "We don't know," she will say. "We don't know."

Camping Out

JAMES WILCOX

Donna Lee and Mrs. Norris went first; behind them in the green, dented eighteen-footer were Donna Lee's father, her brother-in-law, and her nephew, Ralph. Tula Creek was high, and the canoes glided silently, like awkward, heavy-laden clouds, over uprooted trees and clay mounds big as the humped, gray backs of Brahma bulls. Donna Lee was the most experienced canoeist, Mrs. Norris the least, which was the reason they were paired. In the other canoe seven-year-old Ralph was the only one who had mastered the J-stroke, a paddling technique that kept the boat in line from the stern. Donna Lee had tried to teach her father and Henry, her brother-in-law, the J-stroke, but they claimed they already knew.

When they passed the place where the gravel works cut a chunk out of the vine-tangled banks of river birch, Donna Lee looked over her shoulder and shouted back to Ralph that they were out of Mississippi now, in Louisiana. The overloaded green canoe was sliding along sideways, and Ralph's face was red with the effort of trying to get it straightened out. Donna Lee began yelling instructions to her brother-in-law, who was in the stern of the green canoe. Henry was big—six feet eight, a former L.S.U. basketball star—but he didn't know what "draw" meant, which was what Donna Lee was yelling at him. The shouting woke Donna Lee's father, who had been snoozing in the middle of the green canoe with his legs draped over the ice chest, as if the river were his living room. Mr. Keely grabbed a paddle and started churning up the tea-brown water with intense, futile strokes.

Donna Lee couldn't take any more for now. They had been on the river only three hours, including a stop for lunch, but it seemed like days. She was worried about her father—he was overweight and had high blood pressure—and she herself was freezing to death. As she sat in the stern trying to compensate for Mrs. Norris's erratic strokes—they were feathery, artistic, frosting-smoothing strokes—the cold went right through Donna Lee's ancient raccoon coat and lumberjack shirt. The long underwear that she had borrowed from her father hung too loosely on her tall, gangly frame to be any help.

When the bow of the canoe grated on the sandy peninsula where Donna Lee planned to make camp for the night, Mrs. Norris just sat there. Donna Lee politely asked her to try to get out of the canoe. Mrs. Norris, who seemed fairly competent on dry land, had to be told *everything* on the river, as if she had just landed on another planet with a whole new set of physical laws.

Climbing out of the stern, Donna Lee smiled at Mrs. Norris's back. They had met only two weeks ago, in Mr. Herbert's law office in Tula Springs, where Donna Lee, a year out of law school, worked as a junior partner. Mrs. Norris's landlady was trying to evict her. It wasn't a clear-cut case, and Donna Lee had already spent an inordinate amount of time on it, which Mr. Herbert thought unwise. Donna Lee was not concerned; she had decided she wanted to make Mrs. Norris her friend. In her early sixties, Mrs. Norris looked very commonplace, with a bland, weary face and stiff, dyed red hair. But her life had been far from ordinary. Born and raised in South Africa, Mrs. Norris married a French physician who ran a small clinic in Léopoldville specializing in rare tropical diseases. For years she worked alongside him as a nurse, until one day one of the experimental monkeys went berserk— "clear off its rocker," as she had told Donna Lee—and bit the doctor. It was only a minor injury, but he was never the same afterward, and sank into a morose obsession with his stamp collection. They were divorced, and she married her English lover, Mr. Norris, who took her to Bolton, England. Twenty-five years her senior, Mr. Norris died a few weeks later of a heart attack while sparring in an amateur boxing match for a local charity. Next came a Montana ranch, owned by the late Mr. Norris's sister. There, the newly widowed Mrs. Norris was thrown from a snowmobile during a blizzard and nearly froze to death; luckily, all she lost was a big toe. She decided she wanted to live where it was warm, so she moved to New Orleans and had a long, happy affair with a Peruvian who was involved in smuggling something. When New Orleans began to seem too big for her, she moved eighty miles north, to Tula-Springs, where she worked as a nurse for a chiropractor and studied acupuncture.

Donna Lee told Mrs. Norris to sit down and rest while she unloaded the canoe. Mrs. Norris found a driftwood log and sat down on it. "Can't I help?" she called out, but the green canoe had just pulled up, and Donna Lee didn't hear her.

Ralph clambered out of the canoe, with tears making his large dark-brown eyes look even larger. He hurried past his aunt and disappeared into the woods at the end of the peninsula.

"He's too sensitive," Mr. Keely said, lugging the ice chest out of the canoe. "Henry didn't even raise his voice to him."

"Dad, be careful," Donna Lee said. She took the ice chest from him. She didn't want to get into a big discussion now about Ralph. Donna Lee thought it was the nuns who made Ralph so sensitive. Henry was Catholic, and Ralph had to go to catechism on Sundays. He had shown her what he was learning about making his first confession, and Donna Lee did not like it one bit.

After they unloaded both canoes, Ralph emerged from the woods with an armload of kindling and set it down in front of Mrs. Norris, who was smiling absently at the river. "That's my man," Donna Lee said, putting a hand on his shoulder. Ralph was big for his age and exceptionally well coordinated. His father had high hopes for him as an athlete. "Now listen, everyone," she said, keeping her hand on the boy, "the first thing we've got to do is get a fire started. Dad, don't try to put up that tent yourself. Help Henry find some wood. And get a whole lot; it's going to get real cold tonight."

The men trudged off through the sand, followed by Ralph. "I'll go, too," Mrs. Norris said, getting off her log.

"That would be nice," Donna Lee said. Although she was only twenty-six years old, Donna Lee was determined not to let age create a barrier between her and Mrs. Norris. She wanted to treat her like any other girl friend.

Donna Lee unpacked the Coleman stove and lit the colorless gas flame, then noticed that Mrs. Norris was still standing right behind her. "I believe Ralph went over there," Donna Lee said, pointing to a thicket of river birch and sycamore. "Honey?"

"Oh, yes," Mrs. Norris said.

"You can stay here, of course. But I think you'd be warmer if you moved around a little."

"I'll help Ralph; lovely idea." She set off rather mechanically for the woods, like one of "Star Wars"' genteel, battered robots. Donna Lee sighed and shook her head.

After unpacking the food from the ice chest, Donna Lee took a swig of Jack Daniel's to warm herself up. She was sure she was going to get a terrible cold from this camp-out and would spend the rest of the Christmas holidays in bed. She was not happy here, but she couldn't have stood another day with the family milling around the house in Tula Springs. She had her own little apartment a mile from the house, but she felt guilty staying there during the holidays, especially after Henry, Ralph, and Sister, Donna Lee's sister, had come all the way from Houston for Christmas. Sister was at home now with Mrs. Keely. They thought Donna Lee was crazy for making everyone go out in freezing weather, and dragging along poor Mrs. Norris to boot. Mr. Keely tried to explain: "How can you appreciate a nice warm home if you don't rough it?" Donna Lee's mother replied, "You birds—you just don't know when you got it good." But that wasn't it; Donna Lee was not trying to help anybody appreciate a nice warm home. She wanted to make her family experience Reality; Reality to Donna Lee was something like going to the dentist—it was difficult and it sometimes hurt, but it was necessary if you wanted to stay healthy.

Henry and Mr. Keely broke through the undergrowth at the edge of the woods with an impossibly large water oak. Its branches were tangled in python-thick rattan, which Mr. Keely began hacking at with Ralph's Boy Scout hatchet. Donna Lee went over to take a look; the wood was wet and rotted. "Henry, you think it's worth it?" she asked.

"Watch out," he said. Small brown sticktights clung to his salmon cashmere sweater. He had taken off his down vest and jacket. "Dad," he said to his father-in-law, "go up a little further and get that big branch loose."

"Be careful," Donna Lee said, as Mr. Keely inched himself along the trunk, the hatchet drooping from his back pocket. "I really think—"

"What's for dinner?" Henry asked, giving her a tight smile.

"Mama packed some leftover turkey gumbo, and there's that carrot cake Sister made."

"Is that all?"

Glancing anxiously at her father, Donna Lee said, "Well, Henry, if you ask me, Americans eat too much," and walked into the woods to check on Ralph and Mrs. Norris.

They were sitting around a fire waiting for dinner. The tents were set up, the air mattresses blown up, the sleeping bags unrolled. Donna Lee looked at her watch; it was only three-thirty. She turned down the Coleman stove as low as it would go.

"It's so lovely," Mrs. Norris said. She blew into her hands to warm them.

Donna Lee smiled encouragingly at her.

"The trees, the flowing water," Mrs. Norris went on. "It makes me feel like God is so near."

Henry cleared his throat and hugged Ralph closer to him. Ralph's nose was running, and his eyes were bleary. They had already moved twice to escape the heavy smoke from the water-oak fire, which was not very warm. Mr. Keely was practically sitting in it, trying to keep his teeth from chattering.

"I feel like God is near, too," Donna Lee said from her perch on the water oak. They hadn't bothered to chop the trunk up. They just fed it to the fire little by little, root-end first.

"I thought you didn't believe in God," Henry said through a stuffed-up nose. Smoke rose from the rubber soles of his size-12 shoes.

"I believe, but not in your God." Donna Lee's long, big-knuckled fingers clasped the tin cup from which she sipped bourbon, lemon juice, and hot water. "To me, God is that sumac over there, that piece of driftwood, that Chinese tallow."

"That beer can," Henry continued, pointing toward the water's edge.

"Dad!" Ralph said, twisting his head around so he could see his father's face. Henry winked at him.

Donna Lee stood up and walked over to the beer can, which she hadn't noticed before. As she stuffed it into their garbage bag, another shot rang out in the woods. The shooting had started half an hour ago with muffled blasts from what must be deer hunters' guns. They sounded closer now.

"Well, Mrs. Norris," Mr. Keely said, running a freckled hand through his white hair, "how did you like the canoe?"

"Frightfully nice," she replied, sounding a little more British than usual. She plucked a sprig of dewberry from the black leotards she wore under her tweed skirt. "Donna Lee is a smashing conductor. I feel so very safe on the waters."

"Canoeing is really not that hard, is it, Mrs. Norris?" Donna Lee said, sitting down again. "The main thing is, you got to be aware. You can't dream. For instance, remember when we came to that little patch of white water just before lunch?"

"Oh, yes. You told me to stop paddling, didn't you?"

"That's correct. If needs be, only one person should paddle. The bow and stern must be coordinated. You should never fight against each other's efforts." She was looking at Mrs. Norris, but everybody except Mrs. Norris knew she was talking to Henry, who had his eyes closed. "Canoeing should be as effortless as possible. You should always know exactly what you're doing and why."

"Very nice, yes," Mrs. Norris said.

"I think Mrs. Norris is catching on," Mr. Keely said innocently. "A few more times and she'll be—"

"Now, Dad," Donna Lee said, "tell me why you started paddling from the middle of the canoe. You only made things difficult for poor Ralph."

"It wasn't Grandpa's fault," Ralph said, peering out from a moth-eaten army blanket that covered his head like a cowl.

"Maybe not," Donna Lee said.

"Well, it wasn't *my* fault," Henry said, his eyes still closed. "I had a splinter in my hand. And everyone knows that aluminum canoe is harder to steer." His eyes opened. "In any case, I'm sure Mrs. Norris isn't interested in a post mortem. Are you, Mrs. Norris?"

"Oh, don't mind me," she replied. Another shot rang out. It was definitely closer. "But, speaking of post mortems, are we safe here?"

"Of course," Donna Lee said, pulling her raccoon coat tighter about her.

"Well, I must say," Mrs. Norris went on in her mild, singsong voice, "just a few moments ago, when you were down at the river picking up that beer can—why, Donna Lee, with that ridiculous coat of yours on, you looked just like a very tempting big deer."

Ralph laughed, and everybody, including Donna Lee, smiled, because Ralph did not laugh as often as a little boy should. "A beer deer," Mr. Keely said, reaching around and tickling Ralph.

Ralph squirmed in his father's arms. "More Kool-Aid, please," he said.

Donna Lee poured some into his Daniel Boone canteen as her father gave out some annoyingly fake barks of glee. "I hate to sound preachy, but I do think we should all be more careful tomorrow," she said. "We've got about four hours to go before we get to the cars, and there's some pretty tricky bends up ahead. The main thing is, you got to be aware."

"You got to be *aware*," Ralph mimicked, astonishingly well. Everyone except Donna Lee laughed.

They held out as long as they could, but it was still light when they ate. Although Donna Lee thought it was silly, her father tied an orange tarpaulin to a pine near the woods, assuring Mrs. Norris that this would tell the hunters that humans were nearby. She thanked him, then gazed up and admired aloud the big birds that were soaring in the thermal drafts.

"Turkey vultures," Donna Lee said.

"How dreadful," Mrs. Norris muttered. She tossed an acorn into the fire and then made a vague gesture toward the white sky. "They don't *eat* turkeys, do they?" she asked.

"They'll eat anything," Donna Lee said. Reality.

"Mrs. Norris, did a monkey really bite off your big toe?" Ralph asked solemnly.

Donna Lee went crimson. She had told Ralph never to mention Africa or monkeys or toes to Mrs. Norris unless Mrs. Norris happened to talk about them herself.

"More Kool-Aid?" Donna Lee said, holding out the plastic pitcher to Ralph.

"No, Ralph dear, I lost my toe in Montana, during a blizzard," Mrs. Norris said.

"Ralph is going to be in third grade next year," Donna Lee said.

"How nice," Mrs. Norris said. "And what do you want to be when you grow up, Ralph?"

"A priest," the boy said happily.

"A what?" Henry frowned at his son. "You don't want to be a priest, boy."

"I made up my mind. I'm going to be a priest in Africa, a missionary like Mrs. Norris."

"How lovely," Mrs. Norris said. "Of course, Ralph, I was just a nurse, you know—nothing very religious."

"I'll be a nurse priest, then."

Donna Lee glared across the fire at Henry.

Mr. Keely cleared his throat. "Now, Ralph," he said in a hoarse, raspy voice, "you mean you'd like to be a doctor, don't you? Everyone likes doctors."

"No, Grandpa. I have a vocation."

This was too much for Donna Lee. "Here, drink this Kool-Aid," she said, holding out the plastic pitcher again. "Finish it up for me."

"I don't want any more."

"It's fun, you'll like it," she said sternly, pouring from the pitcher into his canteen.

Ralph took the canteen from her, but when he put it to his mouth his eyes welled up with tears. The next thing Donna Lee knew, he was gone, running across the sand to the tent the men would share that night.

"Here we go again," Henry said, sighing as he stood up. He walked off slowly, a little stiffly, toward the tent.

Mrs. Norris pulled the woollen stocking cap Donna Lee had lent her over her ears and moved closer to the fire. "What happened?" she asked. "Is it time for bed?"

"Henry is too soft on him," Donna Lee said, glancing over at their tent. "He's just reinforcing that kind of behavior."

"Donna Lee, let Henry alone," her father said.

"Well, I just can't stand to see poor Ralph get so misguided."

"Misguided?" Mrs. Norris put in. "But he's an angel."

"A little boy should be carefree and obnoxious and dirty and go his own way," Donna Lee said. "There'll be plenty of time to feel guilty when he grows up, don't you think?"

"Ralph can be obnoxious," Mr. Keely said, jiggling a pine branch in the fire. He smiled at Mrs. Norris. "You live way out on Sibley Street, don't you, Mrs. Norris? Those freight trains ever bother you?"

"You have no idea," she replied, shaking her head. "Every night it's the same thing—miles and miles of boxcars. I don't know; somehow it seems so vulgar." She sighed. "Donna Lee tells me you work at the Savings and Loan."

"Yes, Ma'am, I do."

"I hope I'm not being impertinent, but I've always wondered why your office is in a mobile home."

"Oh, the trailer's just a temporary setup, till we get our new office finished. It's that brick building going up by the upholstery shop."

"Of course." She winced as another shot rang out.

Exasperated by this small talk, Donna Lee got up and carried the plates and a few pots to the river. She rinsed them and scrubbed them with sand, the water numbing her fingers and seeping into her jogging shoes. She could hear her father and Mrs. Norris discussing the strawberry wine you could buy at the discount fireworks stand near the Savings and Loan trailer. Donna Lee scoured the plates so hard that a few roses in the dime-store pattern faded away.

"What's become of Ralph and Henry?" Mrs. Norris asked as Donna Lee packed the clean plates into a picnic hamper.

"Want me to go see?" Mr. Keely asked, getting to his feet.

"Oh, I wish you would. Tell Ralph I've got a surprise for him."

"Sure thing." Mr. Keely crunched through the sand to the tent near the woods.

"Margaret—you don't mind if I call you that, do you?" Donna Lee asked. Mrs. Norris smiled. "Margaret, I hope you didn't mind Ralph bringing up your—the blizzard. I must confess, I told him about you. He must have got things a little mixed up—I mean about the monkey and all. But you understand, don't you—you understand why I told him? I thought it was important that Ralph know about these things—the starvation you saw, the leprosy and all that, what life is really like for most of the people on earth. . . ." She faltered. "I mean, you just can't imagine how parochial some people can be. Henry, for instance. His whole world is the Super Bowl and condominiums—he's in real estate. It's really sad. Anyway, I thought Ralph should know that life can be filled with adventure, that there are people like you who aren't content to just drift along, people who have *seen* things and *done* things. Do you understand?"

Mrs. Norris kept her eyes averted, as if Donna Lee were not properly dressed and there was too much showing. "Of course, dear."

Donna Lee was not reassured. "You're not mad at me?" she asked, squeezing her friend's arm.

"Don't be silly."

"You're having a good time, aren't you? I mean, you don't think I've been too bossy, do you? Henry thinks I am; I can tell. I suppose he's right, too." She paused so that Mrs. Norris could contradict her. She didn't. "But I'm working on it, I'm trying to change. And anyway, *someone* has to be responsible, don't you think?"

"You fret so. Really, Donna Lee, stop worrying."

The men were now returning from the tent, with Ralph between them. Frustrated by the remote look in Mrs. Norris's eyes, Donna Lee suddenly reached out and took the older woman's mittened hands. "We will be good friends, won't we?" Donna Lee said as another shot rang out.

"Of course, of course," Mrs. Norris said faintly, freeing her hands. "Oh, I do wish Ralph had something orange to wear."

"Well, here's your surprise, dear." Mrs. Norris handed Ralph a package she had pulled out of her vinyl suitcase. They were all standing around the fire, which had been revived by some fatty pine Donna Lee had found.

Ralph opened the package and took out four long, pointed tubes with strings hanging out one end.

"What in . . ." Henry said, taking the tubes from his son. "Rockets?"

"Fireworks!" Mrs. Norris exclaimed.

Donna Lee began to frown but stopped when she saw Henry's face cloud over. "How wonderful!" she said. "Isn't this exciting, Ralph? Thank Mrs. Norris, Ralph."

"Thank you, Mrs. Norris," Ralph said. He looked over at his father.

"Yes—thank you," Henry said. "Ralph will have a good time with these once we get home."

"Oh, but my dears," Mrs. Norris said, clasping her hands together, "I thought we could celebrate tonight."

"Well, I don't know." Henry scratched his head. "These things can be dangerous. You got to know what you're doing."

"Oh, Henry," Donna Lee said. "There's nothing to it. All you do is light one end and run. Right, Mrs. Norris?"

"Precisely."

Mr. Keely took a rocket from Henry and turned it over in his hands. "Henry is right. This thing looks pretty powerful."

"You babies," Donna Lee said, winking conspiratorially at Mrs. Norris.

"I'm just saying we'll have to be careful," Mr. Keely said. He patted Ralph on the back.

"It's not just that." Henry took the rocket from his father-in-law. "I didn't tell anyone earlier, because I thought it didn't matter so much. But when I was back in the woods getting firewood I saw a no-trespassing sign. We're on private property."

"So?" Donna Lee said.

Henry reached over and took the package of fireworks from Ralph. "So? Well, honey, it just doesn't make sense to attract attention to ourselves. There might be a farmhouse or something on the other side of the woods. And those hunters . . ."

"He's got a point there," Mr. Keely said, rubbing his chin.

"Are we illegal?" Mrs. Norris asked, her smile fading.

Annoyed by the "honey"—after all, Henry was only five years older than she was—Donna Lee knelt beside Ralph and tousled his black hair. "Really, Henry, do you think someone's going to shoot us for camping one night on his beach? What do you say, Ralph?"

Ralph shrugged.

"Oh, please," Mrs. Norris said, "it's too much bother. Take them home with you, Ralph."

"Now, Margaret," Donna Lee said, "it's Ralph's present. We should let him decide. Ralph, look at me." She swivelled him around. "Tell me if you want to have fun tonight or if you'd rather be a stick-in-the-mud like your daddy."

"Donna Lee," her father said.

Donna Lee laughed. "Come on with me, Ralph. You and Mrs. Norris and I will go have ourselves some fun."

"You're too much," Henry said, trying to sound lighthearted. "First you're lecturing us on water safety, and next you're trying to blow us all up."

"Please, Donna Lee," Mrs. Norris said, "we'll do it some other time."

"Ralph?" Donna Lee looked him square in the eyes.

"I think if it's all right," the boy replied, turning to Mrs. Norris, "I'd like to do it at home. Thank you very much."

Donna Lee lay wide awake in the greenish dark of the tent. Beside her, Mrs. Norris tossed fitfully, muttering some sort of nonsense about oleomargarine. Squinting at her watch, Donna Lee saw that it was only eight-fifteen. She decided to try to sleep outside the tent. It would be a little colder, of course, but at least she would have some peace.

"No!" Mrs. Norris cried out. She sat up and looked wide-eyed at Donna-Lee, who was struggling to get her inflated air mattress through the tent's narrow opening. "Don't, please don't."

"Margaret, it's just me, Donna Lee," she said, a little frightened by Mrs. Norris's own fright. "I'm just moving my stuff outside."

Mrs. Norris rubbed her lumpy face. Her red hair was matted on one side, making her head look lopsided. "Oh dear," she moaned. A wide yawn. "Is it morning already? I haven't slept a wink."

Donna Lee gave the mattress a final shove. "It's still night," she said, rolling up her sleeping bag. "I'm sorry I disturbed you."

"Why are you going outside?"

"It's a little stuffy in here. I can't sleep."

"Let's talk, then. I'm not really tired, either." She put her hand on Donna Lee's arm. "You know, dear, you've never told me what my chances are."

"What chances?"

"Of being evicted. All day long it's been preying on my mind. I just don't know what I'll do if I'm tossed out. I love that little apartment so much, and it costs hardly anything."

"I thought the trains drove you crazy."

"I'm used to that by now. So tell me, dear, what do you think? I want to know."

Pettiness, Donna Lee thought. No matter where she went she would be surrounded by pettiness. She felt weary and old, old as the cranky old landlady who was squabbling about the eviction. "I'm going outside, Mrs. Norris. We'll talk about it later—at the office."

Lying alone by the river in her sleeping bag, Donna Lee watched the white moon rise over the river birches. She was a little nervous at first. There were strange noises all around her—a splash, a thump, and farther away, the squeal of tires, a horn blaring. But she was determined not to be afraid.

She must have drifted off, for when she opened her eyes all the way she saw that the woods were not on fire. It had only been a dream. But that rustling, that strange stir coming from the edge of the woods—that was definitely real. Her heart pounding, Donna Lee propped herself up on her elbows for a better look. The canoes, the picnic hamper, the canteen by the ashes of the campfire—everything was visible in the brilliant moonlight. And beyond, only a few feet from Ralph's tent, what looked like a single flame danced wildly, convulsively atop a sumac.

"Damn that tarp," Donna Lee said when she finally realized what it was. Getting up, she stole across the campsite to the pine from which the orange tarpaulin dangled, brushing the leaves of the sumac. Another strong gust from the river shook the tarpaulin as she untied a halfhearted granny knot; the other knots, which had held the tarpaulin still, had already worked loose in the wind. Then, half frozen but no longer afraid, she went back for her sleeping bag and dragged it, along with the tarpaulin, to the sagging, mildewed tent, where, oleomargarine or no oleomargarine, she would ride out the night with Mrs. Norris—Margaret.

Contributors

JOHN BIGUENET says that his short stories "roam across the world from Cincinnati to southern Germany to Philadelphia to medieval France to places where a boy can transform himself into various animals and a ghost can persuade a young couple to become its parents." He is also the author of a novel entitled *Oyster* that is set in and around Louisiana's Plaquemines Parish. His fiction is difficult to classify, as he employs no single voice or narrative form but seeks to find the structure that grows out of whatever conflict is being explored in each story.

JAMES LEE BURKE's fiction explores the characters and cultures of the American South and the American West, regions in which he says he feels at home. He is perhaps best known for his Dave Robicheaux detective novels, but throughout his fiction, readers find people marked by their resilience, courage, and compassion standing up against the charlatans and demagogues of our society. As he says, "The potential in human beings for either good or evil seems limitless."

ROBERT OLEN BUTLER's year of military service in Vietnam, which he says brought him to literature, is readily apparent in *A Good Scent from a Strange Mountain,* which won him the 1993 Pulitzer Prize for Fiction. He is also the recipient of a Guggenheim Fellowship and a National Endowment for the Arts grant. Speaking of Butler's characters, Wendy Wallace says, "Butler brings to life human forms of tenderness who possess a deep longing for love. They're the kind of people whose lives are complex and usually cruelly twisted by fate, but whose souls speak in whispers wanting to be understood and embraced."

KELLY CHERRY is the Eudora Welty Professor Emerita of English and Evjue-Bascom Professor Emerita in the Humanities at the University of Wisconsin—Madison. She recently served as Visiting Eminent Scholar at the Humanities Center, University of Alabama—Huntsville, NEH Professor of the Humanities at Colgate University, and Wyndham Robertson Writer-in-Residence at Hollins University, Virginia. In addition to being a successful writer of fiction, Cherry is also a prominent writer of poetry and nonfiction.

MOIRA CRONE grew up in North Carolina but now lives in New Orleans and directs the M.F.A. program at Louisiana State University. She is the author of three volumes of fiction, the latest being *Dream State,* which, in its humor and irreverence, reflects her sojourn in south Louisiana. Her stories have appeared in the *New Yorker, Mademoiselle, Southern Review, Ohio Review,* and other magazines. She edits *Numen,* a magazine of contemporary writing.

ALBERT BELISLE DAVIS writes in several genres besides fiction, including poetry, drama, and nonfiction. His novel *Leechtime* and his poetry collection *What They Wrote on the Bathhouse Walls, Yen's Marina, Chinese Bayou, Louisiana* were published in 1989 and 1988, respectively. He has received awards for both his poetry and his fiction from the Deep South Writers Conference. His latest novel is *Marquis at Bay.*

CHARLES DEGRAVELLES is a founder of the New Playwrights' Theater and has served as a member of the literature panel of the Louisiana Division of the Arts and as coeditor of the New Orleans Poetry Journal Press. In addition to writing fiction, he has published a full-length collection of poems, *The Well Governed Son.* An active deacon in the Episcopal Church, he was instrumental in establishing the Chapel of the Transfiguration at Angola, the Louisiana state penitentiary.

JOHN DUFRESNE is not a native of Louisiana, or even of the South, though he says the northern part of the state resonates with him deeply. He comments: "Place is not location only. . . . Place is location with narrative, with memory and imagination, with history." In addition to two short-story collections, he is the author of three novels, *Louisiana Power and Light, Love Warps the Mind a Little,* and *Deep in the Shade of Paradise.* He has recently completed his first play, *Trailerville.* All Dufresne's works reflect his belief that "every story is ultimately about the human heart."

RICHARD FORD's fiction is, for the most part, not set in the South. As he commented in an interview in *Harper's,* "Personally, I don't think there is such a thing as Southern writing or Southern literature or Southern ethos." Though whether he is writing about the South can be disputed, Ford's stature is not likely to be. He has been a Guggenheim Fellow (1977–78) and a two-time National Endowment for the Arts Fellow (1979–80, 1985–86). He also was awarded both a PEN/Faulkner Award and a Pulitzer Prize for his novel *Independence Day* in 1996.

ERNEST J. GAINES spent much of his adult life in California before returning to his native Louisiana, but Gaines's most notable writing reflects the rural folk culture in which he spent his childhood. He has received numerous honors, including being named a MacArthur Fellow, Louisiana Humanist of the Year, Chevalier in the Order of Art and Letters, a member of the American Academy of Arts and Letters, holder of the National Governors' Arts Award, and Louisiana Writer of the Year. He was also awarded a National Humanities Medal. He now lives in Pointe Coupee Parish, the setting of many of his books and stories.

LOUIS GALLO has published widely in journals such as *Glimmer Train, Greensboro Review, Missouri Review, New Orleans Review, Loyola Review, Berkeley Fiction Review, Baltimore Review, MacGuffin, Modern Poetry Studies, American Literary Review, Critique, Mississippi Review, Thema, Green Hills Review, Italian Americana, Louisiana Literature,* and others. He has also been active as an editor with the *Barataria Review, Gooks: A New Orleans Review,* and the Pushcart Press. Gallo founded "The Mardi Gras Poetry Readings" in New Orleans, which continue to thrive as "The Maple Leaf Readings."

TIM GAUTREAUX began his writing career as a poet, then turned to short fiction in the late 1970s at the urging of Walker Percy. Since that time he has published two short-story collections, *Same Place, Same Things* and *Welding with Children,* as well as two novels, *The Next Step in the Dance* and, most recently, *The Clearing.* Asked why machinery appears so often in his fiction, he says, "The thing about a properly designed mechanism is that there are no nonfunctioning parts. Everything has a purpose, every bit and tag, screw and eyelet. Good fiction's the same way."

NORMAN GERMAN is professor of English at Southeastern Louisiana University, where he is fiction editor of *Louisiana Literature.* His short stories have appeared in many literary and commercial magazines, including the *Virginia Quarterly Review, Aethlon,* the *Connecticut Review, Louisiana Life, New Orleans Review,* and *Salt*

Water Sportsman. His novel *No Other World* fictionalizes the life of Marie Thereze, the ex-slave who founded Melrose Plantation.

ELLEN GILCHRIST is a writer of poems, short stories, novels, and nonfiction commentaries. Her work is filled with unique characters who are both recognizable and shocking and whose lives are full of surprises. Characters from other stories sometimes appear in new ones, and ordinary events take place in unexpected settings. *In the Land of Dreamy Dreams,* the collection from which "Rich" is taken, was her first book of short fiction, published in 1981.

JOAN ARBOUR GRANT lives in Asheville, North Carolina, but usually writes about New Orleans. She grew up near Audubon Park and graduated from Sacred Heart Academy and Newcomb College. She was awarded the Thomas Wolfe Prize for Fiction at the University of North Carolina at Asheville. Her stories have appeared in *Louisiana Literature* and *Oxford Magazine.* Her first novel, *Sacred Hearts and Lovers,* about a New Orleans girl's search for love in all the wrong places, is in search of the right publisher.

SHIRLEY ANN GRAU is a native New Orleanian who has published four collections of short stories and six novels. She was awarded the Pulitzer Prize in 1965 for *The Keepers of the House.* Her fiction shows keen psychological insight into people of widely varying social and cultural worlds, and her themes are universal: the power of love, the presence of the past, the uses of power. Chester E. Eisinger has characterized Grau as "a novelist of manners who is sharply aware of the collapse of conventional behavior patterns in modern life."

DINTY W. MOORE is the author of three books. His most recent publication is *Sudden Stories,* a collection of stories by writers of "miniscule fiction." He is also publisher of *Brevity,* an electronic journal of concise literary nonfiction. His work has been published in numerous magazines and journals, including the *New York Times Magazine, Harper's, Utne Reader, Arts and Letters, Crazyhorse,* and *Southern Review.* His fiction is often funny but unsettling, humorous but dark.

TIM PARRISH's story "It Pours" appears in his collection *Red Stick Men,* an appropriate title since it presents stories that explore the characters and ambience of Baton Rouge. He re-creates the humidity, pollution, even the Mississippi River, which floods everything from time to time. As he says, "Place isn't simply setting, place is the air and dirt that great characters thrive upon." Parrish was a 2001 Walter E. Dakin Fellow at the Sewanee Writers' Conference and a 2001 Connecticut Arts Fellow.

TOM PIAZZA is as well known for his writing about music and musicians as he is for his fiction. His work has appeared in many publications, including the *New York Times* and *Atlantic Monthly.* His short-story collection, *Blues and Trouble,* won the James Michener Award for Fiction. *The Guide to Classic Recorded Jazz* by Piazza won the ASCAP-Deems Taylor Award for Music Writing, and his essay on the history and nature of the blues, included in *Martin Scorsese Presents THE BLUES: A Musical Journey,* won a 2004 Grammy Award for Best Album Notes.

NANCY RICHARD's fiction has appeared in a number of journals and anthologies, including the *Greensboro Review, Prairie Schooner, Shenandoah, New Stories from the South,* and *Pushcart Prize XXIII.* "What You Do Next" first appeared in the *Hudson Review* and was nominated for a Pushcart Prize. A professor of English at Delgado Community College in New Orleans, she serves as adjunct mentoring coordinator for English and developmental composition and as editor for the SACS Leadership Team.

JAMES WILCOX is the author of eight novels, the most recent of which is *Heavenly Days.* His short stories have appeared in *Louisiana Literature,* the *New Yorker,* and *Avenue.* In 1986 he was awarded a Guggenheim Fellowship, and his novel *Modern Baptists* was included in Harold Bloom's *The Western Canon.* Writing in the *Times Literary Supplement,* Jim Crace commented, "James Wilcox has a sophisticated control of comic pace, his humor the chill of home truth, and his squibs at the expense of small-town America are rarely off-target."

Credits